Lawrence Earle Johnson

# Quantum Fear

A Novel

ISBN: 978-1-7333284-4-9 (sc)

ISBN: 978-1-7333284-5-6 (e)

Clayton Wolfe novels
by Lawrence Earle Johnson

Death Sine
Quantum Fear
Knight Watch

# Prologue

The black-clad figure watched as the target returned to the two-story brick home in the tony suburban neighborhood of Arlington, Virginia. He remained hidden as the man drove his car into the garage, closed the garage door, and entered the side door of the house. The lights came on. Movement continued within the house until about midnight, when the last light in the upstairs bedroom was switched off.

He waited another three hours until three a.m., when he was sure the target was in a deep sleep. There were no street lights, and no people around to see him. He crept silently up the driveway and quickly picked the side door lock. He listened carefully for several seconds, and then entered the dwelling. Having previously checked the layout of the interior, he moved swiftly to the kitchen and to the gas range.

Behind the range he found a flexible metal cable that directed the natural gas into the burners of the stove. He quickly uncoupled the gas fitting on the cable to let the gas flow freely into the room.

Then he placed a device next to the stove that would create a spark and ignite the gas. He set the timer on the device for ten minutes. By then enough gas would have filled the house to cause a terrific explosion. He looked around the kitchen to make sure he had not missed anything. Satisfied, he pressed the *start* button on the ignition device and exited as quietly as he had come, vanishing into the night.

Ten minutes later the device created the spark and a huge explosion leveled the house and everything in it. The black-clad man was close enough to hear the sound of the explosion, and smiled. One down, five to go, he thought to himself, as he proceeded to his next target.

What the black-clad man had *not* seen, however, was that a man had emerged from the upstairs bedroom window at the back of the house and climbed down the gutter. He then ran through the woods behind the home and was safely away when it exploded. The redheaded man, code named *Reaper*, had escaped certain death once again. This time he was going to exact revenge. But first he had one critical thing to do.

Warn the others.

# chapter 1

C layton Wolfe woke early and started his day with his usual exercise of chopping wood for his stove and fireplace. He had worked up a good sweat and was feeling good. His muscles were tight and firm, and with his shirt off, his sweat glistened in the early light of the morning. He loved being out in the woods anytime, especially in the Upper Peninsula of Michigan. It was early October and the smell of fall hung pungently in the air. As the sun rose, he could see that the leaves were reaching their peak color.

Though he spent most of his professional life in the service of his country in various capacities as a clandestine agent, his work was classified at a high level, and he could not divulge the nature of it to anyone. He had just gone through a grueling experience the previous year that nearly cost him his life, and the life of a woman with whom he had grown close. When she returned to Chicago he was again alone with his thoughts and his solitude here in the woods.

The cabin he built on his property provided him all the comforts he needed, though some might think it a bit rustic. But for him it was Nirvana. Peace and quiet. Time to think. Time to get himself centered. He was not working for the government anymore, but there were times when he found it necessary to engage in activities that utilized his special talents—talents that often ended in the death of others. People who needed to die. And that required a period of recuperation. That was what he was doing now.

It was daylight and Wolfe had returned to his cabin where he showered and dressed. He prepared himself a hearty meal of eggs and bacon, toast, hash-brown potatoes, and strong, black coffee. After breakfast he cleaned up the kitchen, then started a fire in the fieldstone fireplace and settled down in his leather chair facing the fire.

His log cabin was pretty much one large room, with a living room area at the front and the fireplace on the side wall. There was a couch and a chair facing the fireplace, with an area rug underneath. At the back of the cabin was the kitchen area, and then off to the side opposite the fireplace, was a door to the bathroom, and next to it another door to the only bedroom.

Wolfe's tastes were simple but comfortable. The only exterior doors were a front door and a back door, both of solid oak. Neither had a window, but there were windows in the front and back of the cabin.

Wolfe had built the cabin himself. He had cleared brush away from the trout stream that flowed through his property, which made it easier to catch his dinner of German browns and rainbow trout that were plentiful during fishing season. He owned one-hundred acres of prime land that provided timber, game, and the privacy that was so important to him. His well gave him plenty of fresh water, and his heat was provided by a wood stove that also heated his water for showers, though he often took them cold.

Best of all, nobody knew where his place was. There were no roads or pathways of any kind. He had taken great pains to make sure nobody knew how to get to him. It was his place of solitude—of security and peace.

He had just settled down and was gazing at the flickering fire in the fireplace.

And then there was a knock on the door.

# chapter 2

Wolfe froze. His mind raced at light speed. He checked off possibilities of who it might be. None of them were good.

Nobody should know where he was, or how to get here. But someone did. Someone with access to information that should not be available—to anyone. And yet somehow it was.

His cabin was a fortress. A place of solitude and reflection. A place of rest.

Not a place of violence.

And yet at this very moment, it just might be. He saw few alternatives. He grabbed his .357 magnum revolver and walked to the solid, windowless door of his cabin. He put his right hand on the door latch. The door opened on the left. His gun was in his left hand. He was as good a shot with his left hand as he was with his right. Maybe that will matter, he thought. Then again, maybe it won't.

Asking who was there was futile. That was what the interloper would expect. He skipped that warning and yanked the door open with one swift motion, while simultaneously aiming his revolver chest high.

The shock showed on the intruder's face, but only for a split-second. It was enough. How quickly the man recovered told him a lot about the man standing in front of him. He was wearing clothes fit for hiking in the woods, not his normal Brooks Brothers attire. He was a shade over six feet tall, with a trim build. He had black hair cut conservatively, and an annoying smirk on his carefully tanned face. Wolfe knew the man. And he despised him.

"Devon Barnes," he said, addressing the intruder. "I hoped I'd never see you again. In fact, I hoped you were dead."

Barnes smiled. "Do you greet all your callers this way, Wolfe?" He gave Wolfe the once over, taking in his blue jeans, plaid flannel shirt, and tan work boots. "Nice togs," he said with clear disdain. "New uniform?"

Wolfe's gun remained steady, now pointing at the man's heart, assuming he actually had one. Wolfe's six-foot frame was made more formidable by his broad shoulders, muscular physique, and the battle scars that showed he had survived numerous physical encounters. But more importantly, the man standing in front of him knew that he was an expert with the weapon, and would not hesitate to use it.

"What do you *want*?" Wolfe asked, steel in his voice.

Barnes looked at the gun and calmly raised his hands. "I have no weapons. As you can see, I'm alone. I'm only here to talk, that's all. You can keep your big gun trained on me the whole time, if it makes you feel better." He stood still, his hands raised.

Wolfe kept his gun trained on him, backing away to keep a safe distance. "Step forward slowly and close the door behind you," he said. Barnes did so.

"How cautious of you, Wolfe. I'm impressed," he said. "I'd like to put my hands down now, if you please."

"First remove your jacket," said Wolfe, watching the man's eyes at all times.

Barnes pulled his jacket open on both sides and held it open as he faced Wolfe. Then he removed his coat, folded it, and carefully placed it over the back of the straight-backed kitchen chair. "You see, I have no weapons with me. I have no need of them for this visit."

Wolfe motioned Barnes to sit in the chair. Barnes complied. "Put your hands on the table and keep them there."

Barnes did so, the smirk still fixed on his face. "Satisfied?" Wolfe put his gun on the table, but kept his hand on it. "I'll ask again. *What do you want?*"

The smirk on Barnes' face faded. "What I want," he began in measured tones, "is for you to do a job for me."

Wolfe stared at him. "I don't work for you anymore. And I don't intend to—ever."

Barnes locked stares with Wolfe. "I beg to differ, *Clayton*," he said. "I think you *will* work for me, and that you will do an admirable job."

"You can't threaten me, Barnes. You may think you can kill me, but that will be a tougher job than you can imagine. That doesn't concern me. Death is always at my doorstep. And I can see by your mysterious appearance here that you have no respect for anybody. Obviously nothing's changed."

"You may not fear your own death," said Barnes, "but you might have at least a slight concern for the life of another."

"I doubt that," said Wolfe.

"Really?" said Barnes. "Hmm. It seems to me that you have had some sort of a relationship with a certain redheaded reporter. Or has that gone by the wayside, like your previous forays into the uncertain world of romance?"

Wolfe's demeanor shifted. His look became even harder, which was difficult to imagine. His stare made most people wither, and though Barnes was not immune, he maintained eye-contact, as uncomfortable as it was. He had seen that stare before, and the death and destruction that usually followed was cataclysmic. Wolfe was like a volcano. He could be civil enough when it suited him. However, when provoked, he could explode quickly and violently, leaving a wasteland of devastation behind him.

Barnes had seen it firsthand, and only survived because he and Wolfe had been working on the same side—sort of. He knew that Wolfe could be a dangerous adversary. The worst kind. He would have to tread carefully if he intended to survive. He decided to change tactics.

"Listen and listen carefully," Wolfe said in quiet, measured words. He leaned forward, moving his face closer to Barnes in a menacing way. "One freckle on her face gets touched, one hair on her head is disturbed, if she even senses she is being threatened in any way, I guarantee you will wish you had never been born. You will think back on all the decisions you ever made and wonder which one brought you to this awful fate. And your thoughts will inevitably return to this one moment.

"So, I'm giving you fair warning, which is more than you deserve. This is the last one you will ever get from me. Now nod and tell me you understand. And give me your answer *now*."

# chapter 3

Barnes' carefully cultivated tan seemed to wash away. He swallowed hard and tried to mask the fear that was suddenly gripping him like a vice. "OK, Wolfe," he said. He chose his next words very carefully.

"Look," he began, trying to soften his demeanor. "Just hear me out. You don't like me and I sure as hell don't like you. We've both done things we regret. Right or wrong, our motives were pure, though the results were sometimes regrettable."

"There was nothing pure about your motives, you . . ."

"Hold on," Barnes cut in, raising his hand. Realizing his error, he slowly put it back down on the table. "Wait until you hear what I have to say. Then you can do what you want."

Wolfe still glared at him but said nothing. Barnes continued. "We have a situation that needs your special talents."

"Go on," Wolfe said. He was pretty sure he knew who *we* was referring to.

Barnes continued. "We need you to locate a person who may be working on an invention that would change the world in a dangerous way."

That got Wolfe's attention. "In *what* dangerous way?"

"We've picked up some signal intelligence—you remember SIGINT, don't you?"

"I see," said Wolfe. "You want something from me and so you begin by insulting me. Is that your grand strategy?"

"No," said Barnes. "Just a reflex action on my part. A thousand apologies."

Wolfe sighed. "Again, in *what* dangerous way?"

"There is a professor of physics who is working on, or maybe has already invented, a method of tapping into something called dark energy."

"Yeah, I've heard of that," said Wolfe. "Science fiction writers' pipe dream for free energy."

"Right," said Barnes. "But it might no longer be a pipe dream. He was doing some research on the subject for DARPA—you know, the Defense Advanced Research Projects Agency."

"I know about DARPA, Devon," Wolfe said acerbically.

"Of course," said Barnes. "No slight intended. Anyway, it appears they had a parting of ways and he was fired. But before he left, he managed to remove critical aspects of his work, including possible working prototypes."

"Oops," said Wolfe, not sympathetically.

Barnes pursed his lips, and continued. "The SIGINT we picked up was from the Soviets, and they seem to think someone here is helping him. It appears to be a woman, from the nature of their conversations, and she may have helped him escape and find a place to hide."

"Really?" said Wolfe. "And how does this involve me?"

"Because," said Barnes, "the Soviets seem to think that this person is located right here—in Marquette County—or close by. The information seems to indicate that they either have some operatives here right now, or that they will soon."

"And we can't let them get their hands on this invention."

"For obvious reasons."

"We need to get *our* hands on this invention, if it exists," said Wolfe, with more than a trace of sarcasm.

"Again, for obvious reasons."

"To share with the world, I would guess?"

"Nothing like that," said Barnes with a sneer.

"No doubt," said Wolfe. "So why don't you, with all your intelligence people and military might and surveillance resources, just swoop down and snatch this danger to the world up yourselves?"

"Birchmont wants to keep a low profile on this," said Barnes.

"General Birchmont?" said Wolfe. "He's heading up this operation?"

"Apparently it's of great interest to him," said Barnes. "Don't ask me why. It's not really his area. But then, who am I to say?"

"Who, indeed?" said Wolfe, taking a jab at Barnes. "Let me see if I can tell where this is going. Because of my familiarity with the area, and my ability to move about and ask questions and look for this person without making too many waves, you would like me to find this guy for you and hand him to you on a silver platter. Am I too far off?"

"Close," said Barnes. "We want you and your team."

"My team?" said Wolfe. "You mean my government team?"

"No, Wolfe. That would be too obvious. We have something much more clandestine in mind."

"You don't mean . . ."

"Yes," said Barnes, cutting in. "That ragtag bunch of *losers* you cobbled together last year that nearly caused World War III. The Sheriff and the Coroner are fixtures here, and will blend in well as they assist you."

"Is that it?" said Wolfe suspiciously.

"Hardly," said Barnes. "The most important person on your team, besides you, of course, would be that girlfriend of yours— one redheaded reporter who can poke and prod to her hearts content without raising any suspicions, seeing as how she is a reporter for the Associated Press. Your girlfriend, Terri Sommers."

"No," said Wolfe.

"No? No, she's not important, or no, you don't want her involved?"

"What do you think?"

"I figured you'd object to her involvement," said Barnes. "So let me put it this way. This is not a request. It's an order. All the way from the top."

"You forget, Barnes. I don't work for you—or *him*."

"Such a short-term memory, Wolfe. I'm surprised at your forgetfulness. You remember that once you reached your level of training and expertise, as well as rank and high level of performance, you can be recalled at any time? You remember that, *Clay*?"

Wolfe bristled at the personal use of his name. "I won't do it. Not for you, not for him. I've done my duty and more than most. Throw me in the stockade if you think you can. But I won't involve my friends again. Period."

"Oh, I believe you will. You see, the world is a strange and unpredictable place. A person could hop in her car, for example, say, heading to an important interview, and suddenly out of nowhere a car runs a red light and plows into her car, maybe killing her instantly, or worse, crippling her for life. Those kinds of tragedies happen every day. And nobody's immune. It would be a pity if such an unfortunate incident happened to Terri, wouldn't you agree?"

Wolfe jumped over the table in a lightning fast move and grabbed Barnes by his shirt, his nose an inch from the other man's face. His jaws were tight and the veins at his temples were pulsing. "Maybe I'll just kill you right now, you worthless pile of crap," he said, threatening with such intensity Barnes' eyes began to water.

"You're choking me," Barnes managed to croak as Wolfe's knuckles pressed against his windpipe.

"That's not all I'm going to do unless you back off," said Wolfe through clenched teeth.

Barnes swallowed hard and forced himself to regain his composure. "Don't threaten me, Wolfe. I hold all the cards. If you kill me, other persons will be sent—ones you don't know —and they will give you no options. Pull your group together and find this person and his invention. And bring them to me. Or you and your associates will cease to exist among the living. Starting with Terri."

Wolfe stared into the other man's eyes with fury. But he knew Barnes was right. He slowly released him and backed away.

"That's better," said Barnes. He grabbed his jacket and walked to the door. Opening the door wide, he turned toward Wolfe. "If you don't do exactly as I say, this beloved cabin of yours will be on the market real soon," he said smugly. "And when it is, I might just buy it—*and burn it down*." Barnes gave Wolfe a defiant stare, then turned and slammed the door.

And Devon Barnes disappeared as quickly and mysteriously as he had arrived.

Wolfe stood there steaming. Barnes had just dragged him into a cesspool, and the last thing he wanted was to have anything to do with him. But then, there was Terri. They had worked together the previous year, and had developed a relationship. If Wolfe didn't help, Barnes wouldn't hesitate to put her in jeopardy.

So Wolfe began the makings of a plan, and the first step was to make sure that Terri was close by so he could protect her. Besides, he thought. He missed her.

# chapter 4

Wolfe stopped at the 7-11 convenience store to make a call on the pay phone.

"Associated Press, Terri Sommers speaking," said the voice on the other end of the line.

"Hi, Terri," he said.

A shocked silence. "Wolfe? Is that you?" she said, recognizing his voice instantly.

"Hasn't been *that* long, has it?"

"Over a year since I've heard from you. Of course, you know that. I thought maybe you died in some forsaken hellhole on the other side of the planet," she said.

"No such luck," he replied. "How've you been?"

"Busy," she said. "I've been promoted and given more responsibility, but no more help, and not much more pay, either. I guess they expect us to just love the job and do it for almost nothing."

"Ingrates," he replied.

"For sure."

"Any vacation time coming?" he asked.

"Lots," she said. "No time to take it so far and I'm starting to max out. Use it or lose, they're telling me."

"That's no good," he said, then paused. "Say. How about I give you an excuse to take some of that time off? Maybe even work into a story you can use? I'd even pay you, if you can believe that."

"I can't," she replied. "Believe that, I mean. But taking some time off might be a good idea. I'm too much of a workaholic to do it myself. This might be just the ticket I need for motivation to take a break."

"Great. Happy to be of service," he said, an obvious smile in his voice.

"You haven't told me what it's about, though," she said. "I might not be interested."

"Well, then, forget it. I have plenty of other women dying for a chance to work with me. I'll just call one of those."

"Nice try, Wolfe."

"No? Then, yes to my proposal?"

"I'll say yes to hear more about it," she said. "Knowing you, this might turn into something more than a cake assignment. In fact, I'll probably find myself running for my life like last year."

Wolfe laughed. "Deal," he said. "When can you come up?"

"I'll come up to hear more about it. I'll let you know then if I agree to work with you. When do you need me?" she asked.

"You're not here already?"

"Funny. I need to take care of a few things and then get my stuff together. I'll leave in the morning and be up there by dinner tomorrow. How's that?"

"Great. Meet me for dinner at the Little Italia. Say, sixish? My treat."

"It'd *better* be your treat," she said. "This whole thing, whatever it is, is going to be *your treat.*"

"I wouldn't have it any other way," he said. "Still driving that old powder-blue Mustang convertible?"

"I am, and don't call it old. I'm keeping it forever."

Wolfe smiled. "Good to know. Hanging on to old things is a good habit."

"Depends on how old," said Terri, smiling, "and *what* things. See you tomorrow. And Wolfe?"

"Yes?"

"This had better be good."

"I guarantee you won't be bored. How's that?"

"It'll do. For now."

Terri was key, and Wolfe was excited to get her involved. He was worried that Barnes and his cronies would try to use threats against her anyway. But that wasn't the only reason. They had developed a relationship last year—one that was made strong through adversity. Then there was the physical and emotional nature of their attraction for each other. He couldn't wait to see her. But first things first.

Next he called the county Coroner, Eino Loukkala.

The phone rang three times before it was answered. "Coroner's Office," came the scratchy voice with a strong Finnish accent. "What?"

Wolfe laughed. Eino had very few social skills and would not suffer fools. Since he figured most people fell into that category, he answered the phone in an abrupt manner that would hopefully discourage foolish questions and inane small talk.

"It's Wolfe, Eino. How the hell are you?"

"Wolfe?" he barked. "Where you been? Ain't heard from you in a month of Sundays. What d'ya want?"

Wolfe pictured Eino in his well-appointed office. The Coroner was tall and thin, over six-two, and the spitting image of the character in *The Legend of Sleepy Hollow*, Ichabod Crane. He had a long nose, droopy head, and a monstrous Adam's apple that bounced up and down like a yo-yo when he spoke. Some said he looked like a vulture, which wasn't totally inaccurate.

"Need your help, Eino," said Wolfe.

"'Course you do," said Eino caustically. "When do you ever *not* need my help?"

"Thanks, Eino. I knew you'd come through for me."

"What?" shouted Eino. "I never said I'd help you. What makes you so sure I will? I'm a busy man, you know. I'm internationally known now, after that last fiasco you got me involved in. I'm in big demand and . . ."

"Terri might be in trouble," Wolfe cut in.

That brought Eino up short. "Terri's in trouble?"

"Not yet," said Wolfe. "But she could be. And if she is, it could be serious."

"Well why didn't ya say so in the *first* place, Wolfe? Why ya always jerking me around?"

"Sorry, Eino. I forgot you need things more direct. I'll remember for the future."

"Yeah, well ya better, Wolfe. Ya know I can't *stand* . . ."

"Yes, Eino. I know your pet peeves. So, you in or out?"

"Well yeah, Wolfe. I'm in, of course. But only if I get to drive my souped-up hearse like a race car again. That was a blast."

"I have a feeling that you might just be able to do that again, Eino. Maybe even more than you want."

"Not possible. I could never get tired of pushing the limits of old Black Beauty. She's a thoroughbred."

"Glad to hear you're in, Eino. So far it's you and me and Terri."

"You gonna call Josephs, too? The Sheriff was pretty helpful last time. He let me drive fast too, and didn't do nothin' about it. I like that guy!"

"Gonna call him next. Thanks, Eino."

Eino's terse response was gruff and predictable. "Ya better," he said as he hung up.

# chapter 5

Wolfe decided to see Sheriff Josephs personally, so he hopped into his Jeep Wrangler 4X4 and headed to the Sheriff's Office. The building was relatively modern looking with a brick exterior, spacious lobby and an open plan with a Sergeant sitting at a desk facing the glass entrance.

"Wolfe!" shouted Sergeant Maki as he walked into the lobby. Maki was short but trim with greying hair, and wore the traditional tan uniform of most Sheriff Departments.

"Hey, Maki. How ya doing?" Wolfe said.

"Just finished one of my homemade pasties. Still one left. Want it?" he said, reaching back toward a brown lunch bag with a grease stain soaking through it.

Wolfe looked at the bag for a second. "What'd you put in it, Maki? Looks like something's leaking out."

Maki looked at the bag, and then shrugged his shoulder. "You know. Same old stuff—ground beef, pork, carrots, onions, potatoes, salt and pepper, all wrapped up and baked in a flour dough pie. You know. Pasty. You sure had enough of 'em."

Wolfe smiled. "I have. And they're delicious. Especially yours." Maki got a big toothy grin. "But I can't right now. I have to see the Sheriff. Is he in?"

"Oh sure. Yeah. Just a minute, eh? I'll let him know. He'll be glad to see ya." Maki scurried over to the Sheriff's door and lightly knocked. "Hey, Sheriff, guess who's here?"

Wolfe couldn't hear the Sheriff's response, but he could see Maki's head bobbing up and down, and hear him say, "yeah, yeah, OK. I'll tell him."

Maki came back over to Wolfe and said, "He says to tell you that since it's been so long since he's seen you, he's gonna have to do a criminal background check on you before you can come in his office. That's what he said." Maki seemed a bit nervous, though he knew the Sheriff was pulling his chain. Then again, he was never totally sure.

Wolfe grinned. "Then you go tell him I'm leaving and he's being kicked out of the band."

The door was still open, and the Sheriff heard Wolfe's response. He got up out of his chair and headed through the door. He was in plain clothes, which for him was a brown suit, brown shoes, white shirt, a fabric pocket badge that slipped over his breast pocket, and a striped tie with a handcuff tie-tac that most cops favored.

He was average height, with salt-and-pepper hair, neatly cut. He had a trim athletic build as opposed to the traditional caricature of the fat, pot-bellied hick. And Wolfe knew he could handle himself.

"I told Maki he should strip search you," he said to Wolfe. "You may be armed." He extended his hand and shook Wolfe's vigorously. "Long time, no see," Josephs said, chewing on a cigar stub that he never lit. "What brings you here? Not trouble I hope. Had enough of that the last time you darkened my door."

"Crazy time, wasn't it, Ed?" Wolfe replied.

"Crazy's not the half of it. C'mon in and tell me what you're up to." Wolfe briefed him on what had transpired with Devon Barnes, and that he had contacted Terri and Eino and they had already agreed to help. "And that just leaves you, Ed. What do you think?

Want to put your life at risk again, with no apparent reason for doing so?"

Josephs sat back in his swivel chair, rocking and staring through Wolfe as he mauled his cigar. "Not a hell of a lot to go on, is it?"

"Nope," said Wolfe.

"You have some bad history with this Barnes fellow, I take it."

"Worse than bad," replied Wolfe. "The man's an unscrupulous egomaniac who will stop at nothing to acquire wealth and power. He's evil through and through and he knows how to manipulate people to keep from being punished."

"And you think you're being manipulated?"

"Oh, I know I am. At least he's trying to. And the same for all of you, if you join me. Fact is, I have no idea if there's actually any substance to his claim, or if it's just someone's wet dream—either his or his superiors. That's not to say that even if there *is* nothing to it, it's not dangerous. Any contact with Barnes is fraught with peril. So I just want to give you fair warning that bad things can happen when he's involved."

"You really know how to make a sale, don't you, Wolfe?"

"Plan for the worst, hope for the best."

Josephs nodded but said nothing.

"So?" prompted Wolfe.

"So," began Josephs thoughtfully, "I'm in, of course. What else could I be?"

"I can think of a lot of things, Ed, but I'm glad you're with us."

"The band's back together?"

"The band's back together."

"I can hardly wait," said Josephs. "I'll restring my guitar." He leaned forward in his chair and reached for the intercom. "Maki," he said as he pressed the lever.

"Yeah, Sheriff?" Maki replied.

"Clear my schedule for the rest of the week. I have an important case I'll be working on that's going to take most of my time. You get an urgent call, page me and I'll get back to you. No radio traffic, OK?"

"Ten-four, Sheriff," replied Maki.

Josephs removed the cigar from his mouth and placed it carefully in the clean ashtray on his desk. "All right, Wolfe," he said with authority. "Let's get to it."

They scheduled a time to meet after Terri arrived. Wolfe gave Josephs as much background on Barnes as he could, including some of the things that they had done together in a previous life. Josephs just sat there in his chair in the conference room, his mouth hanging open at the things he heard.

"You're kidding me, right, Wolfe?"

"Sorry, Ed. Truth *is* stranger than fiction. Things like that are done all the time, but nobody ever hears about it. Because you tell about it, you die."

"But you just told *me* about it. What about me?"

"Oh. Sorry, Sheriff. Too late."

Josephs got in Wolfe's face. "Does that mean *you* are going to die, or is it going to be *me*?"

Wolfe smiled. "Well, if you don't blab, neither will I."

Josephs just shook his head. "But what about Eino—and *Terri*?"

"Don't worry. I wouldn't intentionally put her or any of you at risk. Nothing's likely to happen. Probably we'll investigate this person. We won't be successful because there's likely no such person, and it will be end of story. But if we don't perform due diligence, and they find out about it, well, it could be problematic."

"Problematic?" said Josephs. "*Problematic*?" he repeated. "Is that a euphemism, Wolfe? Does that mean what I think it means?"

Wolfe looked at Josephs. "Kinda. So the band must keep this all on the QT—OK?"

Josephs just shook his head. "Shoulda stayed in bed this morning," he mumbled as he headed back to the sanctuary of his office.

# chapter 6

*R*eaper had cleared the house and had made it several hundred yards away when the house blew up. He dropped flat on the ground and covered his head to protect himself from any possible falling debris. The sound was much louder than he expected, even though he hadn't known for sure that the house would explode. But when he smelled the gas so strongly, he couldn't take time to investigate, figuring a smell that strong had to be more than a leak. Whoever did it was probably pretty sure he was dead, and he would use that to his advantage.

When it was clear he would not be hit by anything from the explosion, Reaper got up and ran to a spot in the woods where he had hidden his emergency bugout pack. He dug it up, and put on the clothes that were folded up inside. He also had weapons that he tucked away in his clothing, including knives, guns, and other defensive and offensive weapons. In addition he had an emergency satellite phone, passports under different identities, and a considerable amount of cash in U.S. and foreign currencies, as well as emergency rations and medical supplies that would sustain him for a limited period of time.

After he had finished dressing and gunning up, he jogged back further into the woods until he came to a lean-to covered with branches and leaves, up against two large trees close together. He pulled the lean-to away from the trees and found his prize Honda motorcycle CM 450 E protected under a tarp. He'd bought it new with his last bonus, and put it out in the woods as an emergency bugout vehicle. He also rode it around the area for fun, and to make sure it stayed in tiptop working condition. He always kept the gas tank topped off and the bike ready to go at a moment's notice. That notice was now.

His first order of business was to contact his team members to warn them of what he suspected was a purge. They all had been on a mission together in a dangerous country where things had been done by others that were illegal, and most likely considered war crimes. None of the team members had participated in those actions, but they all had seen who did. And to that person, they were all a threat. They had considered the possibility that this day would come.

And now it had.

He started making calls on his sat phone, first to his teammates who were closest geographically, figuring that the person who had tried to kill him was moving on to the next closest one to do the same. He first placed calls to Hawk, then Zeb, Otto, and Sparrow in that order. None of them answered, so he left messages. He would have placed a call to Commander Wolfe, but he didn't have a phone number for him, probably because, as far as he knew, Wolfe didn't have a phone.

Then he hopped on his motorcycle and sped off to Hawk's apartment.

He hoped he wasn't too late.

# chapter 7

The place was right downtown Marquette. A business had once flourished there, but the owner had passed away and the business folded. It was a two-story office building that was purchased by a friend of Wolfe's, who then gutted the building and turned it into a luxury townhouse. The exterior remained the same, giving no indication of what, if anything, was on the inside.

Wolfe took his key and entered through the front door. Though the condo wasn't his, it might as well have been, since the owner built it for the exclusive purpose of providing Wolfe a place to stay for as long as he wanted, whenever he wanted. Wolfe had saved the friend's life many years ago, and the man was a multi-millionaire.

He had wanted to give Wolfe money for the sacrifice he had made in saving him, but Wolfe wouldn't take it. So the man built the condo and gave Wolfe a key, with the stipulation that he use it whenever he wanted, and there would be no remuneration. The man took care of all expenses associated with the building, including utilities, maintenance, and any upgrades.

Wolfe looked around. It was fully furnished in a décor and style that suited him. Wolfe didn't really want the condo, but he didn't want to hurt his friend's feelings. So he figured the best thing he could do under the circumstances was to use it occasionally. And this time was as good as any.

He figured while he was working on this problem with Eino, Terri, and Josephs, it would be easier if he stayed in town as well.

Besides. Terri would need a place to stay, and it would make no sense for him to pay for her to stay in a motel when she could stay in his condo. And though he hadn't seen her in over a year, he thought she wouldn't mind. At least, he hoped she wouldn't.

The place had plenty of space with a large living room and dining room, an eat-in kitchen with a prep-island, a large full bathroom, a spacious library/conference room, and a full bar, all on the first floor. He went to the second floor and found four large bedrooms, three with queen-size beds and one larger bedroom with two queens.

They all had walk-in closets and attached bathrooms. Each also had a sitting area and a TV with cable, a round table with four padded chairs, as well as a mini-fridge, coffee maker, and a stocked mini-bar.

The furnishings in the condo were of high quality, including a leather couch and chairs, plush carpets and hardwood floors, with tasteful decorations leaning masculine. Even though Wolfe didn't want it, he did like the way it looked and the comfort was hard to ignore. Normally his cabin suited him better. He liked a minimalist lifestyle. But for now, this would do.

He figured he would have to stock up on supplies and went to the refrigerator to see if there was anything in it. He opened the modern side-by-side and was shocked to see it chock-full of a wide variety of foods, from fresh vegetables and fruits, to beer and wine, juices, fresh meats, chicken and seafood, including lobster tails, shrimp and whitefish. Sparkling water and bottled water were also there, as well as an assortment of condiments.

He closed the refrigerator and went to the cupboards, suspecting that they would also be filled. They were. He shook his head. How did his friend know when he would be there, he wondered? Or did he always have it stocked?

If so, wouldn't the food eventually be ruined, especially the vegetables and fruit in the fridge? Then again, maybe he replaced everything weekly so it would always be ready? Hard to believe his friend did all that, thought Wolfe, but the proof was undeniable, staring him in the face.

Wolfe continued his inventory. There was a sub-level in the building, so he thought he should check that out as well. He didn't expect much because he had been in many basements in his life and there was never anything good in them, and often lots of *bad*.

This basement, however, was like none he had ever seen. It was no different in taste, style and décor than the upper levels, but it had in addition, a pool table, wet bar, another full bathroom, and a giant rear-projection TV—a huge black box that completely filled one corner.

There was also another refrigerator that Wolfe figured was stocked with more beer than food. He checked, and it was. In another room was a wine cellar, stocked with enough quality wines to keep them all inebriated until the millennium.

It was there that he found a note from his benefactor stating that he had a person employed whose job it was to make sure the food in the condo was fresh at all times. This person had her own access to the basement electronic door and was told to announce herself if it was occupied when she came to restock food, wine and linen. The note included her name and the code she would use to identify herself to him.

Wolfe laughed to himself. Now it all made sense.

Continuing his tour, he found a freezer that could hold large quantities of meat for an extended period of time. Maybe his friend figured he was a hunter and needed the storage space, thought Wolfe. He *was* a hunter. But not of deer. And he would not be needing the freezer for *that* game.

# chapter 8

Back upstairs in the library, Wolfe decided he had to think everything through before Terri arrived. He leaned back in the soft, leather chair, closed his eyes, and visualized all the components of this dilemma. He let his mind float off in the distance, with the individual parts of the puzzle free-floating about.

The number of pieces grew as he let his mind expand. There was Barnes—could he believe anything he said? Then there was the unknown person who had supposedly invented the dark energy machine. It sounded like DARPA was his sponsor. Did he work alone? Was the machine ready and operational or only in the design stages? Or somewhere in between? And what about the Soviet probe? Were they GRU or KGB?

Pieces from Wolfe's past floated into view: people he had worked with; people he had killed; weapons dealers; drug dealers; those who stood to lose if the person wasn't found; those who stood to gain by destroying Wolfe's career; those who stood to gain by destroying Wolfe.

And somewhere amidst all those pieces floating in the ether of Clayton Wolfe's mind, a tiny spark of light flickered. It caught his attention, and he tried to focus on it, to bring it closer so he could examine it. But the harder he tried, the more elusive it became, darting around, hiding behind the puzzle pieces, fading out and then popping back up in a different place.

The more he focused, the more the spark played its elusive game of cat-and-mouse. As he chased it, it took him deeper and deeper.

But Wolfe was undaunted. The spark allowed him to believe that this puzzle was solvable, and that he and his team would be the ones to solve it. Wolfe knew it was the spark of truth—of enlightenment. He had seen such sparks before, and they had always led him to success.

And then the sleep he often struggled so hard to come by, found him—and the spark extinguished. But Wolfe slept with the realization that he would find it again. And when he did, those who had caused this mess would pay dearly.

The next morning Wolfe arose early. He unpacked his belongings that he brought from his cabin, which weren't much. When he went to the closet to hang up his shirts, he was surprised to see clothes already there. He looked them over, and found that not only were they the same style as those he usually wore, they were also in his size.

And they were clean. As he continued exploring the master bedroom, he found more clothes—underwear, socks, shoes, bathroom necessities—everything he would need if he was going to live there permanently—which was, of course, exactly what his friend wanted.

Wolfe shook his head and laughed. There was more here than he had ever seen in his life, and he hadn't asked for any of it. He wondered what he would get if he *did* ask for something?

While he pondered that, he stripped off the clothes he had inadvertently slept in last night, found an oversized terrycloth bath towel, and headed to the shower. As he pulled back the curtain, he found a tile shelf with soap, shampoo, conditioner, and a loofa.

He picked up the loofa, turned it over in his hand, and laughed again. Putting it down, he used the rest of the supplies to shower. The water was hot and came in a wide stream that enveloped his body. The heat was therapeutic and washed away a lot of the stress he had been feeling since his meeting with Barnes.

After he dried off and shaved, he wrapped the towel around his waist and went to the closet. He had planned to simply stick to his existing wardrobe, but as he looked at it, he realized that his clothes hadn't been washed recently, and that he would have to launder them before he could wear them again.

He looked back at the clothes in the closet, and decided for the sake of expediency he would wear the new duds. After all, he rationalized, that was the reason he was staying here in the first place.

He pulled on a pair of tan Dockers, navy socks, a dark blue oxford shirt, and cordovan loafers. He found a thick brown leather belt that fit him perfectly. Now all he needed was a jacket. He looked around some more, and found a closet he hadn't seen before near the front door.

Thankfully, inside was a variety of coats and jackets for all weather conditions. He selected a brown leather jacket and slipped it on. Not surprisingly, it fit him perfectly. How his friend was able to do all this astonished him. But he had no time to spend thinking about it. He would do that later and have a frank *discussion* about all this with his friend.

He thought about making some breakfast in his condo, as there were all the necessary foods for his favorite: eggs, bacon, sausage, toast and coffee. But he didn't want to take the time for all that plus the clean-up, so he decided to head to Al's Diner just down the street.

# chapter 9

The diner was a modern version of days gone by. The food was good and there was plenty of it, and the price was right.

Besides that, the waitresses were attractive and friendly, except for 'Big Jack,' who wasn't a waitress at all, but who occasionally waited on tables when things got busy or when he was short-staffed. Big Jack was neither attractive nor friendly, but he did take the orders correctly and he brought the food quickly.

There was no 'chat' with Big Jack, which suited Wolfe just fine. He liked his privacy when he ate alone, and would much prefer thinking and watching the people come and go, rather than to engage in small talk, which he doubted existed in Big Jack's limited vocabulary of sighs, grunts, and eye-rolling.

A young waitress came over wearing a white nametag that read, "Jenny." As the diner had a Fifties theme, she wore clothes of the *Happy Days* era, thankfully sans the roller skates. She seemed perky and had a nice, easy smile. She wore a white uniform with bobby socks and saddle shoes. She had blond hair and blue eyes, a great figure, and looked like she had just stepped off the cover of *The Saturday Evening Post*.

"What can I getcha?" she asked, her order pad and pencil at the ready.

"Hi, Jenny," Wolfe said. "How about a large black coffee, three eggs over easy, bacon and sausage, wheat toast, hash-browns, and a large glass of orange juice?"

Jenny just stared at him, her blond hair and blue eyes framing a shocked look on her face. Her mouth was open in a half grin, as if she couldn't decide whether he was joking or not. Wolfe had seen this look many times before. She had no idea how much muscle was hidden beneath his clothes, nor how high his metabolism was. He looked fit for a six-foot tall man, and he had very broad shoulders. She wondered where he would put all that food.

He ended her suspense. "Yes, I'm serious," he said. "And no, I'm not expecting anyone else."

She nodded her head and refocused. "Right," she said, getting it all down. "Anything else? An order of pancakes? Waffles? Dessert?"

Wolfe looked at her, saw the pixie twinkle in her eye and smiled. "Is there anything else left on the menu?"

She smiled and kind of laughed. "Not much," she said. Her gaze lasted a little more than was comfortable for Wolfe unless they were going on a date, in which case it was more than fine.

"That'll be it," he said kindly.

"Great," she said, ripping off the order and putting her pad away. "I'll get started with that coffee."

She started to walk away, then turned with a minx smile on her face and said, "OK if I bring that coffee a pot at a time? I'll leave it on the table, if that's OK."

"That would be great," he said.

She nodded and turned back toward the kitchen. She had a smile on her face the whole time. Cute, he thought. Pretty *and* a sense of humor. She seemed to like him, but then he reminded himself that she did work for tips. And then he remembered that Terri was coming up in a few hours and realized he had gotten off track with the waitress. He shook his head and changed mental gears.

She brought the first cup and poured it for him, then left the pot as promised, and returned to the kitchen. The coffee was hot, and as much as he just wanted to down the whole cup in one gulp, he blew on it and sipped it until he got enough of the caffeine to his brain to jumpstart his cognitive processes.

While he was doing this, he was scanning the diner, watching people coming and going, eating, talking, or sitting alone—like him. He didn't know most of the people there, though he did recognize a few. It was October in Michigan's Upper Peninsula—prime "leaf-peeping" season—and there were a lot of tourists trying to soak up the ambience, as well as the coffee, for their short trip up north to photograph all the colorful leaves that blanketed the area.

Wolfe wasn't sure what he was looking for, but he needed to be looking for things that seemed out of place, or that didn't look quite right. Barnes had had plenty of time to set things up before he had his meeting at Wolfe's cabin. He may have planted spies of his own to watch Wolfe and his crew—to keep tabs on them.

If he did, Wolfe would find them and turn the tables. It would not just be a matter of spotting them, knew Wolfe. He had a sixth sense about these things. He often got "feelings" about people or situations that were hard to verbalize, but which usually blossomed into full-fledged weeds. So right now, he began looking for the "weeds."

His food came, and literally filled the table top of the booth. True to her word, Jenny took the old coffee pot off the table and replaced it with a freshly brewed pot. "Anything else I can bring you, hon? There's ketchup on the table."

"No, I think you've outdone yourself. Thanks, Jenny."

She got a broad smile and her eyes twinkled. "Why thank you, sir," she said. "My *pleasure.*"

Mine too, thought Wolfe as he watched her walk away. Then Maslow's Hierarchy of Needs kicked in, and he dove into the food to satisfy his primal need for nourishment. First things first, he thought. Always. First things first.

He scanned the diner more carefully between bites. The process engaged his mind, and also his sense of self-preservation. There had been many times in his past while in various eating establishments that by doing so, he had discovered people who were planning to do him ill.

So he scanned and observed, watched and analyzed each person, including those behind the counter and in the kitchen, when they were visible. Everyone was suspect in his world. Everyone was a potential threat unless proven otherwise. Life for Wolfe was better that way—and longer.

After observing for some time, having completed all of his meal and most of the coffee, he signaled Jenny he was finished. She came over quickly, again with a big grin on her face.

"Can I get you anything else?" she said.

"No thanks, Jenny. Just the check please." He smiled back.

"No problem," she said. She ripped off the handwritten slip and laid it in front of him. "I can take that up for you, if you want, or you can pay at the register up front."

Wolfe looked at the slip, dug into his pocket and pulled out a wad of bills, mostly twenties. One of them was her tip. "That should do it," he said as he handed her the slip and the money. "Keep the change, Jenny. Your service was excellent."

"Thank you so much," she gushed. "Please come again."

"You can count on it," he said as he stood to leave. As he did so, he caught a quick glance from a man at the counter he had been watching. He played back in his mind all that he remembered about the man, who was paying his bill the same time as Wolfe.

As he did that, he realized that the man had come in the diner just after Wolfe did. He ordered food and coffee, but not nearly as much as Wolfe. And he got finished much quicker. He also refused the last couple of offers of refills on his coffee, yet he stayed. Wolfe realized that the man had not engaged in any conversation with the employees nor those near him at the counter. In fact, it was like the man was just waiting for Wolfe to finish and leave.

# chapter 10

Wolfe walked toward the front door of the diner, studiously avoiding looking at the man, who was doing the same thing, focusing on some minutia regarding his napkin. Wolfe didn't slow when he hit the glass door and popped it open.

He quickly turned left and went down two doors and then turned left again into a blind alley. There he stopped about three feet back from the edge of the front of the building where he couldn't be seen, and stood with his back to the brick wall, and waited for his tail to come into view.

The man did. But rather than turn quickly down the alley and run into a trap, he moved a few feet past the wall where Wolfe was hiding, and turned to face him. Wolfe did a quick assessment of the man. He had on dark clothing of heavy fabric, solid shoes, and wore a ball cap. What he could see of his hair was dark brown, almost black and he had a swarthy complexion.

He was a large man, about six-two, two-hundred and forty pounds, muscular with minimal fat by the way he walked. He also walked with confidence, like he was used to getting his way, whether by intimidation or by brute force.

Wolfe realized that he hadn't grabbed his gun before he left the condo, so he was at a decided disadvantage if the man was armed. But it was one-on-one, so he still had the advantage.

"Looking for someone?" said Wolfe, facing the man.

The man tried to stare Wolfe down—to intimidate him. It didn't work. Wolfe stared back with a fearless, laser stare.

Finally the man said, "I'm looking for you. I want to talk to you." The man had a strong Slavic accent but spoke English well.

"Well here I am," said Wolfe. "So talk."

The man took a couple of steps forward away from the street and into the alleyway.

"You're the man they call Wolfe."

"That's right," said Wolfe, not budging. "And what might your name be?"

The man blinked, like he had never gotten such a response before. Then he recovered and said, "My name is Vlad. You will remember it."

Wolfe laughed dismissively. "Right. So, what do you want to ask me, *Vlad* ?" Wolfe said his name with more than a tinge of sarcasm, trying to provoke him.

Vlad took another step toward Wolfe. "I want some information. I want to know what you are working on. I want to know who you are looking for. And I want to know where he is. And I want to know, now." Vlad gave his most menacing look, balled up his fists, and clenched his jaw.

"Don't know what you're talking about, big guy," said Wolfe, adopting a much more relaxed stance. "I think you've got the wrong person. I was just having lunch and now I'm going to go back to my apartment and take a nap. Or maybe I'll do a little fishing. Not exactly sure yet. You see, I'm retired. I'm not working anymore."

By the quizzical look on Vlad's face, he didn't know how to take Wolfe's response. He was not used to that kind of reaction. Usually people were afraid of him. They would try to get away.

This was new territory for him. Then he decided to dismiss all that and move ahead.

"No you're not going to take a nap or go fishing," said Vlad. "You're going to answer my questions. And then I'm going to take you apart."

Wolfe smiled at him and said, "Go for it." He had decided that this was not going to be a protracted fight. Considering the size of Vlad, he was going to get in and get it done.

A challenge. Vlad could deal with that. He didn't experience it often, but he certainly knew how to deal with it. "Let me show you," he said menacingly as he took a step toward Wolfe, moving to within striking distance.

But instead of moving away from Vlad, Wolfe suddenly rushed forward, ducking the swing as Vlad tried to land a roundhouse punch, which was usually the only punch he had to throw. Instead, Wolfe closed the distance and brought his fist up from his waist with terrific speed, using all the muscles in his body to force his sizable fist up like a jackhammer into the underside of Vlad's chin.

Wolfe heard the inevitable snapping of the jawbone and saw Vlad's head whiplash back at an odd angle. Then there was another ominous sound as Vlad's head reached its apex backward. Bone and muscle experienced extremes of force that were simply no match for the deadly power of Wolfe's ferocious assault. They both gave way instantly, as did Vlad's legs, when the life force fled out of them.

Vlad crumpled to the ground like a sack of potatoes thrown from a truck. Dead before he hit the ground. Vlad was no longer a threat to Wolfe, or to anybody else for that matter. His days of threatening and intimidating were over.

Wolfe looked down at the lifeless body and wondered who he was and who sent him. He looked around for any cohorts who might be with Vlad. Seeing none, he checked his pockets for any ID, but true to form of operators worldwide, he had no identification on him, and only a few dollars left over after he had paid his lunch bill. Vlad had apparently made no plans for an extended stay, and thought that his job would be over quickly. As it turned out, it was—but not in the way he had anticipated.

Wolfe went back to the diner and used the pay phone to call the Sheriff. He told him what had happened and where the body was. He went into the washroom of the diner and cleaned up, as he had some blood on him from the damage he'd done to Vlad's face. Then he went back to the alley to wait for the Sheriff.

By the time he got back out, Sheriff Josephs was already there. The cruiser was parked at the entrance to the alley, blocking the view of the body from the street. Wolfe saw Josephs standing on the other side of the cruiser where the body was, looking puzzled.

"What's the matter Ed?" Wolfe asked as he approached the Sheriff.

Josephs turned to face Wolfe as he walked up. "OK, smart ass," he said. "What's this all about?"

Wolfe looked over at the body. Except there was no body. It was gone. "What the hell's going on? Where's the body? It was right there," he said, pointing to a spot of blood in the dirt ten feet from where they stood.

"Yeah, I see the blood. What I don't see is the body," said Josephs.

Wolfe shook his head. "I swear it was there five minutes ago when I left to go into the diner to call you. Then I washed up and came back here. I can tell you one thing for sure, though," said Wolfe.

"And what's that?" said Josephs.

"He didn't get up and walk out of here." "You sure about that?"

"Very sure," he said. "The man was dead."

Josephs walked to the blood spot and looked at the gravel. "Yeah, I guess you're right. You can see the drag marks where the man's heels had scraped the dirt, probably when he was moved and lifted into a car or van."

"Well whoever moved him was pretty strong, because this man was large—probably two hundred and forty pounds, about six-two. That's a lotta dead weight, Sheriff—no pun intended."

Josephs shook his head and rolled his eyes. "You get any ID on this guy?"

"No, nothing but the description I gave you. He called himself Vlad. May have been his real name, maybe not. He said it as though he was real proud of it though, so it might have been real. But there was nothing else on him but a few small bills and some change, probably what was left from his meal."

"And where is it?" asked Josephs.

"Still with him, I guess. I put it back in his pocket. Figured it wasn't going anywhere."

"Bad assumption on your part, I'd say," said Josephs.

Wolfe just nodded, and wondered who else was out there that he had to worry about. Somebody bigger than Vlad. Someone who now knew what Wolfe was capable of. Someone who would be better prepared than Vlad was in future encounters.

He decided there was something he had to do immediately.

# chapter 11

Back at his new condo, Wolfe found the gun his friend had left him. It was a Smith & Wesson .45 caliber semi-automatic.

Wolfe was very familiar with the weapon. He had used it, or a version of it, in much of his military/government/clandestine operative career. With it was a note stating that the front door key fit a gun storage safe embedded in the hardwood floor of the dining room, under an ornate Persian rug.

Wolfe moved the rug, opened the safe and found what he was looking for—and more. In it was a shoulder holster rig, an ankle holster for a smaller back-up weapon, a holster for his hip and one to slip in the small of his back. There were a dozen boxes of ammunition and a half-dozen magazines, as well as various other armaments, weapons, and defensive devices, most of which Wolfe left in the box.

He loaded two magazines, and put the others back in the safe. He put one in his pocket and the other into his weapon. Then he racked a round into the chamber, ejected the magazine and replaced that round, then replaced the magazine. That gave him an extra round, or a total of nine rounds in the gun. That also meant that his gun was always "hot" and if needed, all he had to do was pull the trigger which was double-action on the first shot.

None of that wait-until-there-is-a-serious-problem-then-take-the-time-to-rack-one-into-the-chamber-and-make-a-lot-of-noise-to-warn-the-suspect-of-impending-gunplay business, he thought, which is the scenario constantly shown in movies and on TV. That stuff could get you killed in a heartbeat. Plus, he knew he would be dealing with Devon Barnes and his goons.

Little did he know how right he was.

# chapter 12

*R*eaper had his motorcycle helmet on with the smoked plastic face shield, so nobody could see who was on the bike, even though that was pretty much impossible anyway while traveling at night. But he was taking no chances. And he was getting a little nervous because he couldn't reach any of the team. Could be they weren't home or didn't have their sat phones with them. After all, they were the size of a brick and difficult to conceal.

He decided to go to Hawk's house, which wasn't far from him as he cruised down the road on his powerful bike. Hawk was staying in an apartment building, ground floor, in one of the middle apartments in a row of four. He tried the buzzer, but there was no answer. But then it might not have worked, so he went around to the back, where there was an alley and a window to his bedroom.

Reaper was cautious, because the person who tried to kill him might be in Hawk's apartment already, or if not, might still be coming and could catch Reaper there as well. He parked his bike a couple of doors down, and quietly came up to the window. He wondered how he would get it open. He didn't have to worry. It was already open.

There were curtains in front of the window, partially open, which were blowing slightly in the cool, night air. He tried to look inside, but it was dark in the bedroom. He let his eyes adjust to the dark for a few minutes more, then tried again. Now he could see the bed and a form laying on it, but he couldn't recognize who it was.

Finally, hearing no sounds of movement in the apartment, he whispered as loud as he could, "Hawk!" The form didn't move. "Hawk!" he said again. Again, no movement. He looked at the window again, and figured it was large enough for him to get through, but just barely, due to his height and shoulder width. So he put his hands on the window sill and hefted himself up and in.

He crouched on the floor beneath the window, trying to breathe as quietly as he could, listening for any sound, including the breathing of a sleeping man. He heard nothing. His heart began speeding up as all his senses were on high alert. He crept over to the bed, watching and listening for a possible assault by an attacker.

He reached the bed and bent over listening. It was definitely a man lying face down, his face away from Reaper. He whispered one more time. "Hawk!" There was no answer, no movement. He pulled out a small penlight from one of his many pockets and shone it on the man's face. It was Hawk. And he was dead.

Reaper started looking quickly around, swiveling his head from side to side. He flicked the light around the room. There was nothing. He examined his friend and teammate. There was no apparent injury on his back, so he carefully turned him over. His body was still slightly warm. There was a huge pool of blood that had soaked into the bedding and mattress from a knife wound to his heart.

Reaper looked at the body. Death would have been instantaneous. Then why, he wondered, should the assassin turn the body face down? The killer would normally just leave as quickly as possible and not take the time, nor take the chance of leaving more physical evidence around than necessary.

Then he looked at the body again. Hawk was fully clothed.

Maybe the killer needed to get his wallet or things from his back pockets. Reaper turned him back over on his front and checked Hawk's back pockets. Empty. He looked over on the dresser and on the night stand, including in the drawers.

No wallet. That must have been it. But then, assassins don't usually take personal possessions of their victims either. More evidence to connect them with the killing. Must have been something special in that wallet. Reaper checked his watch. He had no addresses for the others, and none had returned his call. It was time to contact Commander Wolfe. He was going to have to fly to Marquette to find him.

Hopefully before it was too late.

# chapter 13

Wolfe had his weapon loaded and firmly seated in the holster behind his back. From his condo he called Josephs to see if he could use the department's firing range. He wanted to sight-in the gun and fire a couple of boxes of rounds through it to check it out. Josephs made arrangements and Wolfe headed to the range. As expected, the weapon was in perfect working order. Then he cleaned it, wiped it down, and put it back in his holster.

When he returned to the condo, he called Eino but there was no answer. So he went to his duffle bag and pulled out a small black device the size of a pack of cigarettes.

His wealthy friend was kind enough to supply Wolfe with two telephone lines in the condo, one in the kitchen and one in the library, so he went to the library, unplugged the phone line, and plugged it into one side of the black box.

He took another short telephone cord and plugged one end into the other side of the black box, and the remaining end into the phone. Then he dialed a long distance phone number, one of several he would dial.

The black box was a device that encoded the message by the use of a highly complex algorithm. Wolfe had previously provided such boxes to his associates when he worked for the Agency, devices which could encode and decode messages as well. All the people he was calling had such a box. He dialed the first number. It rang once.

"Wolfe," said a deep male voice. "Don't tell me you've been activated—again."

"Nope," said Wolfe. "This is different."

"Different how?"

"Different in that I am essentially working alone on this one."

"This one *what*?"

Wolfe explained the situation as briefly as possible.

The man, known as Otto, thought for a minute before responding. "Have any idea who is ultimately behind all this?"

"If you can believe Barnes, it's General Birchmont," replied Wolfe.

"That's not good," said Otto.

"That's where I am—that's why I called you. I'm going to need your help, if you're willing and able."

"Of course I'll assist you, any way I can," replied Otto. "But how much help I will be, well, that is problematic and based on many variables over which I have no control, considering I'm here and you're there. Do you have any other confederates assisting you?"

"Yes," replied Wolfe. He named them and gave a brief background on each.

"They vetted by you personally?" asked Otto.

"I have direct experience with all of them and they're solid."

"That's good enough for me," said Otto. "Let me quietly begin putting out feelers and see if I can get a sense of what may or may not be going on. If it's nothing as you have indicated might be a possibility, it shouldn't be too long before I find out. I'll call you back on this secure system. Do you have the secure messaging system for these calls as well?" asked Otto.

"Yes, as do the others I will be calling."

"You calling your other former associates as well?"

"I am," replied Wolfe. "I don't know how many will be available or willing to assist me, but I'll know that soon enough."

"OK," said Otto. "I'll be in touch. Be careful. You're in treacherous waters here."

"Don't I know it," replied Wolfe. Then he terminated the call. Wolfe made four more calls. He left messages with each and hoped he could get at least one of them to help him. He needed that if he was going to have a realistic chance of success.

And then he thought of Terri, whom he would be meeting very shortly. He quickly switched mental gears and made preparations to meet her for dinner. He only had about an hour to get ready, unless she was early, in which case he didn't really have enough time. He laughed. Who was he kidding? Terri had *never* been early during their time together. In fact, he didn't know if she even owned a watch.

He quickly selected the clothes he planned to wear, disrobed, started the shower, selected the *'desert downpour'* setting, and cranked up the temperature to steam bath. Two showers in one day, he thought. He must be delirious.

He let the hot water and steam relax the knots and tension out of his body and put him in the proper frame of mind for his first meeting with Terri Sommers in over a year. He was feeling a bit apprehensive about seeing her again, especially since they had not talked during the time they were apart. She had seemed OK when he had called her, but in truth, he didn't know what to expect. But he had his hopes.

# chapter 14

*I*n the meantime Reaper was trying to get to the airport. He had already dumped all his weapons in a storage locker on the way, knowing that he couldn't take them on the airplane. He also would need to get a last-minute ticket for a flight to Marquette, which was not going to be easy, and was going to be very expensive. He had enough money, that wasn't the problem. The problem was if he got tagged with a false passport. That would be the end. On the plus side, he reasoned, people in the know believed him to be dead. So nobody would be looking for him under his real identity, to be scheduling a flight to Marquette, or anywhere else, for that matter. In any event, hopefully the false identity on his passport shouldn't cause any suspicion. The photo was of him—albeit a little younger, but it still matched. So he should be OK there.

The trick would be in finding Commander Wolfe once he got to Marquette. He had no driver's license or credit card with which to rent a car. Well, he would just have to worry about that when he arrived—if he arrived.

He decided not to think about that, and made preparations to purchase his ticket.

# chapter 15

Wolfe had decided on casual clothes he found in the well-appointed closet provided by his good friend. In this instance, he was happy to have some alternatives to the severe nature of his normal wardrobe. He wanted to look nice for Terri, but not too far outside what matched his personality. He finally dressed in faded jeans, a longsleeve black t-shirt, and brown leather boots. Then he donned his leather jacket, checked himself in the mirror, and headed out the door.

He found a secluded booth in the back of the Little Italia restaurant where the lights were low, and mostly provided by a red glass globe with a candle burning in it. The tablecloth was red and white checked, and the remainder of the décor was decidedly Italian as well.

Then he saw Terri Sommers enter the room. She appeared to be looking for him. The host pointed him out, and Terri nodded, smiled, and headed his way. He stood and walked over to her as she approached. He smiled and gave her a hug, and she hugged him back.

"You look great," he said. She was wearing jeans as well, with a white crewneck cable sweater, and a green, zip-up safari hooded jacket. His pulse rate notched up a bit. As she went to seat herself in the booth, Wolfe glanced at her shoes. Then he looked up at Terri who had been watching him. "Keds?" he said with a slight smile on his face.

"Why mess with a good thing?" she said, smiling. Her emerald eyes and red hair glowed in the candle light. Wolfe had forgotten how beautiful she was.

"I can think of no good reason," he said as he tried to clear his head. He moved to his side of the booth. As he did, he thought of those Keds. They had been her signature footwear the last time they were together, when they had been successful in fighting off evil men with evil intentions.

He hoped that that would be the case this time, too—if there was an actual case to be working on. He wasn't sure there was, but he guessed that there might be. At the very least, someone was going to a great deal of trouble to make him *think* there was something worth investigating. He put the thought aside as Terri picked up her menu.

"I'm starved," she said emphatically. "I haven't eaten anything since I left Chicago, so you'd better feed me quickly."

Wolfe looked up, saw the look in her eye, and signaled Antonio the waiter.

Antonio came right over. "Yes, Mister Wolfe. What can I get for you?"

"Can you rustle us up some bread and olive oil, and a bottle of your house red wine quickly before my date begins eating the menu?"

Antonio looked over at Terri with a flicker of concern in his eyes. Then back at Wolfe. "Yes, of course, Mister Wolfe. I will have it pronto!" Antonio scurried away not wanting to disappoint a good customer.

Antonio returned with a fresh loaf of crusty Italian bread and a bottle of wine. He poured some olive oil and balsamic vinegar into a dish, added some spices, then took their orders. He poured a little wine in Wolfe's glass for his approval, and after Wolfe sipped and nodded, he poured some in each of their glasses.

After Antonio left, Wolfe raised his glass and gave a toast. "To the past—and the future."

Terri raised her glass. "To both," she responded. They clinked glasses and drank some of the wine. Then Wolfe broke the bread and gave some to each of them. Terri took her piece. "Thanks," she said. "Can't believe how hungry I am. Excuse me if I eat this whole thing."

"Have at it," said Wolfe. "I'm hungry, too."

He glanced at Terri from time to time, as he concentrated on his bread and wine. Terri did the same. After a bit, Terri finished her bread, took a swallow of wine, and set the glass on the table.

"OK," she said. "So tell me about this case." She looked directly into his eyes. He brought her up to date regarding his meeting with Devon Barnes at his cabin, the threat against Terri, and the stated threat that Barnes had hoped Wolfe would fail, and what he would do if he did.

"So that's it?" she said.

"I'm afraid so," said Wolfe.

Before their conversation could continue, their food arrived. Antonio served Terri her pasta carbonara and Wolfe his crab linguini Alfredo. Antonio also brought more bread, and another bottle of wine, since the first bottle had already been consumed. Quite quickly, he thought. He hoped this did not portend some future problems before he got his tip. He quickly left the couple alone.

They began eating and Terri began to summarize. "So, let me see if I have this straight. Barnes appears out of nowhere at your *inaccessible* cabin, tells you that the Agency has intercepted a Soviet communique that seemed to indicate that a person somewhere in or around Marquette has secretly developed a dark energy device, which if it is true, could destabilize the entire world economic system. Is that it in a nutshell?"

"Yes," said Wolfe, wiping his mouth with his white cloth napkin. "But don't forget the threat against you."

"That's right," said Terri. "And against you," she added.

"Right," said Wolfe. "Against both of us. That's one of the reasons I called you—to keep you safe here with me."

"Any other reason?" she said, coyly.

"Well, yeah," he said. "Also so you could help me investigate this mess and find out if there's any truth to it. And if there is, to figure out what to do about it."

"And those are the only reasons?" she continued to probe.

Wolfe paused, thought about where she was going with this. Their eyes locked. He decided to go for it. "And I missed you," he said finally.

Terri smiled, a twinkle flickering in her eyes. "Good to know," she said, breaking eye contact and taking another forkful of food.

Wolfe didn't quite know what to say. She kept him dangling while she ate her food. But not for long. She took another swallow of wine, set her glass down, and wiped her mouth with her napkin.

"I missed you too," she said, finally. "But I must tell you that in the absence of any contact from you for a *year*, I did begin to date."

Wolfe looked surprised. "You did?" Terri nodded.

"Are you still dating someone now?" he asked.

"Well," said Terri playfully, "not right this minute, but, yes. We're still dating as of your phone call."

"Oh," said Wolfe, returning to his food. "Congratulations."

Terri laughed, shook her head. "Well, there are no congratulations in order, Clay. We're just dating. Nothing more than that."

Wolfe seemed relieved. "OK. Just wondering." He decided to switch gears back to their current problem. "Anyway, would you be willing to help try to find this person? You did such a great job last time, and I think that together, we might have a fighting chance." Wolfe took another drink of wine and emptied his glass. Terri sipped her wine slowly.

"Same crew?" she asked.

Wolfe nodded. "You, me, Eino, and Josephs. And maybe a few previous associates of mine, if I can get them."

"Associates?" she asked.

"People like me I worked with in the past. People I can trust."

"Sounds good," said Terri. "I'm in."

Wolfe smiled. "Excellent," he said. "I'll inform the others that the group is back together."

Terri smiled, and wondered what this all meant.

As they finished their meal, Wolfe told Terri about the condo and said that she was welcome to stay there, no strings attached. She would have her own room and private bathroom, and could partake of whatever food and beverages were there during her stay. He explained that the condo would be headquarters for as long as it took to complete the operation, and that it would be a safe place with phones and plenty of other resources.

Terri agreed and told him she would follow him to the condo and retrieve her bags from her car when they arrived. Wolfe paid the bill, leaving a large gratuity for Antonio.

Wolfe showed Terri into the condo and she stopped at the entrance. "Wow," she said. "Nice place."

"I'll give you the cook's tour," he said as they walked further into the room. As he showed her around, she began asking questions, her reporter's curiosity coming to the fore.

"So how'd you come to have this place?" she asked.

Knowing it would be hard to offer a spare description of his benefactor without more probing questions from Terri, he nonetheless gave it a shot. "A man whose life I saved wanted to repay me for doing so, but I told him I didn't want any money.

"However since he was very wealthy, he felt he had to do something, so he decided to make his gifts in-kind services. I wouldn't agree to take ownership of this property, or any other, so he purchased this condo and other items and made them available to me to use at any time, all costs associated with them included."

Terri looked around at the expensive furnishings. "Quite the gift," she said. "No taxes to pay, no maintenance worries—just use the items at no cost—no muss, no fuss."

"That's about right," said Wolfe.

"So who *is* this benefactor of yours?" she said, smiling.

Wolfe shook his head. "He wishes to remain anonymous, and I will respect that," he said.

Terri nodded. "I understand. "I'm still curious, but I understand."

"I appreciate that," said Wolfe. Then, trying to change the subject, he said, "You must be tired from your long drive. Care to get settled in your room and relax some?"

"That sounds like a great idea," said Terri. "I am bushed and I think it's time to turn in. Thanks for the great meal and the wonderful company, Wolfe. I'm looking forward to working with you. Good night," she said as she headed up the stairs to her bedroom suite.

Wolfe realized he was going to have to treat this operation cautiously. But he could make some assumptions. One, he knew

Barnes very well and he could count on him behaving predictably under various situations. That would be helpful.

Two, he knew the types of people Barnes worked for, because Wolfe had worked for them in the past. And even though the names and faces had undoubtedly changed, the types of people who grav-itate to such positions would invariably be the same.

Three, he believed there was probably something going on, although the chance of it being what Barnes said it was, was questionable. Or if the situation described was correct, the end goal was most likely vastly different from Barnes' stated objective.

So, that was that, thought Wolfe. He sat back in his over-stuffed leather chair, and began breathing deeply and exhaling slowly and completely. After several minutes of this, he closed his eyes and started his program of self-hypnosis. He dove deeper and deeper into his psyche, dropping through level after level, until he reached the place where his thoughts began.

He built barrier after barrier, stone by stone, brick by brick until he had built the walls necessary to isolate himself from the emotions that might interfere in his tasks ahead.

# chapter 16

The next morning he was at the Sheriff's Office, waiting for the others to arrive. As he sat in the conference room, consuming a cup of black coffee, Sergeant Maki bustled into the room. "Hey, Wolfe," he said urgently.

Wolfe looked at the distraught Sergeant. "What is it, Maki? You looked stressed."

"I *am* stressed. We just found a body in the Dead River."

"Appropriately named," said Wolfe, with his typical gallows humor.

"Yeah, well, it may not be so funny to you when I tell you that it sure fits the description you gave us of the man you killed."

"Have you examined the body?" Wolfe asked Maki.

Maki looked nervous. "Well, no, not yet. I didn't find it. A fisherman found it snagged along the bank. He went to a camp to use their phone and called it in. And his description was pretty good for your guy," he said. His eyes darted back and forth like he was looking for an escape from the room, and from Wolfe. Then he gulped and continued. "And the fisherman said he was pretty sure the man had a broken jaw and a broken neck. That's what he said. He said he was in the military and he had seen that before, and he was pretty sure that's what had happened to him."

Just then Sheriff Josephs entered the room. "Did you hear?"

"Maki was just telling me about it," said Wolfe.

Josephs turned to Maki. "Maybe we should stop speculating and have the body examined by a professional. What do you think, Sergeant?"

Maki was nervously dancing from foot to foot. "Yeah, sure," he said. "That makes sense. A professional."

"Maybe you should call the Coroner and let him take a look at the scene, then he can take the body back and give it a thorough examination," said Joseph.

"Yeah," said Maki. "I'll do that." He whirled around and exited the room as fast as he could to avoid any further contact with Wolfe.

Josephs turned to Wolfe. "Why don't you come with me to the crime scene, if it is indeed a crime scene, and let's see what we can see."

"Sounds good," said Wolfe.

Just then, Terri Sommers walked into the conference room looking like an ad from Lands' End. "Where are you two going?" she said as they were about to leave. "I thought the meeting was here?"

"It was," said Josephs. "Unfortunately the body of the man Wolfe had a confrontation with just turned up in Dead River."

Terri looked at Josephs. "By *the body*, I assume you mean he's dead?"

"Appears that way, though there has been no official pronouncement as yet. Eino is on his way over to examine the scene now. He's bringing the wagon to transport the body back to the morgue to conduct a full forensic exam."

"Great," said Terri. "The day hasn't even gotten started and already we have dead people showing up." She turned and looked at Wolfe. "*You* have anything to do with this?" she said.

"Kind of," replied Wolfe. "Although Sergeant Maki seems to think I murdered him and I wouldn't be surprised if he's out hustling up a grand jury for an indictment."

Josephs laughed. "Don't worry, Wolfe. You know he's easily excited. Of course, it does look a bit funny, since you do admit killing him."

"Yeah, but it was just one punch, Ed, and he swung at me first."

"If it happened as you say, and I don't doubt that it did, then there's not going to be any inquest. So don't worry."

"I'm not, Ed. It's the others who are still out there that concern me."

The body was where the fisherman said it was. It had been snagged by a branch that stuck out from a fallen tree that had been that way for years, from the looks of it. Eino Loukkala, Sheriff Josephs and Wolfe tried to look at the scene without disturbing any evidence that might be there.

The ground was soggy from a recent rain, and the smell of decay was evident. Wolfe stayed a ways back so his footprints would not be mingled in with the others, further making him a suspect, at least in Sergeant Maki's eyes.

Terri had been invited along as well. Josephs felt that as a previous team member, another set of eyes with a civilian perspective might be of help. Eino conducted the closest inspection of the body. Even though the fisherman had said the man was dead, he had to make sure. But after a cursory exam, true to the fisherman, Eino pronounced the man dead. And a broken neck seemed to be the cause.

Sheriff Josephs got a good look at the man as well. After he finished, he stood and turned to Wolfe. "Well, the man certainly matches the description you gave us, including clothing and physical description."

Wolfe nodded. "Oh, it's him. No doubt about that. I saw him up real close and personal."

"That's what I gather," said Josephs. He took a deep breath, like he was planning to dive under water and stay there for a long, long while. By then a couple of detectives had arrived to preserve the scene. There was no evidence as yet that there had been a crime. But the detectives proceeded as if there had been, as a precaution against losing possible evidence.

"Well," said Josephs, "I'm going to head back to the office so the detectives and Eino can do their work. Terri, why don't you come with me and we can get caught up." It was not a question. "If you would, I'd like you to bring me up to date on what Wolfe has told you, since I feel relatively certain that it will be more than he has told me."

Terri nodded. "Fine, Ed," she said as they walked to his vehicle. "But I'm not so sure you're right about the last part. Seems I might be more out of the loop than usual on this one."

"Well at this point, you're not alone. Unfortunately, I'm not sure how much there is to know, if anything. This is such a weird situation already, and I'm not sure whether we've even scratched the surface."

# chapter 17

Eino's findings after the autopsy were definitive. Wolfe watched each step of the examination and looked over every part of the victim's body. "No signs of any abrasions or contusions, other than to face and the jaw," said Eino as he summed up his exam.

"No puncture wounds, though there was internal bleeding in the head and neck. No water in the lungs, which means that he didn't drown. In fact, it appears the only thing that I can say at this point is that the cause of death is a broken neck."

"I told you that," said Wolfe.

"Right, you did," said Eino. "I guess that has been confirmed. You have been truthful, Wolfe. I think I'll just shove him in the freezer and let him sit unless the next of kin shows up to claim the body. You think that's likely?"

Wolfe smile. "Highly *unlikely*."

"I agree," said Eino. Then he gave the drawer a shove, and the corpse of *Vlad the Unknown* went sliding into the deep freeze of the Marquette County Morgue.

They all finished their respective activities and returned to meet back in the Sheriff's conference room. Once they were all seated around the large, polished wood conference table, Josephs began. "There were no footprints, nor tire tracks, or any evidence as to how the body got to the scene at the river. If I had to guess, I'd say that he was placed in a boat or canoe and floated to that spot, and deliberately snagged on that extended branch."

"Interesting," said Terri. "I wonder why?"

"Good fishing spot," said Josephs. "High probability that he would be found fairly quickly."

"And why would someone want that?" she asked.

"Probably to send a message," said Wolfe. "A warning that that could be one or all of us in that river, and there is nothing we can do to find out who is responsible for putting it there."

"Right," said Josephs. "The fact that he was snatched in broad daylight right downtown on a main city street without being seen, shows how clever—and daring—they are."

"And ruthless," said Terri. "To summarily discard one of their own people so casually. It gives me the shivers."

They all nodded in agreement.

Wolfe clasped his hands on the table in front of him and began. "So, I think it's safe to say that there's something real going on that is behind this surveillance and the moving of the body. This is not just a made-up fantasy by some power-crazed bureaucrat whose train left the tracks long ago. The enemy is playing with enough marbles to pull off this show of intimidation—for that's what I see is the purpose of what happened. Thoughts?"

Eino spoke up, still in his less-than-white lab coat from the autopsy. "I would have to agree. From the way the victim was moved, leaving no other evidence of the crime, the time of day, the location of the abduction, and the obvious way the body was left to be discovered, we have to assume a high degree of sophistication. The type one does not usually get from a private contractor, if you get my drift."

"I agree," said Joseph. "We're dealing with a high level of ability and probably more resources than we have available right now."

Terri cut in. "So, what do we do now? Are we all in danger? Should we be armed? Watch over our shoulders at all times? Have *bodyguards*?"

"In answer to your first question," said Wolfe, "that's what we have to figure out. Quickly. And as to the rest of your questions, the answer is, *yes.*"

Wolfe told the group that for safety's sake, he would be the de facto leader of the group, since the people they were fighting were from his side of the world, and he knew best how to deal with them.

Of course everyone would have input and an important contribution to make through their individual talents and perspectives, but the team needed a leader who would focus on their safety as well as the objectives of the situation.

"I agree," said Sheriff Josephs, "but remember that I'm the county Sheriff and I'm responsible for the safety of *all* the residents and visitors to this county, and that includes you too, Wolfe."

"You're exactly right," said Wolfe. "You have responsibility for all the residents of this county. A big responsibility. And that's why I need to be the leader of this group during this situation. Because my responsibility is for the safety of the four of us, and that's it. Which I will do. The rest of the county, Ed, is yours."

They all nodded. "Agreed," said Josephs.

Wolfe stated that for safety sake and for secure communications, future meetings should take place in his condo, and that they should all stay there, if possible. But Sheriff Josephs and Eino stated that they would have responsibilities in their offices and that they would need to be available to answer emergencies there as well, especially the Sheriff.

Wolfe suggested they go to the condo and familiarize themselves with their quarters. They all agreed, and headed over to the condo.

Once there, Wolfe explained that there were safety features built in by his friend, a benefactor from long ago, and that resources for the group would be available on demand. He gave each one a special key to the front door.

Next to the lock mechanism was a keypad that had a code they would have to punch in before they used the key.

He also explained that they could expect to be followed. They would likely be monitored, including their cars, and homes and offices, which might also be bugged. This was just the nature of who they were dealing with, he explained.

He also explained that he had numerous armaments in his condo, and would give each of them their choice, if they wished. Josephs would probably wish to keep his own weapons that he had already trained on and certified with for years.

But he could have an additional one of Wolfe's weapons if he wished. They would all be trained at the Sheriff's shooting range to become proficient with the weapon or weapons of choice. But since they had little time, they would have to accept the training they were able to get as being sufficient. As he explained to them, this was going to be a battle, and they needed to think and act that way.

They were all pretty shocked at the level of seriousness of his briefing, and wondered if things were all that serious. He explained that they were, and they would soon find out why. He finished by saying that his strategy was to expect the unexpected—and for them to all do the same. Eino asked if that strategy was effective, and Wolfe said it was, at least so far.

Terri asked how he knew that for sure.

Wolfe just smiled and looked at them.

"Because I'm still alive."

Wolfe took them to the floor gun vault and had them select a weapon or weapons as they saw fit. Even though Josephs had his duty weapon and trained on it regularly, he selected an additional one that caught his eye, found the appropriate holster, and put it on his belt. Terri wasn't all that interested in taking one, but Wolfe convinced her that she needed something.

Resigned to her task, she looked through the hardware and finally found one that she thought she could use. She held it in her hand, turned it over and inspected it. Seeming satisfied, she opened her purse, dropped it inside, and closed the clasp. She turned and looked smugly at Wolfe. "There. You happy?" she said.

Wolfe smiled, said nothing, shook his head, and then turned to Eino.

Eino had found a more exotic weapon that delighted him no end. "I'll have this," he said, proudly holding it up for everyone to see.

"Seriously?" said Terri. "*That's* your weapon of choice?"

"It is," he said. "You might be surprised to find how useful it can be."

"How would *you* know?" asked Terri.

"I'm a man of many mysteries," said Eino, who then turned away to examine his new toy.

Wolfe shook his head. "Fine. Everyone has their weapon. Ed, will you take them all to the range and try to qualify them on these . . . items?"

"I'll do my best," said Josephs, "though I'm not sure that a couple of them have any standards involving traditional qualification practices."

"Well, do your best," replied Wolfe. "We might need them sooner than you think, and I don't want any of us getting shot— accidentally or *otherwise*." They all looked at him for a moment, particular Terri. He was looking directly at her when made the statement.

"*What?*" she said, feigning ignorance at his implication. Then she turned to join Eino, who was heading out the door with the Sheriff.

# chapter 18

*Reaper parked his motorcycle in the airport parking garage long-term parking. He wasn't sure when, if ever, he would return to ride it again, but he was hopeful. It was, after all, a new bike that he bought with his hard-earned combat pay.*

*He was very alert to his surroundings as he walked to the airport terminal, watching for any signs that someone was giving him undue attention, or following him—which was very difficult in an airport where mobs of people were going in virtually every direction. Still, he had had excellent training in surveillance and counter-surveillance, and he knew what things to be on the lookout for.*

*But things went smoothly as he approached the ticket counter. He didn't want to use his credit card to purchase his ticket, as he knew that could be tracked, and besides, dead men don't buy airline tickets. If his card was being monitored, those doing the monitoring would know that either he wasn't dead, or that the card had been stolen and was being used fraudulently. Either way, the jig would be up for him.*

*So he used cash to buy the ticket, which in and of itself drew some suspicion. And he had no luggage to check, just a carryon bag—both points of suspicion airline personnel had been trained to look for, along with the fact that it was a last-minute booking. But none of these things could be helped.*

*He did, however, purchase a round-trip ticket, knowing he might never redeem the return portion of the ticket. The woman at the ticket counter took the cash, looked him over pretty thoroughly,* checked his passport and the passport photo that had a picture of him with his broad, freckle-faced grin, and decided he didn't warrant further examination, except perhaps over dinner at a nice restaurant.

Thanking her, Reaper took the ticket and his carryon duffle bag, and headed for security. It was the final checkpoint where everything could go south in a hurry. He had to remain cool, relaxed.

Think good thoughts. Happy thoughts, he told himself. He pictured in his mind his last vacation in the Bahamas, swinging in a hammock between two palm trees on a white sand beach, with crystal clear blue-green waves lapping up on the shore—the sound of the waves putting him in a hypnotic trance of relaxation and peaceful dreams.

"Sir?" said the unpleasant voice from out of nowhere. "Sir!" came the voice again. "Your ticket and ID, please."

Reaper awoke from his reverie and saw the security officer standing there with his hand out. "Oh. Sorry, sir," he said, producing the items. "Just daydreaming, I guess."

The security officer gave his documents a careful look, eyeballed Reaper thoroughly, and reluctantly handed them back. "Thank you," he said perfunctorily and moved on to the next person in line.

Small beads of sweat began forming on Reaper's forehead as he moved through the line. That was a close call, he thought. Be relaxed, but pay attention, he admonished himself. He couldn't wait to board the plane and get to Marquette. He hoped nothing else happened. He had to get to Commander Wolfe, and soon. Lives depended on it.

Including his.

# chapter 19

Weapons qualifications over, the group met back at the condo. "How'd they do, Ed?" asked Wolfe.

"Good enough, I guess," replied Josephs. "I mean, Terri's gun—there were really no qualifying standards. It's a Derringer-type two- shot 'belly gun.' You need to be up close and just aim at the belly. Pretty big target at two to three feet. She did fine, as far as I can tell. She knows how to shoot it safely, and hit the target."

"Great," said Wolfe. "And Eino?"

Josephs laughed. "Well, he knows how to use it, and he can hit the target from about ten feet. Beyond that, or in the wind, it's anybody's guess. It's a *blow gun*, for crying out loud, Wolfe. I sure hope he doesn't hit any of us with those darts he has."

Eino smiled. "Dontcha worry, Sheriff. I've used these before. Never killed anyone one I didn't intend to."

They all looked at Eino. "Really," he said again. "Don't worry. I'm an expert in these things. Once, when I was in South America, I came across this tribe of . . ."

"Enough," Wolfe cut in. "We'll take your word for it. No more stories of you and your exploits in foreign lands. Everyone's scared enough of the local bogeymen as it is."

"OK, Wolfe. Your call. But they *are* interesting and definitely informative. Maybe late some night in a bar, or around a camp-fire . . ."

Josephs chimed in, thankfully sparing everyone. "What I'd like to do is get down to the nitty-gritty, Wolfe. This whole thing seems like it's standing on quicksand. Do we have any firm ground, any facts we can start with?"

"Before we go further," said Wolfe, "let me offer one suggestion here.

"And what's that?" asked Terri.

Wolfe said, "Let's refer to our target, since we're pretty sure it's a man, and that he's a professor, as *professor*. We can make changes in the future as circumstances warrant it."

"Sounds OK to me," said Eino, adding his two cents' worth. "I think it's good enough to move along, anyway. We've got a lot of stuff to get to—as Sheriff Josephs said—'the nitty gritty.'"

Wolfe looked around the room. "Any objections?" He paused. Nobody spoke. "Then let's move on."

"Let's," said Josephs.

Wolfe began. "Fine. So, let's assume, as a starting point, that whatever it is that the professor is working on, it must be something spectacular. And, since the Agency, with all its resources, has been unable to find it, it must be hidden exceedingly well. Agreed?"

"Makes sense to me," offered Eino. Heads nodded in agreement.

"OK," Wolfe continued. "And can we assume that whatever is being worked on, that it's likely that the professor will need to have supplies, equipment and energy, or close access to these things. Agreed?"

"Right," said Josephs. Eino nodded, his blow gun sitting beside him.

"So where would the nexus of all these things likely be located?"

"Somewhere around here, I would assume," said Josephs.

"Why is that?" said Terri. "Couldn't it be anywhere in the world?"

"It could," replied Wolfe. "But it's not. It's in this area. The Sheriff's right."

"Why's that? Terri asked.

"Because," replied Wolfe, "I'm pretty sure they knew I had other resources here, such as you, Terri, or that you would soon be here, and they were most likely aware of the rest of the team since we made quite a splash last time around."

Heads nodded. Wolfe continued. "And with all the resources located here that would be necessary to mount a serious search, not to mention our familiarity with the people and the area."

Eino cut in. "Right. It would make no sense to use this team if there were another location far away they were targeting. Moving us all to another area would be expensive, time consuming, and our advantage of familiarity with the area would be lost. Using a different team of skilled investigators familiar with the area of another locale would make more sense."

"That's correct," said Wolfe. "So I think it's time to work on what we do know, or at least suspect, and see what we can find out. Agreed?"

"Good idea," said the Sheriff. "Time we got moving on this." He looked around the room, and saw heads nodding.

"Great," said Wolfe, as he stood and began pacing around the room. "So to summarize, here's what we know. The professor is in the area fairly close by. He will be close to a variety of stores, shops, and suppliers of various sorts, which again means not too far from Marquette.

"And the last thing," Wolfe finished, " is that there will probably be energy, and maybe water needs that could be substantially higher than normal, which, if to remain unnoticed, would best be 'hidden' in a more densely populated area, as opposed to a more rural one."

"Makes sense," said Eino.

"So until we know more, let's divide up the tasks by type," said Wolfe. "Eino, why don't you look for any unusual purchases of supplies, and other things that might be out of the ordinary, either in terms of type or quantity?"

"Ten-four," said Eino, trying to sound like the cops he heard on the police scanner.

""Ed," continued Wolfe, "you can check for unusual electricity, water, or heat indicators, under the guise of looking for drug-growers."

"Can do," said Josephs, as he stood and stretched. "Actually I probably have some of that information already. I can start by sifting through that before I go out shaking the bushes. Maybe come up with something quick."

"Great," said Wolfe.

Terri finally spoke. "I guess that just leaves me and you," she said, looking at Wolfe.

"Right," said Wolfe. "Since you are already familiar with the campus area and facilities, from your investigation last year at Northern Michigan University, you can reasonably nose around there, looking for any unusual academic or experimental activities, particularly hush-hush research-type stuff. It wouldn't be that unusual for you to be doing that, maybe as a follow-up to last year's inquiry into your brother's death. Being a reporter, that shouldn't look too unusual. Universities often do research on secret projects for the government and private corporations. Maybe this DARPA project was being done at the University, and we can get a lead from there."

"Makes sense," said Terri. "I'll get right on it." She got up and left the condo.

Eino decided to leave, too, but Josephs stayed behind. "So, Wolfe," he said. "What are *you* going to be doing?"

Wolfe smiled. "I'll be looking for the rats that will be trying to kill us once we find the professor—*if* we find him."

"Not much incentive for us, then, is there?" said Josephs as he locked eyes with Wolfe. He held the gaze for a long moment, then turned and headed out the door.

Wolfe watched him go. No, Ed, he thought. Not much at all.

# chapter 20

Wolfe was alone. He liked it that way. He worked best when he didn't have to explain his every move. Besides. He had to do things that he definitely didn't want the Sheriff to see, since they would most likely be very illegal. He didn't want to put Josephs' law enforcement career—or life—at risk.

The unknowns haunted him as he tried to sort through them. He decided to call his contacts and see what they had learned, if anything. Also, he wanted to see if the others he was trying to enlist had returned his calls. He went through the routine of connecting the black box, and made the calls.

"Otto," he said as the first person picked up the phone.

"Right," said Otto.

"Anything?" asked Wolfe.

"Not much," said Otto. "Nobody seems to know anything. Those who would talk, anyway. Everyone seems skittish, which leads me to believe that they do know something, but are afraid to talk about it. And that says something, if they're afraid to talk to me, especially on this secure line that nobody can tap into. I don't know, Wolfe. This is definitely high on the bizarre scale. Maybe I should ask *you*. What have you gotten yourself into, anyway?"

'I wish I knew. If you hear anything, please let me know as soon as possible. I have a bad feeling about all this."

"You got it," said Otto, as he clicked off.

Wolfe saw that he had gotten no returned calls from either the men or the women he had left messages for, so he tried calling again. The first call to one of the men was disturbing. The mechanical voice told him that the line was a non-working number and then clicked off. He stared at the phone, concern on his face.

That was not protocol, he thought, wondering what in the heck was going on. If the line had been invalidated, it just would have been dead—no answer at all. He began to wonder if his contact had been compromised. Or worse.

The second call to the other man was no better. The person who picked up the phone was not his contact. "Hello," said the woman's voice. "Who is calling, please?" That was completely the wrong protocol, he thought to himself.

Nobody was to answer the phone except the person he was trying to reach. Nobody was even to have *access* to it. Wolfe quickly hung up. Whoever answered the phone probably had listened to the message he had left, as well. Something was seriously wrong.

He thought about what these breaches meant. Two of his four contacts had to be compromised. Was he compromised as well? He wondered if he should call either of the remaining two, when the phone suddenly rang.

Wolfe's mind was racing. Should he answer it? Was the whole system blown? What should he say? These thoughts were processed in the space of a second. He decided to answer the phone.

"Go," he said cautiously.

"Sparrow," said the female voice. Before Wolfe could say anything, the voice continued. "Blue Jays have invaded the nest and eaten the eggs," she continued.

Wolfe knew this was bad. *Blue Jays* was code. He developed this simplistic code years ago to communicate with his team. Blue

Jays were intelligent birds, with tight-knit family bonds. And they frequently invaded other birds' nests and ate their eggs. They would also mimic the calls of Red-shouldered Hawks, to frighten away other birds.

Lastly, the true color of their feathers was brown, but the Jays disguised their true color by scattering light through modified cells on the surface of their feather barbs—true camouflage.

This statement in code was one of the most serious warnings that could be made. What it said, in effect, was that his sources had been compromised, and had been *retired*—a euphemism for *killed*. The eggs had been eaten.

Wolfe thought quickly, knowing that Sparrow was most likely in grave danger.

"Any other nests around that the Sparrow could use?" he said carefully.

There was silence on the other end for a few seconds, then the voice said, "No. Migration is a must."

"How far?" said Wolfe.

"Closest," said Sparrow. "Eggs gone, wings tired. Need worms soon."

"Can Sparrow make it to the wildlife preserve?" asked Wolfe.

Sparrow knew that meant a secret and private airstrip close to her location. "I think she's strong enough for that."

"Great," said Wolfe. "I think Sparrow should receive a *citation* for that."

Sparrow knew that *citation* meant the type of plane he would be flying, a Cessna Citation—a small, eleven passenger jet. "I agree," she said.

"Maybe a gross of worms minus a couple of dozen for the trouble."

"Check," said Sparrow.

"Check," said Wolfe. They both hung up.

Wolfe immediately called the Marquette County Airport and ordered the Cessna Citation III to be fueled and readied for take-off. It wasn't his plane, but he had total access to it whenever he wanted it, compliments of his wealthy friend, who also paid all the operating expenses for the aircraft.

In the coded messages with Sparrow, *migration* meant she had to flee quickly. *Closest* meant the closest airport to her location, which was Washington National Airport, in the heart of D.C. But due to the congestion and restrictions of that airport, it wasn't feasible for Wolfe to fly in there and escape quickly—or at all.

So he mentioned the *Wildlife Preserve*, which was code for a small, private airport that Wolfe's rich friend owned. It could handle jets the size of the Citation, and even a bit larger. It wasn't on any map as an airport, and its facilities and the airstrip were disguised to make it look like farmland. It also had the benefit of an enclosed hanger and fueling facilities that could all be accessed on a self-serve basis.

Of course, Wolfe had the codes to all of that, but in this case he would not likely need refueling since the range of his aircraft was over 2,300 miles and his total roundtrip would be about half that, leaving plenty of fuel for contingencies.

References to the *worms* was code for the rendezvous time. So Sparrow would be looking for Wolfe's Citation jet in about 120 minutes—a gross minus two dozen, or 144 minus 24. Two hours should give him enough time to get there, with some time to spare for contingencies.

Finally, *check* meant that they were both starting the clock. It clearly wasn't a sophisticated code, but sometimes the simplest were the best—at least in the short haul.

Wolfe gathered his things for the flight, including his weapon, since he would not be subject to security screening at the private airport. He grabbed his jacket and just before he left the condo, he checked the video monitor he had set up. He ran the tape back to the start time and fast-forwarded through the tape looking for anything unusual. As it ran he noticed nothing until just after the rest of the team left.

Then, as the Sheriff climbed into his unmarked patrol car and began driving off, Wolfe noticed a man who came from behind a building, hopped on his bicycle, and sped off in the direction of the patrol car. Wolfe hit pause on the fast-forward, and looked again closely at the man and the bike. The man was athletic and wiry, wore a back-pack, and looked to be the age of a college student. The bicycle was built for speed – a 10-speed racing bike.

As he looked closer, he thought it could just be coincidence or a clever surveillance.

So he tucked it away in the back of his mind to deal with later, and headed off to the airport. He didn't have much time. And Sparrow's life could hang in the balance. He hoped she could get away, and that he hadn't already compromised both of them.

He would soon find out.

# chapter 21

The Citation was fueled and ready to go when he arrived at the Marquette County Airport. The jet had been pulled from the hanger and was ready on the tarmac. Wolfe had several thousand hours of flying time in the Citation, and could fly it himself, as it was single pilot rated. He went through the outside preflight checklist, then climbed into the cockpit and stowed his gear. Then he strapped in, performed his internal checklist, started the engines and prepared for takeoff.

Satisfied that everything was in order, he contacted the control tower, received his OK and taxied to the runway. Given the final go-ahead from the tower, Wolfe smoothly accelerated down the runway and lifted off. Once at his cruising altitude of 35,000 feet, he leveled off and set his course toward La Guardia, at the plane's cruising speed of 544 mph.

Wolfe left his transponder on so air traffic control could monitor the course of his filed flight plan and verify that he indeed, was headed to La Guardia. But later, once he was between control tower areas, he would cease using his radio, turn off his transponder, and change his altitude and course to the private airstrip where he would pick up Sparrow, safe and sound. Hopefully.

He checked his watch. Thirty minutes had elapsed since he coordinated watches with Sparrow. That left ninety minutes for him to make it to the D.C. area, land at the private airport and pick her up. If she made it. If she was on time.

He liked living on the edge, so this was not anything new for him. He didn't worry about himself. It was other people around him that he worried about. It was Terri. And Josephs. And Eino . . . and now Sparrow.

He shook his head, adjusted his aviator sunglasses, and settled in. He thought about all the things that were going on. Things that disturbed him. Things that could challenge his abilities to the max. That had never bothered him before. But this had too many unknowns.

Too many people involved. Too many ways for things to go wrong. As always he would plan for the worse and hope for the best. Unfortunately, knowing his past history, it was more likely going to be the worse.

Sparrow knew she had to move fast. Her mind was clicking at Mach speed as she talked with Wolfe, listening to him, covertly observing her co-workers, and simultaneously planning her escape. She knew she was under suspicion, or at least a possible target because of what had happened to the other agents. And she only found out about that by accident. But there was no time to waste speculating. The training she had received as a covert agent taught her that speed was of the essence.

Trying to look as nonchalant as possible, she removed her headset and placed it on her desk. At the same time, with her other hand she reached under her desk in her cubicle and snagged the handle of her bag, which was a tote bag that held all her essentials for a quick trip to virtually anywhere.

She then swiveled around in her chair and headed for the women's restroom, looking like she hadn't a care in the world. As she walked by other agents, they looked at her as they always did, which she ignored, as she always did. Sparrow was extremely attractive.

She was graceful, confident, and aware of her sexuality—and that drove men wild. She had dark brown, shoulder-length hair, and a beautiful model-like face with high cheekbones, full lips, and large hazel eyes that could change color depending on what she was wearing, her surroundings, or even her mood. She was nearly five-eight, and had curves in all the right places.

Yet she was trim, and had very low body fat. She was in great physical shape, and she engaged in regular strength training, aerobics, and martial arts. She was blazingly fast, and had a reach with her legs that gave her a great advantage in hand-to-hand combat.

Sparrow was aware of all these attributes and used them effectively in the performance of her job, whatever her assignment. In this case, she used her beauty to distract her director as she passed him in the hall.

A simple smile and an attentive glance was sufficient enough of a distraction to divert his attention away from her deft lifting of his access badge. As a perfect follow-through of her craft, she turned and looked at him as she continued walking away, confident that he would do the same. He did.

Then when he looked away, she moved. She quickly headed for the rear elevator where she used her purloined access badge to gain access. When the doors closed, she swapped out her heels for sneakers and put her heels in her bag. She figured she only had a few minutes before someone would notice her gone, and she had to make the most of it.

Once inside she hit the button for the basement garage where her car was parked. Then she grabbed a big hat and dark sunglasses out of her bag and put those on. Now she looked like a celebrity trying to go about a shopping trip without being noticed.

The elevator doors opened and she moved out with confidence, her head held high, as if daring anyone to look at her. Unfortunately, an attentive guard was there.

"Excuse me, Miss, but I need to see your access badge," he said. "You know the drill."

She smiled her disarming smile. "Of course," she said as she smiled. All comings and goings of the Agency had to be physically checked, because an access badge could be easily stolen—like she just did. Sparrow turned confidently, not breaking her role, and said, "I'm sorry." She reached for her badge and handed it to the guard. "Here it is."

But as he looked down at it, before he could recognize that it wasn't her, she fired a quick jab to his solar plexus that bent him over double, then a quick knee to the chin took him out completely. He was out cold, but for how long she didn't know, and she wasn't going to hang around long enough to find out.

She walked down two rows and found her ubiquitous beige Toyota Camry. She quickly looked around to see if anyone was watching her. Seeing no one, she climbed in and started the car, then headed toward the exit gate.

When she got there, she said in a panicked voice to the gate attendant, "Sir, the guard at the door is laying on the ground unconscious. I think he might be sick or something. Can you go take a look? I think you should call an ambulance. Hurry! He's very pale. Maybe he's dead! Oh do hurry!"

The gate guard forgot about her ID and lifted the gate as he ran to the garage door to check on the guard. Sparrow quickly pulled forward. Looking both ways, she pulled out into traffic and blended in with the other beige cars, disappearing almost instantly.

Feeling like she had succeeded in her escape, but only temporarily, she also realized that the video surveillance tape would be quickly accessed to see her and her car and license number, and which way she went.

There would be an urgent scramble to find her, and find her fast. She had a head-start, but only a small one. She was not out of the woods yet. Turning her concentration to maximizing her speed without drawing attention to herself, she gripped the steering wheel and sped off in the direction of the secret airstrip.

# chapter 22

Sparrow's director, Eric Henderson, returned from the break-room and passed by the security manager. "What are you doing here?" the manager said to Henderson.

Henderson stopped and turned to look at the security manager. "What do you mean, 'what am I doing here?' I'm in charge, that's what I'm doing here," he said, piqued at the almost insubordinate question. "Why do you ask?" He had now assumed an aggressive stance and was glaring at the security manager.

"Oh, sorry. I didn't mean anything about you," the manager said contritely. "It's just that my access control computer shows that you left the building, ah . . ." He turned to look at his computer again, then said, "four minutes and thirty-eight seconds ago." He turned back to see Henderson staring at the screen.

"That's impossible," he said. He reached for his access card. "I have my card right . . . ." His hand had simply swiped the air where his badge should have been. He got a startled look on his face. "What the . . ." he began, and then the realization dawned on him what had happened. "Who's missing?" he barked. "Who should be sitting here but is *not*?"

The security manager looked around, checked the work station monitors, then turned to the director. "Sparrow's not here at the moment," he said.

"I know," he snapped. "I just passed her in the hall a few minutes . . ." Then it dawned on him.

Henderson ordered the security manager to check the women's bathroom, which he quickly did by calling one of his security guards on his walkie-talkie and ordering him to run and check it out. The response came back thirty seconds later. "She's not there, sir," the guard responded. "I checked all the stalls and they were empty. I didn't see her at the water cooler or break area either."

"Shut the building down," ordered Henderson. "Just in case she may still be in the building somewhere. And get someone down to the parking garage to see if her car is still there."

"Too late," said the security manager. "The gate guard said someone coldcocked the garage guard. He's unconscious. Some woman exiting the garage told him about it and he . . ."

"Some *woman*?" said Henderson. "Call 911 and get an ambulance here for the guard. And pull up that security camera pronto. I want to see that woman and her car. And I want it all done ten minutes ago!"

"Yes sir," said the security manager as he dialed 911. Henderson was fuming. Once the security manager pulled up the garage surveillance tape, he said, "Get the make and model, the color, and the license plate number of her car. Now! And get it out to all our agents. And put out an APB to state and local law enforcement, along with a description of Sparrow. Tell them that she is a fleeing fugitive and is armed and dangerous."

The security manager gave an almost imperceptible nod. "I'll find her, sir," he said resolutely. "Don't worry."

"Oh, I *am* worried. You'd better find her—for all our sakes."

For the most part, the flight was uneventful. Wolfe began his approach into the private airport. It was far enough away from the flight path of most of the air traffic headed for Washington National that he could get by without control tower involvement.

He would be flying under Visual Flight Rules, or VFR on his approach, which meant there would be no control tower warning him of other air traffic in his area. He would have to be very diligent watching for any other traffic over, under, behind or around him during this tricky time. He had to be sharp.

As he began to see the airport, he looked for any signs of Sparrow, but saw nothing to indicate she was waiting for him. He hoped that Sparrow got away and was there to meet him, but he had to admit the possibility that she had been detained and would not be able to make it. He decided to circle again, this time a little lower.

# chapter 23

*R*eaper was seated in the waiting area at the gate, hoping to board soon. All his senses were on alert for anything out of the ordinary. And that was the problem. Everything was ordinary.

People were coming, looking for a place to sit. Conversations were going on between friends and family. Some people were sitting quietly, reading newspapers or magazines—or books. Some were sleeping.

Kids were running around. People were going to the restrooms or returning. People were bringing food into the waiting area, mindless of what others were doing or thinking. Beverages were being consumed. Announcements were being made over the PA system continually, advising of flights, parking situations, and paging various important people. It was a cacophony of sights and sounds, smells and chaos.

It was all very ordinary. And yet in the midst of all this ordinary activity, Reaper couldn't help but feel that someone, somewhere, was on a hunt for him—looking, watching, searching for any trace of him. And when they found him, they would pounce like a mountain lion on a runaway dog, and it would be the end of him.

Then he caught himself. He had to think positive. He was going to succeed. He was going to wait patiently, acting bored, until his flight was called. He was going to patiently wait until his row was called, and then he was going to stand in line, slowly moving forward as the line moved. He was going to hand his boarding pass to the ticket taker, smile politely, and walk onto the jet-way and onto the airplane itself.

He was going to patiently wait until he got to his row, stow his duffle bag in the overhead compartment, and take his seat. He was going to buckle his seat belt, close his eyes and think pleasant thoughts until the plane's doors closed, the plane taxied to the runway, and the pilot throttled the engines to full power. And he would feel the increased G- forces press him back into the padded seating as the nose of the jet tipped up and the plane cruised easily and quietly into the bright, blue sky.

And that is exactly what he did.

# chapter 24

The pursuit forces mobilized in full blown attack mode. The problem was that even though they had the license plate number of Sparrow's car, trying to pick that out of the multilane traffic near D.C. at highway speed was nearly impossible. The only other clue they had was the color and make, and that didn't help much, either. Henderson was apoplectic.

Turning to the security manager, he said, "Do we at least know what *direction* she is going in? I mean, can we at least find *that* out? Or maybe where she is heading?"

"We can try," said the nervous security manager. "She could be going to some 'safe' place nearby, where she can lay low for a while. Or," he continued, "she could be going to a train or bus terminal to find a way to get out of town quickly if the roads are blocked.

"We could have checkpoints set up at the bus and train terminals, and also all the major and regional airports in case she is trying to fly out of town. But then she would surely know we will be checking IDs of all airline passengers as a matter of routine, and that she could be easily snagged that way. So that might not be fruitful."

"Let's do all of it," said Henderson. "We can't leave anything to chance. We must find her!"

The security manager ignored the outburst, figuring it would probably end soon with a cataclysmic failure of the director's central nervous system. But until then, he had to keep calm and keep going. "OK, we'll check the bus and train terminals and see if we can catch her there. And notify the local cops and state police to watch for the car and the license plate."

"Do it," said Henderson. "And let me know as soon as you find anything!" Then he turned and headed back to his office.

The traffic was thick, but it was moving along at a good clip. Sparrow was pretty sure she would make it OK, as long as there were no problems. Her car was in good condition, and her reflexes were excellent, so the traffic should be no problem as long as there were no accidents.

She didn't know whether or not she had been found out, but she had to assume that her use of the director's access card would be noticed by someone, not the least of whom would be Henderson himself. Boy, he must have been pissed, she thought, a slight smile creeping across her face. He was not well liked at the office—not well at all.

She was about ten minutes out from the airport when the event she dreaded happened. There was an accident. So close, she thought. The cars all came to a screeching halt, and she could hear the crunch of a few other fender-benders happening around her.

But now there were four lanes of traffic blocked solid between her and the airport. She knew she couldn't stay in traffic. She would have to make a run for it.

She looked around, cranked the wheel of her car to the right, and started moving on the shoulder of the road past all the cars that were stopped. People blew their horns in protest, but she didn't slow down. Then other drivers started pulling over onto the shoulder and doing the same thing.

"Damn," she said. The ones behind her would be no problem, but now drivers in the right lane could see her coming in their rearview mirror and began pulling out in front of her. These were slowing her down and actually blocking her from her run for it.

Not only that, but the caravan of cars driving illegally was bringing unwanted attention to her, and her anonymity was being lost by the second. Taking a last ditch effort, she started driving further to the right of the drivers on the shoulder, off onto the grass, and in some cases, through ditches and culverts. She *had* to make it. She was *going* to make it. No one would stop her now. If they did, she would die. Of that she was certain.

Wolfe made the first approach to the airport from the north side and circled around, looking for any signs of Sparrow. There were none. There were no vehicles anywhere to be seen in the area. The hanger doors were closed and there were no lights on in the seldom used office. Wolfe decided to circle around again, but he couldn't keep doing this without drawing attention from people in the area. *Where are you, Sparrow? Make it. Make it! I know you can do it!*

As Sparrow predicted, her caravan of offenders had drawn at-tention and generated the interest of a police helicopter that spotted the long line of cars avoiding the backup. She heard the chopper and knew it was just a matter of time before she would be nabbed. It would be her end. Her only salvation was that the police cars couldn't get through the traffic any quicker than she could, so she still might have a chance.

Finally she could see the exit she needed, off to the right. So she mashed the accelerator to the floor and bullied her way to the exit ramp, forcing other cars off to one side or the other. Horns blared, fingers were raised, epithets were voiced and flung in her direction, but she ignored it all.

She had one focus—one purpose. Get to the airport before she got caught. She came to the stop sign at the end of the ramp, blew right through it, fishtailing her vehicle in the process. But she was an excellent driver, and she maintained control throughout.

Strangely, she noticed that the chopper had turned and headed back towards D.C., which didn't make sense. If the pilot had stayed over the intersection he would have easily been able to follow her and even land in the open space at the airport and apprehend her there.

But that didn't happen and the chopper left the area in a hurry. Sparrow could worry about that later. Right now she had to make sure that no one else apprehended her—someone who had no problems with violating her civil rights—in the extreme.

She looked around to see if any police cruisers had made it to her location, but she saw none. That was good—and bad. The Agency people would not be driving a marked police cruiser and would not be easily spotted—until it was too late. Sparrow decided to go for broke and headed at full speed for the airport entrance gate.

# chapter 25

On the third trip around, Wolfe spotted the beige sedan shooting off the exit ramp, running the stop sign, and blasting for the entrance gate arm. That had to be her, he thought. He didn't know how she was going to get in because only he had the codes.

He decided he didn't have time to wait, so he quickly descended, lined the jet up on the correct runway into the wind, landed, and taxied to the hanger. He stopped the jet and dropped the stairs. Wolfe had the remote control for the hanger door and ran towards it, pressing the remote as he ran.

Finally it opened just as Sparrow smashed through the gate arm and came careening around the hanger. Seeing the open door, she steered the beige sedan into the hanger and came to a screeching halt. Quickly she grabbed her bag and began running towards the plane.

Wolfe pressed the remote control again and the hanger door began closing. Wolfe bounded up the steps and dove into the pilot's seat as Sparrow vaulted into the jet right behind him and raised the stairs. Wolfe had strapped himself in and was revving the engines just as an unmarked federal sedan came screeching to a halt at the hanger.

Two agents jumped out of the car and tried to get into the hanger before the door closed. They didn't make it, but they were able to see the beige Toyota sedan with the proper plate number before the door closed.

Wolfe had started taxiing away from the agents to the end of the runway. But as he did so, he saw the agents running after him, suit coats flapping in the wind as they both reached for their guns. Not wanting to have his plane filled with holes, he jammed on the brakes and cranked up the jet engines and aimed them at the agents.

As they took aim, he pushed the controls to nearly full throttle. The blast knocked the agents onto their backs, their guns flying from their hands as they tried to cover themselves from the hot blast of the jet engine.

Then Wolfe quickly turned the plane back to the correct direction, and accelerated full throttle down the runway as he rocketed up into the air. As he quickly gained altitude, he looked back to see the agents trying to find their guns and then running back to their car as fast as they could.

He smiled as he kept the plane low until he got free from the local air traffic patterns. Then, still flying VFR with his transponder off, he headed away from the agents and the police and into the safety of the open sky.

Wolfe knew that FAA and other officials would be looking for his plane, but he wasn't worried about it. Even if the agents got a look at his tail numbers, it wouldn't help them any because they were bogus numbers, not registered anywhere. That's because one of the services his benefactor performed for him was to do anything necessary to protect his ward, including falsifying identification documents, including driver's license, passport, license plates and even airplane tail numbers.

In fact, before he left Marquette the true tail numbers were covered up with the alternate bogus numbers. So he was pretty much home free, as long as he didn't do anything more to draw attention to himself. And he had no intention of doing that.

Once he got settled in at cruising altitude and speed, he activated the autopilot and turned to Sparrow, with a big, toothy grin. "So," he began calmly. "How are things?"

She stared at him for a second and then laughed a throaty laugh. "Just fine, Wolfe. Not much going on in my world. How about you?"

"Pretty boring, actually. I could use a little excitement," he said.

She laughed again. "If that was boring, I'd hate to see what you call exciting!"

Wolfe hadn't seen Gina, code named Sparrow, in quite a while. He was her training instructor during certain parts of the academy and had been impressed with her ability to assess danger, and react quickly and instinctively to avoid or resolve problems—which she often did with finality. Then she had been assigned to work with him on several cases where she proved her mettle.

Wolfe took a good look at her. Her charcoal grey pant-suit fit her well, and indicated that underneath it all was still a trim, attractive figure that was filled out in all the right places. She was tall for a woman, at nearly 5'8", and at last check, 128 pounds. She looked to be about the same now, he assessed. He had seen her in shorts and t- shirt during training, and he knew she was fit and agile, and could take down a man twice her size. She could be pretty and demure as well, when she wanted to be—but blindingly fast and lethal when necessary.

She had bright, hazel-green eyes that twinkled, and a cryptic grin that was totally disarming when she wanted to turn on the charm—or mystery. She was very intelligent, and had a great sense of humor when things were more relaxed, or even when things were tense. Wolfe liked her and was glad she had made it.

"So," he began. "I take it things didn't go so well with your departure."

She nodded. "You could say that."

"What happened?"

She settled back in her seat. "After I had talked to you, I excused myself to go to the ladies room. I always keep a jump bag in my cubicle drawer, that's not much bigger than a large purse, but that contains all the items necessary to sustain life—*my* life."

"Is that the one you brought on board?"

"It is," she said, looking over at it on the seat behind her. "Anyway, I grabbed my bag and headed off to the ladies room. On the way there I passed my supervisor, to whom I gave my *special* smile, which he duly returned. His smile was more hopeful, which was the effect I was hoping for. Thus disarmed, I swiped his access ID card and he never noticed.

"I went past the restroom and on to the back elevator, where I used his card to access it, and get to the basement parking garage. And that's where my problems began." She explained the incident with the guard at the garage, and how she got through the gate. "It wasn't pretty, but it worked."

Wolfe checked his gauges, then nodded. "And your hat and sunglasses?"

She had taken them off when she entered the jet and thrown them on top of her bag on the seat behind her.

"Part of my disguise that I put on in the elevator. They became part of my persona. What'd you think?"

"They looked great on you," said Wolfe. "Without them, you look about the same as you did during training. Drinking from the 'fountain of youth'?"

Sparrow laughed. "Hardly. Lots of exercise, good nutrition, meditation—you know. Healthy stuff—body, mind, spirit, and all that."

"Well it seems to work for you. Glad to have you back safely, Gina."

Sparrow gave him a look. "Wow. *Gina*. Haven't heard that in a long time, Wolfe. Surprised you remembered."

"I remember you. Which you are soon to find out. Along with why I contacted you and ended up rescuing you. It's been quite a day."

# chapter 26

"Well we have some time now," she said. "Why don't we fill each other in? And you can start with your real name, because all I know you by is 'Wolfe,' and I know that's your code name."

"Ah, actually," Wolfe began, "Wolfe *is* my real name—and also my code name—only operative with that distinction."

"Seriously?" she asked, looking directly at him. "Please kindly remove your sunglasses, *Wolfe*. I have to see your eyes on this one."

Wolfe removed his sunglasses and looked directly into Sparrow's eyes. "Wolfe is my real name," he said again, not blinking.

She held his gaze for a moment. Finally she said, "But it's not your *first* name, is it?"

Wolfe smiled. "Got me there. OK. Wolfe is my last name, really. Very few people know my first name. So, can you keep it confidential? I only give it to certain trusted people."

"You can trust me, Wolfe," she said. "Now spill."

He smiled a kind smile. "Clayton," he said. "My first name is Clayton. Clay."

"Really?" she said, surprised. "I would never have guessed. But now that I think about it, it does suit you."

"Gee. Thanks. Can I keep it then?" he said playfully.

"I think, yes." She replied. "Good name."

"Thanks," he said. "But you can still call me Wolfe. Everyone else does, and most in the business think it's my code name anyway."

"Great," she said. "And you can still call me Sparrow, for the same reason. How about we only use our real names when we are alone together? Our little secret?"

Wolfe smiled. "Our little secret." He glanced over at her, and saw traces of her enigmatic smile as she looked out the windshield.

Wolfe filled Sparrow in starting with the intrusion by Barnes and his threats, the resurrection of his old team, the events including the surveillance by the man called Vlad, and his death at the hands of Wolfe. Finally he explained their analysis of the situation so far, and their plan of action. When he was finished, Sparrow was quiet for a moment, then said, "So, where do I fit in?"

Wolfe paused, then said, "I need someone I can trust. Someone who knows *the business*. Someone who can handle herself and any of the threats that might confront her. And," he continued, "someone who will have my back. Someone in whom I can have total confidence."

"And what about *my* back?" she said, cautiously. "Who's gonna have *my* back?"

"That will be me," said Wolfe. "And I hope you can have the same level of trust in me, even though we haven't seen each other for years. Think that's possible?"

Sparrow looked at him intently, her eyes taking in all the minute details of his face. Then she nodded. "Implicitly, and without reservation," she said, her eyes locked on his. "If you trust me that much, how can I do any less?" she said. Her caution was gone, replaced by an openness that surprised Wolfe.

"Good," he said, then turned to look back out the windshield, the first to break eye-contact. "Then that's settled. Of course we both have the responsibility to protect the rest of the group as if they were our own family. And I guess, in a way, they are. At least to me."

Sparrow nodded. "I have no family. At least, not anymore. Now it's just me against the world. That's why I have to be so tough—so self-sufficient. Of course, you know that, don't you?" She turned to look at him.

Wolfe didn't look at her, kept his eyes front. He knew her background intimately, as he was the person on the academy staff who screened the recruits.

"Yes, I do know that," he said. "But under all that toughness is a generous heart, which is a great feature. I know all about you, good and bad."

"Good *and* bad," said Sparrow. "So tell me about the bad," she said, playfully.

"Not going there, Sparrow."

"What?" she said, raising her eyebrows and feigning innocence. "Isn't this show and tell?"

"No," said Wolfe. "It's not show *or* tell. We have to keep this strictly business. After all—I'm your former instructor and now your supervisor, more or less. It wouldn't be right."

"Just yanking your chain," she said. "Professional relationship all the way. You got it."

The rest of the trip was uneventful, both of them quiet in their contemplation of the past, and the current situation. What the future held for any of them was a great unknown, but they would tackle it head-on, whatever it was.

After landing in Marquette, the plane was quickly pulled into the hanger, cleaned and prepped, the bogus tail numbers stripped off. Wolfe took Sparrow to the condo and showed her around. She only had one change of clothes with her—jeans, a sweatshirt, and sneakers, plus a light jacket—but that would suffice until she could get some more.

He showed her to her bedroom and left her to change and relax from the harrowing escape from D. C. Everyone had a pager that Wolfe had given them, along with the pager numbers of each individual so they could remain in contact. He would give Sparrow hers when she reappeared from changing and her rest.

Wolfe called Terri's pager and put his number in for her to call him at the condo.

Ten minutes later, she called. "What's up?" she asked.

"There's a new development I'd like to talk to you about," he said, cryptically. "Can you meet me at the condo?"

A brief silence was followed by, "Ah, sure. OK. Just getting started here, but I'll be there shortly."

"Thanks," he said. "See you soon."

Terri came in the door using her own key and the combo lock. "So what's going on?" she asked, as she stood in the doorway. She was wearing a dark green button-down shirt, blue jeans, stylish dark brown leather boots, and a tan suede jacket. Her red hair shimmered in the condo lighting and the whole image took Wolfe by surprise. All he could do is utter, "wow," as he stood there staring.

Terri tried not to smile, but the corners of her mouth worked their way upwards despite her efforts to turn away from Wolfe's gaze without him seeing.

Wolfe took in the vision as she walked past him and shrugged off her jacket. She did so in time for him to see that her jeans fit perfectly, and her shirt, while also fitting just right, did nothing to disguise her amazing figure underneath. Terri turned and plopped down in the soft couch, facing Wolfe.

"OK, what's going on?" she asked, crossing her legs casually. "I was busy on the last task you assigned when you summoned me here. I hope it's important," she quipped, a slight smile still warming her face.

Wolfe came over and sat across from her in an easy chair. He tried to recover some of his dignity by making a quick transition to business. "I was trying to call some of my close operatives to get some support," he said. "Unfortunately, I could only get a hold of one of them."

"What about the others?" she asked.

"I'm not hopeful," he said finally. "And those were my best operatives, too. I could trust them with my life—and often did. It shows what we are up against."

# chapter 27

"Sorry, Clay," said Terri, slipping back into her less formal relationship with Wolfe. "That must be very hard."

"It is," he said, trying to regain his composure. "But we can't dwell on that now. Things are serious and getting worse. And so far, we are nowhere in figuring this thing out."

"What about the other one?" she asked.

"The other one?" Wolfe asked, then realized what she meant. He thought for a moment. This was going to be delicate and he had to do it right. "Ah, that's what I wanted to talk with you about, Terri."

"OK," she said tentatively. "Go ahead."

He explained his flight to rescue Sparrow and the drastic measures that had been taken to prevent her from leaving.

"And she's here now?" Terri asked.

"Yes, she's cleaning up and getting settled in her room. That's one thing I wanted to talk to you about. She only had time to snatch her emergency bag and will need more clothes and some essentials. I'll be introducing her to the group as soon as we can get together, but I was hoping you could meet her first and help her with any things she may need."

Terri looked him in the eye.

Wolfe squirmed uncomfortably. He could see that the third degree was about to begin.

"No problem," said Terri. "But before we begin, what, exactly, is your relationship with this . . ."

"Sparrow," Wolfe cut in. "Her code name is Sparrow. That's the name she will use with us during this operation since her actual name is confidential."

"Sparrow," she said slowly. "Again, what . . ."

"I was her training supervisor back at the Academy," he said, cutting her off before she could throw any invectives his way. "I hired her, vetted her, and trained her. She was my student and, because of her stellar performance, became one of my operatives."

"I see," said Terri. "So am I to assume that she worked for you—or should I say, *with* you—on cases, or operations as you say?"

Wolfe knew he was in dangerous territory, but he had no choice but to push through. "Yes, as a matter of fact we did work together—in both capacities."

"Were these dangerous assignments?" Terri asked.

"Some of them were, yes."

"And how did she do?"

Wolfe adjusted himself in his chair. "Actually, she performed very well. In fact, better than my more senior agents in some cases."

Terri looked at Wolfe in her most penetrating way, searching for any telltale signs of discomfort or deceit. Discomfort she saw. But not deceit. "All right," she said, settling back in the couch. "So when do I get to meet her?"

Wolfe looked both relieved and apprehensive. "I'll check to see if she's ready." He got up and quickly headed towards Sparrow's bedroom. He knocked on her door. "How you doing in there?" he asked cautiously.

A moment later the door opened and a refreshed Sparrow stood smiling at him, makeup on, her hair pulled back in a ponytail. She was wearing a navy blue sweatshirt, light blue jeans and black sneakers. Everything fit well. She looked ready for anything. *Too ready*, thought Wolfe.

"C'mon," he said. "I want you to meet Terri Sommers, the reporter I worked with last year on that big fiasco you may have heard of."

"Oh, I heard of it," she said. "I can't *wait* to meet her. She's a legend."

Sparrow smiled a scary smile, and Wolfe knew he was in trouble. He turned and headed back into the living room.

The two collided like matter and anti-matter. He watched Terri's face as he walked into the living room, Sparrow in tow.

He introduced the two women to each other, and watched their expressions as they shook hands. They sized each other up like a couple of boxers getting ready for a match.

"Nice to meet you," said Sparrow as they shook hands. "Likewise," said Terri. "Welcome to the team."

"Thanks," said Sparrow. "I'm grateful for Wolfe pulling me out of the fire. They almost got me."

"Sounds like it was a harrowing experience," said Terri, her tone softening. "Glad you made it. We can use your assistance."

"Thanks. I'll definitely try to be a help and not a burden. I'll need to get up to speed on your operation. Wolfe filled me in on some of it, but I'm sure there's a lot more to be read in on."

"Maybe not," said Terri. "We haven't gotten very far, and there wasn't much that we were given to work with. It's like, there's a disaster that's going to happen soon, but we don't know where, or how, or when, or who's doing it, or what's going to happen. Just that it's going to be bad. How's that for a good start?"

"Definitely not good," said Sparrow. "I guess I'd better jump in and do what I can to help. Where do I start?"

It looked to Wolfe like the professionalism of the two women was going to keep the chemistry from going critical, so he jumped in. "Everyone else has a function they're working on, so we'll keep that going." Wolfe explained the various roles of the other members.

Turning to Sparrow, he said, "What would be a big help is if you would be undercover and look for covert enemies that might be trying to stop us, or to steal what we get if we're successful. I wish I could be more specific, but it could be anybody looking like anyone doing anything. Helpful, huh?"

Sparrow smiled. "Sounds pretty much like our standard operating procedure."

"What I can tell you," Wolfe continued, "is that we need to suspect everyone. Players definitely include our own people, possible traitors from within our own agency and other agencies who have turned and are working against us. They will definitely be hard to spot because they're from our own government and they know how to fit in, and what we're likely to be doing.

"But that isn't all," he continued. "I think it's safe to assume that foreign agents and private entities will also be targeting us, if the enormity of whatever is being developed is as big as we are told it is.

"On the other hand, the whole thing could be a pack of lies and a major misdirection for something wholly different that's going on. So basically, we have a handful of nothing that everyone could know about but us. An impossible mission with impossible odds. Other than that, everything's perfect."

"My kind of job," said Sparrow, smiling. "If you wouldn't mind, Terri, giving me a hand getting the things I need. Sounds like I might be here for a while, and I would really appreciate it. I have no car and don't know the stores, and you could save me a lot of time getting started."

"Hang on," said Wolfe as he went to a desk drawer and pulled out a set of car keys. He tossed them to Sparrow. "These are keys to a Subaru. License number is on the tag attached. It's a light green car parked behind the condo. There are four spaces marked, 'Condo Parking.' You can use that during this assignment."

"Excellent," said Sparrow, putting the keys in her pocket. Terri said, "Good. But we can take my car for now since I'm

driving you around. Not familiar with the Subaru. I'll leave that one to you."

"No problem," said Sparrow.

Terri looked at Wolfe. "You have any money or a credit card we can use for purchases and gas, or . . ."

Wolfe cut in. "Here," he said, handing Terri a credit card. It was flat black and blank except for the logo, FRB, and a mag stripe. "You can use it anywhere. Just sign your name as *T. Sommers.* It'll get you whatever you want. You can use it for gas." He pulled another card out, same as the other. "Here's one for you too," he said, handing one to Sparrow. "Just sign it, *Sparrow.*"

Wolfe went to the safe and pulled out a wad of bills, mostly twenties. He counted out six hundred dollars and gave half to Terri and half to Sparrow. "That should hold you for a while. If you need more, let me know," he said as he handed them the money. Terri smiled as she put it in her purse. "Good enough for now," she said.

Sparrow looked at the card, a quizzical expression on her face. "I've never seen one of these before," she said, examining the card. "Is this some kind of special government card?"

"No," said Wolfe. "I can't tell you the origin, but it's a private card that works anywhere in the world, and purchases aren't tracked, so don't worry about that."

Sparrow smiled, and looked at Wolfe. "Can I keep it when we're done?"

Wolfe smiled. "Nice try. Just don't lose it."

"Don't worry," Sparrow said, pocketing the card. "I wouldn't think of it."

Wolfe watched the two of them go out the door. "I'll tell you about the code and give you a key to the condo when you return," he shouted after Sparrow. Sparrow looked back, smiled, and nodded.

# chapter 28

Devon Barnes sat in the windowless room. There was one other chair, facing him. The room was sterile with concrete block construction and a concrete floor, all of which were painted an ugly shade of green.

The door opened. In walked Sparrow's director, Eric Henderson, who hurriedly closed the door and took the one remaining seat.

"Nice of you to join me," said Barnes, caustically.

"Got here as soon as I could," said Henderson, obviously out of breath.

"Quite a cluster you've gotten into, wouldn't you say?" Before Henderson could say anything, Barnes continued. "I know you lost Sparrow. We can examine why and how this happened at a later time—and trust me, we will. But for now, what steps are you taking to find her?"

Henderson was sweating though the room was cool. "We, ah, are checking with FAA and all the airports for the plane that she escaped on. We monitored the clumsy and simplistic code that was used between Sparrow and the jet's pilot, but it did take us sometime to analyze it in case there was more to it. We thought it was too simple and that there was probably some deeper meaning."

"Was there?" asked Barnes.

"Apparently not. But by the time we verified everything and realized that she had escaped, it was too late to catch her. We got caught in traffic, and . . ."

"Spare me the gory details," said Barnes. "You lost her. I know that. What I want to know, is who took her and where she is now." Barnes' face was tight and he looked more than a little displeased.

"Well," began Henderson, "that's just it. We know it was a Cessna Citation jet that picked her up, and that it was white."

"Tail numbers?" began Barnes. "Flight plan? Place of origination? *Name*?"

Henderson was now hyperventilating. He shook his head. "No. Nothing. He covered his tracks." Trickles of sweat slid down his face onto his white, starched shirt. "He . . ."

"I see we have a complete mess on our hands and that you have not done your job," said Barnes. "Your career is hanging by a thread. Go back to your office and fix this. Find Sparrow, and you might—just might—save your poor excuse of a career. Go!"

Henderson jumped up, and flew out the door, knowing his fate was in jeopardy. He knew, beyond the shadow of a doubt, that failure now would mean the end of his job, his career, and possibly, his life.

He was in a panic, and that was not good.


Wolfe stopped at the Sheriff's Office to check in with Josephs. He sat in the comfortable chair opposite Josephs' desk, as the Sheriff sat in his swivel chair and played with his favorite toy, a pewter helicopter. He spun the blade as they talked.

Wolfe smiled. "So. Nothing, huh, Ed?"

Josephs shook his head, a grim expression on his face. "Nothing. Nada," he said. "Whatever's going on, there is absolutely no foot-print of it in my county." Josephs leaned back in his swivel chair and turned to look out the window. His brown suit looked a bit rumpled and his equally brown tie was slightly askew. "I hope you have better luck than me," he said finally. "I'll keep my ear to the ground and let you know of anything even remotely suspicious, but for now, I'm sorry. I have nothing."

"Don't worry, Ed," said Wolfe. "I still have no idea of what we're into, but I do know we have a dead body here, and possibly more on my end."

Josephs swung around and stared at Wolfe, suddenly alert. "What?" he exclaimed. "More bodies here?"

"Not here, Ed. On my end, in D.C. All hell is breaking loose." Wolfe filled him in on the most recent events, including Sparrow. "It won't be long before things spill over here, I hate to say, Ed. So keep your eye out for anything strange, OK?"

"Including dead bodies?" said Josephs facetiously.

"Yes, Ed. *Especially* dead bodies."

"Oh," said Josephs. "OK. I just wanted to make sure it included dead bodies I should look out for."

Wolfe's smile remained. "Glad to see you still have a sense of humor. You're gonna need it."

"That's what I'm afraid of," said Josephs.

Wolfe laughed as he left the office.

Wolfe swung by the Coroner's Office to see Eino, but there was a note on the door that he was gone to a conference. The note didn't say where or how long he would be gone. Odd, thought Wolfe. He headed back to the condo and paged the Eino. He waited fifteen minutes for a call back, but nothing came. Eino had his pager number too, so he decided to head over to Al's diner for some lunch— and maybe some company.

# chapter 29

Vikki Taylor was walking down the hall in the academic building at NMU with some books and papers clutched in her arm.

She was about five feet six inches tall, trim but fit, with blond hair and steel grey eyes. She wore a green sweater over a white blouse and had on dark blue jeans and suede loafers. She looked the part of a college professor when she rounded the corner in the hallway and ran into a small boy.

"Whoa," she said as she stopped just short of running into the boy. "Sorry, I didn't see you. Almost ran you over."

"No, I'm sorry," said the boy, who appeared to be about ten years old. He had on a red plaid shirt, brown corduroy pants, and dirty tennis shoes. "I wasn't paying attention to where I was going."

Vikki smiled and said, "No problem either way." Then she looked closer at the boy. "Where are your parents? You're not a student here, are you?" she said smiling.

"Oh, they're in the library looking up stuff. I like walking around campus and seeing what I can see. It's a really neat place," he said. "So much to see and learn. I love it." The boy smiled a big, freckle-faced grin.

"Well that's good to hear," she said. "My name's Vikki," she said, extending her hand. "What's yours?"

"Oh, I'm Quinn," he said. "That's what I go by. Everybody knows me by Quinn."

"OK," said Vikki. "Nice to meet you, Quinn." They shook hands.

"What do you do here?" asked Quinn.

Vikki seemed amused. "Oh, I teach classes, do some research, and write books, mostly. I'm a college professor here, teaching behavioral psychology."

"Wow," said Quinn, all excited. "That's a lot of stuff. You must be *real* smart."

She laughed. "Well, I've studied a lot, if that counts."

"I think it does," said Quinn.

"Well, I must get going," she said. "It was nice meeting you, Quinn. Maybe I'll see you around here again." She put out her hand.

Quinn took it and they shook. "I sure hope so," he said. "Have a nice day."

"You too," said Vikki. "Bye."

"Bye," said Quinn. They both continued on in their original directions before the mishap. But after they had each walked several paces, she turned and looked at him again. This time there was something else in her smile.

Something not so pleasant.

# chapter 30

It was mid-afternoon but the diner was still busy. It was one of the most popular places in town, and was considered a local haunt where people came to meet and get some good, reasonably priced food.

Wolfe looked for a seat at the back of the diner where he liked to sit so he could view all the patrons at one time, and also cover his back with a nice, sturdy wall. But four other men had taken that spot, so he took the last booth, mid-way down the aisle. The place was packed, and he was lucky to find a spot.

Soon he caught Jenny's eye. She was as fetching as ever, in her white formfitting uniform and apron. She flashed him a big, warm smile, winked, and nodded that she would join him soon. She finished taking an order for four at a larger table, put the order in with the cook, and then headed over to see Wolfe.

"What'll it be, stranger?" she said, the big smile warming her entire face.

"So, I'm a stranger now, huh?" Wolfe replied, doing his best attempt to match her smile, and not succeeding.

"Hardly," she said and winked.

"Lunch would be great," he said. "Any suggestions?"

Jenny appeared to be thinking, as if she had never been asked that question. Finally she said, "I'd have to say, double cheese burger with a side of French fried onion rings, and one of our fabulous shakes."

Wolfe nodded, thought for a moment. "Sounds good to me," he said, "except I'll have coffee to drink."

Jenny nodded. "Got it."

The diner was busy and Jenny was hustling about trying to keep up with the orders, so they didn't have time to chat. Shortly she came back with his coffee and food at the same time. "Sorry this took so long, sweetie," she said with an apologetic look on her face. "Had to brew a new pot of coffee so it's all coming at once. Hope you don't mind."

"Not at all," he said.

"I hope you enjoy it," she said, flashing a quick smile as she whisked away to get another order.

"Oh, I plan to," he said.

"Wonderful," she said, another big smile. "It's still quite busy, so if you don't mind, I'll just leave the check with you now, and you can leave the money on the table if you need to leave before I get back. Sorry about that."

"Not a problem," said Wolfe. He just started to eat his burger when he saw a woman come into the diner and look around for a seat. But all seats were taken, including the stools at the counter. The only spot left was the one in Wolfe's booth, across from him. The woman was very attractive. She appeared to be in her mid-thirties, thought Wolfe, as he watched her moving slowly up the aisle. She had on well-fitting jeans, a black turtleneck pullover, and white Adidas sneakers.

She was about five and a half feet tall, slender, and had honey blond hair pulled back in a ponytail. She wore wire-rimmed glasses that complimented her high cheek bones and full lips. But her eyes were what fascinated Wolfe. They shined with the color of polished grey steel. She had little makeup on, but she looked healthy and fit, and had a kind of glow about her.

He realized he was staring when she approached his table, so he turned back to his burger and took a big bite. As he was chewing it and concentrating on the ketchup bottle, she stopped.

"Excuse me," she said politely, almost apologetically, "But I wonder if I might join you and order some lunch?"

Wolfe looked up as if he hadn't noticed her until that moment. She continued. "I wouldn't bother you but you see, this is the last seat in the diner, and I only have a limited time to eat. My next class starts in little over an hour."

Wolfe finished swallowing. "I'm sorry," he said, wiping his mouth with the paper napkin. He pretended to look around to confirm what she had said. Then he looked back at her.

"Sure, of course," he said standing. "By all means. Please join me."

She smiled and sat in the booth opposite him. "Thank you so much, sir," she said offering her hand. "I'm Vikki. Vikki Taylor."

Wolfe shook her hand, and noticed that she had a firm handshake for a woman. "Nice to meet you," he said. "My name's Wolfe."

"Nothing to do with your nature, I hope," she said smiling.

"No, it's just what people call me." He didn't want to divulge any more information about himself to this perfect stranger.

"I'm sorry to interrupt your lunch. Please go ahead and eat. I'll order as soon as I can get the waitress . . ."

Wolfe raised his hand and said, "Jenny?"

Jenny looked over, smiled, and nodded. "Right with you," she said.

A minute later Jenny arrived, saw that Wolfe had a visitor, and asked Vikki, "What'll you have?"

Vikki, realizing she had no menu and no time to make a selection, said, "Oh, just bring me what he's having, except make it a single cheeseburger and instead of the onion rings, can you bring me a salad with oil and vinegar dressing on the side?"

Jenny took it down, smiled and said, "Sure, hon. Back in a jiff." She looked again at Vikki, then at Wolfe, trying to figure out the relationship, then quickly pivoted and headed back to the counter to place the order.

She quickly brought back some silverware, a napkin, and a coffee cup and saucer. "Wolfe's got a full pot of coffee on the table, so if you're pressed for time, you might ask to have some of his to get started and I'll bring more. That OK with you, *hon*?" she said to Wolfe. Her smile had a bit of an edge to it, but it was still there.

"Sure," said Wolfe, tearing his eyes from Jenny and looking back at Vikki. "Of course." He picked up the pot and poured her some coffee.

"Why thank you, Mister Wolfe," she said. "That's very kind of you."

"Please, just call me Wolfe," he said. "I'm more comfortable with that."

"Of course," said Vikki. "Wolfe it is."

Wolfe had his big plate of food and felt a little awkward eating in front of Vikki. She sensed that and said, "Please. Eat. Yours will get cold. I wouldn't want that after you were so kind to invite me to sit with you. Mine will be along in a minute."

Wolfe said, "OK. Well, at least you can have some of my onion rings," he said, nodding encouragingly.

Vikki smiled. "OK. I'll have *one*," she said, and gingerly took the smallest one she could find without pawing through them all. "Thank you."

"Sure," said Wolfe. "Have as many as you want. I've got plenty." Vikki smiled and took small bites of her onion ring, interspersed with small sips of her coffee.

Wolfe took small bites too, so as not to be talking with his mouth full, following her admonition for him to eat. He was kind of between a rock and a hard place, socially speaking. He decided to wage small talk until her order came.

"So, you mentioned you have a class starting soon. Are you a student at the University?"

Vikki smiled. "Not exactly," she said. "But thanks for the age reduction. I'm actually an adjunct instructor at NMU where I'm currently teaching a class in deviant behavior."

"Wow," said Wolfe. "A teacher, huh? You looked so young. You could easily have passed for a . . ."

"No more flattery, please," she pleaded. "Let me just thank you for your assessment and move on."

"No problem," he said, taking another bite of his burger to insure that he wouldn't have to speak for a minute or two.

# chapter 31

Vikki decided to talk until her food arrived. "I was born in Austria, though I've spent time in Australia, England, Italy and Canada before coming to the States."

"Interesting," said Wolfe, who then took another bite of his burger, hoping Vikki would be encouraged to continue her monologue. "You don't seem to have any accent at all. I would never have known you weren't born in America."

She smile and continued. "English is my second language, but I've worked hard to adopt the dialect of the country and region I visit. It makes for an easier time, if you know what I mean."

Wolfe looked at her, pausing for a moment. "I *do* know what you mean."

Vikki and Wolfe locked eyes for a second, some kind of non-verbal communication taking place at the subconscious level. Then she blinked and continued.

"I've done research in those countries and others on behavior modification, mostly on humans, though I've done work on animals as well. The whole field of study has intrigued me since I was a child. You know? What makes people tick? Why people do what they do—and what causes them to change their behavior and become deviant."

Wolfe swallowed his last bite of burger, and drained the last of his coffee. "So I take it you studied Skinner? Pavlov?"

Vikki smiled. "Yes. Of course. I studied the basics. But so much more. You'd be surprised what you can make people do with some basic techniques."

Wolfe looked up at Vikki, now quite intrigued with this woman. But just then Jenny arrived with her food, and that put an end to the serious conversation, at least as far as Vikki was concerned. Then the shoe was on the other foot when Vikki said, "Tell me about yourself, Wolfe. What's your background?" She took a bite of salad and he was on the hot seat—a place where he was least comfortable.

Wolfe finished chewing and drank some coffee to wash it down. "I, ah, have been around, too," he said, trying to be sociable without revealing too much information about himself.

"Oh?" she said.

"Yeah, I was in the military and had assignments in various parts of the world. Since I've retired, I've been an adjunct instructor working part-time when there is a need. In between teaching assignments, I assist local law enforcement when they ask me. Otherwise, I go fishing."

"Well, it sounds like you've had some interesting experiences," said Vikki. "Have any particulars you'd like to add? Like where you were stationed in the military, what your specialty was? What you teach?"

Wolfe remained intentionally vague. "I teach criminal investigation mostly. Other than that, my other experiences have been amazingly boring. Just routine stuff. I won't bore you with the details. I'd rather learn more about what you teach. That sounds much more interesting to me."

Vikki smiled. "I guess I'm like you. We each find our particular occupations mundane. Talking about them is like a busman's holiday, wouldn't you say?"

Wolfe laughed. "I guess you're right. I'll let you eat in peace." They ate their lunch in relative quiet, both contemplating, wondering about the other. When they had finished, Wolfe signaled Jenny and she quickly came over.

"All set?" she asked with her pleasing smile. The edge was gone. "All set," said Wolfe. "Put hers on my ticket." He turned to Vikki. "My treat."

"You don't have to do that," said Vikki. "I didn't intend for you to pay for my meal when I asked to join you. Letting me sit in your booth was plenty generous of you."

Jenny looked at Wolfe, eyebrows raised. Wolfe handed Jenny two twenties and said, "That's for both. Keep the change."

Jenny smiled, beaming at the huge tip. "Why thank you, hon," she said. "How kind of you." The smile had spread ear to ear.

"My pleasure, always," he said. "See you soon."

"Looking forward to it," said Jenny, who gave him a wink, and an extra wiggle as she walked away.

Vikki was watching this mating ritual with interest and amusement. "She seems to like you."

Wolfe looked back at Vikki, forcing himself to take his eyes off of Jenny's derriere. His smile faded when he saw the look on her face.

"Should I say, get a room?" said Vikki.

Wolfe got a little embarrassed, shook his head. "Oh, no. She flirts a lot, is all. They work primarily for tips, you know."

"I know," said Vikki. "Apparently she's good at it."

"Yeah, I guess she is," he said, putting his now much lighter wallet away.

Vikki was looking intently at Wolfe, a pensive smile on her face. "Say," she said. "Since you bought me lunch, how about I return the favor? I hang out a lot at a place called Boh's near campus. It's comfortable, eclectic, and has a variety of things to eat, though not in the vein of Al's Diner. What do you say? It's a little less hectic than the diner and much more relaxing."

Wolfe thought about it for a minute. He didn't want to offend her, but he really didn't want to talk much more about himself, and he was pretty sure that's what she wanted. But he couldn't think of anything to say to get out of it gently, so he agreed. "OK. Sure," he said. "Though I didn't buy your lunch with the intention of a reciprocation."

"Oh I know you didn't," she said. "But I feel like I owe you something and I would prefer to be on equal footing, if you know what I mean."

Wolfe smiled. He knew exactly what she meant. "I understand. I'd be happy to meet you at Boh's sometime. I don't know when it would be, as I'm a little busy right now, but I can giv  you a call when things settle down a bit, if you'll give me your number."

"Overwhelmed with your, ah, sporadic teaching, or maybe your intermittent consulting?" she asked, poking fun at his attempt to wiggle out of the invitation.

Wolfe was embarrassed again. "No. Of course not. I can see why you might think that I was trying to get out of your kind offer. So let me put an end to this uncomfortable mess I seem to have gotten myself into. I'm free for dinner tonight, if you are. After that, I have no idea when I'll be free."

"Perfect," said Vikki. "How about I meet you there at seven-thirty? You know where it is?"

"Seven-thirty sounds great," said Wolfe. "And I do know where it is."

Vikki stood and extended her hand. "Then it's a date. See you there." She smiled a knowing smile that Wolfe found unnerving.

He stood and shook her hand. "See you at Boh's." He smiled as well, but his smile was less certain than hers was, and he wondered what that meant. He guessed he'd find out soon enough.

# chapter 32

Wolfe went back to the condo, took a shower, and dressed quickly in jeans and a black V-neck sweater. He went to his closet and pulled out a dark brown corduroy jacket and laid it over the back of the easy chair in the living room. Terri and Sparrow weren't back yet from their shopping spree, and he began to wonder if he hadn't made a terrible mistake sending them out together. Just then he heard some talking outside the front door. He heard the key inserted in the lock and the alarm system deactivated.

Sparrow was first in. "Hey Wolfe," she said as she spotted him. "Got the code and the key from Terri, so I'm all set." They both had an arm full of packages and smiles on their faces, which made him very nervous. He wondered where Terri got the extra key.

"I see you bought some things," he said tentatively. "Get what you needed?"

Both Terri and Sparrow responded simultaneously. "We did." They looked at each other and laughed. "I needed a few things, too," said Terri. "Hope you don't mind."

Wolfe shook his head. "Of course not. Go ahead and get those things put away and then join me down here. I have to bring you up to date."

"Back in a jiff," said Terri. They both bounded up the stairs like a couple of schoolgirls back from the mall.

Wolfe decided to try Eino again, so he dialed his number at the morgue. Still no answer. So he tried Eino's pager again, and plugged in the condo number. Hopefully he would hear back soon. Eino could take care of himself, but he was getting a little worried.

He checked his watch. Four-thirty. Plenty of time to make a phone call and take care of a few things before heading to Boh's to meet Vikki for dinner. He shook his head to clear out the cobwebs, picked up the phone and went through the security process to call Zeb. But the line went dead immediately, which was a bad sign. He was hoping they hadn't gotten to him already, but it looked bad.

He hung up and went through the same process to call Otto. A voice came on the line that sounded like Otto, but it was whispered so he wasn't sure. "Otto?" he said softly.

"Wolfe," came back the whispered voice. "Things are bad here. You're on your own. Housecleaning here's terminal. There appears to be a *purge* of your team. They're razing the place. Don't call again. I'll contact you later—if I can. If not, see you on the other side. By the way—Reaper called. They blew up his house. He's on the run and headed your way. I hope he makes it. Help him if you can."

"Otto, I . . ." Wolfe began, but the line went dead. He hoped that wasn't Otto's fate as well. He hung up the phone, a bad, sinking feeling in his stomach. He wondered how Reaper would get hold of him. He didn't have any phone numbers for Wolfe and didn't know where he was living, especially not his cabin or the condo. Well, he thought, Reaper was resourceful so he'd wait until he heard from him. There wasn't much more he could do. Then he thought of a possibility. Reaper knew about last year's caper and the people he'd worked with. If he were Reaper, he'd probably contact Sheriff Josephs, because he was a trusted member of the inner circle, and he would probably have the greatest chance of knowing where Wolfe was, or how to find him. He decided to call Josephs as soon as he was done with the briefing.

Suddenly he heard voices again, as Terri and Sparrow came down the stairs.

Wolfe cleared his head. "You two all set?" he asked.

"Sure," said Terri. "I have some new alternative surveillance clothes. See?" And she did a quick spin around to show off her new outfit.

"Me too," said Sparrow and did a turn as well.

"Very nice," he said, admiring their forms rather than the clothes. "Have a seat," he said, pointing to the couch. "I need to brief you on recent events."

Then he told them about his recent phone calls to Zeb and Otto. He didn't mention Reaper. After he had finished, Sparrow said, "Holy crap. This is really getting out of hand."

"It is," responded Terri. "And then factor in the reality that we are looking for people trying to watch us in the hopes that we find whatever we are looking for—and when we do find it, they will most likely take whatever it is we find, and eliminate us too."

Wolfe took a deep breath. "That about sums it up. So you see how important it is that we take all these precautions seriously and try to survive for as long as we can."

"You mean, *survive, period*, right Wolfe?" asked Sparrow, a serious look on her face.

"Yes. That's what I mean," he said. "We're all going to survive."

"Good," said Terri. "Then we'll get to our respective assignments."

Wolfe nodded. "And be careful. Don't be seen together, and page me if you find anything suspicious—anything at all."

"OK," said Terri.

"You got it," said Sparrow. They both left the condo, much less chipper than when they'd arrived.

After they left, Wolfe called Josephs, and explained the latest information. "Well that's a hell of a lot of bad news, Wolfe," the Sheriff said when Wolfe had finished.

"True," said Wolfe. "But at least Sparrow and Reaper are still alive, and maybe even Otto, too, if he was able to get away. That one's kind of iffy, though. The others being murdered in cold blood has all the earmarks of Barnes cleaning house. He's using this operation as a means of eliminating all the witnesses to his previous crimes."

"Sounds like a lovely bunch of guys you've associated with, Wolfe."

"Didn't have much choice, Sheriff. I didn't pick and choose the people I had to work with. Besides. Most all of them were solid patriots who continually risked their lives for their fellow operatives. It was basically just Barnes who turned out to be the black sheep of the group—and what a black sheep he was. We've got to get rid of him, Ed—before he destroys more lives."

Josephs nodded. "I agree."

Wolfe changed gears. "So if you hear from Reaper, you can give him all my contact information, including my sat phone number. If he has one, he can call me on that. I'll have mine with me at all times. Otherwise, let me know where I can meet him.

"I'd like to keep him separate from the others—I have some special assignments for him, and the fewer people who know about him, the better. I'll put him in the basement apartment. There's a hidden separate entrance to that, and I'll give him a device to access it."

"Will do, Wolfe. Don't worry. I'll take care of him and see that he finds you. And mum's the word."

"Thanks, Ed. I really appreciate it."

"No problem," said Josephs. "You know I'll always have your back."

"Ditto," said Wolfe. They both hung up. Then Josephs called his dispatch center and gave them strict instructions that if any man called up and asked to speak directly to him, and wouldn't leave any information, to patch him directly through to Josephs. They said they would. Josephs vowed to keep his police walkie-talkie with him at all times after that.

# chapter 33

*A*t that same moment, Reaper was winging his way toward Marquette, wondering how he would find and contact Commander Wolfe. All he knew was that he was living somewhere in or near Marquette, and that he didn't know Reaper was coming. He sat back in his chair, reclined it as far as it would go, which wasn't far, and closed his eyes. He tried to relax, and think back to his experiences with Commander Wolfe, and what he would do in Reaper's shoes.

Then it hit him. Last known contact. That was what he was taught. Go back to the last person you knew who had contact with the person you were looking for. One of those was Terri Sommers, but he didn't know how to get hold of her. He had no number for the Coroner, Eino Loukkala either. And even then, he probably wasn't there half the time.

Then he lit on the one person who was always reachable. The Sheriff. He could contact him and he would most likely know where Wolfe was. He decided he would call Sheriff Josephs as soon as he landed at Marquette County Airport and hopefully he would be able to make contact for him.

That was his plan. And he hoped word of his survival and escape had not leaked out and armed guards were not waiting for him with handcuffs, to cart him away to dark places in unknown lands.

He hoped.

# chapter 34

It was Terri who first spotted the man on the bicycle. He fit the description Wolfe had given her, and of the bike as well. But she couldn't be sure, so she followed him. Maybe she could spot some furtive action that would give him away.

She was on foot on the university campus when he actually rode by her going in the same direction. They were on a curved path that wandered through campus, with many pine and hardwood trees carefully spaced throughout. Since it was early October in Marquette, the leaves were at their peak color in shades of bright red, deep red, orange, yellow, and rust brown. Terri delighted in the vivid colors, and how beautifully they contrasted with the deep greens of the white pine and blue spruce.

The grass was still green, but it was beginning to go dormant, waiting for the killer frost that would drive it deep into hibernation for the winter. Other plantings were still hearty, but they, too, would succumb to the inevitable cold and snow that would be blanketing the area soon enough.

But this day was beautiful, with the late afternoon sun back-lighting the leaves, making them shine with a brilliance that made them appear as if they were lighted from within. Terri marveled at the beauty, thinking that it all looked like a child's candy-land.

Her observing of the environment was perfectly in keeping with her surveillance of the subject on the bike, who had stopped ahead to look around as well, though maybe not for the same reason.

There was a wooden bench next to the pathway, so since her subject was stopped, Terri sat down just like any passerby might do. She had on comfortable, warm clothes, but only two layers, a shirt and a jacket—and jeans.

The air was crisp and cool. But one could easily get too warm if the surveillance took on a faster pace. She had on black sneakers more substantial than her normal Keds, which provided good support for walking, as well as jogging, running, and jumping—which she hoped she wouldn't have to do.

While they were both stopped, she tried to get a better description of him, and of the bike. He appeared to be in his mid-twenties, but it was hard to be sure. His hair was sandy colored with a slight wave to it, and was on the long side, but neatly trimmed.

He climbed off his bike and looked around. Standing, he appeared to be slightly under six feet tall. He seemed strong and athletic, having had no trouble pedaling around campus at a good clip. The bike was a relatively new 10-speed racing bike, green in color.

Terri watched him as he looked around campus much as a tourist would, except that he did not look like a tourist. His gaze seemed to be constantly moving, side to side, as if looking for someone or something—his gaze did not linger on the brightly colored leaves that were all around him.

To him, they appeared incidental. Indeed, almost unnoticed. His pants were dark and non-descript, stretchy enough to ride the bike easily—or to run, chase, or jump over objects or fences, if need be. He had on a darker jacket, loose-fitting but serviceable, and, she thought, large enough to hide a firearm.

Terri reached for a campus map that she had picked up at a kiosk when she first got on campus, though she was pretty familiar with the area from the last adventure she had here with Wolfe.

But she had a more pressing reason for bringing it with her now, as it provided perfect cover for her role as tourist.

Just as she pulled out the map and started opening it, the subject turned and looked at her. She wasn't looking directly at him, but she could see his movements with her peripheral vision, which happened to be excellent. She focused on the map, turning it around a bit and then flipping it over to look at the other side, which had a more detailed map of the central campus. As she studied it, he studied her. More likely, stared. That made Terri uncomfortable.

So she decided to go on the offensive. Terri quickly looked directly over at him, locking her stare on his. She maintained eye contact until he looked away, which he did fairly quickly.

But not before sending an unwritten message—he was watching her. That also told her she was on the right track. She would be watching him, too. So much for covert surveillance, she thought. She grabbed her camera and began taking pictures as he quickly climbed back on the bike and sped off down the path.

She took as many photos of the subject as she could, some Polaroid and the remainder with her Nikon that she used for her AP reporting, and then returned to the condo to report in. However when she got there, it was empty, so she went to see Sheriff Josephs.

"What've you got?" Josephs asked as Terri entered his office. "Photos and a summary of my blown surveillance," she
responded.

"Lemme see," he said as he leaned forward in his chair. "Hmm. Man on a bike."

Terri laughed, tossed the Polaroids on his desk and sat down. "Good description," she said. "I have others I've taken, before and after he spotted me. Maybe you can have them developed in your photo lab?" she asked expectantly.

"What photo lab?" Josephs asked, eyebrows raised. "You think we're made of money here?"

Terri smiled. "Worth a shot," she said. "Where do you recommend I get them developed?"

Josephs said, "Give me the film. I'll take it to a private developer who does these things for me on the QT. He'll do it right away, if he's in his office."

"Thanks, Ed," she said. "I feel strongly he's one of our adversaries, and the sooner we identify him and find out who he's working for, the better."

"I agree," said Josephs. "I'll call him right now."

"I'll get back to what I was doing before I spotted him. I'll be in touch," she said as she left his office. Josephs nodded as he picked up the phone and dialed.

# chapter 35

The man on the bicycle watched as the woman turned and left the area. He was pretty sure she had been watching him too, but he wasn't positive. He decided to call it in. He found a payphone in the lobby of the student union, and placed his call.

"Go," said the serious voice on the other end of the line.

The man gave his code name, Serge. "I believe a woman has been following me."

"Describe the woman and the situation."

Serge did. "What do you want me to do?" he asked, looking around to make sure nobody was listening.

"She sounds like that AP reporter who is working with Wolfe," said the voice. "See if you can spot her again, and let's turn the tables on her. See if you can find out what she's working on. Then report back."

"Got it," said Serge, then the line went dead. He went back, but could not find the woman.

Terri went back to the campus and decided to try the direct approach. She went directly to the administration building and up to the university president's office. There was an attractive woman at the reception desk, who looked to be in her sixties. She had well-styled grey hair and a conservative outfit befitting her many years of experience.

"May I help you?" the woman said, looking up from her desk.

Her tone of voice was professional, but had no warmth.

"Yes," said Terri as she pulled out her press credentials. She showed them to the woman, who carefully looked them over, nodded and handed them back.

"And how can we help the press," said the woman, a reserved smile on her face.

Terri replaced the credentials in her pocket. "I'm researching a piece on the important role colleges and universities play in the advancement of scientific development," she continued. "Cutting edge projects are my primary interest, you know, how scientists and universities collaborate on new developments in biotechnology, agriculture, space exploration, energy, and so on. I was wondering if you could direct me to any personnel that might be working on such things here, or anything else of a similar nature."

A student employee was working on some files at the other side of the room. Finishing her work, she gathered up her papers and left the office, glancing at Terri as she did.

The woman sat up straighter in her seat, preparing her remarks carefully. "Well, Miss Sommers, we here at the university pride ourselves on cooperating with the press, of course, and we do work on a number of advanced projects in conjunction with scientists, industry, and the government. However," she continued, her artificial smile fading slightly, "I'm sure you are also aware of the fact that most of these programs are classified, or are of a confidential or proprietary nature, and thus cannot be publicized during their ongoing development." She relaxed a tiny bit, leaning back in her chair. She had the ironclad look that said she was finished, and that nothing more would be gained by Terri remaining in her office, or on campus for that matter.

"So, then nothing at all you can show me that I can print?" said Terri.

"I'm afraid not, Miss Sommers. I'm afraid there's nothing I can do for you."

Terri held her gaze for a moment. Then she said, "I see." She put away her notebook and pen. "Well, thank you," she said as she prepared to leave. "I'll make sure I write a glowing report on the great cooperation I received at this *public* university." Her sarcasm was lost on the secretary, who prided herself on protecting the university.

Terri then left the office, leaving the door open.

The woman at the desk maintained her pose as she watched Terri walk down the hall away from her. The frozen face, however, began to crack, first a little bit, then a lot, as she began contemplating the ramifications of what she had so self-righteously just done. She had a bad feeling in the pit of her stomach—a knot that seemed to tighten and grow as Terri reached the end of the hall, turned, and headed toward the elevator.

# chapter 36

As Terri was walking away from the administration building, mulling her unsatisfactory visit with the president's secretary, she heard a voice behind her.

"Miss?"

Terri stopped and turned around. There, hustling down the sidewalk towards her from the building was the student worker who had been in the president's anterior office filing papers. "Yes?" said Terri.

"Can I talk to you for a minute?" The young dark-haired girl had no jacket on, just jeans and an NMU sweatshirt and sneakers.

Terri took a couple of steps towards her and let the student catch up. "Sure," she said. "How can I help you?"

The student caught her breath and got up close to Terri, as if passing some confidential message. "I overhead your conversation with Mrs. Kaswell—that's the President's secretary—sorry. Didn't mean to eavesdrop, but . . ."

"Go ahead," said Terri, a little impatient, but also interested in what she might have to say.

The student said softly, "My name is Kara Dugan, and when you asked about cutting edge projects, well, I know of one at least, that you might be interested in."

"How do you know about it?" asked Terri, "if it's so hush, hush?"

Kara looked back at the administration building to see if anyone was watching her, then satisfied no one was, turned back to Terri.

"There was a professor who worked in the physics department who had been working on a secret project for a government agency—I think it was *drapa,* or something like that."

"You mean *DARPA*?" Terri asked, suddenly very interested.

"Yeah, that's it," said Kara. "Anyway, I was a student assistant for him too, and so I got to learn a little bit about what was going on just by doing office work, being a 'gofer' like bringing coffee or materials to his lab, and so on."

"Can you tell me his name?" asked Terri.

"Yes, ah, his name is Professor Dejanovic—Jonathan Dejanovic," she said. "He's a nice man but very reclusive and quite paranoid," she continued. "He always felt that someone was looking over his shoulder, monitoring his phone calls, even following him home."

"Yet he trusted you?"

"Well, yes, I guess so. I don't think he saw me as much of a threat, being so young and naïve." She blushed then continued, "I think he thought I was cute and he liked me. We got along pretty well, anyway."

Terri had taken out her notebook by now and was entering information as Kara kept talking. "Why did you think Professor Dejanovic's work was cutting edge?"

"Because of lots of little things," Kara said, moving even closer and almost whispering to Terri. "Like, he'd be talking on the phone and discussing things about his experiment, and it seemed that whoever he was talking to, wanted things to move faster. I think that person was someone who was funding the project, maybe even paying the professor's salary."

"Do you think that person might have been from DARPA?" asked Terri.

"Maybe," said Kara. "I did hear him one time say in a heated exchange, words to the effect that if they didn't like his rate of progress, that DARPA could just shove it up their collective . . .well, you know, it was a crude expression," she finished, blushing again. "I also heard during another conversation the term, 'above top secret,' though I can't say for sure that it was in reference to the professor's project or not. But I'm guessing it might have been."

"Very interesting," said Terri, scribbling away. When she had finished, she looked at Kara and noticed she was shivering. The slight breeze had shifted direction and was now an onshore wind coming off of Lake Superior. The temperature had suddenly dropped at least ten degrees. "You're shivering," she said to Kara. "Shall we go inside somewhere and finish our conversation?"

"I should get back to the office," she said, looking around nervously. "I have another half-hour to work before my time is up."

Terri looked around and spotted the student union. "How about you go back and finish your half-hour, then meet me in the student union and we can finish up then. I have a few more questions to ask you, and I'll buy you a cup of coffee and a bite to eat if you want. How's that?"

Kara thought about that for a few seconds, still shivering. "OK," she said finally. "I'll meet you there in half-an hour." She then headed quickly back to the administration building and the welcoming warmth inside.

Terri walked to the student union and found a corner with a small table and a couple of chairs. She then went to the counter and bought a cup of coffee for herself, and went back to the table to review her notes and plan her strategy. She might just have the clue they were looking for, she thought. Wouldn't that be nice?

A little over a half-hour later, Kara found her, wearing the jacket she had previously left in the administration building office. "Hi," she said as she walked over to the table.

"Hi," said Terri. "How do you take your coffee?"

"Cream and sugar," said Kara.

"Anything else I can get you? A snack? Bagel? Something else?" Terri asked.

"No, coffee's fine. I'll be having dinner soon. I've already paid for that. You know. Room and board?" She smiled weakly.

"Sure," said Terri. She got the coffee and brought it back.

"Thanks," said Kara. "That'll help warm me up." She took a sip.

"You're welcome. Now, if it's OK, I'd like to continue our previous conversation and ask a few more questions."

"Shoot," said Kara.

"Can you tell me where the professor's office is, so I can contact him?"

Kara took another sip of coffee. "That's a problem," she said cautiously. "Because he no longer has an office on campus."

"Really?" said Terri. "Why's that?"

"Well, I really don't know how to say this, but he was removed from his office by campus police three weeks ago."

"Removed?" asked Terri, surprised at the statement. "You mean, *fired*?"

"That's where I'm not sure," said Kara. "There was no official announcement of anything, and nobody told me anything, which is strange because I was working for the man. I was just contacted and told to report to Mrs. Kaswell to finish out my hours."

"Did the professor say anything to you when he left, or afterward?"

"Well, nothing at the time because I wasn't there when the campus police came and got him."

"Was he *arrested*?" asked Terri.

"I don't think so," said Kara. "I mean, there was no announcement in the student paper or anything like that. It was like, one minute he was there, and the next minute he was gone. No explanation, no information. Just gone."

Terri nodded, then looked at her notes for a few minutes while Kara sipped her coffee. Both of them looked around the room every so often, obviously concerned about being observed together or being overheard. But nobody seemed to be paying any attention to them.

Finally Terri said, "You said the professor said nothing to you at the time, because you weren't there at the time of his removal from the office."

Kara said, "Right," and nodded her head.

"Has he contacted you since then?"

Kara looked down at the table, and fidgeted in her chair. She said nothing.

"Kara?" asked Terri again. "This is all confidential, so don't worry about anything getting out. You're totally safe." Then she added, "And so is *he*."

Kara looked up at Terri and held her gaze. Finally she sighed, sat up straight, opened her mouth—and out came the mother lode.

# chapter 37

Wolfe showed up at Boh's a little early so he could check the place out. He wasn't exactly sure how he had gotten himself roped into this date, but he had, and so he decided to make the best of it. There was something about her that intrigued him—something elusive, hidden just under the surface. He would have to keep his eyes open with her.

As he looked about the low-lit room, he took in the eclectic nature of the design and furnishings. It was bohemian in style, hence the name Boh's. The dark tin ceiling, twelve feet high with wood paddle fans gently circulating the air, set the atmosphere. Comfortable, used furniture of varying styles and generations were scattered around in different groupings, from tables for two, to couches and soft chairs grouped for five or six, or more.

Windows along the right side as he entered the door looked out onto Washington Street, while at the opposite side of the room were a few steps up to the counter area, where various offerings of cookies, brownies, pies, cakes and biscotti were stacked on the counter or displayed in clear, plastic circular displays. Also available there were numerous kinds of coffees, teas, and flavored drinks of a bygone era, plus an assortment of gourmet stuffed sandwiches. The whole place was carpeted in dark reds and browns. The carpet was old and worn, threadbare in some places, but clean.

He found a corner towards the back of the seating area that had a solid wall behind it, which provided an expansive view of the entire establishment, especially the front, and as far as he could tell, the *only* door. Once settled he began his usual scan of the patrons and the staff, checking for any signs of dangerous or unstable people.

The place was only about half full, but he expected that it would fill up pretty quickly as it was a popular spot with college students. It was definitely interesting, Wolfe observed.

Finding no threats, he put his jacket on the chair, and went to the counter to order a plain black coffee. After an extensive interview by the clerk regarding which of the infinite combinations and variations of coffee and flavorings he would like, he was finally able to get through to the young man that plain black coffee meant exactly that. Plain. Black. Coffee. The man finally shrugged his shoulders as if he had been talking to a cretin, and poured him his cup, placed it on a saucer, and handed it to Wolfe, who paid him and headed back to his table.

The coffee was indeed hot, so only after sitting down and blowing on it for a couple of minutes was he was able to take a sip without scalding his palate. As he did so, he kept his eye on the front door, periodically scanning the patrons and staff for any unusual behavior. Still, the place looked normal and unthreatening.

Finally the door opened and in walked Vikki, confident and poised as she scanned the room until she spotted Wolfe. She smiled as she deftly picked her way around the chaotic scattering of tables and chairs to the corner where Wolfe sat. As she approached his table, he rose to greet her.

"Hi, Vikki," he said.

"Hi to you, Wolfe," she said, and sat down opposite him. She still had on jeans, but had changed her turtleneck for a green NMU sweatshirt.

"What can I get you?" asked Wolfe.

Vikki thought for a moment, then said, "A chai latte, if you don't mind, and maybe a chocolate and almond biscotti. But remember. It's my treat. So, what do *you* want?"

Wolfe smiled. "Well, as you can see, I already have my black coffee, which by the way, is not as easy to order here as one might think."

Vikki laughed. "No doubt," she said. "I imagine they were quite taken aback at such a prosaic order. In fact, I'm surprised they even knew how to fill it."

"I'll admit, it appeared to be quite a struggle."

"So?" asked Vikki again. "Your order?"

"Oh. Sorry. Ah, I saw a particularly high-calorie chocolate brownie with nuts that I'd take if you don't mind."

"I'll do my best," she said as she turned and walked up the three steps to the counter.

Wolfe watched her go, admiring her walk and the cut of her jeans. So far, it was pretty nice being with her, thought Wolfe. *This might not be so bad after all.* Another voice said, *be careful.*

The phone rang deep in the bowels of the Kremlin in Moscow, headquarters of the Soviet Union. The phone sat on a massive wooden desk in an ornate, paneled office. A man reached out his pudgy hand to pick up the receiver. "General Morozov," he barked into the phone.

"General, this is Major Kozlov," said the man on the other end.

"Dmitry," said General Borya Morozov, head of the KGB.

"What have you to report?"

"Some bad news, I'm afraid," said Kozlov. "Vlad has been killed at the hands of that agent, Wolfe."

"Killed?" barked Morozov. "How?"

"In a fight," he said. "Vlad put up a tremendous fight, General, but Wolfe took him by surprise and got the upper hand."

"How is this *possible*?" shouted the General. "He was one of our best men. He was a *tank*!"

"That is true," said Kozlov. "All I can say is that it happened."

"I hope you have better news than that," said Morozov menacingly.

"I do have *some* good news," said Kozlov. "Contact has been made by Comrade Dunayevsky. A relationship is being formed as we speak."

"Well that's something," said the General. "Anything of value yet?"

"Not yet, but maybe by this evening we'll know something more."

"For your sake, I hope so, *Major*. You know how tentative these ranks can be."

Major Kozlov gulped nervously. "Yes, General. I understand. I'm right on top of this."

"Report as soon as you have something," ordered the General. "Time is running out."

"Yes, General, I . . ."

But the line had been disconnected and Major Dmitry Kozlov was left holding the now dead phone in his hand, a trickle of sweat slowly working its way down the side of his face, in spite of the cool October evening in Marquette, Michigan.

Vikki was enjoying her chai latte and biscotti, while Wolfe devoured his chocolate brownie in two bites, and was draining the rest of his coffee. They had exchanged small talk revealing nothing much about each other.

"How about some real food?" Vikki said, finally. "I'm supposed to be buying you dinner, and so far these are barely appetizers," she said, smiling. "Actually, it looks like you have already had dessert. Got it backwards did you?"

Wolfe smiled. "I didn't want to seem like I was taking advantage of your generous offer. But I could eat. They do have an excellent deli here, and they make great stuffed sandwiches. Would you like one?"

"Do they have menus here, or are we supposed to use ESP to divine the offerings?"

"No menus," said Wolfe. "Just a chalk board behind the counter. You want me to go look?"

"Stay put," said Vikki as she rose to go to the counter. "I'm supposed to be doing this. You've been here before. Do you know what you want?"

"Pastrami and Swiss on Rye, with mustard, and kettle chips," he said. "And more coffee. And another napkin."

Vikki just looked at him. "Anything *else*?"

"No," he said. "That should do for now."

Vikki nodded. "Back in a minute."

Wolfe watched her go to the counter, admiring her again.

Vikki came back with another chai latte and Wolfe's coffee. "It'll be a few minutes," she said. "They'll bring it over as soon as it's ready."

"What'd you get?" he asked.

"A ham and cheese on wheat with mayo," she said. "Wow. We are real conversationalists, aren't we?" she said with a trace of sarcasm.

"OK," said Wolfe. "What do you want to talk about?"

"Well for starters," she said, leaning forward, "who *are* you?"

That took Wolfe back. He wondered what she was getting at. Did she know more about him than he had revealed? Which was nothing? Finally he said, "Who am I? I told you at Al's Diner."

"OK," she said a little impatiently. "We can turn this into an interrogation if you wish. How about a little bit more? What are your hobbies? What kind of music do you like? What's your *sign*?"

"OK, OK. I get your point," he said. "I'll tell you if you tell me about yourself."

She laughed. "So, it's, *I'll show you mine if you show me yours*?"

"Something like that," said Wolfe smiling.

She nodded. "OK. You first."

Wolfe was saved as the sandwiches arrived and they both took a few minutes to dig in to their food. It was dark outside and the place had a cozy, comfortable feel to it. Most of the furniture was now occupied, and there was a soft hum of conversation in the room. There was music playing in the background, instrumentals of a nondescript and eclectic nature, which perfectly matched the atmosphere of the place.

Vikki had finished her food, rather quickly he thought, and was leaning over the table, closer to him. "OK, Wolfe. Spill. Give me your deepest, darkest secrets." She was smiling a rather enigmatic smile, and her unblinking silvery eyes drew him in.

Wolfe was getting a little disoriented. Maybe it was the music, or the low lights—it was definitely something. He felt like he had had several drinks of alcohol. That was a feeling he was familiar with. But not one created by two cups of coffee. Something was off.

"What's the matter?" said Vikki. "You look a little tired."

"It's been kind of a long day," he said. "A little stressful, I guess."

Vikki leaned back in her chair. "Say. Why don't you come over to my place where it'll be more comfortable? Then you can have a drink and relax. No more grand inquisition. I promise. I can see you've had a tough day."

Wolfe thought about it for a minute. Then he said, "What the hell. I could use some R & R."

"Great," she said, getting her jacket. "We can take my car, or you can follow me—whichever you wish."

Wolfe thought about it for a moment. Something told him in the deep recesses of his mind that he should drive his car. "I'll follow you," he said finally. He put on his jacket, stood and swayed for a moment, then getting his bearings, he followed her out the door. He noticed she had a white Land Rover as he got in his Jeep Wrangler, started it up, and pulled up behind her. He was a little wobbly, but he managed to follow her to her house at one-ninety-eight Lincoln Avenue. The house was not far from Al's Diner, thankfully, and they were there in a few minutes.

Wolfe did not feel good about Vikki. His instincts were ringing alarm bells and his suspicions were growing. Why did she push so hard to meet him for dinner? Was the first meeting at Al's Diner just a coincidence? Maybe he was being overly cautious but he felt there was some subterfuge with Vikki, and if that was the case, why? What was to be gained? Could Vikki be a part of the pursuit of the professor and his invention? Could she have set up this persona as a college professor just to get to him?

Wolfe did not have the answers to these questions, but of one thing he was certain. Going to Vikki's house now was risky. Especially after he was drowsy after drinking the coffee that *she* had gotten for him. Had he been drugged? If so, he should be heading for the hills right now instead of into the lion's den. But if she was after him to find out what was going on, the only way he was going to find out was to follow through with this *date*, and do his own investigation—into her.

He only hoped that he was not going in too deep to recover.

# chapter 38

Wolfe stepped out of his car and looked up at the old, three-story home. "You can park on the street in front if you want," said Vikki.

"This house is *yours*?" he said, surprised at its size and location, which was prime real estate not far from the University. It was a large Victorian-style home with pale-yellow stucco on the upper two levels, and red brick on the lower level. Trim around the windows was white, and on the third floor there was a corner turret room. The shingles were dark grey, and though the house was old, it had once been quite the mansion.

Vikki laughed. "It is, but I rent three rooms out to college students while they're here during the school year. The extra income is kind of nice. But they're not here now. The others have gone on a trip together, so I have the place to myself for a few days. C'mon," she said, motioning to him. "I'll show you."

The cool night air had revived Wolfe a bit. He walked with Vikki up several steps to the covered porch. White railings enclosed the porch, with fieldstone posts at each corner, and large windows looking into the front living room. Vikki pulled out a key from her purse and opened the front door. They both entered the large vestibule. The living room was furnished with a mix of period antiques and vintage used furniture.

Vikki showed Wolfe around the main floor. Past the living room was another spacious room with more furniture, then a large dining room, with an eat-in kitchen off the back. There was a bathroom off the middle room, and a stone, wood-burning fireplace in the living room. Wolfe took it all in, though everything looked a little out of focus.

Vikki then took him up to the second floor where there were three bedrooms and one bathroom off the central hall, then on up to the third floor where her bedroom, the master suite, angled off of the turret sitting room. The master suite included another fireplace, a bathroom, and a large walk-in closet.

Vikki said, "Why don't you go down to the living room and make yourself comfortable? Just relax a bit, if you don't mind, while I go to the powder room. I won't be long. There's a bottle of wine in the kitchen on the counter. Would you open it for me? There's a corkscrew in the drawer below it, and a couple of glasses in the cupboard above. Pour me a glass, too, if you would."

"Sure," he said. Wolfe went downstairs, found the bottle of Cabernet and corkscrew, and clumsily pulled the cork. His fingers felt thick and seemed unable to perform the commands his brain was sending them. He was woozy, but still managed to complete the task. The cork came right out, and he placed it and the corkscrew, which he didn't bother removing, on the kitchen counter. He still hadn't had anything to drink, and he was beginning to think he shouldn't have any now.

But then he figured one glass wouldn't hurt, so he found the two wine glasses, filled them half full, and took them into the living room. He put them on the glass coffee table and plopped down on the couch. He sat there a moment and looked at the glass. His fuzziness didn't seem to be getting any worse, so he figured, what the hell, and took a sip. Then two.

The phone call took only a minute. "Kozlov," said the voice. Major Kozlov was KGB and assassin Viktoriya Dunayevsky's handler.

"Dunayevsky," she said.

"Comrade Dunayevsky—Vikki—so good to hear from you. What have you to report?"

"I made contact. He's at my house. I drugged his coffee. It shouldn't be long. I drugged his wine, too."

"Good. Let me know as soon as it's done." They both hung up at the same time.

Kozlov called the General and updated him. "Get it done tonight," ordered General Morozov. "Or else." He hung up.

# chapter 39

Wolfe sipped his wine, finishing the glass by the time Vikki reappeared from the powder room. "Feel better?" she asked.

"A little," he replied. "I feel a little funny, though. Kind of dizzy—disoriented. Maybe I'm coming down with something."

She sat next to him and felt his forehead with the back of her hand. "I don't think you have a fever," she said. "I think it might be from working too hard. What have you been doing lately?" she asked, innocently enough.

Wolfe knew he had to be careful, but his thinking was getting hazy. "Just trying to help some friends of mine who are in a bit of trouble," he said finally.

"Oh," she said, nodding slightly, then changed the subject. "Mind if I put on some music?"

Wolfe shook his head. "No. Not at all. What kind of music do you like?"

"All kinds," she said. "But for a quiet evening of conversation, I like relaxing music—instrumentals, mood pieces, that kind of thing." She went over to a rack of eight-track tapes on the wall next to her stereo system and perused the titles. "Ah. Here's one I like," she said, pulling it out of the rack and popping it into her tape player. "I love eight-track tapes, don't you?" she asked, as she set the volume level on her stereo.

"Oh, ah, yeah," said Wolfe, trying to shake away the fuzziness that seemed to be enveloping his brain. "They're great." He had no idea what she was talking about but he decided to agree with her. It required less brain power—something he seemed to be lacking at the moment.

Vikki nodded. "I like the way it automatically moves from one track to another until they're all completed, and then automatically starts up again at the beginning. That way if you're playing something you really like, you don't have to keep jumping up to restart it, like with a record."

Wolfe nodded, his eyelids at half-mast. "Like a record," he repeated, not realizing that his response made no sense.

Vikki smiled a knowing smile. She finished her glass of wine, and said, "Let me get us some more wine. Be right back."

"K," said Wolfe, getting sleepy.

Vikki went into the kitchen and poured more wine, but as she did, she took out a tiny bottle from the back of the food shelf and squeezed two drops from the bottle stopper into Wolfe's glass. "That should do it," she said to herself. She brought the glasses into the living room and gave one to Wolfe, being careful to give him the one she had just drugged.

She nudged him a little as his eyes were closed by the time she had returned. "Wake up, sleepy," she said. "Not time for bed just yet." She held the glass in front of him.

"What?" he said, sitting up straight. Then he focused his eyes and saw her holding the glass. "Oh. Right. Thanks." He took the glass from her and smiled. "Not sure I really need this," he said, stalling.

"Who does?" she said. "Might make your headache go away though."

Wolfe didn't know he had a headache, but in fact just as she said that, it was beginning to throb. "Maybe some aspirin would be better," he said, some logical thinking fighting for a chance to be heard.

"Try the wine first," she said. "If that doesn't work, I'll get you some aspirin."

Not wanting to argue, Wolfe said, "OK," and swallowed some wine. Strange, he thought. He couldn't seem to taste it.

Then he noticed the music. It was like no music he had ever heard before. It was slow and rhythmic, pulsing about one beat a second—kind of like his heart beating. He listened carefully. The volume slowly increased and then decreased, over and over again. Like the waves on an ocean beach. He liked it.

Reaper's plane came in for a landing at Marquette County Airport. As soon as it landed, he grabbed his duffle bag from the overhead compartment and headed into the airport terminal building. Still not sure whether those out to kill him had figured out where he was, he was acutely alert to anyone acting strangely or seeming out of place. He scanned every face as he entered the building, from the airport workers in one kind of uniform or another, to families coming to welcome their fellow travelers.

Reaper stood just inside the entrance, watching each and every person for a full minute before he ventured further. Nothing raised an alarm with his finely attuned instinct for survival, so he went to the bank of phones and placed a call to the Marquette County Sheriff's Office. The phone rang two times before it was answered. "Sheriff's Office," came the voice at the other end of the line.

"I'd like to speak to the Sheriff," said Reaper.

"May I ask who is calling?" responded the male voice.

"Just tell him it's a friend of Wolfe's," said Reaper, hoping that would fly. He couldn't identify himself without risking capture.

Fortunately the voice said softly, "Just a moment, please." Ten long seconds went by when a voice came on the line.

"Sheriff Josephs. Dispatcher said you're a friend of Wolfe's, that right?"

"Yes," said Reaper. "I need to talk to you. I need to get in touch with Wolfe quickly."

"You at the airport now?" asked Josephs.

"Yes," said Reaper. "And I have no transportation to get to you. All I have is my duffle bag and the clothes on my back. The rest is gone."

Josephs thought for a moment. "I'll come get you and give you a ride to my office. If I can find Wolfe, I'll take you directly to him. But he's a slippery soul, and I'm not sure I can find him right at the moment. Hopefully by the time I get you to Marquette, I'll have tracked him down. Now, describe yourself so I know who to look for when I arrive."

"It shouldn't be hard to identify me," said Reaper. "I have red hair, freckles, and stand about six feet, two inches tall, at about two hundred and twenty-five pounds. You miss me, you must be blind."

Joseph laughed. "I'll be there shortly. Be watching," he said, then hung up.

"Oh, I will," said Reaper to the now dead phone.

Reaper stayed to the side of the lobby, as far away as he could from the mainstream traffic. He tried to tuck himself in the corner and be as unobtrusive as possible while waiting for the Sheriff. He stayed alert, watching all the people coming and going, and kept a close eye on the vehicles pulling up to the curb.

Then he started wondering what the Sheriff would be driving. If he had a marked patrol vehicle, that wouldn't be hard to recognize, though he still didn't know what the Sheriff looked like. It would be bad if by chance a different deputy pulled up not knowing about his arrangements with the Sheriff. He started to worry.

Finally a silver Plymouth pulled up to the curb, stopped, and a man in a brown suit got out and headed to the terminal entrance like he owned the place. Slowly Reaper moved slightly away from the corner so that the man coming in could see him. His senses were on full alert in case this was not the Sheriff and worse, was someone coming after him to finish the job.

But the man came in with his head on a swivel, swinging from left to right, scanning the lobby looking for someone. Then his eyes locked on Reaper and he walked directly over to him. "Wolfe's friend, I take it?" he said, putting out his hand.

Reaper shook his hand. "I am," he said, "and I'm definitely glad to see you."

"Let's get out of here," said Josephs. "I guess you don't need any more exposure than is absolutely necessary, right?"

"Right," said Reaper, a big grin on his face. He grabbed his duffle bag, threw it in the back seat of the Sheriff's car, and climbed in the front, moving the seat all the way back. "Hope you don't mind," said Reaper. "I need a little extra room."

Josephs looked over and smiled. "Obviously." Then he pulled away from the curb and headed off to try to find Wolfe.

# chapter 40

The eight-track tape player clicked from track to track, one after the other, until it reached the end, at which time it clicked back to the first track and started all over again. Wolfe pondered the mu-sic. There seemed to be no beginning and no end to it, musically.

One stanza led seamlessly to the next, and so on.

Wolfe let the music lead him along through waves of sound and tempo, getting a little louder, then softer, picking up tempo, then back down again. The average beat still seemed to be about one beat per second though—again, matching his heartbeat.

Wolfe could feel the music pulsing through his body, putting all his organs in harmony with each other. It was like being in a boat on the water, with gently rolling waves moving him up and down, back and forth. It was hypnotic. He liked it.

Between the alcohol and the music, he felt himself slowly slipping out of reality into a comfort zone of peace and tranquility. He was *so* relaxed. It was a nice feeling, he thought. He could live here in this zone—wherever it was. He gave no thought to his other life—the one of mystery, intrigue, excitement and danger.

That had faded into a distant memory, as if the boat was slowly receding from the shore, heading further and further out to sea, until the shore eventually became invisible, and all he could see was the horizon in every direction.

Then he noticed that the boat rocked like it was going to tip, then it righted itself. His eyes were closed, but everything felt right again. Then slowly he became aware of a presence near him. It was saying something softly, ever so softly as it moved almost imper-ceptibly closer and closer. He sensed the touch of the entity. It felt pleasant. Then he sensed the warmth of breath on his ear, and soft words spoken as lips touched the very outer layers of his ear. He strained to hear the words spoken, but the music masked them and he couldn't make them out.

There was more movement in the boat, then he seemed to be transported to another place, soft and warm. His eyes were still closed and he was curious where he had moved to, but try as he might, he couldn't raise his lids. Then he thought he might raise them with his hands, but he couldn't lift his hands, either. What a strange dream, he thought.

Then the words resumed again, but this time he could almost make them out. The music had gotten softer and he sensed someone asking him questions. He tried to hear the questions, and he had a strong urge to answer them. But he couldn't.

There were more words, more questions, then he smelled a wonderful smell. Perfume, he thought. Exquisite. It filled his senses with feelings, thoughts, memories, sensations. Good ones. He found himself slowly coming awake from his dream.

Finally he was able to open his eyes, and he saw another pair of eyes, close and looking into his. They were Vikki's eyes. They were steel-grey and hypnotic. He felt they might swallow him up.

He became aware that she was lying next to him on a bed—in her bedroom. How did he get there? He looked at her for a minute, trying to wake up. Trying to clear his head.

"Wow," he said finally. He lifted his head up and looked around the room. "I'm sorry, Vikki," he said, shaking his head to try to clear it. "I must have fallen asleep." He got up on his elbows. "I think I had too much to drink."

Vikki looked at Wolfe, a satisfied smile on her face. "That you did."

Wolfe got a funny look on his face and rolled over on his side toward Vikki. "We didn't, ah, I mean I didn't . . ."

"No," Vikki cut in. "Nothing happened. In fact, I had too much to drink too, and we just came into the bedroom, laid down on the bed and almost instantly passed out. I just woke up a minute before you, in fact." She smiled warmly at him, and he smiled weakly at her.

"OK," he said, hesitantly. "Good. It's just that I had a weird dream that I . . . we . . ."

"I know," she said as she swung her legs over the side of the bed. "You were mumbling something, and I think that's what woke me up. You seemed to want to say something, but you couldn't. That make any sense to you?"

"Yes," said Wolfe. "As a matter of fact, it does. I guess that's all it was."

"I'm sure of it," said Vikki, standing and smoothing her clothing. "C'mon," she said. "Let's . . ."

Suddenly Wolfe's pager went off. He seemed surprised and looked down to see the screen, but it was no longer clipped to his belt. Looking to where the sound was coming from, he saw it over on a table several feet away. He looked at Vikki, who had a funny look on her face.

"How did my pager get over there?" he asked.

"Oh," she said, her eyes darting around as she tried to think of an answer. "Ah, it seemed to be digging into your side when we came in here to lay down, so you took it off and put it over on the table."

Wolfe thought about that for a minute, then said, "Yeah, I guess that makes sense, though I don't remember doing that."

"Honey," she said, "I'd be surprised if you remembered much of *anything* that happened after all that alcohol."

"But I didn't drink hardly any . . ." began Wolfe.

Vikki cut in. "You did, Wolfe. You just don't remember it. You were pretty plowed and maybe some of your memory was blacked out. That happens sometimes, I can tell you. It's not that unusual."

Wolfe looked at her. "Well, I guess you should know, being a shrink and all."

"Yeah. *Shrink*," she said. "We love that term in the field of psychoanalysis."

"Oh. Sorry," said Wolfe.

She laughed as she went to the table and brought him his pager. "Here," she said. "Better check it out. Might be a national emergency," she said, smiling, a twinkle in her eye.

Wolfe took the pager and looked at the number. It was code from Sparrow to meet up with her as soon as possible. She also gave the code for the location.

"Gotta go," he said, clipping the pager to his belt and checking to make sure he had his wallet and keys.

"Where to?" she said. "What's so important that you have to run off after such a nice evening? It doesn't have to be over, you know?"

Wolfe looked at her. "Can't talk about it," he said, rushing toward the door.

"Can I come along and keep you company?" she said as a last ditch effort to stay with him.

"Sorry, Vikki. I'll call you. Bye." He closed the door and rushed down the steps to his Jeep, trying not to stumble and fall and look like a fool.

"Bye," she said after he had gone, her soft voice suddenly gaining an edge.

Her steel-grey eyes turned to arctic ice as she watched him through the window.

Her efforts had been futile. It was time to change tactics, she decided. It was time to bug out and follow the girl. Hopefully she would lead her to the professor.

# chapter 41

Wolfe drove to the bar Sparrow had indicated on his beeper. It was a small establishment called The Whistle Stop, with beer and wine and a limited menu, which was frequented mostly by blue collar workers.

There were stools at the bar itself, plus a row of wooden booths directly opposite it. By the time Wolfe arrived, Sparrow was already seated in the back booth with her back to the wall, as he expected she would be. As much as he hated it, he sat across from her, his back to the rest of the patrons. This was getting to be a bad habit. One he would have to break—soon.

Wolfe looked at her. Even in the dark lighting, she attracted attention.

Sparrow leaned forward and softly said, "I know you don't like sitting with your back not against the wall, so I thoroughly scoped out the people before you arrived. It all looks good."

"So you've got my back?"

"I've got your back."

"Then I can relax," he said, not relaxing.

"Of course you can—though I know you won't."

"Astute," he said, a slight smile on his face. "Must have had good training."

She smiled back. "The best."

"OK," he said. "Why the urgent message?"

"I did as you asked," she began, as she leaned forward and lowered her voice. Her eyes kept roving as she talked, taking in each person's actions, looking for any sign something was not right.

She found nothing. She focused back on Wolfe. "I took the Subaru and cruised the town, looking for anything suspicious. I also pretended to do shopping, bought a scarf and got a store bag with it to help with the ruse. I also stopped in various restaurants and bars, bought a bit of food or drink for a quick scope of the people, and then moved on to the next."

"That's all great," said Wolfe. "But what did you find that caused you to give me an urgent page?"

"I'm getting to that," she said, somewhat piqued.

"Sorry," he said. "Go ahead."

"As I was cruising the streets, I saw what looked like one of our agency's undercover cars—an Impala. And someone was sitting in it, engine running, drinking what looked like a cup of coffee."

"That's not so unusual," said Wolfe. "Lots of cars look like agency undercover cars. They were meant to fit in. What made you think it was an agency car?"

Sparrow glared at him. "Because," she said, "I recognized the man inside. He was one of the men from my office."

Wolfe jerked to attention. "You sure it was him?"

"Saw him every day," said Sparrow. "Name's Dan Jenkins. A real bastard. Not a covert agent, but part of the Agency, nonetheless. He knows me, too. And he thinks he's hot stuff. Macho man.

"I was approaching his car from the rear and when I saw his face in his rearview mirror, I recognized him instantly. He wasn't looking at me, so I looked to the left as I passed his vehicle so he couldn't see my face. I glanced once in my rearview mirror to double check to make sure, but it was him.

"He was pretty consumed with drinking his coffee, which appeared to be hot, since he was blowing on it as steam rose from the cup. I'm sure he didn't see me. But he was here. And the question is, why? And how did he find us?"

Wolfe's mind was racing through time, back and forth—searching for all possibilities. Finally he said, "I don't think he followed us. I think that they are just covering their bets by sending people to locations where you might be. And you being with me was not much of a stretch. Also, this would be a good place to start since it was the locus of the area we were tasked to search from the beginning."

Sparrow nodded. "Makes sense, I guess."

"But we'll have to be extra careful," he said, "since they're hot to find and 'recover' you, so you can be *retired*. You should consider him armed and dangerous, because his orders might be to bring you in, dead or alive. And his preference might be, dead."

"I'm not too worried about that, Wolfe. This guy thinks he's Don Juan. He'll want to play before he does whatever he's been ordered to do. And that will be his downfall. Trust me."

"I do trust you," said Wolfe. "But just remember, the stakes are high and I wouldn't make too many assumptions about anything or anyone, including him. OK?"

"Point taken," she said.

"Good," said Wolfe. "We'd better disguise you from now on, so even if you are seen, you won't be recognized."

"Already bought clothes, wigs, and everything else I need for that when I was with Terri. Just didn't think I'd need it so soon."

Wolfe nodded. "Better get back to the condo and change up as quickly as possible. Make sure you're not seen, and always wear your disguises until this is over."

Sparrow nodded, and gave Wolfe a description of the car and license number. Then she put some money on the table for her drink. Wolfe pushed it back to her. "On me," he said. "It's the least I can do."

She scooped up the money and put it away. "It is," she said with a quick smile. Then she got up and went quickly out the door.

# chapter 42

Terri had suggested they find a more private place to talk, so Kara recommended a coffee shop nearby, which was run by a French woman who had brought her European style to Marquette. Kara said she often came here to get away from campus and enjoyed the quiet casual atmosphere and good food and drink. Terri had never been there. She checked out the high, tin ceilings with slow moving paddle fans, the soft ambience, and lazy, swirling architecture. The name of the place was Boh's. She liked it.

They found a quiet corner with two comfortable over-stuffed chairs and a small round table. Kara dropped her things on a chair and asked Terri if she wanted anything.

"Sure," said Terri. "How about a chocolate biscotti and a large chai latte? I'm buying, so get what you want, too. I know what it's like on a student's budget." She handed Kara some cash.

"Thanks," said Kara. "Back in a minute."

The service was at the counter, and was very relaxed—read that, slow, thought Terri. But the place was so peaceful. She didn't mind. As she looked around, there was no particular period of time that the place reflected. The architecture, furnishings, pace—it was almost timeless. Nothing fit, and yet, everything fit. This was a place where she could hang out on a regular basis, she thought, if she only lived here. She contemplated that.

And then she thought of Wolfe. From their harrowing experiences of a year ago, they had cemented an attachment. A relationship had bloomed, although a tempestuous one for sure. Still, she felt strongly about him, and was disappointed he didn't call, though they never set anything up officially. Maybe they were both waiting for the other to call. Maybe that didn't happen because they were both stubborn.

So she had developed another friendship with a man in Chicago, a financial manager named Brent Davenport. They met one day at a coffee shop when both of them were bustling around in a great hurry. There had been some confusion, and they had each gotten the other's coffee by mistake. By the time tempers had settled and they had rectified the error, they had both felt a spark of attraction, which led to a phone call, which led to a date, which led to an unsettled relationship.

But their busy schedules, with Terri running off here and there to cover stories, and Brent's work hours often going late into the evening, made for difficult times getting together. Still, it worked somewhat. It was not totally satisfying, she thought, but it worked well enough so that neither one of them wanted to give it up. But she never stopped thinking of Wolfe, and her attraction to Brent did not come close to that which she had for Wolfe. But then, Brent was there and Wolfe wasn't.

Kara returned with the food and beverages and placed them on the round table. Terri was grateful for the distraction. Her line of thought about Wolfe and Brent was not productive.

"Thanks," said Terri. They had both gotten chai lattes, and Kara had brought a couple of biscotti as well as a cookie and a cruller, just in case she missed dinner. They munched and sipped for several minutes, and then Terri said, "OK. Spill. And I don't mean your chai."

Kara looked at Terri and laughed, appreciating the bit of levity before she launched into what was probably a life-changing event for her. "So, as I said before, I was a student worker for Professor Dejanovic, and I did typical clerical work that a student would do—make copies, file papers, get supplies, get coffee and sometimes lunch when he didn't have time to go out—all that stuff."

"Go, on," said Terri, taking another bite of biscotti, then picking up her pen and paper again as Kara began speaking.

"Well, it didn't seem like anything special at first. I mean, his work. Just a scientist doing scientist-type work that I didn't understand, but I didn't care about, either. Then one day he got a phone call that upset him. I didn't know who called, but his secretary took the call as usual and told the caller he was busy. But the caller insisted, so she went into the lab and asked him to come out and take the call. That's the part I heard—at least his half of it."

"How did he seem?" asked Terri. "Was he agitated, angry, nervous?"

"Angry, I think," said Kara. "At least, mostly he was. And I think, maybe a little bit scared. I got the impression the caller was threatening him. His face got red, then he shouted, *go to hell*, and slammed down the phone."

"Any idea what the call was about?"

"Not really, except it seemed that it might have something to do with what he was working on, because after that he quit working on his research and began quietly removing things from his lab, mostly after the secretary went home."

"How did you know that?" asked Terri.

"Because he asked me to change my work hours, somewhat. Come in later in the afternoon and work more into the evening."

"What did you think about that?"

"I was fine with it," said Kara. "I mean, I worked my study hours around his schedule, and there was less busy work to do in the evening, so I got to help him with lab stuff more."

"You mean you helped him with his research?" asked Terri.

"No, but I helped him move things out of the office and I got to ask him questions about his work."

"Wasn't that confidential?" asked Terri. "I mean, wasn't his research classified?"

"Well, yes," Kara said tentatively, "but he didn't seem to care about that anymore. You see, the reason he was having problems with DARPA was that he had stopped working on their research, and he had begun working on his own secret invention. On his last phone call, he was angry and resentful, and pretty much told his funder to go screw himself."

"So he talked to you about what he was working on?" asked Terri, hoping for the bonanza. She got it.

"Oh, yeah. He was excited about it. That's why he quit working on their project. He was proud of *his* work."

"I see," said Terri, as she concentrated on her notes, afraid to ask the next question. Then she looked up at Kara, focused on her eyes, and said, "Can you tell me what it was?"

Kara smiled and said, "Oh sure. His own invention isn't classified. He had found a way to use Nikola Tesla's theory of resonance and quantum physics to tap into something he called, 'dark energy.' He said it was the answer to the world's energy problems forever, and that it was essentially free for the taking. He was talking about going public with it."

"Wow," said Terri. "That must have been exciting."

"It was," said Kara. "But now everyone is searching for him, because he's disappeared. And he took all the equipment and notes on his own invention with him. The stuff he left at the lab was what DARPA had paid for, and was essentially worthless."

"What if he's never found?" asked Terri.

"Oh, that's no problem," said Kara.

Terri looked up from her notes. "And why's that?"

"Because I was the one who helped him move his equipment, notes and stuff out of his office."

"You . . . moved all of his stuff to . . ."

"To his new hideout, ah, location." Terri's eyes got big as she stared at Kara. "That's right," said Kara, taking her last swallow of chai latte. She put the cup down and smiled.

"I know exactly where he is."

# chapter 43

After Sparrow left the bar, Wolfe stayed and had some coffee. He shook his head, tried to clear it. He thought of Terri. He had the strongest feelings for her, without a doubt. He found her stimulating and very sexy. There was an emotional bond there, and he missed enjoying that with her. But he never called her after they were last together, and she had found someone else. Not surprising, he thought.

And now she was dating another man. That hurt the most, but he couldn't think what he could do about it in the middle of the assignment. He had to focus on finding the professor and whatever invention he was working on that could threaten so many people.

Suddenly his mind cleared. Puzzle pieces fell into place. Wolfe threw some money on the table and jumped up. He now knew what he had to do.

After Sparrow had left Wolfe at The Whistle Stop, she didn't go back to the condo as she was supposed to. Instead, she pretended to walk away, like a carefree college student after a few drinks. She kept her eyes open as she did so.

Across the street she saw a man smoking a cigarette, loitering on the corner. She kept an eye on him as she walked by. He glanced at her, then looked away, concentrating on the door to the bar she just came out of.

Normally a man would take at least a second look at her as she walked by, and often one would eyeball her the entire time she was visible to him. Or even make a pass. But this one didn't. Maybe not into women, she thought. Still, he seemed to be focused on that door, and who might come out. She decided to walk around the block and come up on his blind side, to observe him unseen. She stayed hidden in the doorway of the business next to the one he was in front of.

The man, about thirty years old, looked very fit, and of foreign origin. His cigarette gone, he popped another one out of its pack and lit it. The cigarettes had a dark color and were probably foreign as well. It was when he dropped the spent cigarette on the ground and crushed it out with his shoe, that she noticed the other cigarette butts littering the ground by his feet. He had been there for quite a while.

Suddenly the door to The Whistle Stop swung open and Wolfe stepped out. As he did so, the man slid back into the shadow of the doorway where he was standing. At that point he was going to be invisible to Wolfe, who turned right, away from the man and Sparrow, and started down the street.

As soon as Wolfe walked away from the bar, the man dropped his newly lit cigarette to the ground and crushed it out with his shoe, all the while keeping his eyes focused on Wolfe. He came out of the shadows and started directly after Wolfe. As he walked he began reaching for something in his pocket.

That was enough for Sparrow. She quickly approached him from behind just as the gun in his hand emerged from his pocket.

Quickly she drew her gun, dropped to one knee, and yelled in a commanding manner, *"You! Drop it!"*

The man, with his gun now drawn, suddenly spun around pointing his gun at what he believed to be the source of the threat.

But before he could get off a shot, Sparrow put two rounds into his chest. He dropped instantly, and stopped moving.

Wolfe heard the shout and turned around just in time to see Sparrow bring the man down. He drew his own weapon and came running over to her, scanning the area for other possible assailants as he did.

Sparrow did the same, then stood up as Wolfe approached her. "He was gunning for you. I saw him loitering around, so I hid myself in the doorway and watched. As soon as you walked out, he started for you, pulling a gun as he did. I only had time to distract him and shoot him in self-defense. In *your* defense. So you see," she said as she put her Beretta away, "I *do* have your back."

"No argument from me," he said. "Thanks, Sparrow. C'mon. We'd better check to see if he's still alive. Maybe we can find out who he is."

After a quick check, it was plain the man was dead. One of Sparrow's bullets entered the man's side while the other round struck something vital, either his heart or his aorta, either one of which would be almost instantly fatal.

They searched his pockets, but found nothing but a second loaded magazine and a piece of paper with a name and a number. The name was in Russian—Alexei, and the number was 84A95B. It meant nothing to either of them, so Wolfe put the paper in a cellophane bag and stuck it in his pocket. People were starting to stop and stare, so Wolfe told Sparrow to go use the phone in the bar and call Josephs to have him come quickly and to send Eino for the body.

Wolfe looked down at the man's face. He looked Eastern European.

Sparrow came back from calling Josephs. "He's on his way and he's bringing a passenger. He's coming lights and siren, so he should be here quickly."

Even then Wolfe could hear the siren off in the distance.

"Good," he said.

A minute later Josephs came roaring up in his unmarked car and squealed to a stop in front of Wolfe and Sparrow. He told Reaper to stay out of sight in the car, then jumped out and came over to Wolfe. "What happened?"

Wolfe explained. Sheriff Josephs stood there with his mouth open. He found it difficult to believe that Wolfe almost bought the farm. "Damn good thing you rescued Sparrow," he said finally. "Looks like she literally had your back."

Wolfe nodded. "Proof positive," he said, still in a bit of shock. Two deputies arrived and blocked traffic from both sides to

protect the scene.

"Busy night, huh?" said Josephs sarcastically. Then Wolfe told him he had more bad news. "You're kidding me, right?" said the Sheriff. "Could it *get* any worse?"

"Probably," said Wolfe.

"By the way," said Josephs. "I just picked up your guy at the airport. He's in my car right now. What do you want me to do with him?"

"Leave it to me," said Wolfe. "Don't let anybody see him. No one is supposed to know he's still alive."

# chapter 44

Wolfe went to his Wrangler Jeep and pulled it next to Josephs' car, blocking the view of Reaper. He put his finger to his lips, indicating to Reaper to quietly slip from the Sheriff's car into Wolfe's, which Reaper quickly did. Wolfe drove away and headed towards the condo. On the way he filled Reaper in as much as he could about what was going on with his team, including the threat from Barnes and all the things that had happened since, up to and including the dead man in the street, most likely a Russian named Alexei.

"Jeez," said Reaper. "And I thought what was going on in D.C. was bad. Well, in retrospect, it *was* really bad. And still is, I guess."

"Unfortunately, it appears so," said Wolfe.

Reaper filled Wolfe in on what had happened to him, including finding Hawk murdered, and ending with his escape to Marquette. When they arrived at the condo, Wolfe pulled around to the back of the condo. Reaper grabbed his duffel bag and got out of the Jeep. Wolfe produced an electronic door release device and pressed its only button. An otherwise invisible metal door with no external handle popped open, revealing a back staircase to the basement area.

Wolfe directed Reaper to head down the stairs, after which he followed, and then pressed the electronic door release button again, causing the door to close silently. Once shut, an electronic lock slid into place making the room ultra-secure. There was a similar type door lock-release mechanism at the top of an internal staircase that led to the top two floors of the condo, where the rest of the team would be staying.

"Go ahead and get settled in," said Wolfe. "I think you'll find what you need here. You're probably tired, so get some food and something to drink. There's plenty here for you to choose from. There are towels in the shower, and a terrycloth robe hanging on the back of the bathroom door. Also there are clothes in the closet, but I can't guarantee they'll fit you. You can try them on if you want.

"There's a phone on the table next to the leather chair. Press button one to dial upstairs and I'll answer. Press two for a secure outside line. And here's another remote door-release you should carry with you." Wolfe tossed it to him. "You'll need it to get in or out once the doors close. Any questions?"

Reaper shook his head as he looked around at the sumptuous room. "Plenty," he said as he stared in amazement. "But I'll save them until later. You're right. I'm bushed and need some food and rest as soon as possible. Let me know when you need me. Otherwise, I'll be out like a light."

Wolfe laughed. "So glad to see you, Reaper. You don't know *how* glad."

"Me too," said Reaper as he grabbed a bottle of water out of the fridge. "Talk soon."

Wolfe nodded, and headed upstairs, securing the electronic door behind him.

# chapter 45

Two paramedics showed up with the rescue truck at the scene of the shooting. Josephs came over to the lead medic. "Where's Eino?"

"Gone to some conference, I guess," he said. "I stopped by the morgue, but he wasn't there. The door was locked and there was a faded note on it that said, 'Gone to a conference. Back soon.'"

"I sure haven't seen much of him," said Josephs. "Come to think of it, once he picked that blow gun as his weapon of choice, I haven't seen him hardly at all. I'll try him again, while you're here." He went to the patrol car, used the police radio to call dispatch, and then told the dispatcher to call Eino's number and to put the call through to his police radio so the medic could hear too. It rang three times, and just as Ed was about to click off, there was a click and a voice came on the phone. "Eino, you old buzzard," he began. "Where . . ."

But Eino's voice cut him off as a recording began, without deference to Josephs.

It said, *"Hello, this is Eino Loukkala, Marquette County Coroner. I'm away at a conference right now, but I have hired someone to fill in for me until I return. He should be here soon. His name is Aaron Beecher and he's well- trained.* (At this point, Josephs' eyebrows were raised as he looked at the medic. The voice continued.)

"He will take care of your Coroner needs and answer your questions in my absence. However, in the event that there is a serious emergency that Dr. Beecher cannot handle, or if it is of such a nature that you absolutely must get in touch with me, I do have an answering service that you can reach during the hours of nine AM to four PM Monday, Wednesday, and Friday, ten AM to six PM Tuesday and Thursday, and noon to four PM on Saturday and Sunday. But if it's a super emergency, you can call the Sheriff at . . ." Josephs clicked off.

"How *long* is that cassette tape?" asked the medic. "He must have used up the whole damn thing just with his *instructions*."

"I don't know," said Josephs. "All I know is that I won't live long enough to find out. That was a life-shortening experience."

They laughed. "Maybe he's trying to drum up business?"

"Not from me," said Josephs. "I'll never call *that* number again. Can I assume that this *Doctor Beecher* wasn't there when you stopped by?"

"You assume correctly," said the medic. "The place was dark."

"Gonna have to have a talk with that man, when he returns," said Josephs. "In the meantime, would you guys take the John Doe to the morgue and put him to bed until either Doctor Beecher or Eino shows up? Who knows when that will be, but we should keep him in the deep freeze until then."

"Sure," said the medic. Then he went to get the other medic and they loaded the dead man into the rescue truck and headed to the morgue.

Josephs left the scene in the hands of the deputies and headed off to the condo. Sparrow did likewise after giving her statement to the deputies.

A few minutes after Wolfe went upstairs, Sheriff Josephs came into the condo. Before he could say anything, Wolfe said,

"Hey, Ed. Can I bounce something off you?"

"Sure," said the Sheriff, plopping down in the comfortable couch. "Whatcha got?"

Wolfe sat across from him. "First, before I forget, I got some information on someone following us—probably one of the bad guys—probably one of *ours*, unfortunately."

"All right," said Josephs, as he got out a pen and pad of paper.

"One of the people from Sparrow's office is here, sitting in a tan Chevy Impala in front of Woolworth's." He gave Josephs the tag number.

"I'll check it," said Josephs. "Probably a rental, though. Hang on a sec." He used his walkie talkie to call their dispatcher and gave him the number to check. They did so while he was still on the line. A minute later they gave him the info and he hung up the phone. "Yup. Avis out of the airport rental counter. Not gonna be much help there," he said.

Wolfe nodded. "Thanks for checking."

"So Sparrow saw him but he didn't see her, is that it?" asked Josephs.

"Yup. She says he didn't see her, but she was sure it was him. We don't think he tracked us here through the jet I flew to D.C., because I took serious precautions to see that no one could. All I can figure is that since we were tasked by Barnes to look for the professor in this area, it was a likely place to send an agent to see if he could spot her."

"Makes sense," said Josephs.

"So I thought if an *anonymous* complaint was called in to your office that a suspicious man had been seen stalking a woman and he fit the description, you could ID him, check his driver's license and any other ID he might have on him, including credit cards . . ."

"Yes, Wolfe. I know the drill," said Josephs sarcastically. "I'll take care of it and let you know what I find."

"Thanks, Ed. I owe you one."

"One?" said Josephs, with a shocked look on his face. "They're really stacking up like cordwood. More like, one-*hundred*."

"Well, better make it one-hundred and one," said Wolfe. "I need another favor from you."

Josephs rolled his eyes, took out his pad of paper and, and said, "What now?"

Wolfe told him about Vikki and the strange feelings he had when he was with her in her house. "There's something not right and it's bothering me," he said. He explained his dizziness right after they had coffee at Boh's, and how it continued after they went to her house—that he only had one and a half glasses of wine, and apparently passed out. "That doesn't happen to me, Ed. Something was really off.

"What I'd like you to do is to run a background check on her, without her knowing about it, if you can. Also, I'd like to find out if she really owns that house, and whether or not she's renting it to three college girls. It would be great if you could find that out." Wolfe gave Josephs all the information he had on her. "And see if you can verify that she is a professor at NMU. She claims she is, but right now, all I have is her word on everything—even her name."

Josephs was scribbling things on the note pad. "OK. Anything else?"

"Well, actually, there is. I'd like to get into that house while she isn't there. I need to take a look around. She seemed to have some equipment partly hidden in her closet. I didn't get a good look at it, but I have an idea what it might be. Also I'd like to check the place for bugs, two-way mirrors, and also the other bedrooms where these girls are supposed to be staying. I have a feeling this whole thing's one big setup. And if it's being done by the people I think it might be, they're very good at what they do, and we are in deeper trouble than I ever imagined."

"Wow," said Josephs. "That's quite the scenario."

"I know, Sheriff, and I wouldn't ask you if it wasn't so critical. But if I'm right, and I hope I'm not, then you're the only one I trust to handle this so it doesn't blow back on us all."

"Consider it done," said Josephs. "I'll find a pretext to get in the house—gas leak, complaint from neighbors of some sort, you know the drill."

"I do," said Wolfe. "Thanks a bunch, Ed. I owe . . ."

"Better stop right there," said Josephs. "Don't want to have to put you in debtor's prison, now do I?"

Wolfe smiled. "Thanks, Ed. Talk to you soon."

Just as Josephs was leaving, Sparrow arrived, so he filled her in on what he had discussed with Josephs. At least, on most of it. He did leave out the part about Vikki. No point in muddying the waters, he thought to himself. But he knew it was more about protecting his own reputation, such as it was.

Wolfe hoped he was wrong about Vikki. But he was getting a bad feeling about her. He sensed that she was not the person she had said she was. And if she wasn't, who the hell was she? He was definitely getting that feeling on the back of his neck where the hairs stand up straight. He'd had that happen before and he knew what that meant.

And it scared him.

# chapter 46

Terri stopped for a minute, staring at Kara and considering all the implications of what she had just said: I know exactly where he is. If this man was the person they were looking for, and what he was working on was the thing they were all freaking out about, then Wolfe and his team, and now Kara were right on track—and in mortal danger.

If the enemy could find the professor before they did, then there would be no reason to keep them alive, and every reason to eliminate them. They already knew too much. These thoughts flew through Terri's mind at the same speed as it took Kara to finish swallowing her sip of latte.

"OK," began Terri seriously. "I don't want to freak you out, but you have stumbled into one of the biggest and most dangerous operations of the century."

Kara's eyes got suddenly very wide. "What? What do you mean you don't want to freak me out? How could I *not* be freaked out after you saying that?"

"I know. But I didn't know how else to say it, and I wanted to let you know right off, the gravity of the situation we all are in."

"All in? All who?" asked Kara.

Terri took a breath, then slowly let it out. "I will fill you in on what's going on, because I have no other choice. But you have to promise you will not reveal any of this to anyone else. Not your friends, not your family, not the police, not anybody. Your life and ours depends on that."

Kara thought for a moment, then said, "OK, I guess."

"No," Terri came back quickly. "You don't *guess*. You know. Or else I can't tell you anymore, and I will have to immediately place you in protective custody, where you will be held incommunicado until this is all over, whenever that is. *Now* do you understand the gravity of the situation?"

Kara started to become indignant and was about to shout about her constitutional rights, when Terri reached back behind her underneath her jacket, and revealed a pair of handcuffs. The look on her face said she was deadly serious. Of course, she had never used handcuffs before, and she had no authority to use them now, nor deprive Kara of her freedom. Wolfe had insisted she carry them when he issued her a gun. But Kara didn't know any of that.

"Well?" said Terri. She discreetly displayed the cuffs to Kara. "This is a matter of national security, and many, many lives are at stake. Your cooperation with us now is of critical importance. And we must act quickly. I'll explain more after we go to a safe place."

"But what about my classes? My exams?" said Kara.

"That will all be worked out later," said Terri, "*if* we succeed and survive. If we don't, well, all those concerns become moot. Get my drift?"

"Yes," said Kara, looking pale. "I agree. But you'd better explain everything to me or I'm gonna be in deep, deep . . ."

"Don't worry. Right now, let's get you to a safe place and we can make arrangements from there."

"OK," said Kara.

"C'mon," said Terri as she got up. "I'll drive you. My car's parked near here. Don't worry. Everything will work out," Terri said, hoping she believed her own words.

"Sure," said Kara, having an equal amount of doubt.

They found her blue vintage Mustang with its white convertible top, and Terri drove them both to the condo. On the way, Terri explained as much as she could to Kara about the situation, the team and who they were, and about the condo, where they would make provisions for Kara to stay during the duration.

They arrived and Terri showed her in. "Nice digs," said Kara."

"Yeah, they're not bad," said Terri. She gave Kara a tour of the condo, including Terri's bedroom. "I have plenty of room, so you can stay with me," said Terri.

"Let me go back to my dorm room and get my stuff so I . . ."

"Sorry," said Terri. "I'm afraid you can't do that. You're in grave danger now, and if anyone you knew saw you on campus, you could lead those who are out to get us right to this condo."

"But I have . . ."

"We'll replace anything you need, Kara. Right now your safety is our primary concern."

"OK," said Kara, hesitantly, seeing her life turned upside down in an instant and not knowing what she could do about it. She certainly didn't want killers chasing her like dogs on a fox hunt.

"You can use the restroom if you want, then we should get down to the debriefing. If you want something to drink, let me know and I'll get it for you."

"Thanks," said Kara as she headed to the bathroom. "Just water would be fine."

# chapter 47

A few minutes later they were both sitting in the living room, Terri in the soft chair and Kara on the couch. "OK," began Terri. "Let's start from the top. I'll summarize the first part. Stop me if I'm wrong about anything."

"All right," said Kara.

"So you were assigned to work for Professor Jonathan Dejanovic as a student worker. There you did 'gofer' work for him, filing papers, typing documents, bringing him his coffee, getting him supplies when he needed them, and so on."

"That's right," said Kara.

"Did I miss anything so far?"

"Nope," said Kara. "Go on."

"Then one day you heard him on the phone talking to someone whom you assumed was the financial supporter of his project, and he seemed angry. In fact, you feel he was threatened, right?"

"That's right," said Kara. "From what I heard on the one side of the conversation, there was concern about the speed the research was progressing at, or maybe I should say, the *lack* of speed." Kara took a sip of water and leaned back in the couch.

"What happened then?" asked Terri.

"Well, it was about at that point that Jon—I mean, Professor Dejanovic—I called him Jon—began taking me into his confidence about his research and his invention. He had to trust someone and he decided that I wouldn't have any reason to betray him. Plus, he kind of liked me and, well, I kind of liked him, too," she said blushing. "I even called my mother and told her about him."

"You didn't tell her about his *work*, did you?"

Realizing her mistake, Kara quickly said, "No, not really. Not specifically. I just told her that he was working on an amazing energy device that would change the world, and that it was super-exciting to be a part of it."

Terri rolled her eyes. "Anything *else*?"

"Not really," said Kara. "I mean, we talked a lot, and I may have said some other things, but I don't remember everything I said. I think that was all I talked about regarding Jon and his work, though."

"I see," said Terri, scribbling in her notebook. She decided to not comment on the danger Kara had put herself in by having that conversation with her mother. "So, was it then that he asked you to help him to secretly begin moving his research out of his lab?"

"Yes, that's right," said Kara. "He had a faculty apartment on campus, but he had secretly purchased a place off campus too, so that was when he switched my hours of work so that I would be there later in the evening. That way, the secretary and campus administrators were not likely to see us."

"But what about the campus police?" asked Terri. "Wouldn't you be more noticeable skulking around campus with equipment, papers, and so on in the evening? And wouldn't it appear more suspicious if the two of you were seen together after normal work hours?"

Kara nodded. "Yes. That's why we never went together. After I left he would wait ten minutes, then he would leave and go in another direction."

"Pretty clever," said Terri as she put down her notebook and smiled. "Sounds like you have already done some clandestine work."

"I guess," said Kara. "It was kind of fun, you know, sneaking around, secret research, spies and stuff."

"Spies?" asked Terri.

"Oh, yeah. Well, you know, Jon told me that his research was so important to the world, that he was sure there were people spying on him and other scientists, to get the jump on important technology advances, especially regarding free energy and things like that."

"Did he think he was being spied on already at that time?"

"No, I don't think so," said Kara. "At least he didn't say so. He just said we had to behave as if there *were* spies trying to steal his work, and that we needed to be careful not to do anything suspicious."

"I see," said Terri. "That makes sense. So you didn't think he was acting abnormal, like paranoid?"

"No, not really, though we did take some extraordinary precautions to get his equipment out of his lab. But it just seemed like the logical thing to do, under the circumstances. No, he didn't seem like, mentally ill-type paranoid. I guess I would have done the same thing under the circumstances."

"OK," said Terri. "So tell me where he lives."

Kara looked nervous. "I will in a minute. First, let me explain. I moved his lab stuff there, and then once he was set up, I would bring him any supplies he needed as he continued his work."

"Good," said Terri. "When was the last time you were there?" Kara got a strange look on her face, like she was going to betray her friend. She seemed reluctant to say.

"In for a penny, in for a pound," said Terri.

"What?" said Kara, having never heard that expression.

"You're committed now, Kara. Whatever you feel for Professor Dejanovic, the only safe thing for you to do is to take us to him so we can protect both of you. Otherwise, sooner or later, *bad people* will come and get you both—and it won't be pretty."

The color drained from Kara's face as she knew what she would have to do. And she hoped Jon would forgive her.

Just then Wolfe walked in, and saw Kara and Terri in the living room. He looked at Kara, then at Terri. He wasn't smiling. "Terri?" he said. "Can I talk to you for a minute? In the *kitchen*?" Terri knew Wolfe was upset. She got up and walked back to the kitchen.

"Who is *she*?" asked Wolfe angrily as they entered the kitchen.

"I can explain," she said hurriedly.

"It'd better be good."

# chapter 48

Terri quickly told Wolfe all that had gone on with her visit to the campus administration building, her conversation with the president's secretary, the overheard conversation by Kara Dugan, Kara's declaration to Terri about Professor Jonathan Dejanovic, their meeting at Boh's, and Kara's last statement that she knew where Professor Dejanovic was and what he was working on. She explained that she determined that Kara was now in danger with the rest of them, and why she saw the only action to take was to bring her in and house her at the condo for the duration.

"Was I wrong?" asked Terri.

Wolfe was calmer now. "No, you did the right thing, under the circumstances. Good job, Terri."

"Thanks," she said, and meant it.

"Do you think he's the person we're looking for?" asked Wolfe.

"I don't know for sure, but he's the closest thing we've found so far," she said.

"I agree. If it looks like a duck . . ."

"Right," said Terri.

"OK. You'd better introduce me to Kara and keep the circle close and tight. I think things will be coming to a head soon."

Terri gave him a quizzical look, but said nothing.

"By the way," he said. "Where's Sparrow?"

Terri thought for a moment. "Actually, I don't know. When I brought Kara back here I didn't see anybody, so I'm not sure where she is."

Just then Sparrow came walking down the stairs, her hair a muss. "What's all the fuss about? Who're you looking for?"

"You, as a matter of fact," said Wolfe.

"Oh," she said. "I was tired so I took a nap. Things have been stressful lately and I haven't had much rest. Who knows when I'll have time again, right?"

"More right than you know," Wolfe half mumbled.

Wolfe and Sparrow introduced themselves to Kara, then Wolfe brought them all up to date on events so far, including his situation with Vikki. Sparrow was quiet when he was finished—unusually so, thought Wolfe.

"Something on your mind?" he said, looking at Sparrow.

"I don't know," she said. "I don't want to offend you, but back at the agency I was doing research on Soviet moles and clandestine agents, and I came across one that kind of matches the description of Vikki. And something rang a bell, which I can't put my finger on."

Wolfe said, "Don't worry about offending me. I've been having my own thoughts concerning Vikki, and in fact, am doing some digging as we speak. Can you find out more about the M.O. of this Soviet spy?"

"I do know some things," said Sparrow. "The woman I'm talking about is very pretty, but there are no photos of her. She lures and hypnotizes her victims. She uses hypnotic chemicals, audio programming, knockout drops, post-hypnotic suggestion, and scopolamine—used as truth serum—on her victims.

"Then after she's done extracting information and getting whatever else she wants, she poisons them and they die very unpleasant deaths. Overall, a real nice lady. Why? She your girlfriend or something?" Sparrow said laughing. Her laughter slowly died when she saw nobody else laughing. "What?" she said. Wolfe just shook his head.

Just then, the phone rang. It was Josephs. "Hey, Ed," he said. "Let me put you on speaker. Terri's here with me, and Sparrow, too. They need to hear this as well." He purposely didn't mention Kara. "What do you have?"

"First off, I rousted that guy you thought was surveilling Sparrow. His driver's license showed he was a resident of McLean, Virginia, thirty-two years old, white male, which you already knew, and had no wants or warrants—not even a speeding ticket. Said he was a pharmaceutical representative and this was part of his territory. I asked him how many pharmaceuticals he sold sitting in his car for hours smoking cigarettes, and he got kind of angry. He said it was also his vacation and he was taking in the sights. Sounded bogus to me, but I had nothing on him, so I sent him on his way. He didn't look happy."

"I imagine not," said Wolfe. "But I think you got it right, Sparrow," he said, turning to address her. "I think he was here looking for you and maybe the rest of us."

"Got anything else, Ed?"

"I do, but you're not gonna like it."

"Probably not," said Wolfe. "Hit me with it. Bad news is better than no news in this game."

"Well, I checked on the address and history of ownership of the house Vikki said was hers, and it seems that she doesn't own it after all."

"Then who does?" asked Wolfe.

"Not clear," said Josephs. "Seems it went through several layers of ownership, and quickly, too. Almost like they were trying to hide the true owners. That make sense to you?"

"It's beginning to."

"Well, there's more. The current title is held by a company called Barrymore Properties, Inc."

"And who owns that?"

"Don't know. It's some kind of holding company out of the Cayman Islands, and that's as far as I got."

"Great," said Wolfe. "Tell me Ed, what *do* you know?"

"Well, ignoring that tone of disapproval for a minute, I found a few things. Like, she's not renting it to students. I checked with the University for their list of approved housing for their students, and the property isn't listed as approved. In fact, it's not listed at all."

"That's not good," said Wolfe.

"No, it's not," said Josephs. "I also checked on her affiliation with the University, and it seems that she's not a professor there. In fact, they have no record of her being employed there, in any capacity."

"So she lied to me the whole time."

"It appears so," said Josephs.

"I think I need to get into that house, Sheriff. And *soon*."

# chapter 49

Wolfe, Terri, Kara, and Sparrow were all together in the condo. Wolfe looked around. It was time for action. He looked at Terri. "I know this looks bad, and on the surface, it probably is. But when you know the full circumstances . . ."

"Forget it," said Terri.

"OK," said Wolfe. "Right now we have to move on. Is Kara staying with you? You have a second queen-size bed in your room. Is that the plan?"

"It is," said Terri, looking over at Kara. Kara nodded.

"She obviously can't go back to the university, so we have to get her some clothes and other provisions. We should also disguise her appearance as much as possible, since I think it's safe to say we all are now under surveillance and totally at risk."

"Ah, at risk of what?" asked Kara.

"Death," said Wolfe, gravely. Kara blanched. "So we have a number of things we have to do, and quickly. Josephs and I will search Vikki's house and see what we can find to verify some of the things Sparrow just told us. If Vikki is the Soviet spy she described, we need to verify that and act quickly.

"Second, as soon as possible, we need to get over to Professor Dejanovic's new residence and do all we can to secure his invention, papers, and everything of relevance in his home lab. And," he continued, "We need to safeguard the professor from abduction, and whatever the abductors might have in store for him, including torture, and death."

Kara practically wilted at Wolfe's description.

"Wolfe," began Terri, "Kara and Professor Dejanovic are having a relationship. Isn't that right, Kara?"

Kara's face turned red.

"I'm sorry, but embarrassment is the least of our worries. I think saving his life and his life's work is much more important now, don't you?"

Kara nodded, looked at the floor, and uttered an almost inaudible, "Yes."

Terri looked at Wolfe. "So would it be possible for you to crank down the rhetoric just a bit? I think we all know the dangers here, and scaring everyone half to death won't help us do what we need to do."

The condo was uncomfortably silent for several seconds. Then Wolfe said, "You're right. Sorry, Kara." She nodded but said nothing, still looking at the floor.

"Let's work out the plan," Wolfe continued. "I don't think we have much time. We have one dead body, Vlad, and another dead body, possibly named Alexei, and also probably Russian KGB. Plus we have the man on the bike who is still on the loose. We have an agent Sparrow recognized from her office, doing surveillance here—fishing for information, I think, or he'd be much busier than just sitting in a car watching people. And we have the people who were, and apparently are, after Sparrow, the people who also probably killed some of my contacts in the spy world."

He turned to Kara. "Have you made plans to see him again?"

"I'm supposed to bring him some food and batteries tonight," she said. "I told him I would show up around ten o'clock, and . . . had planned to stay the night."

"Good," said Wolfe. "That'll work. He's expecting you, so you just continue with your plans. Don't do anything out of the ordinary from your normal routine. Stick to your plan for tonight, and then tomorrow we'll all follow you to his house and take him and you to safety. OK?"

Kara looked nervous, but seemed to be holding up. The prospect that she could still see Jon again seemed to bring her around. "I can do that," she said.

"Great," said Wolfe. "Let's do it."

Wolfe called Josephs and they agreed to go over to Vikki's place in Wolfe's Jeep so as to draw less attention. Then he went to his suite and made a private call on his own secure line.

He picked up Josephs from his home which was near his office. He had changed clothes and was now dressed much the same as Wolfe—black pants, shirt and jacket, black soft-soled shoes, and snug black gloves. They both had their weapons and backup weapons, small black flashlights, and handcuffs.

Wolfe passed the house and pointed it out to the Sheriff.

"That's the place?" said Josephs. "Pretty nice for an adjunct instructor," he said as Wolfe drove by.

"Yeah," said Wolfe, displaying disgust at the situation he had gotten himself into. "How do you want to do this? You're the law here."

"Thanks for reminding me. And now I'm going to break it."

"For the greater good, though."

"So say you," replied Josephs. "It had better work out that way or we'll be Sing-Sing-*ing* a different tune—and not a pretty one."

Wolfe parked the car and they got out. The place was dark. Vikki, or whatever her real name was, had been there when he left to take Sparrow's page. He stood on the sidewalk and looked around.

He wondered where Vikki was. He hoped she had gone out somewhere, but it was getting late and she might have been tired, though he was sure she hadn't drugged herself, like she probably had drugged him. If she went to bed, this break-in would be very difficult. But if she had gone out, where could she have gone?

They were committed to going in and they had to make it quick. As they walked to the back of the house, a chill ran up his back. He shook it off, but it wouldn't go away. He would have to be ultra-careful. When he got those feelings, there was usually trouble.

Lots of it.

# chapter 50

Wolfe picked the lock to the back door of Vikki's house while Josephs stood lookout. Fine thing for an upstanding Sheriff to do, Ed thought to himself. *I get in more scrapes when I get together with Wolfe than I . . .*

"I'm in," said Wolfe. He carefully opened the wood door, which had glass panes in the top half. He stopped and listened carefully for a few seconds.

"Will you get going?" whispered Josephs. "You're leaving me with my ass sticking outside for everyone in the world to see!"

Wolfe moved slowly forward, trying not to make the floorboards squeak. "Ed, I don't think the whole world *wants* to see your . . ."

"Never mind," whispered Josephs. "*Move.*"

They had entered the kitchen but saw no signs of Vikki—no coffee on the stove, no dishes on the table. All was in order. They quickly moved into the living room at the front of the house. They moved quietly, in case Vikki or someone else was sleeping on the couch. But no one was there.

They crept silently upstairs, their small flashlights providing just enough light so they could see the steps. One by one, they looked into the empty bedrooms where the renting students were supposed to be sleeping. The rooms looked neat, and the closets were empty. The bedrooms looked like they hadn't been slept in for weeks or longer.

"So much for the renters," whispered Josephs. "Looks like our intel is panning out."

"Right," said Wolfe. "Let's move on to her bedroom." The door was open, but they were slow and cautious anyway, in case Vikki was asleep in her bed. The room was empty. "Let's check her closet." They opened the closet door slowly. They found some clothes, but not a lot. But as Josephs looked down on the floor at the back of the closet, he saw something strange. He pushed the clothes aside on the clothes rack and shined his flashlight at the back corner. "Well, lookee here."

Wolfe took another step and bent forward. What he saw confirmed his suspicions. It was a reel-to-reel tape recorder, with a tape still in place. "There's a power cord plugged into what looks like a makeshift electrical outlet at the back of the closet, Ed."

Josephs took a look. "Odd place for a tape recorder, wouldn't you say?"

"I would," said Wolfe.

"Let's see what's been recorded," said Josephs, kneeling down and reaching for the rewind switch.

"Maybe we'd better not," said Wolfe, trying to think back on all the things he might have said—or done.

"Don't worry, Wolfe. Your secrets are safe with me. Besides. She may have revealed something that will help us in our investigation." At that, Josephs flipped the rewind switch and let it run a bit, then flipped it to 'play.'

[Woman's voice.] "*. . . Shouldn't bother you. I just want to get to know you better. So, what are you working on?*"

[Man's voice, slurred speech.] "*Nothiiing.*"

[Woman's voice, soft and encouraging] "*Oh I don't believe that, Wolfe. A man as important as you must be working on something very exciting and important, like national security, or something, don't you think?"* [Long pause] *"Hey, I have an idea. Why don't you tell me about your friends? And about your job? And about who you're trying to find?"*

[Man's voice, slurred speech again.] *"You're my friennnd, Vikkki. I'm trying to find you—under all theese clothes. I meeen, why d'ya have soooo many buttonnzz? You oughtta have zipperzz— eezzier to . . . unn . . . unn . . . unndooo."* [Silence ensued.] *Wolfe? Wolfe? Wake up. Wolfe!* [Silence for a full minute.]

Wolfe reached around Josephs and flipped the switch to 'stop.' "That must be when I passed out. Anyway, I think we've heard enough."

"What? That was just gettin' interesting," said Josephs, a big grin on his face.

"Clearly she was interrogating me, Sheriff. Even a novice like you could see that."

"I guess you're right," said Josephs. "But I think we should preserve that tape for evidence of . . ."

"We don't need any evidence, Ed. There isn't going to be any criminal prosecution. These are war crimes—spying—espionage. Tribunal stuff. So. No evidence. Got it?"

"Spoilsport," said Josephs. He stood and left the closet as it was. They walked back downstairs.

"Did you notice that *her* speech wasn't slurred?" said Wolfe.

"I did," said Josephs.

"And yet she drank as much alcohol as I did, maybe more."

"Maybe it wasn't *alcohol* she was drinking." said Josephs.

"I think you're right, Ed," said Wolfe. "I think this whole thing has been planned from the beginning. I think she's a spy who came here pretending to be a professor, *knowing* I was going to be assigned the case. Knowing it before *I* knew it. Knowing I would frequent that diner. Now, how would she know all those things, Ed? Who else knew all those things about me? My patterns, habits, behavior in different circumstances?"

"Not me, that's for sure," said Josephs. "In fact, I don't care to know that much about you *now*."

"Thanks, Ed. That's comforting."

"No problem. I'm here to help."

"I can see that. You're a *big* help, Sheriff."

"Don't thank me. Just doin' my job."

# chapter 51

Wolfe shook his head. Thought about the situation for a minute. Then, "Seriously, who would have profile information on me, Ed? I mean, nobody other than my closest friends—and I don't have many of those . . ."

"I wonder why?" Josephs said under his breath.

Wolfe glared at him.

"Sorry," said the Sheriff. "You were saying?"

"Vikki knew information about me and my assignment that only the Agency knew. Now, how'd she get ahold of that?" said Wolfe.

Josephs thought for a second, then said, "Sounds like a mole, to me."

"Exactly," said Wolfe. "And not just any mole, but a mole who knew *my* mission, *my* assignment, and *my* history. There's only one person I know of who knew all that."

They stepped outside the house. Josephs stopped, looked up at the dark sky, and said, "I believe that would be our beloved Mister Devon Barnes, if I'm not mistaken."

"Bingo," said Wolfe, climbing into the Jeep. "Barnes has his fingerprints all over this fiasco. He probably leaked this mission to the Soviets, just to take me down."

Josephs looked back at the house. "So, where do you suppose Vikki is?"

"I have a pretty good idea, and we'd better get moving before she finishes her sinister plan. She sure played me for a sucker," said Wolfe.

"She could have played *anybody* for a sucker, Wolfe. Don't beat yourself up."

Wolfe cranked up the engine on the Jeep and peeled out, heading for the condo.

"She's not going to win this one," he said as he slammed the Jeep into second gear and mashed the accelerator to the floor.

"And neither is he."

Wolfe got back to the condo in record time, the color somewhat drained from Josephs' face from the wild ride.

Josephs said, "We found information indicating that Vikki is probably a highly-trained spy. We found secret recordings made of their evening together, and they showed her interrogating Wolfe, who was under the influence of alcohol and probably some truth serum-type drug."

Wolfe added, "We think she's working for someone in the agency, who's feeding her information on my background and confidential information. Probably yours too, Terri, based on your past involvement with me."

"That's awesome," said Terri, her voice ripe with sarcasm.

"Yeah, well it might very well include everyone here," added Josephs, "since we're clearly being monitored by several people that we've spotted—and I'm sure there are more we *haven't* spotted. So whatever we do, we have to be clever about it. And quick."

"Right," said Wolfe. "Vikki's not at her apartment, and my guess is she bugged out right after I got Sparrow's emergency call."

"Where do you think she is?" asked Sparrow.

"Wild guess?" said Wolfe. "If she has an inkling of where the professor is, she'll make a beeline there, or send some of her associates there, or both."

Terri piped in. "What do you think, Kara? Have you two been careful to keep your movements secret? Is there any chance someone could have spotted either you or Jon going to his hideout?"

"I'm pretty certain nobody followed us," said Kara. "Every time we went there, we went separately at different times, and took circuitous routes, always different. We didn't follow any pattern, and took extreme caution to lose a tail—in the front door of a store and out the back, all around the university with its endless halls, rooms, entrances and exits, elevators, and food courts, where someone not of the university would stand out—that kind of stuff. And more."

Wolfe looked at Kara with new eyes. "That's quite an understanding of tradecraft, Kara. Where'd you learn all that?"

"Oh, I'm a big fan of spy novels, movies, TV, that kind of thing. I find it very interesting, and this gave me a chance to try it out. It was actually lots of fun, in a scary sort of way."

Sparrow spoke up. "If you're ever looking for a job in the clandestine services, let me know," she said. "We could use a person with your skills, who doesn't *look* like a spy."

"And what's a spy look like?" asked Josephs.

"*Not* Kara," said Sparrow.

"OK," said Wolfe. "Then if Vikki doesn't know where the professor is, the next best thing she could do is to follow one of us until we lead her there."

"Who do you think she would pick?" asked Wolfe, to no one in particular.

"Me," said Kara.

"Why?" asked Terri.

"Because if they've been trying to follow anybody, it would be me, especially with me taking such complicated routes to lose a tail."

"Makes sense," said Terri.

Wolfe said, "Kara? Looks like you're going to have to do your regular routine today, and go to the professor's house like you normally would. Take whatever supplies or things you already agreed to, and play it straight with him. Stay the night. The only thing is, you'll have to make some excuse to leave his place early tomorrow morning so you can resume your normal schedule on campus.

"Then tomorrow, we'll follow you there and catch whoever is following you, *if* someone is following you. If no one is, then we're home free. We'll go to the professor's house, explain things to him, and secure him and his invention, papers, and equipment until he can finish his work in peace and quiet. Sound good?"

Kara looked uncertain. "So, how will you secure Jon—Professor Dejanovic—and his invention? I mean, he's kind of secure *now*, isn't he? At least until I lead you to him?"

Josephs listened to all this, and finally spoke up. "You make a good point, Kara. And you're right. He is secure at the moment. But it's only a matter of time until evil forces find him, and then it'll be too late. They'll probably abduct him, make him finish his invention if he hasn't already, provide them with all his notes and papers describing the invention. And then most likely, kill him."

# chapter 52

"If they are unable to do all that," Wolfe added, "they'll kill him anyway, and destroy his invention and all his files and papers so no one else can get them. Either way, he's a dead man if we don't remove him and his effects to a safe place where we can protect him and his invention. Make sense?"

"I guess you're right," Kara said softly. "I'd better head out now. It's almost ten."

"Need a ride anywhere?" asked Terri.

"No, I have what I need. I packed it with me this morning in this bag." She had a large cloth bag with a long shoulder strap. "I can do my routine from here. Works better to change up my start point anyway, to make sure I really lose my tail."

"Good point," said Terri. "Good luck and we'll see you back here tomorrow by, say, noon?"

"OK," said Kara. "See you then."

It was quite dark when Kara left the condo. The night was cloudy with a new moon. As she began her new circuitous route to Professor Jonathan Dejanovic's secret location, a tall figure in black clothing slithered up behind her. The person wore black clothes, a black ski mask, and black gloves. The person's face had been blackened generating almost total invisibility. The figure slid noiselessly behind her, from tree to light pole, to mailbox—to whatever would provide cover.

This was a tail she would not shake.

After Kara left the condo, Terri and Sparrow went into the kitchen to go over their plan for the following night. Wolfe and Josephs stayed in the living room.

"How about that film Terri gave you, Ed? Get that developed yet?"

"Oh, crap," said Josephs as he reached inside his jacket pocket. "I forgot about these." He handed them to Wolfe. "Afraid they're not much. All you can see is a man on a bicycle, or a man standing next to one."

Wolfe looked carefully at each photo in turn. "Guess you're right," he said, giving them back to Josephs. "We'll have to keep an eye out for him. Make sure you have a camera on you at all times. Never know when he's going to turn up."

"Dammit, Wolfe. You think I don't know how to do my *job*?"

"Sorry, Ed," said Wolfe. "Always trying to cover all the bases with my novice helpers. Terri's not bad at this stuff, but Kara— well, I'll have to think of everything for her. You and Sparrow, you're both awesome and I don't mean to insult . . ."

"Forget about it. Just yankin' your chain. Gettin' easier and easier to do that these days, ya know. Things gettin' on your last nerve?" Josephs said, trying to lighten things up.

"I guess," said Wolfe. "Too many variables and possible scenarios to consider. I think this whole operation is getting out of hand. One thing goes wrong and it could be catastrophic."

"True," said Josephs. "On the other hand, it could all go right and we could solve one of the greatest cases ever. So, think about *that*."

"You're right," said Wolfe. "I will." But he didn't.


Comrade Viktoriya Dunayevsky, *Vikki*, took her encrypted phone out of her handbag and dialed a number.

"Things did not go as planned," she said to her handler, Major Dmitry Kozlov. "He was . . . resistant."

"You're supposed to be the *expert* in this sort of thing, Comrade. The best. What happened?"

"He had been prepared for my techniques, apparently. His psychological blocks were very deep—and strong. They must have been placed there long ago."

"Why do you say that?" asked Kozlov.

"Because I have been trained to defeat all the current types of blocks. And would have, if they had been used. But I've never seen any this deep or powerful. We had no information that such blocks existed, and thus had no preparation to defeat them."

There was silence for a moment on the other end of the line.

Then Kozlov spoke. "What's your plan now? We can't lose this one. Everything depends on it."

"I know," she said. "I will track the student. She will lead me to the professor eventually. She's a novice who thinks she's good, but she's no match for me. I'll get Kara—and the professor, *and* his invention."

"Good," said Kozlov. "I want that device. I don't care about the professor. That device means everything to me, and I mean to have it. Understood? You'll get your share, I assure you. And it will be more money than you could dream of spending."

"Oh, I have big dreams . . ."

"Never mind that. Just remember—this stays just between the two of us. No one else can know, I don't care who they are. And I want that agent, Wolfe, dead. He's responsible for the deaths of two of my best men and he must pay the price. Understand?"

"Of course," said Viktoriya, softly, but menacingly. "It will be done. With *great* pleasure. Nobody makes a fool out of Comrade Viktoriya Dunayevsky. *Nobody.*"

Major Kozlov broke the connection, as did Vikki—naked, raw revenge firing from those now cold, steel-grey eyes.

# chapter 53

Kara hurried off into the night, excited about the prospect of seeing her beau, Professor Jon Dejanovic. Sure, he was much older than she was, but she was mature for her age, and he was young for a college professor, even with a PhD in physics and amazing work experience.

She thought he was attractive, though a little eccentric, but they talked and got along well. And he was proud of what he was doing, and didn't mind explaining some of it to her, at least the part that she was likely to understand. And that was fine with her.

She even thought about a possible future with him, in addition to their romantic relationship. He was obviously going to be very famous when his discovery came out, and with that would come a lot of money.

She was absolutely sure of that. Not that the money was all she cared about. Not at all. She cared about him in her own way. But there was nothing wrong with money, either.

And she had plans of her own, outside of his interests.

She was studying psychology and hoped to open her own practice someday, counseling people with their mental problems. After all, she liked to talk, and she thought that would be a natural occupation for her. Of course, she didn't like people much, so that might be a bit of an impediment to being a good psychologist.

But then, she had other plans for money, and those plans would come to fruition much, much sooner. In fact, they might provide all the money she needed and she wouldn't have to bother with the professor. Or psychology. With all the money she was getting, she could surely find a younger, more attractive man to meet her needs. Yes, she thought. That would be nice, too. One or the other would be fine with her.

As she wound around the town and campus taking a new route to Jon's house, she fantasized about her future. As she did so, she carefully looked around to see if she was being followed. On campus she entered a large building with offices and classrooms, labs, and study spaces.

She went in the front door, into an elevator, got off at the third floor, went to a stairway and walked down one flight, went into an office and asked directions that she didn't need, watching to see if anyone came to the same office, and loitered outside in the hallway.

She went into another building, walked up the stairs to the second floor, waited to see if anyone came up after her, then walked through the hallway and down another set of stairs, and exited through the loading dock door. She repeated this at several more buildings before she was through.

Outside again, she walked across the lacrosse field and then the marching band practice field. There was no cover on either of those, so she could spot a tail following her from a long way off, if there was one. She felt good about her skills, and she was consumed with seeing Jon again, and what they would do to each other when she arrived.

Not once did she notice the black clad person following her at a discreet distance. Even at the fields, as she looked around, the person became literally invisible as he dropped to the ground and lay flat, leaving no profile.

She laughed to herself as she remembered those conversations in the condo where they all guessed that Jon was out a long way from campus, out in the remote wilderness somewhere. Little did they know he was only five miles from town, then off the pavement and down a dirt road about a mile.

He had found an abandoned farmhouse and fixed it up so it was livable. Jon was safe for the time being. At least until they could find a new place. Earlier that day she had left the pickup truck they had been using to move off campus over on the edge of town. She had her own plans now.

Of one thing she was certain. She was not going to lead Wolfe and Terri and the others to him so they could "protect" him, because that meant they would control his movements, and thus be his jailers until they chose to release him. That was *not* going to happen.

She was going to warn him tonight, and they would pack up and leave before dawn—before anyone knew what happened. She would keep him safe in her own way. And she would even bring his nephew—or whatever relation he was—Quinn—along, too. She had a big heart that way.


Professor Jonathan Dejanovic busied himself in his lab, getting ready for his visitor. He'd had a long week, and it was tiring with no adult companionship, other than when Kara visited. Which she was going to do tonight. Pretty soon. He couldn't wait.

"Anything I can do, Professor?" came the young voice from the back of the room. The boy came in quickly on ten-year-old legs, with boundless energy.

The professor looked around the lab. "Uh, yeah, Quinn. Can you get those five jars over there by the window and put them away where they belong in the cupboard?"

"Sure, Doc," said Quinn. He quickly did as requested, having done this many times before.

"We're going to have company shortly, and I want the place to look as neat as possible."

"Kara coming?" said Quinn eagerly.

"Yes she is, son," said the professor. Quinn was not his son, nor was he related to him in any way. The boy had just wandered into his lab on campus one day, asking lots of questions. The professor at first was annoyed and wondered where he came from and how he got in.

The boy said his name was Quinn. But he would give no more information about himself. After realizing the nature of his questions and the ten-year-old's seemingly advanced understanding of quantum mechanics, the professor let him stay, curious as to how he knew so much, at such a young age.

But then one day Quinn left without a word when the professor's back was turned. He was startled to find Quinn missing, and a little taken aback. He wanted to question Quinn more about his background. But he was gone. The professor had then turned back to his work, which was behind schedule according to his financier.

However, the next day Quinn showed up again, and so their conversations continued. The professor stayed away from asking any more questions about Quinn or his background, because he didn't want to chase him away again. But he began to notice some details about Quinn's appearance that told part of the story.

Once he got Quinn talking about particle physics, he noted that Quinn was quite thin—even for an active young boy—and he thought he might be undernourished. As Quinn came in for a couple of hours each day at about the same time, the professor started bringing in extra food—sandwiches, fruit, milk, and other nutritious items. These were quickly gobbled up by Quinn—another testament that he was not being fed or taken care of properly.

The professor knew he should report this to Social Services and have Quinn properly attended to. But with Quinn's aversion to giving information about himself, probably for fear of being returned to an unhappy home situation, he would likely be placed in a foster home which the professor doubted would be good for Quinn. So he decided to let the boy continue to come, and he continued to feed him and discuss nuclear physics.

Then one day, he noticed that Quinn's clothes were stained with dirt and debris. He asked Quinn where he had gotten his clothes all dirty. Quinn quickly told him that he was playing football with his friends and got tackled several times and knocked to the ground.

A good answer, thought Jonathan, but he felt that there was another explanation—that he was sleeping outdoors or somewhere away from his home—and was homeless, probably by choice.

Being the countercultural maverick that he was, the professor decided to do the illegal thing and offer to let Quinn stay with him in his home. He would tell people that Quinn was his cousin's stepson, and he was watching him for a while. He could also say that he was homeschooling Quinn, which accounted for him being with the professor during the day.

However, things at the University had not been going well for the professor, and DARPA was breathing down his neck. So he had been stealthily removing his essential materials and papers from his lab to a secret location.

Kara Dugan was a trusted student and had been helping him move his things. She also knew the real story about Quinn and was fond of the boy as well.

Then one day the Campus Police showed up at his office, informed him that his services to the University were no longer needed, and that he was being terminated immediately. He was not allowed to take anything from his office. But he had already removed everything of value to his project.

He had to hand over his faculty ID card, office key, and keys to his file cabinets, after which he was escorted directly off campus. The police then gave him a court order to stay off campus, and a gag order that he was not to talk to anyone about his research or inventions. Violation of these orders would lead to his immediate arrest and imprisonment, he was told, for contempt of court and violations of national security. So he went home, packed up his remaining things, and moved to his new, secret location in a remote farmhouse.

Professor Jonathan Dejanovic's new residence served as his new lab, and also as his temporary home and hideout. There were living accommodations for him, Quinn, and Kara, whom he hoped would stay for more than the night.

However, unbeknownst to Quinn and the professor, this would be the last evening they would ever be in the farmhouse.

Because all hell was about to break loose.

# chapter 54

Kara decided to leave her bag in the truck. Climbing in, she turned the key to check the gas gauge. The tank was full as she remembered, ready for their escape. Satisfied, she locked the truck and returned to campus, to continue her circuitous route for another fifteen minutes.

She was in no rush, because there would be no raid on his house 'til the next night—plenty of time to get Jon and Quinn and all the equipment and papers moved out.

She had another place in mind to hide them, but had not had time to work out all the details. So tonight she was going to have to play things by ear. But she was sure it would work out, because she was pretty smart about these things.

The black-clad figure followed Kara to the truck, wrote down information on the license number, VIN number and other information. He placed a miniature battery powered radio transmitter underneath the wheel well and turned it on. Then he raced back to town to pick up his car and position it near the truck to watch when she returned.

A second person in black was out and about looking for Kara, too. She knew some of Kara's haunts and routines, and that she mainly did her route around town and the campus where she was familiar enough with the terrain, and where she felt she could easily lose anybody trying to follow her. She decided to wait on campus and watch to see if Kara would appear. It wasn't long until that very thing happened.

But the second person in black did not know about the truck that Kara had ready for her escape. Kara left and the second person in black followed, confident she would not lose Kara again.

And the chase began.

While Terri and Sparrow were doing their planning in the conference room, Wolfe and Josephs were in the living room out of earshot of the women. Wolfe started to get up to go into the kitchen for a drink when the encrypted phone rang. He gave the proper code, nodded, and went to get Sparrow.

"Encrypted call for you, Sparrow. Why don't you take it on the extension in there?" suggested Wolfe. "Terri, why don't you join Josephs and me in the living room?"

Terri felt humiliated by having to leave the room because of Sparrow's *special* phone call. She found herself getting really fed up with things. She stood and stomped off into the living room.

"Nothing personal, Terri. These are just highly classified and compartmentalized calls. Nobody could be privy to that call except Sparrow. Not even me," Wolfe said.

Terri softened a little. But only a little. "I thought we were a team, Wolfe? Working together? Helping each other out? Sharing information? I don't feel like that's happening here," she said. "Too many secrets are being kept."

Just then Sparrow came into the room. "We know who Vikki is," she said. All eyes were on her. Josephs woke up from the catnap which he often took in the midst of personal conflicts.

"Well, spill it," said Wolfe.

Sparrow looked around the room. "Her real name is Viktoriya Dunayevsky. Spy and assassin in the KGB."

The women were both looking at Wolfe. So was Josephs. But for different reasons.

"How'd they identify her?" asked Wolfe.

Sparrow explained. "Because I followed you to Boh's, Wolfe, and saw you meet with her. I wanted to have your back, so I continued to follow you to her house. Then I called a friend in Records, and gave her the description. It matched a KGB agent on file, down to the M.O. she uses to interrogate and eliminate the competition."

"Where did your friend find this information?" Wolfe asked.

"Evidence from another case where it was certain that Vikki Taylor was the perpetrator of an assassination," finished Sparrow.

"I had suspicions," said Wolfe. "Although we both had been drinking, Ed and I believe she also used some sort of truth serum on me, which when mingled with the alcohol and the hypnotic music she was playing over and over again—was a triple whammy. But I resisted her questions, pretended to be only interested in getting her clothes off and having sex. When Sparrow's emergency call came on my pager, I used that as an excuse, and made a hasty exit. Thanks, Sparrow, for getting me out of there."

"Thank goodness for you, she did," said Josephs. "At least the bitch didn't have time to poison you."

"I doubt she would have done that yet," said Wolfe, now nearly recovered from his embarrassment. "She still didn't have any of the information she was tasked to get. I imagine she is in some hot water with her superiors. And you know what that means in the Soviet KGB, right?"

Sparrow responded. "If she wasn't as good as she has been in the past, she'd be dead by now. Unfortunately, we can't count on that. I think she's out right now trying to redeem herself. And I think she's now more ruthless and dangerous than ever."

"Probably right," Wolfe said. "We're now at red alert. Everyone and everything should be considered dangerous. Everybody 'gun-up' and be prepared for anything. It's life or death from now on. Let the deaths be *theirs*."


Vikki Taylor, now identified as KGB assassin Viktoriya Dunayevsky, was the second person in black who was following Kara. Kara was no match for the KGB assassin, who had trained for years in the art of covert surveillance. She followed Kara until she stopped at a pickup truck parked on the road. Vikki, dressed all in black, was able to hide while Kara stopped and looked around. Satisfied no one was watching her, she reached in her pocket, pulled out a set of car keys, and unlocked the door.

Viktoriya was shocked. She had not anticipated this. She had no vehicle. Maybe Kara was just getting something from the truck and would continue on foot—she hoped. But that didn't happen. Kara opened the door, climbed in, and started the engine. The assassin was panicking. Quickly she looked around for some kind of transportation, but there was nothing close by. She watched in horror as Kara put the truck in gear and drove off north on the paved, two-lane road.

"No!" she exclaimed out loud. She watched to make sure the truck was continuing straight down the road, then ran as fast as she could in the opposite direction, looking for a car she could steal.

The other person in black, the one who had been following Kara all night, watched this fiasco with mild amusement.

He watched her run as fast as she could in the other direction from the truck until she was out of sight, then he started his vehicle.

He had an electronic tracking device by his side that showed on its screen exactly where Kara's truck was because of the transmitter he'd earlier attached to it. The transmitter's range was about three miles, so he put the transmission in gear and took off after her before he lost the signal.

# chapter 55

Meanwhile, the KGB assassin came upon a car parked in a driveway. The house was dark and the car was locked. She smashed the driver's side window with her elbow, and unlockedthe door.

Brushing away the broken glass, she ducked down under the dash, grabbed a handful of wires, and pulled them out where she could see them. Holding a small flashlight between her teeth, she found the two she wanted.

She pulled out a vicious looking knife and cut the two wires. Dropping the flashlight, she put the two ends in her mouth and stripped the insulation off with her teeth, baring the two ends. Quickly she twisted the two wires together, resulting in the car's engine coming to life. The electric shock didn't faze her. She, herself, was wired.

She pulled herself up onto the driver's seat, put the car in gear, and tore off down the road in the direction of the truck. She hoped the truck hadn't gotten too far ahead, or turned off on a side-road somewhere. She was furious at herself for allowing Kara to escape so easily. She *had* to catch her. She pushed the gas pedal to the floor and hoped nobody was foolish enough to get in her way.

She would stop for *nobody*.

As the man in black followed the tracker, he saw that Kara had turned left about a mile or so ahead. Just then he spotted a pair of headlights behind him, coming up fast. He had a thought as to who it might be, but he waited and watched, keeping his speed a steady sixty mph. About a half-mile further the car overtook him, going, he estimated, one-hundred-plus miles per hour. As he glanced to his left when the car roared by, there seemed to be a woman driving. A woman with blond hair, what he could see of it. And if he wasn't mistaken, it looked like the driver's side window had been busted out, too.

The man let her get out of sight, then he slowed as he came up to the road Kara had turned left on according to his tracking device. He turned and headed up the dirt road. He doubted the assassin would find it, even if she came back, as it was an unmarked road. The road was a little bumpy, since it had not been graded in a while. But it was passable if you didn't try to do the Indy 500 on it. So he took it easy, and kept a look out for any more turns. But as he watched the blinking light on the tracker, Kara didn't make any more turns, and soon she stopped.

Kara pulled up to the farmhouse where the dirt road ended, and turned off the truck's engine. Suddenly the front door slammed open and out ran Quinn. His longish sandy blond curly hair flopped around his head as he ran. He ran straight to Kara, wrapping his little arms around her waist.

"Kara!" he shouted. Then he looked and said, "You brought a truck!"

"Yes I did," said Kara. "Let's go inside. I've got to talk to Jon."

They walked up the steps to the wraparound porch, and into the front door of the farmhouse. "Hey Jon," she said. They hugged. "Good to see you."

"Good to see you, too, Kara," he said. "I heard Quinn say you brought a truck?"

"Long story, but I've got to keep it short." She brought him up to date.

The man in black parked a ways back off the drive to the farmhouse, tucked up in some bushes where he couldn't be seen. His car was as black as his outfit, perfect for surveillance. Well, *kind* of perfect, he reflected, since he knew the car was not totally invisible. But he was close enough to see everything that was going on, though he couldn't hear the conversations.

After about ten minutes, something strange happened. The professor and Kara came out of the farmhouse carrying boxes. They carried them over to the pickup truck and loaded them into the back. Even Quinn was carrying small boxes.

This was definitely not according to any plans *he* had heard about when he was in secret communication with Wolfe. Kara was supposed to stay the night and act normally, until Wolfe and his associates raided the house tomorrow to secure Professor Dejanovic and his work. Something was wrong. That something was probably a blond KGB spy. He wondered how they knew she was on their trail. But there was no time to think about that, because just then he could hear a car engine roaring up the dirt road, bottoming out on the suspension as the car hit various ruts and holes.

The car was traveling much faster than the road would allow. The man in black had some implements and tools that he carried with him, and he gathered them up and took them out of his car and into the bushes. As he moved around in the dark, he was nearly invisible. He positioned himself near the truck, still out of sight.

Kara and Professor Dejanovic heard the car, too. They froze in their tracks holding their boxes, as the car pulled directly up beside the truck. A blond woman got out dressed in black, a pistol of unknown make in her hand and pointed at Kara.

"Do you like this girl and the kid, Professor Dejanovic?" she said in flawless English.

He was speechless for a moment.

"*Professor!*" she said more insistently, pointing the gun first at Kara, then Quinn, then at the Professor—back and forth.

"Yes! I like them!" he shouted, almost in a panic.

"Well, if you want them to stay alive, you do exactly as I say. Otherwise I will shoot them both in their cute little heads right before your eyes, and you will watch them die."

"No, don't!" said the professor, freaking out. "I'll do whatever you say."

"Good. Then all three of you might live to see tomorrow. Now take the packages you were loading into the truck, and finish loading them."

The three looked at her for a moment, not understanding what she intended, then they slowly started moving.

"You're going to continue loading the truck with your equipment, experiments, papers and anything having to do with your work, professor," she ordered. "I can see you were planning to move anyway tonight, so I will provide you with some additional encouragement. And don't bother with your personal things. There's no time for that. Hurry up now. There's no time to lose," she barked. "Get moving!"

They all started moving quickly, taking boxes, equipment and papers out of the farmhouse and loading them into the bed of the truck.

The man in black had moved forward to where he could hear the conversations now, and he knew that he was going to have to take some action to prevent this abduction—and maybe a triple-homicide. He had brought various weapons with him, but he had one that was perfect for this situation. He was waiting for the right opportunity so he would hit only one person. The blond in black—with the gun.

# chapter 56

The professor, Kara, and Quinn were just about finished loading when Kara said, "You're going to kill us anyway, aren't you?"

The blond lady smiled. "As a matter of fact, you're right, Kara. I really only need the professor and his inventions. You and the kid are of no use to me now," she said, "now that you loaded the truck for me." An evil grin spread across her face.

"Time to clean house. I should say I'm sorry about this, but I'm actually going to enjoy it." She pointed the gun at Kara. "Say good bye."

"No!" shouted Quinn as he turned and took off running.

Viktoriya swung her gun around and aimed at the fleeing Quinn. But before she could pull the trigger, something stung the back of her neck. The gun went off but the round went wild, into the air. She grabbed the back of her neck and started to say, "What the fuu . . ." but she never finished her sentence. The gun fell from her hand, then she crumpled to the ground.

The man in black came out of the shadows with his long blow gun, and knelt down by the KGB agent. He pulled the small poison dart out of the back of her neck and put it in a special satchel. He then put his bony fingers on her neck, on the carotid artery. He felt for a pulse.

He waited, couldn't find one, and then examined her pupils. Her pupils were fully dilated. And she appeared to have stopped breathing. He closed her eyelids and stood, his full six-foot-two-inch frame towering over Viktoriya.

"I believe she will no longer be a problem to you," he said calmly. The two just gawked at him. "Let me introduce myself. My name is Eino Loukkala, and I'm the Marquette County Coroner. Here are my credentials."

He pulled them from a concealed pocket in his outfit, and presented them to Kara and the professor. They both looked at them in turn, and nodded. He put them away.

Then he turned to them and said, "Going somewhere?"

Just before things got hot and heavy at the farmhouse, Eino had called the Sheriff's Office on the police radio that the Sheriff provided him for his souped-up Hearse-mobile, which he had named Black Beauty, and told dispatch to send the Sheriff and Wolfe, and whoever else was available to his location.

He added, shots fired, which hadn't been the case at the time, but which he was pretty sure would be by the time things were over. He checked his tracker and provided the dispatcher the precise location.

In answer to Eino's unasked question, Kara was embarrassed. "I couldn't lie to him," she said. "Jon trusted me and I couldn't lead a gang of feds, or whoever you all are, to his place to do who knows what. What he's working on is earth-shattering and valuable to the whole world. Nobody has the right to keep it from the public."

Eino could hear sirens off in the distance. "Very idealistic of you, Kara. And loyal. But you need to understand the realities of the world today. Anything that powerful could also be very destabilizing to the power structure—business, government—everybody.

"So you see, your life-span and the life-span of Jon and probably Quinn can probably be measured in weeks, if not days, as you can see here." He pointed to Vikki/Viktoriya, who lay dead on the ground.

"She's a spy and assassin for the KGB—a highly trained clan-destine operative who is skilled in surveillance, abduction, interrogation and torture. She has been tasked to find Professor Dejanovic, abduct him and take all his papers, devices, and inventions—and to get him to tell her how they all work."

Kara swallowed hard. The professor was white as a ghost. "And no matter how much the professor cooperated with them, he would ultimately be tortured and killed. So you see, you really have no options at this point. You have no life of your own. The only life you have is tied to me and the people who will be here any minute, who are dedicated to doing whatever is necessary to keep you all alive for the rest of your natural lives. Do you understand me?"

Kara nodded. "Yes. I'll cooperate fully from now on."

Professor Jonathan Dejanovic said, "So will I. I knew things were getting bad when DARPA's threats got worse and worse. And then they fired me and escorted me off campus with warnings of dire consequences if I ever came back, or revealed anything I'd been working on. I'd just like to keep working on my research and inventions, if that's possible."

"We'll see what we can do," said Eino. "In the meantime, our main task is to keep you, and all of us alive. So let's start with that. OK?"

"Yes," they both said simultaneously.

"Great," said Eino. "And Quinn?"

They all looked around. He was nowhere to be seen. "Quinn?" they all yelled. They looked in the farmhouse. They looked all around the area. "Quinn? Quinn? C'mon back. Nobody's going to hurt you," they shouted.

Kara tried her own technique, knowing he had taken a strong liking to her. "Quinn? You can stay with me. I promise, I'll take care of you! You can stay with Professor Jonathan and me. Please! Come back!" But it was to no avail. Quinn had fled the area when the assassin fired her gun at him. And they would never find him in the dark.

The professor said, "I wouldn't worry too much right now." They all looked at him. "He's got street smarts, and I have a feeling he was living on his own in the wilderness for some time before he came to me."

Just then the posse showed up. Cars came screaming up and skidding to a stop. Wolfe, Josephs, Sparrow and Terri, along with two deputies flew out of the cars. A slower, but equally noisy rescue squad came flying up seconds later.

"We brought the works," said Josephs. "What with hearing from Eino for the first time in a fortnight and his urgent message, we didn't know what to expect. Since Eino didn't stay with the radio to keep us updated, we could only fear the worst," he said.

"Well gee, Ed," said Eino, "I was kinda busy, you know, eh? What with a homicidal assassin ready to take everyone out and no backup, I had to take steps." He nodded to the corpse of the KGB spy.

Wolfe looked at Vikki, shook his head. "Sure took me in," he said.

"Looks that way," said Terri and Sparrow together. They turned and looked at each other.

Josephs bent down to look at the body. "What'd you shoot her with, Eino? A *bb*? I don't see any bullet hole."

"Roll her over," said Eino. "Look at her neck. See that spot of blood?"

"What?" said Josephs? "That little spot? It's tiny. I can barely see it."

Eino reached into the satchel and pulled out the tiny dart, held it in his gloved hand. "Don't touch it, Sheriff. It's a poison dart. Can be absorbed through your skin just by touching it. I have gloves on, you notice. Very fast acting and very effective, as you can see." Josephs looked at the dart, and then up at Eino, a questioning look on his face. "Yes, I can see that, Eino. Let's sit down and talk about this . . . blowgun of yours. How'd you . . ."

"That's where I've been, Sheriff. At a training program on blowguns, types of darts, disabling agents, doses, paralyzers, and fatal poisons. Fascinating stuff, really."

"I'll bet it is," said Josephs. "But let's put it away for now. I have no idea what the law is on this stuff, but I think I'd better find out quickly."

"No problem," said Eino. "I know how to handle it safely."

The Sheriff looked over at the body. "I can see that." He looked back at Eino. "Let's meet soon."

"You got it, Sheriff."

# chapter 57

The rescue squad left to transport Viktoriya's body to the morgue to put it in the freezer next to the John Doe they got earlier.

Josephs ordered two deputies to guard the body at the morgue so it wouldn't disappear, as had happened a couple of times on the caper last year. They were going to meet the rescue squad at the Coroner's Office and stand guard there. This was a corpse they *weren't* going to lose.

The rest of the crew decided to meet at the Sheriff's Department until they could sort things out. They had to try to come up with a plan to keep everyone safe. And that was getting harder and harder.

The deputies arrived at the morgue before the rescue squad, and they were standing there waiting as it pulled up. "Hurry up, guys," said one of the deputies. "I've had a long day and I'm dead tired—no pun intended," he said, looking at the other deputy.

"None acknowledged," said the other deputy.

"Oh ha, ha," said the first deputy.

The two paramedics got out of the rescue vehicle and opened the back doors. They looked inside, then looked at each other.

The body was gone.

Back at the jail, everyone had arrived at the conference room except Quinn, when the call came in. A deputy poked his head in and motioned for the Sheriff to come to the door. Josephs got up and walked to the deputy.

"What is it?" he barked. The deputy whispered in his ear, not knowing whether or not the information was to be heard by the others.

"She's what?" exclaimed the Sheriff. "Gone? How's that possible?" The deputy whispered something. "Fine. Get them on the phone. Pronto!"

"What is it?" asked Terri.

"Apparently our corpse went missing between the time she was loaded into the rescue truck and the time they stopped at the morgue—if you can believe *that*."

"Did they stop anywhere along the way?" asked Wolfe.

"Nope," said Josephs. "Other than for the stop sign at the end of the dirt road. Unless she got out there and went for a walk, she just up and disappeared."

"That's impossible," said Terri. "A corpse doesn't just . . ."

"This one did," interrupted Josephs. "My guess is, she wasn't dead, despite Eino's superb evaluation of her at the scene. Probably woke up, not happy with her situation, and jumped out the back, either at the stop sign, or sometime when they slowed down for a curve in the road, or other traffic."

"You'd think the driver would have noticed that," said Kara, chiming in.

"You'd think," said Josephs sarcastically.

Eino had been in the bathroom while all this was going on.

When he walked back into the conference room, Josephs said, "Lost another one, Eino," referring to a previous case.

"What?" said Eino, incredulous. "You mean, our Miss KGB is *gone*?"

"Guess she wasn't dead," said Josephs. "Pretty sloppy work if you ask me. Coroner can't tell if a client is dead or not. Be really bad for the mortuary business," he finished, sarcasm dripping like a tenement water faucet.

Eino thought for a minute. "I must have gotten the potency wrong. It was supposed to kill her—and it very nearly did. I couldn't detect any breathing or pulse. And her pupils were fully dilated. I guess the dose was just enough to lower her biological readings to make her appear dead, but they were still functioning at that extremely low level."

"It would appear," said Wolfe.

"Oh, this is bad—very bad," said Eino. "She's going to be really pi . . ."

Wolfe cut him off. "Wrong word, Eino. I think the word is, *homicidal*. And you're at the top of her list, no doubt."

"I think," said the professor, "that most of us are at the top of her list."

"I think the professor's right," said Josephs. "Eino for shooting her, though I doubt that she saw you or knows what you did. Kara and the professor for hiding out and escaping in a truck that she hadn't anticipated and for thwarting her planned abduction. And Wolfe for resisting her failed interrogation."

"And that's just *one* person after us," said Terri. "There's also the unidentified man on the bike, Sparrow's follower Dan Jenkins, and the people that they report to, as well as the people Viktoriya Dunayevsky reports to—her handler, for sure, and probably others. Although, after she's messed up twice now, I imagine she'll be running from them, too."

"What a cluster," said Josephs.

Terri was also quite disturbed by the fact that Quinn took off, and was surprised when it didn't seem to bother Kara that much.

"What are we doing about Quinn?" said Terri. "I'm worried about him."

"We already dispatched our search and rescue team of deputies and volunteers," said Josephs. "We also have tracking dogs. I think they're already at the site. If there's a trail, they'll find him."

"I hope so," she said. "The thought of him wandering around in the wilderness, all alone, and . . ."

"Don't worry," said Wolfe. "Sheriff's right. They're a crack team. They'll definitely find him."

"OK," said Terri. "I won't worry, then." Of course, that was not true at all.

Josephs took the floor. "Short term, everyone can stay here tonight until we figure out what to do. We have an excellent kitchen and you will all be fed. My staff and I eat here quite a bit, and the food is good and plentiful.

"There are a few rooms we have for guests, and you can parcel them out. I guess, the Professor and Kara can share one—I think that was the original plan for this evening anyway, right?" They nodded, embarrassed.

"Sparrow and I can take a room," said Terri. "That OK?" she said, looking at Sparrow and then the Sheriff.

"Fine with me," said Sparrow.

"Good," said Josephs. "Wolfe and I can share the third room. It's best we all stay together here, both for safety and communication. We have a lot to do, and it's late, so let's hit the sack. We'll get up early in the morning, have breakfast and discuss a plan."

"What about Eino?" said Wolfe.

Josephs chimed in. "Oh, we have a dog house out back for him. He'll be in it for quite some time until he can learn to hang on to his corpses."

"Ha, ha," said Eino. "Very funny. I don't need your damned accommodations. I have been taking care of myself quite well, thank you, and I already pulled Kara, Jonathan and Quinn's bacon out of the fire. And as far as I know, nobody knows me as part of your team, Wolfe. I think it's best we keep it that way. I'll be quite at home with my 'guests' who don't talk back to me."

"Let's hope it stays that way," said Josephs. "With you, ya never know," he said, laughing. "They might just decide to go for a walk." Eino turned and stormed out in a huff, vowing to show them all.

# chapter 58

Early the next morning, the search and rescue team leader came in to report to the Sheriff, who was still reeling from the loss of the KGB assassin. The search leader stuck his head in the Sheriff's office doorway.

"No luck," he said, of the search for Quinn. "We took the dogs and everything, and we searched throughout the night. We found his initial trail away from the farmhouse, but after a while, it fragmented and so we split to follow the different paths, but they all ended in a dead end.

"So we went back to the main trail and stuck with that to the very end, but that one just stopped, too. I mean, it's just like he was lifted up by a crane and carted away. The foot prints just ended. It was so weird," he finished.

Josephs just shook his head. "Man, this job is going from bad to worse. I've never lost so many people in a single day in my entire career. What the *hell's* going on?"

The search leader sympathized with him. "I don't know, Sheriff, but I hope this streak ends soon."

"Me too," said Josephs. "Me too." He turned to his phone as the search leader left the office.

Just then Wolfe came in with two large coffees from the kitchen and handed one to Josephs. "They made it the way you like it," he said.

"Glory be, aren't you the saint," said Josephs as he took his first sip.

"Yeah, well everyone else is eating breakfast and they told me you hadn't been up yet, so I thought I'd send my own rescue party. I heard about the search being called off on the way here, and figured you'd need all the sustenance you could get."

"Got *that* right," said the Sheriff, drinking as much as he could without scalding his mouth.

Wolfe took a drink of his own coffee, then sat down in the chair opposite Josephs' desk. "I've been thinking," he began.

"Glad somebody has," said Josephs. "I'm not sure I'm functioning all that well right now."

"Well, let me run this by you. You can just sit and listen, and then tell me what you think."

"Sounds good," said Josephs. "I'm a good thinker."

"First, I think we can assume that we're being watched by multiple bad guys, some of whom we know about, and some, or even many, we don't."

"I think that's a sound conclusion." The Sheriff drank some more coffee. His eyelids seemed to rise slowly, from half-staff, to three-quarter-staff.

"Right. And at the present time, we're all nicely corralled in one tight space in the jail, except for Eino at his office, and Quinn, who knows where."

"An astute observation."

"OK," said Wolfe. "Now we believe that we are safe unless and until the bad guys get hold of the professor and/or his invention, of which we know almost nothing."

"True," said the Sheriff. "Go on." He was starting to come alive as the coffee was having its effect.

"You and Eino are pretty visible and easy to find, because of your jobs. But if we were to find another location for the professor,

Kara, and Quinn—if we ever find him—then they, and *we* will be much safer."

"Except for one thing."

"What's that?" said Wolfe.

Josephs leaned forward in his swivel rocker and put his hands flat on his desk. "The fact that you not only have a highly trained KGB assassin gunning for the professor and his invention, but she's also now undoubtedly gunning for you too, for embarrassing her by ruining her seduction-interrogation and getting away alive. And also for catching two of her cohorts and killing them."

"Yes, Sheriff. I'm well aware of that. However, for the record, Sparrow killed one of them."

"Trying to save your life," added Josephs. "Which she did admirably well, I might add."

"Yes, she did," said Wolfe. "So I guess she's also a target of this mad assassin."

"It would appear," said Josephs.

Josephs looked intently at Wolfe. "Do you suppose Vikki is in hot water with her superiors over all this?"

"Ed, I think she has screwed the pooch, so to speak. She's the walking dead for such blatant and visible failures. She won't be trusted anymore, and will be considered to be a grave liability to their cause. She will certainly be terminated, if they can find her. So, her life is over. There's nowhere for her to run where they ultimately can't find her.

"As I see it, her choice is to turn herself in and be summarily executed, or she can spend her remaining days on earth hunting me down to seek her revenge and go out in a blaze of glory. I don't see any other paths for her, and in her psychotic frame of mind, I'm confident of the direction she'll choose."

Josephs took a deep breath and slowly let it out. Finally he said, "I agree, as much as I hate to admit it." He slowly leaned back in his chair. "What do you suggest?"

"Misdirection," said Wolfe.

"What?" said Josephs.

"A shell game," said Wolfe. "Which shell is the pea under, you know? The old con game."

Josephs nodded slowly, then leaned forward again, his attention perked up. "OK. So how do we do that?"

Wolfe explained in detail how it would work and what resources he would need.

Josephs leaned back in his chair and stared at the ceiling. "There's no way on earth I can get you the kind of things you need from the county budget."

"I'm not asking you to, Ed," said Wolfe.

"But then where . . ."

"I can get it," said Wolfe. "I just wanted to go over the plan with you to see what you think."

Josephs thought about that for a minute, then said, "This isn't coming from that mysterious, rich friend of yours, is it? The one who got you the condo and furnished it better than the Vanderbilt House, and the weapons and food and, well, who knows what else?"

"What of it?" said Wolfe. "It's no skin off your nose."

"I'm just kind of wondering who this person is, you know? I mean, are you in debt to him for all this? Does he have something over you?"

"Look, Ed," said Wolfe. "All I can tell you is that he is very, very rich, and I did something for him and his family that he feels indebted to me for. I never asked him for any money or anything—

just told him I was doing my job, though I wasn't working for anyone at the time, including the government.

"But he wants to do things for me, and that's how he wants to express his gratitude. I told him I didn't need anything. But he has so much, and it makes him feel good to do it. So I let him. I guess I'm kind of his pet project."

Josephs adjusted himself in his swivel chair, pulled out a stogie, snipped off the end with his cigar cutter, put it in his mouth to dampen it with his saliva, stuck the end in his mouth and then, unlit, clamped down on it with his teeth.

Finally Josephs said, "Think he needs another *pet*?"

Though the Sheriff was smiling when he said it, Wolfe didn't blame him.

"No, you best stick with your law *enforcement* and leave the ways of the wealthy to me. You'll be much happier."

"You say so," said the Sheriff.

"I do," said Wolfe. "But now I have to go back to the condo and take care of a few things. Try to hold things down while I'm gone, will you?"

"Aside from the fact that you are now violating your own rule about leaving the sanctity of my facility, I think it is *you* who should be careful. And I mean it."

"I will. I won't be too long. Just be sure to let me in, OK?"

"I'll think about it," said Josephs, smiling as he chomped on his unlit cigar.

# chapter 59

Wolfe left the confines of the Sheriff's Office and, looking around cautiously, made his way to his Jeep. But before getting in, he slid to the ground and inched underneath the vehicle to inspect the undercarriage. He was looking for any signs of tampering with the brakes or the addition of an explosive device that would be designed to take him out of the game—permanently. Finding no evidence of either, he checked under the hood for any such additions, and also in the interior of the Jeep Wrangler. Finding none, he hopped into the driver's seat and gingerly turned the ignition key. The engine roared to life, but that's all that happened, so he shifted into first gear and headed over to the condo to meet with Reaper and to develop him into his secret weapon. Arriving at the condo, Wolfe parked in back in one of the condo parking spaces, and used his electronic door opener to access the back stairs to the basement. He tried to be a little quiet because he didn't know if Reaper was still sleeping or not, but he had a lot to do and little time to do it in, so he hoped he was awake.

He came down the steps and saw Reaper sitting on the couch in a robe, finishing a breakfast sandwich and coffee as he watched the news on TV. Wolfe smiled. "Glad to see you're up."

Reaper swallowed the last bit of his sandwich and said, "Absolutely. Up and ready to go." Then he looked down at his robe and said, "Well, almost ready to go."

"Did you bring a change of clothes with you, or did you look in the closet to see if there was anything that might fit you?" asked Wolfe.

"Actually, I did both," said Reaper. "I did find some clothes in the closet that fit pretty good, so if you don't mind, I'll wear those now because mostly what I have in my duffel is old military fatigues, t-shirts, and things like that. I figured I might need clothes that would blend in with civilian life a little better. What d'ya think?"

"I think you're right," said Wolfe. "I have some things to discuss with you when you're ready. Time is of the essence, so if you don't mind, I'd like to get going."

"No problem. Let me just throw some of those new duds on and I'll be ready."

"Go for it," said Wolfe. "I'll just watch a little TV, see if we made the news."

Reaper threw Wolfe a questioning glance, but grabbed his things and went into the bathroom to get ready.

A few minutes later Reaper rejoined Wolfe, grabbed another cup of coffee and sat across from Wolfe, ready to receive instructions. "Fire away," he said.

"First I want to say that I'm so glad you were able to get away from the assassins sent to wipe out me and my team."

"I'm kinda glad myself," said Reaper.

"As I told you before, things have gotten pretty hot and heavy here, and I believe they're going to get worse. So far our small group has done pretty well. We killed two KGB and avoided being the victim of a third, but she's on the loose now, hell-bent for revenge."

"Do you know her identity?"

"Actually, we do. She presented herself to me as Vikki Taylor, college teacher, but in reality, her name is Comrade Viktoriya Dunayevsky, KGB assassin and spy for the Soviet Union. She's lethal, and uses drugs and poisons on her victims."

"A real sweetie," said Reaper.

"More than you know," said Wolfe. "And there's definitely another one out there who is her handler, and probably others. But that's all we know for sure on that score."

Reaper took another sip of his coffee, and nodded his head. "OK."

"So between her and her obsession with getting me, the professor, Sparrow and Terri, there's a man on a bicycle reporting to somebody unknown, and Dan Jenkins from Sparrow's Agency sent here to look for us. Add to that Devon Barnes, who has been the instigator of the purge that almost got you and did get Hawk, and probably many or most of the others of our previous team—and we've got a real disaster on our hands. I believe he wants to wipe out all witnesses to his war crimes in that infamous operation we were privy to years back."

"I remember," said Reaper. "Hard to forget."

"For all of us," said Wolfe. "I can't believe nothing was done regarding our report on the incident. Something stinks somewhere."

Reaper looked at Wolfe intently. "What can I do to help?"

"Glad you asked," said Wolfe. "You're going to be my ace in the hole. Nobody knows you're alive except me and Josephs, and I'd like to keep it that way. I'd like you to pursue a separate track from the rest of my team. We have found and *rescued* the professor, Jonathan Dejanovic, and his girlfriend, Kara Dugan. They are lodged in protective custody at the jail, as are the rest of the team, except Eino Loukkala, the Coroner, and we still don't know where Quinn is."

"The young boy at the hideout."

"Correct," said Wolfe. "After Vikki tried to execute them all, he took off and hasn't been seen since."

"I guess he's pretty resourceful, from what you've told me already."

"He is," said Wolfe. "Let's hope he keeps being resourceful until we can find him and take care of him, too. I think Vikki would love to nail Quinn as well, for spoiling her plan."

"So, where do I fit in?" said Reaper.

"I want you to set up an offensive action in the place where our final battle happened on my mission here last year—up at the compound on Lake Superior."

"I've heard of it, of course. That was a legendary battle. I think it's in the textbooks now at the War College."

Wolfe laughed. "Wouldn't surprise me. Probably as a lesson in what *not* to do."

"I doubt that very much, Commander," said Reaper, forgetting Wolfe's request to drop the military formality.

"Well in any case, I hope this one turns out better. And you will be a big part of that plan. I believe the forces against us will soon try to take us out, and I plan to lead them straight to that same compound, luring them into thinking we'll be sitting ducks for their plan to annihilate us in one major assault. I have a friend who wishes to remain anonymous, who seems to have bottomless wealth, who will fund pretty much any action I ask for. He paid for this condo and all the furnishing and the food you've been eating, as well as a private jet, weapons, and a pretty fancy credit card for any incidentals."

"Wow," said Reaper. "Now that's the kind of friend to have."

"It is, and I'm counting on him supplying you with anything you need to mount this counter-offensive against the action I'm sure they're planning. We need to have an overwhelming response to neutralize whatever forces they bring. I don't know what that will be. But whatever it is, we need to be ready. And unfortunately, you will be a team of—one."

"OK," Reaper said slowly.

"Of course, there will be me and Sparrow, Sheriff Josephs, Eino, Terri, and the Sheriff's SWAT team, and we'll all be armed as much as we can be. But that's the extent of our manpower. My goal is to protect them, and the professor and Kara, and Quinn, if he ever shows up again. We'll try to take up a defensive position as best we can, and we'll try to be on the offensive as well, but protecting them will be my priority."

"I see," said Reaper. "So you want me to plan for, and implement an overwhelming response to whatever attack they are planning."

"Yes," said Wolfe.

"What about my resources in terms of equipment, firearms, ammunition, and so on? What can I requisition?"

"Anything you want, Reaper. Anything one man can conceivable use, deploy or activate to cause incredible mayhem and disruption to their plans. You can get it, and I'll tell you how. But we must act now to get this ready. You need to have everything in place and ready to respond before we arrive there. After that it will be too late."

"You know, there's a hell of a lot I can do on my own," said Reaper. "You know I love to destroy things. And I'm good at it. Just give me the tools."

"Anything you want, you got it."

"Anything?"

"Anything. Just make out your Christmas wish to Santa, and don't hold back. Just remember the time limitations. It has to be in place by the time we arrive. Here's the number to call on this private, secure line," said Wolfe, pointing to a phone next to the refrigerator. "Just tell the person that your name is Reaper and that Wolfe sent you. He'll give you whatever you ask for.

"This part of the operation is yours to set up however you like—method of deployment, weaponry, and if you think you can get it, additional manpower, though it won't be much, if any. But you can try. So now I guess it's my turn to call you *Commander*."

Reaper smiled. "I'll try to live up to your expectations," he said.

"One more question."

"Yes?"

"How much time do I have?" Reaper asked.

"Twenty-four hours."

# chapter 60

All hell was breaking loose in Washington, D.C. Back at Sparrow's agency, Eric Henderson came into the office, his hair all messed, his clothes in disarray, his eyes blurry, and no tie.

It was one o'clock in the morning. Most of the offices were dark, but the night staff were busy and looking worried.

"What the hell's going on that you have to drag me down here at this unholy hour?" he shouted.

The night supervisor took a deep breath and stood to greet him as he stormed through the office door. "Sorry sir, but Agent Dan Jenkins just called and said that there's suddenly a lot of activity at the jail where our subjects are staying."

"What kind of activity?" barked Henderson.

"I'll let you talk to him, sir, if you don't mind. I still have him on the phone." He handed Henderson the phone, which was snatched from his hand.

"Jenkins!" snapped Henderson. "What's happening? And it'd better be good!"

"Well, sir, three large rock star-type buses just pulled up to the sally port at the jail. That's where they load and unload prisoners."

"I *know* what a sally port is," said Henderson. "So why is that so important?"

"Ah, they're big buses, sir. They each might sleep as many as ten to twelve people, with plenty of room for gathering, eating, and other things."

"What *other* things are you alluding to, Jenkins?"

"I don't know, sir. Secret experiments, maybe?"

Henderson's eyes lit up. "And how many of these buses are there?"

"Three, sir. So far."

"What? You think there may be more?"

"I don't know. Only three have shown up so far. They kinda came in a caravan, like a rock band."

"So you think that our 'gang' might be loading on the bus to be transferred somewhere else?"

"It's a possibility, sir," said Jenkins.

"Can you see anybody getting on or off the bus?" said Henderson.

"I can see some movement. People are getting on, but they're dressed in dark clothing with hoods, so there's no way I can identify them."

"All right," said Henderson. "Keep an eye on things and let me know of any further developments. You able to follow them if they pull out?"

"Yes, I have a rental car," said Jenkins.

"Good!" said Henderson, who slammed the phone down. To the rest of the staff—"get everyone up! We've got a serious problem! Let's *go* people!"

Deep in the bowels of the Kremlin, things were blowing up. The General in charge of the KGB, Borya Morozov, had a call in to Comrade Viktoriya Dunayevsky's handler, Major Dmitry Kozlov.

"I hope you have some good news for me, Major. I've been hearing some very disturbing rumors from other sources. I hope, for your sake, they are not accurate."

Major Kozlov gulped and said, "Dunayevsky's gone, General. She's in the wind. We're using all the assets we have to locate her, but if she doesn't want to be found—well, you trained her to be the best—at everything. Where else can we look?"

The General said, "Find the professor, and you'll find her. Or find Wolfe. I know she'll want to find him and kill him in the most horrible way she can imagine. And she can imagine many."

"Isn't she running for her life, now?" said Kozlov. "I mean, she can't screw up like she did, *twice*, and get away with it, can she?"

"No," said General Borya. "She will be terminated when we find her, and she knows that. Incompetence cannot be tolerated. Sets a bad example for the others. But in the meantime, if she can accomplish her goal of capturing the professor and his invention, she will be redeemed in memoriam. What she does with Wolfe, is on her. I hope she gets her priorities right. And I hope you do too."

The General ended the call.


Viktoriya Dunayevsky had her eyes glued on the middle bus— the one behind the one at the door of the sally port. She knew this was where Wolfe and the professor would be. She could go without sleep for days if need be, and with the added incentive of killing Wolfe, she knew she could stay awake until her tasks were completed. She had never failed before, and she wouldn't start now, even if she had made some mistakes.

What the Kremlin did to her was up to them. She was a devoted Communist and would be until the day she died. Which would probably be sooner than later. Better that than spending old age hooked up to tubes and IV lines. Blaze of glory. That was the way she was going to go.

The plan had been explained to everyone and they agreed. The truck with all of the professor's possessions had been taken inside the Sheriff's Department where the patrol cars parked, and unloaded near the sally port to be ready to load into one of the buses. The buses would provide excellent accommodations.

There was room for Professor Dejanovic to conduct his experiments and work on his device, and there would be protection for all concerned, except Eino and Quinn, wherever they were. They had tried to contact Eino again but got his painfully long taped message instead.

Neither of the watchers was aware of the other. They were both watching the buses and both had cars. Viktoriya Dunayevsky knew she had a problem. She was one person with one car—and there were three buses. Unless they all went together, like in a motorcade, she would have to pick one to follow and hope it was the right one. She thought about it. If it was like a motorcade, the principal, or key figure, would be in the middle vehicle, with protection from the lead and tail vehicles. She decided that if the three buses split up, she would go with the middle bus.

Agent Dan Jenkins was also monitoring the scene and was in the same quandary. But he figured that if the first bus left and he didn't follow it, and none of the other buses moved, then he would lose everything. He knew about motorcades too, but he decided to follow the first bus, figuring he had a thirty-three percent chance of being right, and a bird in the hand was worth two in the bush— or so the saying went.

They both watched.

Finally the first bus driver put his bus in gear and slowly pulled away from the sally port two bus lengths and stopped. The second bus pulled up to the sally port where the first bus had been, and the third bus pulled up behind the second.

Jenkins was getting nervous, second-guessing himself, vacillating back and forth between the buses. He started biting his nails.

It was getting cold outside. The fall air was turning damp and a breeze was picking up. The temperature had fallen to the high forties. Jenkins gave an involuntary shudder, and cranked up the heater fan.

Suddenly people started coming out of the door to the sally port, dressed like the ones who came off the first bus—dark clothes, hooded. Several people got on, maybe eight or ten. Jenkins tried to count, but they moved too quickly. It was late afternoon and there had been thick cloud cover all day. It was practically dark outside, though the sun wouldn't set for another hour or so.

They continued to wait. Five minutes. Ten minutes.

Then the first bus started moving and drove quickly away. The other buses stayed put. Jenkins waited as long as he could, looking expectantly at the other buses. But they did not move. There was not going to be a caravan. He finally decided. Dropping the gear shift lever into Drive, he hit the gas and gave chase. Well, he thought, *a bird in the hand* . . . thirty-three percent. Then another thought crossed his mind and put him in a panic. Thirty-three percent chance of success—*sixty-six* percent chance of *failure*.

Suddenly the odds looked horrible. He could see his career going down the toilet. If he was wrong, Henderson was going to be livid.

# chapter 61

The phone rang on the desk of Archie Fox, FBI agent in charge of the ongoing surveillance of Wolfe, Terri, and the others.

Fox picked up after one ring. "Yes?" he said. It was the man on the bike, code name, Serge.

"It's a squirrel cage over here," said Serge. "A three-ring circus."

"What's going on?"

"Basically all the key players have been secured in the jail until just recently."

"Is the professor among them?"

"He is."

"Are we sure he's the target everyone's after?" said Agent Fox.

Serge responded. "We're sure. He's been working on a free energy device, tapping into dark energy, or some such crap. I don't understand it, but our operative has seen it work, albeit on a small scale. But apparently it works, and he who controls the energy, controls the world."

"OK," said Fox. "Just wanted to make sure that we're after the right person and the right technology."

"If it isn't this," said Serge, "I don't know what is."

"OK," said Fox. "What happened next?"

"Anyway, then three rock star buses pulled up to the jail and began loading passengers."

"What? Who were they?"

"Couldn't tell. People had dark clothing on, and hoods covered their heads."

"Go on."

"Well the first bus fills, at least takes on all it's going to, and pulls up away from the sally port—and stops. The second bus pulls up to the sally port and does the same thing, with the loading of the unrecognizable passengers. The third bus pulls up behind the second one."

"Then what?" said Fox.

"Then we waited. About ten minutes later, the first bus takes off. A minute or so later, a rental Chevy pulls out and takes off after the bus, in a big hurry."

"Do you think it was following the bus?"

"Looked like it," said Serge. "The driver was a middle-aged white male, as far as I could tell. That's about all I could see."

"What's your plan?"

"Well, I have no idea who's on the bus and who's not, and who's still waiting inside, if anyone. Our main targets could all be on the first bus for all I know, or all still inside."

"And you have no car," stated Fox.

"And I have no car," said Serge. "But I don't need one. Because we have our operative on the inside."

"Yes we do," said Agent Fox, confidently. "And we'll be informed every step of the way, won't we?"

"Yes, we will," said Serge, equally confident.

"Then we won't worry. Just let me know the next time our operative contacts you and bring me up to date."

"Will do," said Serge. He broke the connection.

While Viktoriya watched the last two buses, the door to the sally port opened and one more person, equally disguised as the other passengers, got on the second bus and the doors to the bus and the sally port closed.

Sticking with her plan, the KGB assassin grabbed her car keys, sprinted to her vehicle, a Land Rover with a V-8 engine and four wheel drive, and cranked it to life. She sat there for several minutes before the bus brake lights came on. The driver put the bus in gear and drove off, not waiting for the other bus to pull up. That was different, she thought, but she was committed now. She began following the second bus. *Motorcade*, she thought to herself—middle vehicle—she had to be right.

"Wolfe?"

"Eino?"

Eino Loukkala had fashioned a couple of two-way radios that broadcast a lot like Citizen Band radios, but at a much higher frequency—higher than anything the government used. The range was only a few miles, but the transmissions were clear and worked in buildings. He had given one to Wolfe and kept one for himself.

"Yes it's me—Eino Loukkala, Finlander wit' a strong accent. Can you tell it's me now, Wolfe? Eh?"

"Of course I can," said Wolfe. "You just took me by surprise, that's all."

"Likely story," mumbled Eino.

"Eino," said Wolfe, exasperated, "I assume you have a reason for calling me."

"I do, I do," said Eino. "Two cars took off after the first two buses, just as you expected. The first driver was a man and the second was a woman. The first had a rental car, and the woman had a Land Rover."

"Thanks," said Wolfe. "We'll load the third bus, just in case there's another person watching, and go through the same scenario. Are you prepared to follow a car if there is one?"

"Yup," said Eino in a disgusted tone of voice. "I know the drill. I'm not stupid, ya know. Everyone assumes I'm stupid just because I don't sound like one of them New York City radio announcers. I mean, frankly, dey don't sound so hot to me."

"Nobody thinks you're stupid, Eino. We all know you can drop the Finnish accent anytime you want to."

Eino ignored him. "And if nobody follows the third bus, *I* will. How's dat?"

"Ha, ha. Very funny, Eino. You ought to do stand-up comedy."

"I do. I do stand-up comedy when I do an autopsy. I crack all kind of great jokes and no-*body* complains. Good one, eh, Wolfe? I crack me up."

Wolfe shook his head. "Just stay out of sight and don't get caught."

"You can count on me. Eino the Finlander out."

"Wolfe out."

The third bus pulled away from the sally port. The first bus had headed south and east. The second bus had headed west. And now the third bus headed north. Eino watched for some time to see if there was a third car trying to follow that bus, but none did. Since Eino knew where they were going, he could afford to give the bus a longer lead. But not so long a lead that he would be out of range of the radios.

As it turned out, nobody followed the third bus, which was good, because that was the bus with Professor Dejanovic, Sheriff Josephs, Kara, Sparrow, Terri, and Wolfe on it, plus all of the professor's papers and inventions and equipment, along with the bus driver and five SWAT-trained deputies. They were Josephs' pride and joy, and his best kept secret. They were going to provide security for the bus, which they labeled, Assault Vehicle One, or AVO, for operational purposes.

The bus was driven north up a remote road until it came to a dead end with a large turnaround circle at the end. It took about twenty minutes for the bus to make the trip. After the bus got turned around, the driver kept the engine and all auxiliary functions turned on, at which time the SWAT team took up protective positions outside the vehicle. They all had night-vision goggles, plus all the armament they would need to defend the bus.

When things settled down, Wolfe got the professor aside. "OK, doc. Why don't you tell me what all the fuss is about? Somebody, or many *somebodies*, seem to want you and your invention pretty bad. People have died over it. More might. So I need to know what it is, how it works, and what its uses are. And also, what you plan to do with it."

The professor suddenly became defensive. "And why should I tell you?"

"No reason, really," said Wolfe. "Except that the only people who are keeping you alive, and from being tortured, are me and my team. I think you saw what Viktoriya Dunayevsky was planning to do to you and Kara. And were it not for Eino, another one of my associates, she would have succeeded. Lucky you."

"And who is this *person*, anyway?" asked Professor Jonathan Dejanovic, PhD in physics.

"Only the Soviet Union's most deadly KGB assassin, who really enjoys her work."

The professor gulped loudly. "I see," he said. "Then I suppose we should get down to business, shouldn't we?"

"I suppose we should," said Wolfe.

# chapter 62

They all gathered in the living room area of the rock star bus. Professor Jonathan Dejanovic set up a table in the center of the area, and placed his experiments on the top. The rest of them, Wolfe, Terri, Sparrow, Josephs (in charge of the protection team), and Kara sat in a rough semi-circle in front of the professor. Class was about to begin.

"I'm going to simplify this as much as I can," he began, "because there is a lot of physics behind the operation of this device, particularly in quantum mechanics."

"We'll try and keep up," said Josephs.

"Good. Well, the first basic conceptual change is that what you have learned about 'space' all these years, is wrong. Space is not empty. Space is filled with either matter or energy. Wherever there is no matter, there is energy. OK?"

"We're with you," said Terri.

"Good. Next misunderstood concept regarding reality is that things, like bricks or pieces of wood, are solid. A piece of wood, or a rock, or anything we consider 'hard' is actually, over 99.999 percent space."

"Which is energy," added Wolfe.

"Correct. But to our mind's eye, there is 'space' between atoms and electrons and protons, and so on. But you're right. That space is really energy. There is no such thing as a void where nothing exists."

"Are we going to be graded on this?" said Josephs. There was some snickering.

The professor ignored him. "Moving along, wherever there is no matter, there is energy. It is everywhere throughout the universe. It surrounds us all. It is in this room. It *is* this room—and the bus—99.999 percent what we call space-energy."

"So if I shot you right now with my .45 caliber semi-automatic pistol," began Sparrow, shocking the room into total silence, "there's an infinitely small chance that the matter in this bullet will collide with the matter in your body, right? It should pass right through, undisturbed."

The professor looked at Sparrow askance, somewhat alarmed at her analogy. "No, that would *not* happen," he said hastily, "for reasons not pertinent to our discussion at hand."

"Oh," said Sparrow. "I just thought that a demonstration would be a . . ."

"Let's move on," said the professor, nervously.

"Let's," said Wolfe, giving Sparrow the evil eye. She just raised her eyebrows and shrugged.

"The point is," continued the professor in front of the unruly students, "that there is energy all around us that we call dark energy—because we can't see it—but we can tap into that energy, just like we do with the sun's energy using solar cells. It's there, everywhere around us when the sun is shining, and it's free as long as we can find a way to collect it and turn it into useful electrical energy."

"Same with wind power I assume," said Josephs.

"Right, said the professor. "We don't usually see the air moving, or wind, but we can feel the effects of it and can harness that wind to produce useful electrical energy through the use of windmills.

Again, it's free for the taking, and like sunlight, we don't use it up and worry about running out of it. For our purposes of illustration, it's always there."

"But the wind doesn't always blow and the sun doesn't always shine," said Terri, finally getting her two cents worth in.

"Right again," said the professor. "But that's where dark energy differs from all the other forms. It never runs out. It's always . . . on."

"But where does it come from?" asked Kara.

"We don't know. That's an interesting and valid question, but the only answer I can give is that it's always there and has always has been. Just like matter."

The security forces were still positioned in a perimeter surrounding the bus, invisible to the naked eye, but they were there watching in all directions, covertly scanning for any sign of intrusion. If one came, they were ready—almost eager for it.

Meanwhile, most of the clandestine world was in a lather. "Where are they?" yelled Henderson, furious that he was in this predicament because of Sparrow, his ungrateful and insubordinate employee.

"Who do we have left?" he shouted at Wilton, one the two last remaining employees in the room.

"Ah, no one, sir," said the nervous neophyte. "Just me and Symington."

"Well, why aren't *you* doing something to find her?" Henderson knew his anger was misplaced, but he was so angry at her betrayal—he had been so nice to her—he thought she liked him. Then she stabbed him the back like the traitor she was. Embarrassing him like this in front of everyone, ruining his career. He was so angry he couldn't think straight.

Symington and Wilton were at his mercy. But Wilton did the only smart thing he could do. "What would like us to do, sir?" he said. "We'll do whatever you ask." Wilton thought that was a safe bet. Put it back on his Director. Show him deference. Respect. Unfortunately, that didn't work so well.

Henderson's head whipped around to look directly at poor Wilton. "What? You're asking *me*? What I want you to do is get your *ass* out of this building and find her and bring her to me. *Now!*"

# chapter 63

"Let me move on to the thing everyone is after and why they are after it," said the professor."

"Sounds good," said Wolfe.

"OK," said Dejanovic. "Let me show you my first primitive invention." He brought out a four-inch by four-inch piece of one-quarter-inch plywood. Attached to the piece of plywood was a small circuit wired to a small black knob. Also attached to the circuit was a wire with an alligator clip on the end, and another wire with a regular connector for a nine-volt battery on the end.

Sitting next to the board on one end was a huge capacitor that looked like a metal tube about an inch in diameter and about three inches high, with two metal connectors on top. The professor set these devices on the card table in front of them.

"OK," he began, "These are the basic pieces of my device—a circuit, a knob that turns the device on or off, and which also acts as a rheostat—you know, that turns left to lower the frequency or right to increase it—and the metal tube which is a capacitor that stores energy. This one is huge, so it will store a lot of energy."

Then the professor brought out an electrical device called a volt-ohm-amp meter, or VOM, and showed it to them. He could hold it in his hand, and it had two wires that plugged into the meter, one red and one black.

At the other end of each wire was a metal probe that you could touch to one end of anything metal to measure current flow—

one probe on one terminal, one on the other. He explained how it worked, with a meter that showed volts or amps or ohms of whatever device was measured.

He then took the VOM and touched one probe to one terminal of the capacitor tube, and one probe on the other end, and turned on the meter. The meter showed no stored electricity in the capacitor. Then he reached into his pocket and brought out a brand new nine-volt battery with the wrapper still on. He passed it around.

"Brand new," he said. "When you're done examining it, one of you take off the wrapper and hand the battery to me." Josephs offered to do that. "Thank you, Sheriff," he said.

"This is like a magic show," said Sparrow.

"It will look like magic before I'm done," he said, taking the battery from Josephs. "Now watch as I check the voltage on the battery." He touched one probe to one terminal of the battery and the other probe to the other terminal on the battery. The meter immediately jumped to life, and the needle swung over to nine-point-one on the dial.

"Everyone see that?" he said, holding up the meter. "This shows that this brand new battery is producing nine-point-one volts of electricity, which one would expect." Then he took the battery and connected it to the battery connector wire from the circuit board.

Then he connected two alligator clips on the ends of the other wires and clipped one onto one of the capacitor terminals, and one onto the other capacitor terminal.

"Now we have a complete circuit, with the battery producing power on one end, my circuit in the middle, and the electrical storage unit—the capacitor—on the other. Right now the circuit is closed as my on/off switch/tuning knob is all the way to the left, in the off position."

Everyone's eyes were starting to glaze over as the professor droned on.

"OK, Mister Wizard," said Josephs. "Get to the point. You're putting us all to sleep!"

"Watch," said the professor. He turned on the circuit and began turning the knob looking for a certain frequency. When he found the frequency he was looking for, he put the VOM probes on the capacitor terminals. It showed that the capacitor was filling with electricity. "See?" he said. "Look at it filling up. Pretty cool, huh?"

"No, not cool," said Sparrow. "So what? So you're draining the battery and storing the charge in the capacitor. Big deal. Nothing new about that."

"No, you're right—Sparrow, is it?"

"*Yes*," she said sarcastically. She thought about renaming him Ten-second Jon, in light of his apparently deficient short-term memory.

"But what *is* new," continued the professor, "is that the capacitor has already stored much more energy than is available from the battery. That excess energy is coming from the ethos—from all the space around us. It is dark energy, and *that* is what is being stored in the capacitor. That is what I just tapped into." They all looked at each other, still not quite comprehending.

"Want to see some proof?" said the professor.

They all nodded.

"Watch."

Dan Jenkins was still following the first bus. It was heading east towards Munising. He had no idea how long he was to follow the bus, or what he was to do if it stopped. But he sure as heck hoped that it would stop, because his bladder was filling up from all that coffee he drank to keep himself awake. He had not properly planned for this surveillance. He would pay dearly for this failure.

Viktoriya Dunayevsky was following the second bus that was heading west, towards Iron Mountain. She was sure the targets were on that bus. Her instincts had never failed her yet. She just had to wait until the bus stopped for gas or a bathroom break, and she would deal with its occupants in her unique way. And she had plenty of restraints, gas, and weapons to take care of a small army. She was gleefully waiting for that time to come.

And nobody had followed the third bus. Yet.

Reaper had called the secure number Wolfe had given him and talked to the anonymous benefactor about his equipment needs. The man didn't seem to flinch at his list, so he decided to add a few things more that he thought would be nice. It was all approved and would be delivered at the compound within the time frame given. The man even threw in a bonus that Reaper hadn't requested, but which would make his assignment much more effective.

Reaper couldn't believe that the things he ordered could be delivered so quickly, and he wouldn't believe it until he actually saw them on-site. But if it all came as planned, it would be incredible.

He took the detailed maps of the compound that Wolfe had given him, and began mapping out his plan of attack. He knew what he was capable of with limited equipment and supplies, and if he got *half* of what he had requested, the attackers were in for a big surprise.

This was his own operation from beginning to end. His first.

And he couldn't wait for it to begin.

# chapter 64

Professor Jon Dejanovic, PhD in physics, was ready to wow his captive audience. They didn't seem too impressed so far, but that would change.

Sparrow, bored by the lackluster presentation, could hold her tongue no longer. "So you proved, I guess, that you could produce electricity 'over-unity.' That is, your output was greater than your input—the nine-volt battery. So, how much over-unity was it? Anything significant?"

The professor smiled. "Not dramatic enough for you? Watch this." He brought out a one-inch-thick by six-inches-wide piece of pinewood board, three feet long. On it were mounted six light fixtures with six regular sixty-watt incandescent bulbs screwed in.

He handed the board to the spectators. "Please. Examine the board. You will see that there are no hidden wires, no hidden power supply, nothing but a pine board. Go ahead."

Sparrow, Terri, Wolfe, and Josephs each in turn, examined the apparatus, then passed it on until it came back to the professor. Kara did not examine the board as she had seen him put it together.

"Satisfied?" he said, much like a magician before his prize magic act.

"Looks OK to me," said Josephs.

"Me too," said Sparrow, followed by the others.

"Excellent," said the professor. Then he removed his circuit and on/off switch from the first demonstration, and attached one set of wires to a fastener on the board of lights, and the other to the same nine-volt battery. "Ready?" he said dramatically.

"Go for it," said Terri drily.

Professor Dejanovic held up the board with his left hand, and gripped the knob with his right hand forefinger and thumb. "Please prepare to shield your eyes," he said. They all looked at each other as if he was an imbecile.

"Here goes," he said. He turned the knob until it clicked on, and the light bulbs all came on simultaneously with a very dim glow.

"That's not very . . ." Josephs began, then the professor turned the knob slowly to the right. Gradually the lights got brighter and brighter until they were as bright as normal lights would be. But then he continued turning the knob, at which time the lights got brighter and brighter still until they were so bright, the group could no longer look directly at them.

"Holy crap!" said Josephs as he shielded his eyes. "That's bright!"

"There's more," said the professor as he cranked the knob more and more to the right. The light got so intense, that the occupants of the bus had to turn away from the demonstration and cover their eyes with their hands. The professor and Kara had already donned protective eyewear.

"Turn it off!" said Terri. "You're going to blind us all!"

The professor turned the knob to the left and reduced the lights to a comfortable, dim level. Slowly the occupants removed their hands from their eyes and looked back at the display.

"How'd you do that?" said Wolfe.

"Yeah," said Terri, "without burning out the filaments? You must have created a lot of heat."

"Check it out," said Professor Dejanovic. "Go ahead. Feel the bulbs. They're cool to the touch."

They did so. "You're right," said Sparrow. "No heat at all."

"Now feel the battery," said the professor.

Terri did. "It's cool, too."

"So, two things happened," said the professor. "First, I opened the circuit and accessed the dark energy the same way I did in the first experiment. Secondly, I increased the frequency that the bulbs were operating on from sixty cycles per second, which all our electric appliances and lights run on in our homes, to thousands of cycles per second.

"I won't give you the exact number because that's proprietary confidential information. But to your concern, Terri," he nodded to her, "about the filaments burning out, at the higher frequency they don't burn out at all. In fact they will last many, many times longer than standard bulbs. Maybe indefinitely.

"So you see, we have virtually free electricity from space. All it takes to get it started, is a nine-volt battery. And of course, my circuit. Once the circuit is opened, you can disconnect the battery and the power will continue pouring in, indefinitely. You never have to turn it off."

They all looked at him in shock. "The implications of this are staggering," said Wolfe, finally speaking. "Free energy—free electricity." Then, as a secondary thought, "The power companies. Oil. Gas. Coal. Nuclear power. The infrastructure. Commerce. Third world countries."

"Yes, yes, yes," said the professor, excitedly. "It will change the world. Free power for everyone. Limitless power. No more pollution!"

They sat there in stunned silence, thinking of the possibilities, both good and bad.

"What about use in automobiles?" said Terri. "If we had electric cars, you could use your device to power them too, couldn't you?"

"Absolutely," said Professor Dejanovic. "In fact, electric cars were the preferred method of transportation in the late 19th and early 20th centuries. The only limitation was range and time to recharge the batteries.

"With this device, you wouldn't even need batteries to run it, just one to start the process. The electric motors would be fu-eled from dark energy. As long as you never turned it off, you would never need a battery again. And it's all solid state," he said. "No moving parts. Except the on-off switch. Nothing to wear out. Theoretically, it could run forever."

Terri chimed in again. "What about electricity for your house? Would this work for that? Or businesses?"

"Same principle," said the professor. "I could build one to power a house, or a factory, or a car or an airplane or a boat or submarine. Even a spaceship. Simply a matter of scale. The possibilities are endless."

"Yes, they are," nodded Wolfe, slowly. He was thinking of the downside of all of this. "This is very exciting, professor," he said. "I can see the reason for your secrecy and enthusiasm."

"Yes, yes," he said. "I can hardly contain myself. It's revolu-tionary. It will change the *world*."

"It will," said Wolfe. "And that's why your life is more in danger than it has ever been. In fact," he continued, "you will be lucky to survive another week once this gets out—and I think it probably already *is* out, at least in part. That's why all these people are gunning for you—for *us*."

The professor's face fell. "But why? I'll give it to the world for *free*. I don't even want to make money on it. It's my contribution to the world—the environment."

Kara's face changed perceptibly, noted Wolfe. This was apparently news to her. He watched her. She looked at the professor with questioning eyes. "Ah, Jon," she said, forgetting protocol, "I thought we were going to share this as partners? Surely we can make *some* money on it—I mean, after all the work you did on it, I..."

"Oh, sure we'll share, sweetie. But we'll share the glory, not the money. This must be free to the world. It's my gift to mankind. *Our* gift to mankind. Surely you can see that."

The expression on her face showed that she did *not* see that. In fact, it was the exact opposite of what she thought would happen. Surprise was replaced by shock, followed by resentment, then anger.

She'd been used. Duped. Well, two can play *that* game, she thought to herself. She had another agenda—a hidden agenda the professor knew nothing about. She was going to get her revenge for his betrayal. But right now she needed just one thing—a phone.

She had to call a special person who had offered her a substantial amount of money—an amount that would set her up for life—if she agreed to play ball with him and his agency. Well, the time had come. The person was reputable and would guarantee that the funds would be available to her on completion of her part of the bargain. That person was Archie Fox, Special Agent with the FBI. He wanted information on how the search for the professor was going, and also information on the status of the invention.

Well, she could see that Jon was reneging on his promise to share his inevitable fortune with her, so she had no compunctions about switching teams. She could get revenge on Jon and cement her future with one quick phone call. She just needed to find a damn phone.

# chapter 65

They all sat back, their thoughts spinning wildly. Wolfe's, however, were focused. He could see all of the things that could, probably *would*, happen, and none of them were good.

He finally spoke. "How's your team doing, Ed?" he said to Josephs.

The Sheriff came out of his own reverie and tried to shake his head clear. "I'll check," he said. He walked to the other end of the bus, pulled out his walkie-talkie, keyed the mic and said, "Unit one to Leader. How's it going?"

There was a short pause, and then, "Leader to Unit one. Everything's quiet."

"Your people need anything?"

"Negative," Leader responded. "Ten-four," said the Sheriff. "Let me know if you do."

"Copy," said Leader.

The Sheriff walked back to the group. "Nothing to report," he said. "And under the circumstances, that's a good thing."

"I'm still worried about Quinn," said Terri. "Out there all alone, in the cold and dark. No coat. I can't stand it."

"Tried to find him," said Josephs. "Sent my best search and rescue team, and their dogs. They usually can find anything."

"What does that mean?" she replied.

"It means," he said softly, "that Quinn doesn't want to be found—and he's good at it. I think we have to assume that he's OK for now. He's a survivor and he's smart. He'll be OK."

"I agree," said the professor. "He seemed to be able to take care of himself when he was with me. He came and went, and sometimes didn't need any food when I offered it to him. He must have a place to crash and a source of food and water somewhere."

"Yes, but we weren't near town when he took off," said Terri. "Maybe he couldn't make it back there."

"Nothing we can do about it now, Terri," said Wolfe. "First chance we get we'll try to look for him, but it's hard to know where to start. And we have bigger concerns right now."

"Right," said Sparrow. "Like keeping all of us alive, including Eino. Quinn will just have to wait. Anyway. It sounds like he can go it alone for a while. We, on the other hand, are now sitting ducks—a situation that needs to change soon."

Wolfe spoke up. "Well it looks like nobody followed us, so I think we can assume that the decoys have done their job. At least for now. A good time to relocate and get more permanent quarters." They all perked up. "Where?" asked Terri, voicing the question in all their minds.

"You'll see," said Wolfe, as he watched Kara. Her eyes were darting around, like a cornered animal. "Sheriff, have your team scout the road ahead and make sure it's safe to head out," he continued. "Then we'll pick them up at the end of the road as we leave."

"OK," said Josephs. He grabbed his radio and gave instructions to his team. "They'll report back as soon as it's cleared. Shouldn't take too long."

"Good," said Wolfe.

"Now, I have the same question," said Josephs. "Where you taking us to?"

The bus Jenkins was following made its way into Munising on U.S. 28 and slowed down. Jenkins suddenly came alert, aware that something might be happening besides slowing for the reduced speed limits in the city.

Sure enough, the bus slowed even more and then made a left turn into the parking lot for the Pictured Rocks Cruises that operated out of the Munising harbor on Lake Superior. The bus pulled up close to the building where the tickets were sold, so Jenkins pulled into a parking space where he could see the door to the bus.

Several people on the bus, still with their heads covered, got off and went into the building. Jenkins tried to see what they were doing, but his view was blocked. He thought about getting out as he had a very full bladder, but he was afraid if Sparrow was there, that he would be recognized. So he waited.

Suddenly he saw a large boat steaming into the harbor, which slowed and made a quick turn so the bow would be facing out toward Lake Superior. It docked where the cruise boat would normally be. Before Jenkins could decide what to do, the people from the bus boarded the boat, which was a large yacht that Jenkins estimated was at least a hundred feet long. He quickly jumped out of his car to see what he could see, and if he could identify any of the passengers.

But by the time he got inside, the passengers were already aboard and the lines were being cast off. He ran to the edge of the dock as the boat was pulling away, but all the passengers were inside and out of view. As the boat quickly accelerated he tried to see the name on the back, or any identifying characteristics.

He pulled a pair of small binoculars out of his coat pocket and scanned the boat for any information about its identity, including the name, registration numbers, and so on. But he saw none and the boat quickly slipped from view.

Jenkins ran back inside and asked the woman at the ticket counter what the boat was that had just left. She was an older lady with grey hair and wire-rimmed glasses.

"Gee, I don't know, Mister," she said. "Never seen it before. Just came up, loaded some passengers, and took off again."

"Do you know who the people were who got on?" a panicked Jenkins asked. "Did they buy tickets? Use a credit card?"

"Oh, no," she said. "They weren't part of the Pictured Rocks Cruises. We had no idea who they were, where they came from, whose boat it was—nothing. I'm as surprised as you seem to be," she said. Then she looked at him dancing around with a panicked look on his face. "You like to use our bathroom?" she said sympathetically. "It's down the hall on the right."

"Thanks," said Jenkins, as he made a mad dash down the hall.

# chapter 66

The bus Vikki was following drove into Ishpeming, circled around, and drove back towards Marquette. "What the hell?" she said, anger getting the better of her. But she dutifully followed the bus back along U.S. 41 towards Marquette.

However, before arriving at Marquette, the bus slowed and turned off at the entrance to the Marquette County Airport, in Negaunee. "No!" she said to herself as she looked on in disbelief. The bus pulled into the general aviation area up to a private hanger. The door to the hanger slid open, and the bus pulled inside. The hanger door then closed.

Shouting a Russian obscenity, she pounded her fists on the steering wheel. Quickly she pulled her car up behind the hanger and jumped out to see if she could find a window to peer into, or a door she could breach.

But as she was doing that, the hanger door opened again and the bus pulled out and started heading for the airport exit. The bus's windows were blacked out so she couldn't see if anyone was still onboard.

She ran back to her car and had a decision to make. Follow the bus, or check inside the hanger? She thought for only a second, before an airplane tow-tug began pulling a King Air Turbo Prop out of the hanger. It was large enough to carry all the people she was after. The man operating the tug saw her and looked up at the cockpit of the airplane, and got a signal.

The plane was nearly out of the hanger, so the man quickly disconnected the tow-tug and pulled it out of the way. Simultaneously the engines started on the airplane, first one and then the other. Vikki quickly tried to look in the windows of the airplane, but they had been darkened as well.

The plane's engines were now powering up and the plane began moving towards the runway. Viktoriya started the Land Rover and began pursuing the plane. She pulled out her weapon and tried to get in front of the plane to threaten the pilot to stop, but the plane was picking up speed, violating all the aviation rules by racing to the runway.

Airport officials suddenly started scurrying around, trying to stop the pilot, calling on the radio, but they were suddenly more concerned about the lady with a gun in her Land Rover chasing the plane.

"Drop the weapon!" one of the deputies finally shouted at her, out of breath but close enough to hit her as she drove towards him.

Quickly she snapped off a couple of shots above the head of the deputy, who quickly ducked and headed for cover as she chased after the plane. She thought she might be able to block it with her vehicle, but her options were running out now that the police were chasing her in their patrol vehicles.

She raced her Land Rover across the grass and up onto the runway in front of the plane, but the police were in their cars and pursuing her at high speed. She looked at them and at the plane, and she knew she was out of choices and out of time. Better to live to fight another day, she thought, as she wheeled around, headed straight for the police cars in a deadly game of "chicken."

As the vehicles raced towards each other, the police cars veered away at the last possible second, fearing death and destruction more than she did.

Now with a clear path, she rocketed towards the exit. She had to stay free to finish her objective or she might as well die now, she decided, with grim determination.

Vikki knew the police would catch her quickly if she stayed to the main roads, so she decided to put her off-road vehicle to the test. After she had gone up U.S. 41 for a few miles and out of sight of the airport and the police, she pulled off the road and headed north towards Triple-A country, which was mostly wooded wilderness with a few rugged logging trails that were unimproved tracks in the dirt at best.

She knew the vehicles they had as patrol cars couldn't follow her. But she also knew that the Coast Guard had helicopters that could be up and searching for her in short order. Her only option was to stay under the cover of the trees and hope that they didn't know where she left the road and which direction she was headed in.

Right now she was running on pure adrenalin, but she was used to that. It would sustain her to the conclusion of her mission—or until she was caught or killed. Either way, she thought, the end was coming soon.

And master assassin Viktoriya Dunayevsky was definitely looking forward to this, far more than the Soviet firing squad which would come as sure as the sun rose in the east. She would go out in a blaze of glory, one way or the other.

Henderson was angry with his shrinking subordinates. "Jenkins did *what*?" he snapped. "He *lost* them?"

Wilton and Symington were still holding onto their assignments, tenuously, but they remained hopeful that he wouldn't fire them—mainly because they were the only two people left in the office besides him.

Symington spoke first. "Ah, yes sir. The bus pulled into a park-ing lot next to a scenic boat tour facility in Munising, and the people on the bus got off, went into the ticketing building, and then quickly boarded a large yacht. By the time he got in the building, the people had all boarded and the lines had been cast off. The boat was pulling away from the dock much faster than wake speed."

"Did he see any of them, recognize any of their faces?"

"No," said Symington, moving back away from the supervisor, out of spittle range. "He also looked for a name on the boat, but there was none. And there were no registration numbers or any other identifying characteristics, other than that it was about one hundred feet in length, and was white."

The director snapped his attention over to Wilton. "That true, Wilton? We have *nothing* to go on?"

Wilton's voice was just barely above a whisper. "I didn't take the call, sir. You'd have to ask . . ."

"I've already asked him, *Wilton*," he cut in. "Didn't you *hear*? He knows nothing!" Henderson looked at them both. "You know," he began, a little less volatile, "You guys are worthless. Get the hell out of here. Go find another job. Try pumping gas or flipping burgers or something closer to your skill set."

They both stood there, eyes wide open, frozen—afraid to move.

"Leave!" he shouted.

Wilton and Symington bolted from the office and headed for the exit, not happy, their careers now gone in a puff of smoke.

# chapter 67

T he third bus came to life when Josephs' team called in that
the way was clear. "We're moving out," said Wolfe. "Take your
seats, this may be a bumpy ride until we leave this area." They all
found a seat and something to hold onto.

Wolfe looked at Kara. She didn't look good. She was sweating,
though it wasn't too warm in the bus. Her breathing was shallow
and rapid, and her pupils were constricted. Her eyes darted all
around the bus, like a trapped rat in a cage.

""What's the matter, Kara?" said Wolfe. All eyes moved to her,
especially Terri's and Sparrow's. "You don't look so well."

"I'm *not* well, Wolfe," she snapped. "I've been uprooted from my
classes, I'll probably lose my credits for this semester, my parents
don't know where I am, or where I'm going—heck! *I* don't know
where I'm going." She got up and paced around, even though the
bus was moving along at a pretty good clip over the bumpy and
rutted road. "I didn't sign on for this. And now you tell us that
our very lives are in danger, all for trying to do something for the
benefit of the world?"

"And you," said Wolfe softly.

"What?" said Kara. "What do you mean, me?"

"Get off it," said Wolfe. "You were in it for the money, and
maybe fame, though you didn't invent anything. You worked for
the professor, and saw an opportunity for a meal ticket. Maybe
even, *Mrs.* Jon Dejanovic? You know, *share* in the profits, fifty-

fifty as husband and wife? Fame as the wife of a world famous inventor and philanthropist? Of course, all that goes up in smoke if he gives it all away. No money, no profit, no fame. Well, maybe a little fame. Not what you had in mind, is it?"

"No, it's not," she said, angrily. "Particularly not if I'm *dead*," she said, quickly gaining her equilibrium.

"But that *is* what you had planned, wasn't it?"

"What of it?" she retorted. "What's wrong with going for the American Dream?"

"Yours," began Wolfe, "or *his*?" he finished, nodding to the professor.

The professor was thunderstruck. "Is this true, Kara? Was that your plan?"

She looked at the professor. "What's so wrong with that? You liked me, I liked you. It seemed like a good idea."

Terri chimed in. "Wouldn't it be better if the concept of *love* were part of your equation?"

"I've never *loved* anybody," said Kara. "I think *like* is good enough."

"Well, I don't," said the professor. "I love you, Kara. I thought you loved me."

Kara walked over to the professor and put her hand on his arm. "We can still do this, Jon," she said imploringly. "If you would just retain the rights to your invention and we could make some money, we could help people that way. Finding causes where people needed money and giving it to them directly, rather than letting others decide who gets what. You could maintain control to spend it the way that's consistent with *your* beliefs—*your* philosophy."

The professor looked into her eyes and saw something he had not seen before—greed. "That's not going to happen," he said.

"*We're* not going to happen. I had no idea you were like this, Kara. I'm afraid our relationship is over," he said angrily. "You're not the person I thought you were."

"No!" she admonished. "You can't do that! We had an *agreement!*"

"Based on false pretenses, I'm afraid," said Josephs. "Not a binding contract. Your dream of fame and fortune is over."

Kara was fuming. "Well you can't do this to me. I want off. Right now! This is kidnapping—false imprisonment. You'll go to jail!"

"Sure," said Josephs. "No problem." The driver stopped the bus and opened the door. "Go ahead. Get off. We're not holding you. You're free to go, here and now."

"You can't be serious," she said. "I can't get off here. I don't even know where I am. I'll die out here!"

"Your choice," said Josephs. "You're probably gonna die anyway. We're *all* probably going to die anyway. So it doesn't make a lick of difference if it's here or somewhere else."

Kara stared at him. Then she looked around the bus, looking for any sign of support. But she saw none. Her shoulders slumped and she dropped her head. Very softly she said, "No, I'll stay. I'd just like to make a phone call, if that's OK. To tell my mother I'm all right and when I'm coming home."

"Sorry, Kara," said Wolfe. "We have no phone here. And if we did, you couldn't use it. Not now. Not until this is over—whatever happens."

"That's not fair," she exclaimed. "I never signed on for this."

"Yes, you did," said Josephs. "You did when you decided to hitch yourself to the professor's star—let him propel you to your desired fame and fortune. Unfortunately, he's a better person than you. He cares about people. You on the other hand . . ."

"Go to hell," said Kara, as she left the common area and stomped to the back of the bus.

Everyone was silent for a moment. Terri looked at Wolfe, studying his face. "What?" she said.

"Huh?" he said, looking up.

"What're you thinking? I know that look—I've seen it before," said Terri. "Something's bothering you, isn't it?"

Josephs looked at Wolfe, and so did the professor. "Well?" said Josephs. "You going to answer her?"

Wolfe looked up, refocused his eyes from his thousand yard stare, back to the present. "I think we have a mole in our midst," he said. "She was too eager to use the phone and coughed up a poorly acted lie to try. I think she's been sharing our plans and actions since she came aboard. Fortunately it's been a while since a phone's been available."

Josephs thought back. "Right. She doesn't yet know our whereabouts or our current plans." He sat back in his chair and thought for a moment. "In fact, *I* don't know our current plans."

"And it's a good thing I didn't reveal them, isn't it, Ed?"

Josephs said grudgingly, "I suppose."

"Well, you'll know in a minute. You'll all know—except Miss Dugan. She'll henceforth and forevermore not be privy to our plans."

"Good," said Josephs. "So? Where're we going?"

"We'll be there in less than an hour," he said with a cryptic smile on his face. "Terri's been there before."

Terri looked up, then it dawned on her where they were going. "You don't mean back *there* again, do you?"

"I do," said Wolfe.

"After what we did to the place?"

"All is forgiven," he said. "At least, there's no longer a problem. It's the safest place for us now."

"I'll believe it when I see it," said Terri.

"It'll be OK. You'll see," said Wolfe.

# chapter 68

Viktoriya Dunayevsky was bouncing around the Triple-A country trying to stay under the cover of the trees and off the beaten track, where the police would not be able to get to her. Even the Coast Guard helicopter would not be able to find her while she was in the woods.

Her only limitation was the amount of gas she had, and she had taken the opportunity to not only top off the tank of gas, but to also fill up the auxiliary gas tank that the Land Rover had built in. She would have enough for what she needed to do.

The KGB assassin had studied Agent Wolfe's history and his last mangled operation, so she knew where his haunts were. She also knew of the forces that were allied against him, and they were considerable. He would know that, too, and she didn't want to underestimate him. That would be a fatal flaw, and it was one she didn't intend to commit—again.

She had a pretty good idea where he would go, if given the chance. She didn't know which bus Wolfe and the others were on, or where the other buses went. So that avenue of finding them was closed. Now she had to rely on her instincts, which may have already failed her once, if the targets were on the airplane that took off. There was no way to confirm that. So she had to try something else.

This time it had better work. She thought she knew him through her research and through her attempted seduction and interrogation. In the latter case, she was outsmarted. So now she was down to her research that helped her to know her adversary, and she felt pretty comfortable about that, though her confidence was shaken. She had to come through on this one. For her, time was running out.

She wasn't working for the Soviet Union or General Borya or her handler, Major Kozlov, or the KGB anymore. No, Viktoriya Dunayevsky, master assassin, was working for herself now—to complete her mission—to hold her head high. To kidnap the professor and confiscate his plans and inventions. Or if that wasn't possible, to kill the professor and destroy his plans and inventions.

But above all, she must kill and destroy her nemesis, that thorn in her side, the one person who got away and humiliated her in front of her superiors—the American clandestine agent Clayton Wolfe, whom she hated with an anger that bordered on the psychotic.

And as she bounced around the woods and rutted paths, she plotted how she would do it. The very thought of that lifted her spirits and gave her new energy she had never before experienced.

The police commanders at the airport were in a fit. "How could you lose her?" yelled the captain of one of the departments. "She was *one person* in one car! And how many of you are there?" he said to no one in particular. One of the officers started looking around and counting. "It was a rhetorical question, you idiot! You had her blocked. You had her out-gunned! What were you *doing*? Sitting on your thumbs? Drinking coffee? Eating *doughnuts*?" That same officer looked down at his shirt to see if any powdered sugar had spilled onto his dark blue uniform shirt. Big mistake. His sergeant glared at him, then shook his head slowly as a warning of what was to come.

"Get out and find her!" shouted the captain. "Put up road blocks. Put out APBs. Call the Coast Guard and try to get their chopper. Put a broadcast out on radio and TV. Above all, find her! Do it! *Now!*" The officers started running to their cars. Sergeants who knew how to handle emergency situations got together to map out who was going to do what. Assignments were given. Everyone was sud-denly in motion. Whether or not they knew what they were doing, they were going to *look* like they did. Above all, they got out of the line of sight of the command officers as quickly as they could.

Moscow was in an uproar. Fists were pounding the tables in the Kremlin, voices were raised. Panic was in the room and coronaries were in the making, if the strokes didn't hit first. There were no cool heads.

First strike, was considered. If the invention got out and distributed, their fragile economy would falter. Nobody would need their oil. Third world countries would get rich almost overnight. Free energy. What a ghastly concept, thought General Borya Morozov. The Party Chairman was in total agreement. It had to be stopped, no matter the cost. Or they would all be shot. Or *worse*.

But then if there was a first strike, it would be their last, they all knew. The retaliation would be catastrophic for them, and for the world. Either way, their world was coming to an end unless they could get the professor and his invention before anyone else. And that eventuality was becoming more remote by the minute. Despair ruled. Comrade Viktoriya Dunayevsky was their last hope.

The bus with the endangered six, plus the bus driver, moved quickly along the roads back to Marquette. Breaking no traffic laws, the bus looked natural, or at least as natural as a rock star-type bus could look. But there had been three of them driving around town for a while, so it wasn't too much of an attention-getter—they hoped.

Once through the downtown area, the driver turned north on North 4th Street and then west on Hawley Street which then became County Road 550.

"I know where we're going," said Josephs. He turned to Wolfe. "We are, aren't we?"

Wolfe smiled. "That makes three of us who know."

Terri smiled knowingly. She was back with the in-crowd. And she liked it.

"Well I don't want to know," said Professor Dejanovic. "At this point, the less I know the better."

"I would have to agree," said Josephs.

Kara poked her head out from the back room. "Well, I *don't* know, and if I'm going to be a sacrificial lamb, I have a right to know."

Josephs saw a car that looked familiar following the bus, but said nothing. He watched it make all the same turns the bus was making.

"You have *no* right to know," Wolfe said to Kara. "You have intentionally inserted yourself into Professor Dejanovic's life for personal gain, and now you are a useless pawn in a high stakes chess game, which you undoubtedly don't play."

"No I don't," she said sarcastically. "It's a stupid game for eggheads who don't know how to live life. They just move pieces around a board for hours and hours. How more boring could they be?"

"Go to the back of the bus and be quiet," said Wolfe, "before I tape your mouth shut. We've heard more than enough from you."

"Screw you!" she said as she stomped to the back of the bus.

# chapter 69

They were on the outskirts of town now, moving quietly along when an alarm sounded on the bus driver's panel. They all looked. It was an indicator light. It was indicating that the back door of the bus was open. It was readily apparent what had happened. Kara had figured out how to open the door and did so. They ran back to see, and saw her laying in the middle of the road. She jumped up and ran to the driver's side of the car that was following the bus. She said something to the driver, then nodded and ran around to the passenger side and got in. The car started up and made a U-turn behind the bus, then headed back to Marquette.

The professor looked alarmed. "She's getting a ride back to town," he said. "She'll get away and betray us *all*."

"No, she won't," said Josephs. "She's in capable hands. Don't worry."

"I don't care about capable hands, and I don't care about her. Not anymore. I just don't want to die because she wants to be free."

"You won't," said Wolfe. "She just jumped from the frying pan into the fire. Eino's got her locked in the hearse and she's going where she won't get away."

Professor Dejanovic didn't look so sure about that, but he shrugged his shoulders and went back to his seat. She had turned out to be a real disappointment, he thought to himself. Good thing he didn't marry her. He breathed a sigh of relief and looked out the window at the passing scenery.

Eino Loukkala, county Coroner and now novice commando, took Kara back to his office to be restrained until further notice. He told his assistant fill-in guy, Dr. Aaron Beecher, to detain her until they returned. He told him where the restraints were, and where he could keep her, and to order in food and beverages for her.

He told him to make her comfortable, but to watch her like a hawk. He warned the doctor that some nasty people might try to find her and kidnap her or worse, so he should be on the lookout for trouble. Dr. Beecher did not seem pleased about his new assignment, but said nothing. He began contemplating an imminent move to a warmer climate—far, far away.

Eino knew where Wolfe and Josephs were going. He grabbed a few things, and then hopped into his classic ride and headed north to the bus's destination. He knew he could catch up, and relished the opportunity to put the pedal to the metal.

Wolfe's bus continued out of town and stayed on County Road 550. It seemed that everyone knew where they were going except Professor Jon Dejanovic and Sparrow. Jon was resigned to whatever fate his "captors" had in store for him. However, Sparrow was not so inclined.

"OK," she began, in a fit of pique. "I realize I'm not a card-carrying member of your secret little *rat pack*, but I would like to know, if it's not too much trouble, where the *hell* we're going."

"Sorry," Wolfe began. "We only did that to keep Kara from knowing." Josephs' head turned.

"Wonderful," said Sparrow. "Now that we've got that little *lapse* of protocol out of the way, would you please tell me where we're *going*?"

Wolfe gave Sparrow a weak, semi-apologetic smile. "We're heading for a place where we can be safe for a while—hopefully long enough to do what we need to do." He looked at Sparrow who was waiting, her question still unanswered. He quickly continued. "It's a place at the end of the road where there used to be a private conclave of very wealthy, very elite people who would meet, and sometimes live there."

Terri caught Wolfe's eye. "Used to be?" she said.

Wolfe nodded. "Yes. They're no longer there. After a rather dramatic incident that occurred there not long ago, the place was no longer private due to the publicity surrounding the event. So they sold the place."

"Someone else bought it?" said Terri.

"In a manner of speaking," said Wolfe.

"Who?" she pressed.

"A friend of mine who has lots of money," he said, getting a little uneasy.

"That wouldn't be that friend of yours who ponied up money for the condo, is it?" asked the Sheriff. "And the airplanes, and buses and food and equipment and cars and . . ."

"Yes," cut in Wolfe. "One and the same. Now can we get off this subject, please? He needs to remain anonymous. I promised him that his identity would never be revealed and I intend to keep that promise."

"Fine," said Josephs. "No problem. My lips are sealed." Wolfe glanced at him sideways. Josephs had his lips pursed,

and made the motion of locking his lips with an imaginary key and throwing it away.

Wolfe said, "I trust you, Ed, only because I haven't already revealed his name. And I intend to keep it that way."

Josephs just shrugged his shoulders. "So many secrets," he mumbled under his breath, as he turned and looked away.

The KGB assassin was bouncing and twisting around through the trees, sometimes on a trail, mostly not. She knew roughly where she was going. She had a compass, but most of her driving was by dead reckoning, which she was especially good at.

She had studied all the files on Wolfe and Terri Sommers, and their previous exploits. She also knew that there was only one place they could go that might supply a safe haven, temporary as it might be.

And that was where she was heading. She just hoped she could beat them there in time to set up a proper ambush. She knew if she could, there would be no escape for any of them. They were in for a big surprise.

The bus continued on up County Road 550 to Big Bay, where it slowed down going through the small town. Wolfe turned to Terri. "Bring back any memories?"

She looked at him. He had a warm smile on his face, and any feelings of agitation she had felt, melted away. "Yes," she said, sending a slight smile his way. In a previous engagement when they had been together in a life or death flight from numerous forces, they had traveled this very route. They had also had a strong romantic attachment at that time, though it had never been totally without tension. The sparks had flown between them, but instead of causing an explosion, they had fanned the flames of a warm fire that burned long and slow.

"Hopefully the end result will be better," she said.

"The very end result?" he said.

"Not the final end result," she said. "I mean the intermediate end result. You know. With all the shooting and stuff."

"Oh good," said Wolfe. "I thought you meant the very end result. Because I thought that was pretty good."

"Yes," she said, now frustrated. "The very end result was good. But I was referring to the very, *very* end result. You know. Where it is now."

Josephs finally cut in. "Will you two lovebirds please kiss and make up? We all know what you're trying to say in code. But it seems everyone here knows more about what you mean than you two do."

Terri blushed. Wolfe smiled. The professor stared out the window. And Josephs shook his head and laughed to himself. What a group.

# chapter 70

Wolfe's bus left Big Bay and headed into an eerie forest of trees that hadn't been touched in ages. Trees died and fell and just laid there over the decades, decaying and providing food for different forms of life, from insects and birds to fungi. The canopy pretty much covered the sky, so that even in the daytime it was almost twilight.

Wolfe had felt an otherworldly presence when driving through it, and so had Terri. The same feeling for both of them had returned, bringing that uneasy feeling that made the hairs stand up at the backs of their necks.

But after about twenty minutes they were through the forest and had come to the end of the road.

"We're here," said Josephs as the bus slowed down and stopped at the turnaround circle. Across the circle at the front of another wooded area stood a guard shack and a metal gate arm. Wolfe got out of the bus and walked over to the guard shack. There was nobody in the shack, and it was unlocked, so Wolfe stepped in and walked over to a control panel with lots of dials and levers. He pressed one lever and seemed to be talking to someone. About twenty seconds later, he let up on the spring-loaded lever and stepped out of the shack. Suddenly the gate arm rose and remained up. Wolfe got back on the bus and the driver started through the gate. Once the bus was through, the gate automatically lowered and locked.

Wolfe then stood and turned to explain things to Sparrow and the professor, which was also a refresher to Terri and Sheriff Josephs. "This looks like a normal wooded area with a dirt road leading through it. There appear to be no monitors nor access controls other than an automatic gate control that is opened only by a phone call and a code.

"It looks like a normal fiberglass gate arm, but in reality it's made of a titanium alloy. There are also three bollards that could rise up out of the ground in half a second, which rise four feet high and are reinforced steel approximately a foot in diameter. So you see, access is not quite as easy as it appears."

Sparrow listened intently, and then made an observation. "That's all well and good, but what about the open woods on either side of the shack and gate arm? What would prevent people from just walking around it?"

"Good point," said Wolfe. "Actually, there used to be armed guards with machine guns scattered through the trees on both sides, and if someone tried to do that, they would be met with an unfriendly response."

"But what about now?" responded Sparrow. "Are there people in the woods now?"

"No," said Wolfe. "Instead there are electronic devices imbedded in the trees and the ground that send a signal to a central monitoring station at the main compound further on, and also to a remote monitoring site as well. In addition, there are cameras, for both day and night, as well as audio microphones. These are recorded and stored on tapes also at the monitoring station. If an intruder is detected, a board with a map of the place lights up with a red dot where the intrusion took place, and the video and audio can automatically rewind to the event the intrusion began.

It also simultaneously sends a signal to the person monitoring, or if no one is, to the owner of this estate warning of the intrusion."

"So," continued Sparrow, "is there anyone here to respond to the threat? Any *armed* people?"

"Unfortunately, no," said Wolfe. "However there are many automatic systems that can detect a person or persons entering the area illegally that can deploy countermeasures that would incapacitate any interlopers."

"*Incapacitate*," repeated Sparrow. "Interesting word."

"It is," said Wolfe.

"May I be so bold as to ask what the nature of the incapacitation is?" she said. "Is it pits dug in the ground? People nets sprung to capture them? Or maybe, more lethal measures?"

Wolfe smiled. "Let's just say that the measures are appropriate to the threat, and very effective. People will not be coming uninvited, I assure you."

"Good to know," she said, not happy that she didn't get a full read-in. "I'll stay out of the woods—for now."

"I highly recommend that you do," said Wolfe.

He continued his spiel as tour guide. "If you noticed the road, it looked like packed dirt, and the bridges looked like wooden structures." Sparrow nodded. The professor just continued looking out the window. "In reality," Wolfe explained, "they are steel-reinforced under the surfaces and on the bridges, and the road surface is made of an ultra-strong composite made to look like packed dirt. They are designed to easily support a fully loaded eighteen-wheel semi-trailer."

"Impressive," said Sparrow, still not pleased.

Wolfe continued. "You will see buildings coming up in a minute, both on the left and right sides of the road. On the left side you will see a grocery store, gas station, fire/rescue station, a security/police station, a recreation area and a hall with a swimming pool.

"There are also tennis courts, a fitness center with weight-lifting free weights and cardio machines, a bowling alley, a movie theater with two screens, a hospital/urgent care center, and other buildings including an administrative center."

"Looks like a city," said the professor, speaking for the first time. "At the end of the world. A dead city with multiple services and no people. Very weird. Creepy."

"It is a city," said Wolfe. "Complete with water, sewer, restaurants, and all supplies one might need in a small town. And yes, there are no people to provide services and no people to receive them. So, to your point, I'd have to agree. Except for the creepy part."

"And who's this all for?" asked Sparrow, looking out the window on the left side of the bus.

"If you look to your left," said Wolfe, "you'll see a large number of houses, made from materials and colors designed to fit in to this wooded environment in the least obtrusive manner."

"But where are the people?" asked Sparrow.

"Gone," said Wolfe. "There was a great battle that took place here not long ago, and people died—property was damaged or destroyed—and the members moved out and the place closed. It was ultimately put up for sale, and finally purchased by one man."

"Your anonymous friend," said Terri.

"That's right," said Wolfe.

"So, where is he?" said Sparrow.

"Not here," said Wolfe. "He operates this place remotely, or has people who do so. But the place is devoid of humans right now, except us."

"Great," said Terri. "So how do we get food, and use the facilities you just showed us?"

Wolfe took an unusual looking radio from his belt and held it up. "This allows me to communicate directly with the operators and they will turn on and operate anything we need, including automatic food preparation with just about anything one would want. Just order it like you would from a takeout restaurant. And it's pretty good, too," he finished.

Josephs finally spoke up. "So, you telling me that we're all alone here?"

"That's right, Ed. And I aim to keep it that way for as long as we need."

"And how long is that?" asked Sparrow.

Wolfe looked at her, then said, "As long as we need. But hopefully, not long."

# chapter 71

Unbeknownst to the passengers of the bus, Eino Loukkala, Coroner and amateur commando, had caught up to the bus by the time it had reached the guard shack at the entrance to the compound. As the passengers waited for Wolfe to enter the shack and activate the lift gate, Eino parked his car in the trees behind the bus where it couldn't be seen.

Then he quietly sprinted to the back of the bus, his weapons in a carrier slung over his back, where he climbed on and grabbed the hand rails on the back. From there he scrambled quickly to the top of the bus and laid flat as the bus entered the wooded compound. With his black clothing, soft black shoes, black gloves, and black head-covering, he became virtually invisible to any watchers.

Just before the bus stopped at the end of the road, Eino hopped off the bus and melted into the woods behind the village buildings. There he scouted the area, looking for any signs of interlopers or waiting assassins, though he doubted they could get into the compound without getting caught—or shot.

Wolfe stood at the front of the bus before anyone got off. "Here's what we're going to do," he said. "I'm going to assign living quarters, and show you the mess hall, which is next to the recreation hall. That's where meals will be prepared and where we'll eat together. You can also take snacks from the hall to your residences to eat in the evenings or at a later time.

"Professor Dejanovic will continue working on his invention, and his lab will be set up in the recreation hall. He may need assistance so some of us will help him as needed. Sheriff Josephs' unit will continue to provide perimeter security, but they will only need to deploy out to a hundred yards or so, as the remainder of the compound has electronic detection and intrusion countermeasures throughout.

"Sheriff Josephs will take care of providing relief for those deployed, and they will remain as a self-contained unit. They are not to be bothered. Keep in mind that we must consider we are in hostile territory, and any intrusion should be considered to be deadly, and we will need to respond accordingly. Understood?"

Terri, Sparrow, Professor Dejanovic and Sheriff Josephs all nodded. They all had weapons, except the professor.

"Good," said Wolfe. "The housing is on the right as you get off the bus. They are referred as 'cottages,' and each is named after a bird. Terri will be in Starling, Sparrow will be in, well, Sparrow," he said smiling. She didn't. "Sheriff Josephs," he continued, "will be in Ibis, I will be in Condor, and the professor will be in Blue Jay. Stan," he nodded at the bus driver, "will sleep in one of the beds on the bus."

"There are many other cottages but they are all empty. But we can use them if we need to. They're all clean and operational with electricity, water, sewer and heat and cooling. No phones or TV in any of them however. So don't look. We're here to work—and survive."

Josephs' team fanned out, one guarding the road in, one on each side of the compound, one at the boat dock which was right on Lake Superior, and one who was the team leader who stayed with the Sheriff and Wolfe. The professor unloaded his materials and carried them to the recreation hall to set up his lab.

Meanwhile Josephs, Wolfe, Terri, Sparrow and the SWAT team leader went to the security monitoring center. It was a clean room with fluorescent lights, a couple of padded chairs with rollers on the bottom, and a bank of monitors with maps of the compound clearly displayed.

Wolfe had been briefed by the owner on how they worked. He explained to the others. "The compound is divided into sectors, with video, audio, and underground pressure sensor lights that display if activated.

"For example, if an intruder tries to get in, one of the sensors will activate and sound an audible alarm here and to my portable radio. It will also send an alarm signal to a central alarm monitoring off site, that is monitored 24/7. They also have the capacity to respond if nobody here does. But it obviously will take a lot longer, due to our remote location. So it's kind of up to us."

Sparrow asked, "How does the map work?"

Wolfe said, "If an intruder trips an alarm, a colored dot will appear in the sector and at the location within the sector where the trip occurred. Also an audible alarm will sound, unless silenced. Speakers hidden in the trees will play a recorded warning message that they are trespassing on private property and must leave immediately, as deadly force is authorized. Also, a recording will begin of the cameras and audio devices at the site.

"If the intruder continues and trips another sensor, a yellow dot will appear and a voice alarm will sound. However, if a countermeasure is deployed, a red dot will appear, meaning the person has been incapacitated in some manner and we will need to deactivate the rest of the sector alarms to retrieve the trespasser."

"Incapacitate," repeated Sparrow. "Interesting word. I think I've said that before. Care to elaborate now?"

Wolfe nodded. "Sure. That could mean anything from being rendered unconscious, trapped via a snare of some sort, or even killed if the threat persists."

Terri asked, "What methods would be used to render the intruder unconscious?"

Wolfe said, "Oh, gas most likely—sprayed directly in the intruder's face and surroundings. Usually sprayed up from the ground in a small explosive charge to disseminate it quickly. Very effective, in the demonstrations I've seen."

"Oh," said Terri. "Great."

Just then one of the intrusion alarms went off. It was a green dot, in sector seven, behind the rec hall. They watched the dot move. Josephs had the leader send his closest team member toward the location of the dot, with another one moving over for backup.

Then a louder, more persistent alarm sounded as the green dot turned yellow. It was approaching the back of the rec hall. Then the leader's radio crackled and the voice of the officer came over the speaker. "Cancel further security measures," he said. "I have two subdued and in custody."

"Two?" said Josephs.

They all ran outside around back of the rec center and stopped short by what they saw. The security officer had handcuffed two people together and was bringing them in. One was a tall, gangly man with a large Adam's apple and a beaked nose, all dressed in black, who was handcuffed to a small boy wearing pants, shoes and a short-sleeved shirt.

"Look what I found?" the tall man said, smiling.

Wolfe shook his head. "Eino! What the heck are *you* doing out here?"

Terri saw the small boy and said, "Quinn! You're OK," and ran toward him.

Quinn said, "Of course I am. I can take care of myself, you know."

"I know," she said, "but where have you . . ."

"Let's get those cuffs off them," said Josephs, walking up to Eino.

Quinn said, "OK," and slid the handcuff off over his small hand. "I was just being polite. Didn't want to cause a ruckus by running away."

By the time the officer got his key out to remove Eino's cuff, his was already off, too. He handed the handcuffs to the officer and held up his own key, a big grin on his face. "I always carry one of these, for emergencies," he said.

The officer just shook his head and replaced the cuffs in their pouch.

"All right," said Wolfe, "we'd better reset the alarms in sector seven." He went into the building and did so, then came back outside and confronted Eino and Quinn. "Now what I want to know, is how you two managed to slip in as far as you did before getting caught?"

"It wasn't too hard," said Quinn. "I just kind of felt where the sensors were and avoided that area."

"You felt . . ." Wolfe began. Then thought for a moment. "Why didn't you avoid the one you triggered?" said Josephs.

"I figured that the response of the system would get progressively worse, and I didn't want to get shot, so I deliberately set it off," Quinn explained.

Wolfe looked at Eino, who shrugged his shoulders. "I caught up with the bus, then when you stopped, jumped on top of the bus and rode in with you all. Then I got off just before the bus stopped, and headed into the woods to look for trouble. And I found him as he was coming towards me. Good thing I found him first."

"I think it's more like, good thing he found *you* first, Eino," said Josephs. "You were closer in and more likely to trigger a volatile response than Quinn."

"Guess you're right about that," said Eino. "Better count my lucky stars."

# chapter 72

The KGB assassin bounced and twisted through the wooded country by dead reckoning. Her compass helped some, but it was impossible to keep checking at every turn since she had to avoid trees and rocks, and occasional gullies.

She was going as fast as she could in her Land Rover, but it was such a jarring experience she had to keep slowing down, especially if she didn't want to break a spring or axle.

Her frustration mounted due to her failure to find Wolfe and his compatriots. The airport fiasco almost cost her her life, had she not ditched her plans to verify passengers either on the bus or the airplane.

They may have been on either the first bus, or even on the second or third—or maybe they were still at the jail and never left. Such speculation was pointless, so she decided to press on and go for broke. If they weren't where she was headed, it was over anyway.

Regrouping in the dining hall, Wolfe and his crew went to the automated machines and began making selections. While they were doing that, Terri began looking around for a jacket Quinn could wear.

"Don't worry," Quinn said to Terri, when he figured out what she was doing. "I'm fine. The cold doesn't bother me. I've been used to being out in it most of my life. Besides," he said. "I doubt you'll find anything my size here anyway."

Wolfe said, "He's right, Terri. The most you'll find here is a blanket he can wrap around him. I can get one if you want."

"That's OK," said Quinn. "Really. I'm fine." He smiled an impish smile at Terri. She finally shrugged her shoulders, her mothering instinct temporary sidelined.

The food was brought to the table and they all dug in, being quite hungry. Strangely, Quinn ate some, but not as much as Terri had expected. She wondered if something was wrong with him, being so small and all, but said nothing. He obviously didn't want any attention, but she decided to keep an eye on him, just the same.

Changing tack, she put her investigative reporter hat on. "So what happened to you, Quinn?" she said. "I realize it was dangerous when the crazy lady pulled her gun and threatened to kill us, and it made sense for you to run off until the danger passed. But where did you go? The Sheriff's search and rescue team, along with their tracking dogs, weren't able to pick up your trail. They searched everywhere, but couldn't find any trace of you."

Quinn just smiled. "Evasive maneuvers I learned over time," he said. "Duck and run, misdirection, false scents, hide in plain sight—just be somewhere the pursuers aren't," he said cryptically.

"But why didn't you want to be found?" she asked. "I mean, they were only looking out for your own good—to take you to safety."

"Yeah," said Quinn. "Well, you knew that but I didn't. I didn't know any of those men and I didn't know what their intentions were. I've been chased by men and dogs before and believe me, *they* didn't have my welfare in mind at all."

Terri got a quizzical look on her face, and was just about to ask another question, when Wolfe cut in.

"I think he's had enough questions for a while," he said. "Let's let him get settled and get some rest. He must be tired. Terri, he can stay in your cottage, if it's OK with you and him, as long as you don't pester him with questions and let him be."

"Sure. He can stay with me," said Terri. "That OK with you, Quinn?"

Quinn gave her a quick smile. "Sure, Miss Terri," he said. "I promise I'll be good."

Terri thought that that response was a little strange, like everything about the boy, but she temporarily dismissed her feelings.

"Great," she said. "Then let's get you settled. C'mon," she said as she offered her hand. Quinn walked up beside her, but did not take her hand. Terri was puzzled again. Very little Quinn did made sense to her. More and more questions that she could not ask—yet.

Viktoriya Dunayevsky, KGB assassin, kept plowing through the woods until she reached a clearing. She abruptly stopped just before she left the cover of the trees, and assessed the situation. From the recon maps she had studied about Wolfe's previous battle in this area, this looked like the right place.

There was a road coming from the south that ended in a turn-around circle right in front of her. There was a guard shack with a gate arm that blocked further movement up the road. The guard shack appeared empty, but at this point, she was going to take nothing for granted.

She sat and watched for some time, looking for any furtive movement, or any signs that the entrance was being watched. She saw none. Carefully she got out of her vehicle and probed the edge of the forest, looking for signs of activity, including broken twigs or foliage, disturbed ground, or footprints.

She saw nothing. Until she came to the car. Actually, it was an old hearse. It was black as a hearse would be, but it appeared to have had some modifications, such as bigger tires, stronger suspension, and probably a bigger engine, due to the large, dual exhausts that she also observed.

She felt the hood of the car to see how long it had been there. It wasn't hot, but it wasn't cold, either. A little warm, indicating that had been driven, maybe an hour ago, but not longer. She looked around some more before she went back to her Land Rover.

She thought about what type of security equipment and procedures such a place might have. She opened her valise and pulled out the documents that contained information on the previous owners of the compound.

She knew that there had to be electronics installed, probably very current technology and sophisticated ones at that. She would have to find a way to circumvent them if she ever hoped to penetrate without being discovered.

But penetrate, she would.

# chapter 73

Everyone got settled in their cottages after eating, and Eino got the cottage named Hummingbird. He liked the name. As Coroner he hovered over his "clients" in the morgue, as he performed his professional duties on the dead.

However, with his new avocation he silently hovered as well, flitting from place to place, moving at once quickly, and then hanging motionless in one spot, sensing—watching. Yes, he thought. It would suit him well.

Wolfe, Terri, Quinn and the professor returned to the rec hall, now referred to as the 'lab.' Josephs and Sparrow were assigned to walk the compound, performing internal security in case someone slipped by the other security measures.

Professor Jonathan Dejanovic gathered his equipment and supplies, as well as his extensive notes and plans, and set up shop on numerous tables. He sorted and arranged items until he had them exactly the way he wanted. When he was completed, he looked up at Wolfe. "What now?" he said.

Wolfe said, "How long before you can complete your invention or inventions, Professor?"

The professor shrugged. "That depends on what you mean by being completed," he said. "The preliminary demonstration projects have been completed. They did what they were supposed to do, and showed that my theory works, and that I have found a way to tap into so-called, 'dark energy,' though it is called other things too, like ether, for example."

"I understand, Professor," said Wolfe. "But what about the other devices you had talked about? The device to power electric cars? Or the device to provide free electricity to homes? Or businesses? What about those?"

"Oh, those," said the professor dismissively. "Those are on the drawing board right now. I haven't had time to work on them yet. The casings have to be designed, higher power outputs need to be checked for safety measures, and so on. I'm not an engineer, so I will need someone to do those types of things.

"But the key thing is to make sure that the software and hard - ware are in place to limit the amount of dark energy we draw. As I said before, the availability of this energy is limitless, and so would the use of it be limitless. Theoretically, if we kept the energy level coming without any checks on the flow, it could conceivably keep growing in brightness and intensity until it incinerated the whole earth. Or the whole solar system, for that matter. Or . . ."

"I get your drift," said Wolfe. "It can be dangerous."

"Very," said the professor, only just now seeming to realize the tiger he had by the tail.

Wolfe thought about it for a minute, then said, "What do you have right now that would be so valuable to these people who are after you?"

"Basically," said the professor, "it's my circuit." He picked up the demonstration model and held it in his hand. It was the two-inch square piece of black plastic with a plastic knob in the center, attached to a small piece of plywood with a small circuit board with wires and other small items attached. "This is what opens the portal to dark energy. This is what I presume people are after."

Terri looked at Wolfe. "Seriously?" she said. "*That's* what all the fuss is about?"

"I believe so," said the professor. "This is what opens the reservoir of limitless energy."

"Well I guess that would do it, wouldn't it Wolfe?" said Terri.

"I would say so," said Wolfe.

Then Terri said, "That's not your only one, is it?"

The professor got a strange look on his face. "Well, actually, it is. I'm not going to let copies of this float around for people to steal, reverse engineer, and make some for themselves only—to *control* energy. Energy should be free. And that's why I'm going to give it to the world. Free energy. Not to just a handful of greedy elitist moneygrubbers," he finished, indignantly.

There was a pause as they all looked at each other. Except for Quinn. He was quiet and noncommittal—just observing. Or so it seemed.

Terri chimed in, trying to be positive. "That's great, Jon," she said, trying to sound supportive. "But have you figured out just exactly *how* you're going to do this? Give it to the world?"

The professor looked pensive. "Well, no, but it can't be that hard, can it? I mean, I'm giving it away *free*. I would think people would be beating down my *door* to get one. I'll make a bunch of the devices, make a press announcement, and then just hand them out—like candy on Halloween, right?"

Terri looked at Wolfe and shook her head. Then she turned and addressed the professor. "Ah, have you thought about all those moneygrubbing elitists who might knock *down* your door instead, and *take* it from you? And take your plans, and then kill you? Or maybe they would kidnap you and force you to make your devices for them? Lots of them? And show them how to make them?

Have you ever given that scenario a thought?" Her friendly and supportive tone began to sound sarcastic and shrill towards the end of her statement, try as she might not to do so.

"Oh, no, I would never do that," said the professor. "I would never help them do that. I would destroy it before I would let *that* happen."

Wolfe looked at the professor, incredulous at the naivety of this learned man. "But, professor, what if they tortured you to get you to cooperate?"

"I still wouldn't do it," said the professor stubbornly. "They couldn't make me."

"OK," said Wolfe. "Just for the sake of an argument, let's say you could withstand hours and days and weeks and months of torture and still refuse to help them." The professor's eyes were getting wider and wider as the significance of reality was beginning to sink in. "So let's say they change tactics. Let's say instead of torturing *you*, they decide to torture someone you love—In front of you? Say, a family member? Like your mother?"

The professor's eyes were darting back and forth, as he was imagining such a thing happening. His breathing was becoming shallow and more rapid.

"Or if you don't have family you care about, what about an innocent child, even one you don't know?" continued Wolfe.

Suddenly the professor became quite agitated. "Stop it!" he shouted. "*Stop it*! Don't say anymore!" His eyes were scrunched shut and he had his hands over his ears, and was shaking his head back and forth, trying to get these now vivid images out of his brain.

"Sorry, professor," said Terri. "We had to make you see how dangerous this is. A great deal of effort and lost lives have gone into either capturing you and your invention, or killing you and all those around you—just to stop you from doing what you plan to do. They would rather kill you and destroy your invention than take the risk of it getting out to the world for the benefit of others. They would rather do that, than lose control of their vast power."

Professor Dejanovic was stunned. He looked around like he was seeing life for the first time. "I, I guess I didn't realize life was so brutal. I've lived in my quantum world of physics pretty much my whole life. It was a safe place for me. I wasn't a social person at all. I was terribly shy. So I buried myself in my studies. Electrons, neutrons, positrons—they became my friends."

Terri watched the professor try to make sense of things. "They may be your friends, but they are dangerous to many of the world leaders and corporate magnates. They fear that your little sub-atomic particles will ultimately uproot the world's economies and topple governments. That they will change the world as they know it. As *we* know it."

"I fear that's what's happening," said Professor Dejanovic.

"That's *your* fear," said Terri. "And others fear ruination of their carefully crafted system of power. It seems that fear rules the day."

"I don't get it," said the professor.

"Your quanta are causing fear on both sides," said Terri.

Suddenly Wolfe joined in. "Sounds like a severe case of quantum fear," he said. They both looked at him and nodded. He headed out to check on Eino and the security detail.

# chapter 74

Eino Loukkala, Coroner and amateur sleuth, slipped quietly out of his cottage. Dressed all in black, he slung the strap of his weapons case over his shoulder and looked around until he had found a perfect observation spot, high up a tall white pine tree. Though tall and skinny, Eino was wiry and very strong. Climbing the tree, while not easy, was accomplished quickly and quietly in the deep night of the woods.

Once settled, he pulled out a small telescope and checked the area surrounding the grounds, looking for any signs of intrusion. He was able to spot Josephs and Sparrow moving across the central area, around the buildings, and near the perimeter of the open area. They seemed to be engrossed in conversation as they looked around.

He could also see a ways into the woods surrounding the compound, but beyond a few dozen yards, trees blocked his sight. He did, however, spot three of the Sheriff's security team, one on each side of the compound, and a third down near the marina on Lake Superior. The one down the road was out of sight, presumably closer to the guard shack. He then continued his surveillance.

Elsewhere, *Vikki* Dunayevsky, assassin and psycho on a single -minded mission, had been skulking around the perimeter of the woods surrounding the compound. Because of her intelligence research prior to her arrival, she knew the layout of the area quite well, and knew the likeliest spots for intrusion equipment to be placed.

She also knew that each one had to be periodically inspected, and sometimes adjusted, and that would require the physical pres-ence of security personnel to come to each such location.

And to do that would leave traces of those inspections, such as foliage trampled down, branches broken, footprints or other disturbances around the area. She was good at tracking and looking for such signs, even in the dark.

She also had infrared goggles and a night vision scope that am-plified ambient light thousands of times, giving her great advantage.

She continued working her way around the side of the compound, identifying many security intrusion detectors along the way, and giving them wide berth. Finally she had made her way all the way around the compound and had come to the shore of Lake Superior.

She stopped and listened. She knew there had to be a sentry somewhere around there, so she would have to wait for that person to make himself visible to her. And that would be his big mistake.

Terri had taken Quinn to her cottage after the demonstration and conversation with Professor Dejanovic. She thought it might be a bit much for him, plus she had some questions for the boy. She found some chocolate chip cookies in the cupboard and milk in the fridge.

After checking to make sure it was fresh, she poured him a glass, and prepared him a plate. Quinn sat in a wooden chair at a square wooden table, and readily accepted the offering. He then proceeded to consume it with vigor.

Terri decided that this was the right time to ask her questions. "So, Quinn," she began. Quinn looked up at her, but continued to chew his cookies. "Tell me. Where did you go after you fled the assassin, and how did you get up here?"

Quinn nodded his head and kept eating. He held up a finger indicating he needed a minute to answer. Finally finishing his cookie and after a good swallow of milk, he sat back in the chair and shrugged. "I don't know," he said, noncommittally. "I just ducked and dodged, and used tactics I have used my whole life to evade adults."

"Where'd you learn those tactics?" she asked, her reporter's instincts kicking into high gear.

"Don't know, really, Miss Terri. I mean, I can't remember when I didn't know them. I don't remember anyone specifically teaching me. I just seemed to know how to do them—kind of instinctively, you know?"

"Hmm," she said. His answer sounded evasive, she thought.

Quinn was going to be a tougher nut to crack than she had imagined.

"Fine," she said. "Let's switch gears. How did you get from where you ran away, to this location where Eino found you? That's probably thirty miles or so. How'd you *do* that?"

Quinn again shrugged dismissively. "Hitchhiked," he said. "Got a ride from a man up as far as Big Bay, and walked the rest of the way."

"Well, that's wonderful," Terri said, suppressing her frustration. "But how did you know where to go? Wolfe didn't tell any of us where we were going until the bus was already on the way up here. How did *you* know?"

"I didn't really," said Quinn. "I mean, how many possibilities are there up here? There aren't that many houses, there aren't hardly any stores, and it's mostly woods everywhere from here. I just had to get away *somewhere*, and this man was going to Big Bay, and that seemed as good a place as any."

"OK," said Terri, not giving up. "But what drove you to walk through the spooky forest away from Big Bay? I mean, how would you know to go through there, and how did you know what was up there?" She knew she had him now.

But Quinn had an answer for everything. "Well, I could clearly see that the bus wasn't there. That thing sticks out like a sore thumb up here. So I asked around to see what else was up here where a big bus could go?

"Nobody seemed to know, until one nice lady at the gas station told me that there was a place up here where people used to go—big caravans of limos and expensive cars. She told me that the place was closed down now, though.

"So I thanked her and started walking. I figured that if you guys were going to hide somewhere, then that would be the place to go. I mean, where else is there?"

Where else, indeed, thought Terri.

# chapter 75

Far away from the Michigan compound, Devon Barnes was sitting in the Pentagon in a chair across from a very concerned military man—General Chester A. Birchmont, head of NACOM— North American Command. His job was to deploy military operations in North America whenever overt foreign military actors threatened the United States of America. He was drilling a look at Barnes, unhappy at the information he was receiving.

"What do you mean, you lost him?" General Birchmont snapped. "You had all the resources in the world to deploy Wolfe to find this professor, take his invention that he was working on for DARPA, and bring both to me. Wasn't that your task, *Mister* Barnes?"

"Yes, it was, sir," replied Barnes, as respectfully as he could. "But the professor quit working on DARPA's project, which he never finished. Then he started working on his own secret device, and when he was fired, he had already removed his own secret device and he proceeded to disappear into thin air."

"And so you lost him and the device?"

"In a manner of speaking, yes," said Barnes.

"And please tell me why you haven't completed that relatively simple task. Wait. Let me guess. Is it because you've had this long running feud with Agent Clayton Wolfe, and you wanted to make sure this would be a lose-lose situation for him, and a win-win situation for you? Is that why?"

"No, sir," said Barnes. "I have not let my personal life . . ."

"Stow it," snapped the General, cutting Barnes off mid-sentence.

"I don't want to hear any of your lame excuses. You knew where the professor was for some time, but you waited for Wolfe to get sucked into a losing situation so you could 'retire' him 'with extreme prejudice' and then bring the prize directly to me yourself, without getting your hands dirty, isn't that right? But you waited too long, and the professor skipped town, and you lost him and the device. Isn't that what happened, *Mister* Barnes?"

Barnes upper lip had a gleam of nervous sweat forming. The sharp crease in his pants and the starched collar of his expensive shirt were beginning to show signs of being less than crisp. He was not used to feeling as uncomfortable as he was now.

"It's not like that, General," he responded lamely.

"No, it's *just* like that, Barnes. Now what I want from you is this professor, alive or dead—and right now I don't care which it is— and I want that invention in here too, or you're gonna find yourself at a post so remote that the Eskimos will have to go *north* to find you! Do you understand? Do I make myself *clear*?"

"Yes, sir, I . . ."

But the General cut him off again. "No, I don't think you do. I want *your* ass on the front line of this little endeavor. I want you *personally* to find Wolfe *and* the professor, and that little student helper of his, if she's still around, and bring them and the inventions to me. I want to tie up this little operation and I want it to go away, for good. Understand? And I want them here yesterday! Now get out!"

"Yes, sir," said Barnes. He rose and turned in one swift move, and exited the General's office as fast as he could.

Barnes climbed onboard the Agency jet along with his crack hit team of sixteen ultra-lethal mercenary assassins, and closed the door. Once they were all belted in, the jet took off and headed at breakneck speed toward Marquette. "Where can we land up there?" asked the pilot.

"K.I. Sawyer Air Force Base," said Barnes. "We'll have choppers standing by to take us the rest of the way." The pilot nodded and set his course accordingly. Barnes pulled out his satellite phone that looked like a giant brick, and made a call to his inside man.

The man on the other end answered softly. "Yes?" he said. "We're on the way," said Barnes. "How's it look?"

"All calm," said the man. "Everyone's in place. People are in bed or getting there. Should be easy pickings. I'm keeping tabs on the professor. The girl's not here."

Suddenly Barnes was alert. "Not there?" he echoed. "Why? Where is she?"

The man laughed. "She got free and jumped off the bus. Right into the hands of the Coroner who took her to the morgue and handcuffed her there for safe keeping. She's no problem now."

"Unfortunately, you're wrong about that," said Barnes. "I need her freed, and I need her dead. She knows too much. *Way* too much."

"Not much I can do about that up here. We're all tied up and I have no transport, even if I could get away."

"Looks like I'm gonna have to do it when I get there. I'll drop off one of my guys to take care of it and we'll get by with fifteen instead of sixteen. That should still be plenty, from the sounds of it."

"I agree," said the man. "Gotta go now. Someone's coming to relieve me. Out."

Barnes was not happy. Another problem to deal with. Well, that's why he got paid the big bucks, he thought. Always putting out fires, solving unsolvable problems. What's one more to deal with?

Vikki was hidden at the marina behind some boxes in the back of the boat building. She had worked her way close enough to hear the security guard's conversations on his walkie-talkie, but there had been nothing of interest so far. Just status reports and coffee runs. He took care of his bathroom breaks in the boathouse bathroom.

Then something happened that made her sit up and take notice.

"Unit five," came the call over the radio.

"Five," the guard answered, keying his radio. "Looks like we're gonna have company your way."

"What? Why?" said the guard. "Nothing's supposed to be coming all night."

"Special supply run," came the reply over the radio. "Just found out. We hadn't been told about it. Slip up somewhere, I guess."

"Great," said the guard. "What's coming in and when?"

"Don't know," came the communication. "Some kind of odd transport, somewhere around three a.m."

"Seriously?" said the guard, obviously unhappy about the development.

"Sorry," said the man on the radio. "We just got notified."

"Yeah, right," said the guard. "I'm out."

The KGB assassin heard it all and suddenly her way in was on the way. The boat would be a perfect distraction as the supplies were being unloaded, to slip in and locate her targets. First the professor and his inventions, then Wolfe. She could hardly wait. If it all worked out well, her failings might even be forgiven. Maybe she would get a medal. Probably too much to hope for, but she was very good, and who knows. Stranger things have happened. She checked her watch and then hunkered down and waited for the boat.

After Wolfe met with Eino, he went back to the cottage to see Terri and Quinn. Terri was just tucking Quinn in.

"He needs his sleep," said Terri softly. "We'll have to be quiet."

"Of course," said Wolfe. "He must be one tuckered out little hellion."

Sheriff Josephs and Sparrow had gotten the update on the supply delivery, as well as all of the security detail since they were all on the same radio frequency. Eino didn't receive that information however, as he did not have a radio and nobody knew where he was. Nor did Wolfe nor Terri get the info, as they were occupied in the cottage with Quinn.

# chapter 76

Barnes and his crew of assassins were making good time. He had told the jet captain to "kick it in the ass," so to speak, so he did just that. The trip would take less than two hours, and that would give him time to grab the chopper and make it to the compound while everyone was still sleeping. Perfect timing, he thought.

He had made another call to Sawyer AFB to have a Coast Guard helicopter available for his guy to be flown to the hospital helipad in Marquette, which would put him very close to the morgue. There he could steal a car, modify it in a way to make it 'unsafe at any speed,' and take care of that problem pretty smoothly.

Terri had tucked Quinn into bed in the second bedroom, and he seemed fast asleep. Wolfe and Terri were sitting on the couch in the living room, too tired to sleep, but also keyed up for what was likely to come, although they weren't sure what that would be.

Wolfe looked at Terri and said, "Tell me about Brent."

"Who?" said Terri, surprised at the sudden question.

Wolfe smiled. "You know, Brent. Your boyfriend—or whatever you call him."

Terri looked at him, not quite knowing what to say. Then, gathering herself up, she said simply, "Brent. That's what I call him. That's his *name*."

"OK, back to my original statement. Tell me about Brent."

"Why do you want to know?" she asked.

"Just curious," he said. "You've been dating for a while, and I figured he must be a pretty good guy for you to be with him, so I wanted to know what kind of a guy he was. Tall? Handsome? Funny? Polite? Rich? Anything. What's he like?"

"I still don't know why you want to know," she said cautiously. Then she decided to answer him. "He's a nice guy, yes, good looking, not so tall, but average, has a good job as an accountant, drives a nice car, dresses well—basically a very decent guy. Now, why do you want to know?"

Wolfe said nothing, lost in thought for a minute, carefully choosing his words. "I wanted to know how serious it was between you two."

Now it was Terri's turn to think. "And why do you want to know *that*?" she said, an impish smile forming on her face.

Wolfe shrugged his shoulders. "You know. Because we were serious about each other at the end of our last time together, and I just wondered if any of that was still left, or if you've totally moved on."

Terri turned on the couch to better face him. She looked him in the eye. "I moved on because you were nowhere to be found," she said. "And I got kind of lonely. Brent and I were both getting coffee at the same place one day and there was a mix-up in the order—I got his and he got mine. By the time we got it straightened out, we had a laugh, and then he suddenly asked me out. I was taken by surprise at first, but then I thought, he was nice, a good looking guy, and he had a pleasant personality, so why not? So we started dating."

"Is it serious?" asked Wolfe again.

"Well for pity sake," said Terri now flustered. "I don't know. It's nice, it's comfortable, it's . . ."

Wolfe cut in. "But is there fire? Sparks? Passion? That's what I'd like to know. Is there *heat*?"

"*Heat*?" she exclaimed. "How can you ask me that? That's very personal, and none of your business."

"It is if I want to be back with you again," he said, deadly serious now.

This took Terri by surprise, though he had given her plenty of signs of where he was going with this line of inquiry.

"Do you, Clay? *Do* you want to be back with me again?"

"I think I've made that pretty clear. But just to make sure there's no doubt, yes. I do."

"Wow," she said. "I had no idea. I mean, with Waitress Jenny trying to charm you and your apparent willingness to be seduced by a college professor/KGB assassin, well—I would have thought you had your hands pretty full, no pun intended."

"OK," said Wolfe. "Jenny just likes to flirt, and Vikki . . . well, she seemed to take a fancy to me, at least until I found her trying to interrogate and probably poison me. That took the edge off a bit."

There was a long pause, then Terri said, "Yes."

Wolfe looked at her, searching her eyes again. "Yes, what?" Terri looked intently at him. "Yes, there is still something between us—you and me."

"And?" said Wolfe.

"And there's no fire in my relationship with Brent. It's just—nice. That's all."

Wolfe smiled a warm smile. "That's good," he said.


One of the Sheriff's security detail looked around to see if anyone was watching. His name was Hal, and he was also Barnes' *guy* on the inside. Seeing no one around, he silently went over to the housing unit and began checking the cottages to see who was where, under the guise of a security check.

He noted the names on the cottages, which was the only way to identify each one since they all looked the same and had no numbers on them.

First he checked Condor, but nobody was in there. He didn't know who was assigned to that one, so he moved on to the next one which was Sparrow and he knocked on that door. No one answered there, either.

Hell's bells, he thought. Isn't anyone where they should be? This is never going to work if they're all scattered, roaming the compound. He was getting nervous.

Next he checked Ibis and Hummingbird, but both were empty. *Damn*, he said to himself. *Somebody's* got to be home. When he checked Blue Jay, he again found no one there. He moved on to the last one.

The name on the cottage was Starling. "Security check," he said as he knocked on the door. He saw Wolfe and Terri through the window. Bingo.

Wolfe opened the door. "Security check?" he said. "When did we start doing that?"

"Ah, just tonight," he said nervously. "Sheriff authorized it just to make sure everyone's OK. People on edge, I guess. Sorry to bother you."

"Just doing your duty," said Wolfe. "Goodnight."

The deputy decided not to push his luck. He knew where Wolfe was, and that was good enough. No point in raising suspicion at this point. He went back to his post, pulled out his satellite phone, and called Barnes.

"Yes?" said Barnes, speaking into his own satellite phone on the jet.

"I have what you need."

"Excellent. What've you got?"

# chapter 77

"All the cottages have bird names," said Hal. "That's the only way to identify them. There's the name of the bird and a wood carving in the shape of the bird on the front of each cottage, next to the door."

"OK, go ahead," said Barnes.

"The key one is the professor, and he's supposed to be in Blue Jay. But he's not there."

"So where the hell is he?"

"I don't know," said the deputy, "but I'll keep looking. Terri was in Starling, though, when I went there. Wolfe was there too."

"A twofer. Excellent. Next?"

"Nobody else was in their cottage, so I don't know which is which. Nobody told me. I was just sent to a post and told to keep my eyes open."

"That's all right. The rest won't matter for long," said Barnes. "As long as I get the professor, his inventions, and that damned Wolfe. I want him bad. *Real* bad. And I'm absolutely sure that this night is going to be the last one for him on this bloody planet."

"Yes, sir," said Hal. "Gotta go now."

Barnes clicked off and looked over his list. "This is going to be great," he said, more to himself than anyone else on the jet.

Just then the captain announced that they were nearing the air-space over K.I. Sawyer Air Force Base, a part of the Strategic Air Command that had a fleet of B -52 bombers always in the air with an arsenal of nuclear bombs. It was part of the Triad of responses to nuclear attack by other countries.

That's what made it a little tricky to fly a civilian plane onto the base, even one approved by the CIA. If it wasn't one of the military's planes, it was viewed with serious attention. The captain of the jet knew all the protocols, though, and they were cleared to land without incident.

As soon as they did, they were searched, and the plane was gone over with a fine-tooth comb to make sure that nothing dangerous or illicit was being transported onto the base.

Satisfied, they were all released with their weapons to board the two helicopters—one military, heading straight to the compound, and one Coast Guard, unknowingly taking a killer to the hospital heliport to carry out his assignment.

Devon Barnes was in his glory now, the excitement of the chase and ultimate killing of his nemesis, Clayton Wolfe, now closer than ever. That ragtag group of misfits would never be a match for Barnes and his highly skilled, highly trained killers who were extremely capable and extremely dedicated to their profession. And extremely well-paid. Wolfe was done. And Barnes would be there to watch it happen, live and in color.

The Coast Guard helicopter began its approach to the Marquette County hospital heliport and came in for a smooth, soft landing. The killer jumped out without a word, and proceeded to the hospital parking lot to find a car to steal.

It would not take long. The Coast Guard crew took off again, heading for their rounds, unaware of the mayhem they had just released on this unsuspecting city. Of course, this would be nothing compared to what was going to happen further north.

The killer found an appropriate car and hotwired it. He then drove it out of the lot and onto an empty warehouse parking lot, around the rear of the building. Quickly he opened his bag of tools and went to work to modify the vehicle from a safe, American car into a very unsafe deathtrap. It didn't take him long.

The man then drove the vehicle to the Coroner's Office, where the hapless Kara Dugan was handcuffed to a temporary bed and the very unhappy assistant to Eino Loukkala, one Doctor Aaron Beecher, was sound asleep on his own makeshift mattress.

Suddenly the ultra-quiet morgue erupted with a startling sound, that of a man banging on the door. "Open up," he shouted. "Emergency!"

Doctor Beecher jumped off of his mattress and stumbled to the door. "What is it?" he shouted, rubbing his eyes awake.

"I was sent to pick up Miss Kara Dugan," the man said, holding up an official government ID card with his photo on it. "It's an emergency."

# chapter 78

Beecher quickly unlocked the door and let the man in. He began looking for his handcuff key, when the man said, "I have one of my own." He unlocked Kara's cuffs and helped her up off the bed. "Thanks, Doc," he said as he helped Kara to the passenger side of the car. Then he went to the driver's side and got in, started the engine, and drove quickly away.

Doctor Beecher was relieved to see his charge gone. Now he could go back to his apartment and sleep like a normal human being. Tomorrow he was going to look for a position in a large city where none of this foolishness happened—where people were *civilized*.

The killer drove Kara to the entrance of the road that led to the professor's former hideout. He got out and led Kara around to the driver's side and helped her in.

"You know the way to the professor's place?" he asked.

Kara nodded that she did.

"OK," he said. "Just head up there and he'll be waiting for you. People who support you have made arrangements for you both to get away together, including transportation and money." Kara started to say something but he cut her off.

"No need to thank me. I'm just following orders. Just get up there as quickly as possible. There isn't much time. Everybody's looking for him." She nodded, put the car in gear, and drove away. She had been so nervous, then she was scared being handcuffed in the morgue, and now this. She didn't know what to think.

But she knew the way to the farmhouse where they had planned to stay, so she decided to go there and see if what the man was tell-ing her was true. If it wasn't, she had a commitment from Agent Fox, and she now had a car that she could use to get away from everything and start a new life somewhere else. Somewhere where people weren't trying to *kill* her.

Wolfe stepped outside the cottage where Terri and Quinn were staying, and pulled out his own satellite phone. He placed a call. A person answered. "We're ready. They'll be there any time now," he said. He got the acknowledgement, and put his phone away. Everything was in motion now. One way or another this was all going to be over soon. He hoped things would turn out the way he had planned. Often that was not the case.

The control center operator got the call from the supply boat that it would arrive shortly. He quickly told Josephs and Sparrow. Josephs went to Terri's cottage where he assumed, rightly, that Wolfe would be, and knocked on the door. "Rise and shine," he said.

Wolfe opened the door. "Supplies coming in," said Josephs.

"Things are set and in motion," said Wolfe. "You know what we have to do. Get Stan and your deputies on the bus and tell them to get out of here immediately. We'll meet you down by the marina."

"Let's hope for the best," said the Sheriff as he ran over to the team leader to give the order. Wolfe shut the door.

He turned to Terri, who was still sitting on the couch in a very mellow mood. "Things are coming to a head. I think it'll all work out, but everything's in motion and all things are moving targets. Let's hope we aren't among them."

Just then they heard a voice behind them. They turned around and saw Quinn standing in the bedroom doorway, fully clothed and alert. "I'm going too," he said, surprising both of them.

"No, you're not, Quinn," said Terri. "This is too dangerous. You stay here and stay out of sight. There could be a lot of commotion pretty soon, and you need to be safe."

"I'll be safe with you," said Quinn. "And besides," he continued before they could say anything, "you're going to need me." He had managed to find a jacket, and he had a duffle bag over his shoulder, presumably with all his worldly possessions in it.

Wolfe started to say something, but Quinn cut him off. "What are you two going to do, watch me all night? Handcuff me to the bed? Tie me up and gag me?"

They looked at each other. "Guess not," said Wolfe. "OK. Let's go."

Terri looked at him. "Are you *serious*? We can't take him along."

"You heard him," said Wolfe. "Besides—we're going to need him. He just said so. So I think we'd better take him at his word." Quinn smiled.

"Thanks, guys. You won't regret it. I even have a few surprises for you."

"Your whole existence is one big surprise," said Terri, under her breath. "OK, Quinn. Let's do this," she said finally.

"Great," he said. They all headed out the door together.

# chapter 79

Kara couldn't believe her luck! She had escaped twice, and was now on the road to see Jon Dejanovic. Her lover. He must have changed his mind about her. That was not surprising. He never had much in the way of convictions, one way or the other. No matter, she thought. She would wrap him around her little finger, get him to change his mind about giving away his invention, and get at least half for all her trouble. Yes, she was going to be rich. Maybe later she would find a handsome young guy to satisfy her personal

needs, but the meal ticket would stay. She was really on her way. The dirt road was bumpy and wasn't much more than two ruts in the grass. She was probably driving too fast, and the holes and bumps bounced the car around pretty good. But she didn't mind. The sooner she got there, the sooner her new life would begin and her old life would be over.

She was almost there. One more bend in the road and she would see the place they were calling their own.

Then she hit the brakes. Right across the middle of the two-rut road a small tree had fallen, blocking her way. She quickly jumped out of the car and ran over to it. She lifted one end of the tree and was moving it away from the car and off of the road when there was an inaudible click underneath the driver's seat. A circuit was closed, causing a huge explosion that knocked Kara flat and enveloped the car in a raging fireball.

Kara was bruised, but otherwise OK, except for the tremendous heat. She was in shock, but she still jumped up and ran away from the burning car to the farmhouse, up the steps, and into the kitchen, only to find that it was empty. Nobody was there, least of all, her boyfriend, Jon.

Suddenly it dawned on her. It had all been a ruse to lure her out there. To get her into a remote area where she could be murdered with no witnesses, and no identifiable body. She looked out at the car, still engulfed in flames, now unrecognizable, as she would have been if she had not had to stop for the fallen tree. She shuddered, then dropped to the floor, hugged her knees, and began to cry.

The crying did not last for long, though. She had not been crying for Jon or anyone else. She had been crying for herself and her crushed dreams. Well, she thought as she collected herself, that was over now. Maybe those dreams were gone, but she was a survivor, and she would make her own plans now—plans independent of anyone else.

Kara got up, looked around the kitchen. No phone. Then she looked around the farm property, behind the house, by the outhouse, and finally in the large barn/garage. There was no lock on the door, but it was large and heavy, and it opened only with great difficulty. But she finally got it open, and stood in the doorway, letting her eyes adjust to the darkness. The moon peeked out from under the clouds a little as she stood there, and illuminated the interior enough for her to navigate inside.

Careful to avoid dangerous farm implements, she finally made her way to the back of the barn and saw a dirty tarp covering something large. Venturing carefully forward, she took the edge of the tarp and slowly pulled it back. What she saw put a smile on her face. It was a tractor. She pulled the tarp the rest of the way off and then began looking at the controls, and to see if there was a key of some kind.

After careful examination, she found no key, but she did see a button on the dashboard. She decided to give it a try. She climbed into the driver's seat, put her hands on the steering and on the brake, clutch and gas pedals to see if they were reachable. Satisfied, she closed her eyes and pressed the button.

The engine of the tractor turned over a few times but didn't start. She let off the button. She waited a few seconds and tried again. Still nothing. Then she remember something she had seen her uncle do on his tractor to get it started, so she tried the same thing. She pushed the button again and this time she held it in as she pumped the gas pedal. At first it was the same result. But then, a few seconds later, the engine sputtered a few times and then came to life.

She pumped the gas pedal to keep the tractor running, and then let it idle as she took stock of where she was and what she was going to do. She looked at the shift lever and wondered what the configuration pattern was, since there was no diagram on the shifter. She had driven a stick shift before, but this would be purely an experiment.

Cautiously, she depressed the clutch, and moved the shift lever until she thought it might be in first gear. She gave it some gas to keep it from stalling, and slowly let out the clutch. To her surprise and chagrin, the tractor moved backwards and hit the rear wall of the barn. She quickly put the clutch in and hit the brakes. She made a note of the shift lever position and tried for a different gear, one hopefully moving forward this time.

After some unpleasant grinding sounds and a period of trial and error, she determined the shift pattern, found the switch for the headlights, and made her decision. She put the tractor in first gear, let out the clutch, and slowly moved forward out of the barn and down the dirt road. She kept it in first gear all the way down the path until she got to the paved road. Then she turned right, and headed back toward town.

Kara thought about what she would do. One thing was for sure. She was out of this place and away from everyone in it. She would start a new life. She had a credit card with no limit, which would only be good for a short while until the first bill came to her parents, but that would be long enough.

She would buy a one-way airplane ticket to Los Angeles, change her name, and hang out at UCLA until she found some students she could befriend and sponge off of until she could get a job and find a place of her own. No more people trying to kill her. No more government agents. No more KGB assassins. No more crazy Coroners with blow guns. No. She was done with all that.

And as she trundled along the two-lane blacktop country road heading toward town, mostly in second gear, she made her plans, and calmed down. She was in control of her life again. She had a plan. She was confident. She was a survivor.

And she would survive.

# chapter 80

The supply boat lights came into view, but the boat itself was not yet visible. Hal, the SWAT team deputy who was assigned to guard the entrance to the marina, tried to see the shape of the boat as it was coming in, but it was dark out, and all he could see were its lights.

He started to walk out to the edge of the dock to have a better look when Comrade Dunayevsky quickly slid around the boat house, pulled her silenced Makarov pistol and shot deputy Hal in the back, not knowing he was the traitor working with Barnes.

She quickly turned toward the central area of the compound when she suddenly stopped short. Standing right in front of her was her nemesis, Clayton Wolfe, and his girlfriend, Terri Sommers. And there was someone hiding behind Terri—someone peeking out from behind her. It was that brat kid, Quinn, she thought. The one who had caused her shot to go awry. The one who disrupted all her plans. Well, that wouldn't happen this time.

Eino was still in his tree, when he saw Viktoriya come into view and shoot the deputy. He was too far away to get a clear shot with his blow gun, and there was too much movement of the target to get a good shot with his firearm. He would have to get closer.

Much closer.

The KGB assassin's gun was already raised and aimed right at Wolfe's heart. "Well, well, *Clay*. That's what your lovers call you, isn't it? *Clay*? We meet again. Under less pleasant circumstances,

I imagine—at least for you," she said, an evil smile crossing her otherwise beautiful face. "The one that got away—but not for long."

Viktoriya started walking towards the three of them, now less than six feet away—then five, then four. Then she stopped. Terri was slowly inching away from Wolfe, to his left. Quinn followed her, remaining tucked carefully behind her. Wolfe knew he could not draw his weapon and fire before the assassin did. He would be dead before it could clear its holster.

Vikki smiled her wicked smile. "Pity, Clay. Your time's up. I wish I could prolong the last minutes of your life, and make you suffer the exquisite pain I usually inflict. But we're running out of time. So say goodbye to your girlfriend, Wolfe. Don't worry. She'll be next, right behind you. And then that brat, Quinn. That'll be an added bonus."

The assassin was staring intently into Wolfe's eyes. He was doing the same to her. Neither blinking.

"I want to see the life go out in your eyes, Wolfe," she said menacingly. "To see the light extinguished in them as your pupils dilate before your body slumps forever to the ground. I'm going to relish this moment."

Then suddenly there was a quick motion to his left and two loud shots rang out. Wolfe quickly looked over and saw Terri with her Derringer pointed straight at Viktoriya, the gun just two feet from her heart. Viktoriya stood there for a second, a look of amazement in her quickly fading eyes.

When Wolfe looked at her black clothing, he saw two red plumes of blood spreading from her now lacerated heart, flowing through the two, well-placed holes in her chest.

The gun dropped from Viktoriya's hand, but she still stood, unable to let go of life, victory snatched from her in such a cruel manner—her last quest forever unresolved. Terri walked over to her as her legs collapsed, dropping her to the ground.

"Oh," said Terri. "I forgot to tell you, *Vikki. Drop your gun, or I'll shoot.*" She looked at Wolfe. "I guess I messed up. Oh well," she said. "Maybe next time."

Wolfe just watched her, like watching a play—mesmerized by what he was seeing. Josephs and Sparrow came running over after hearing the gunshots. "What happened?" said Sparrow, breathing heavily.

Wolfe looked at her. "Terri just blew Vikki away," he said.

"Wow," said Josephs, looking at the body. "She sure did."

"Good for her," said Sparrow, giving Terri a nod. "And good riddance to the bitch assassin from the Kremlin," she added looking down at the KGB spy.

They all stood transfixed at the scene for a moment, but that's all they had. Because the sound of military chopper blades slicing through the air, the engines throbbing, wump, wump, wump, wump . . . filled the air.

"That's not ours," said Wolfe looking up. "Let's head for cover!" Wolfe grabbed Terri who grabbed Quinn, and they started for the cover of the boat house.

"No," said Quinn. "This way. Hurry. I know a better place." Terri and Wolfe looked at each other and made an instantaneous decision to follow Quinn. Josephs, and Sparrow quickly followed. Quinn ran towards the cottage area, past the ones that had been assigned as housing for the group. He ran past Blue Jay, Condor, Sparrow, Ibis, Hummingbird, and Starling. There was one more cottage at the end of the row—Phoenix. Quinn headed up the steps of Phoenix cottage and popped the door open. "Quickly! In here!"

They all ran inside. Eino had been watching all this from his perch in the tree and was about to put another poison dart into Comrade Dunayevsky when Terri took care of the problem. He scrambled down, saw Sparrow and Josephs running toward them, so he joined in, too. He didn't know where they were going, but anything would be better than what would likely be waiting inside the military helicopter.

As the chopper was landing, Devon Barnes saw Wolfe and the others running for the cottages. "Set this bird down!" Barnes shouted to the pilot. "They're running away! Grab your weapons!" he shouted to the fifteen assassins. "We're gonna hit the ground running and mow every last one of them down. No one lives through this!"

What Barnes didn't see while he was concentrating on Wolfe and his fleeing comrades, was that the so-called supply boat wasn't a boat at all. In fact, it was an M 113 Armored Personnel Carrier with a mounted fifty caliber machine gun. It was climbing out of the water just as the chopper was landing. The APC had amphib-ious capabilities, and doors that could be opened before it was totally on land.

Suddenly Reaper jumped out loaded with weapons and explosives. He sloshed through the water, ducking down as low as he could, and headed towards the back of the administration build-ings, and behind where the helicopter was landing. He ran quickly through the trees, dropping explosives behind several of the buildings and at the base of some trees as he went.

After he had planted several of them, he ran back to the boat-house, pulled out a transmitter with buttons on top, numbered one through five, grabbed his own machine gun and a number of hand grenades, and waited, watching for the right time to set them off. Wolfe watched as a marine, code-named Viper, jumped out of the other side of the APC loaded with weapons and explosives, including a Gatling gun. Viper ran along the shore towards Phoenix Cottage. Stopping halfway to the cottage, he turned to help fend off the assassins from the frontal assault. As the APC clambered up out of the water just as the helicopter touched down, Wolfe shouted, "Cavalry's here!"

# chapter 81

A bout half of the assassins made it out of the helicopter and were charging towards the fleeing targets when Wolfe gave the order. "Take them out, now!" They all began shooting. Wolfe nailed one immediately, which caused the remainder of the assassins to run for cover.

The assassins began returning fire when suddenly their attention was diverted to an entirely different problem. An operator on the APC manning the fifty-caliber gun began flinging hot lead at a furious clip towards them and the men leaving the chopper. The assassins who had already taken up protected positions once Wolfe and crew started firing on them, now had another menace to worry about behind them.

The operator on the APC was firing at all the assassins he could find. Some scattered into the administrative building, while others tried to run into the woods behind the buildings and the chopper.

Viper set up the Gatling gun behind a large tree next to Phoenix Cottage and began spraying lead toward the helicopter and the buildings the assassins were using for cover. They had no place to go, and couldn't advance on Wolfe and his team without exposing themselves to deadly gunfire.

Suddenly there was an explosion in the trees behind the buildings. Reaper looked down at the control panel for his explosives. He had not set them off yet. He wondered what caused the explosion. He looked over to where the sound came from and saw one of the assassins lying dead next to a hole in the ground. Was someone else firing at them? If so, Reaper was not happy because he was in a position to become a casualty as well.

Then there was another slight pop. He looked in the direction of that sound, further back in the woods, and saw a cloud of gas enveloping another assassin. The assassin stumbled around trying to get away from the gas, but was overcome and dropped to the ground, inert. Must be some automatic countermeasures, Reaper decided, and turned his attention to the problem at hand.

Everything was in commotion. Viper was firing his Gatling gun at the assassins and the cottages and buildings where they were hiding. The man in the APC was firing rounds at the helicopter and at the assassins still visible. Reaper decided to add some chaos of his own. He flipped the switch to the on position on his detonators, and pressed number one. Instantly the building farthest from the helicopter exploded into a million pieces, with a fireball demanding everyone's attention.

Then he pressed button number 2. The next building closest to the chopper did the same, causing great consternation amongst the assassins hiding in the remaining buildings. Suddenly they started bolting from the buildings like rats from a sinking ship, trying to make it to what they thought was the safety of the helicopter, to make a hasty escape while they still could. Reaper took his machine gun and made sure that those who weren't mowed down by the fifty cal. didn't make it either.

Then Reaper pressed buttons three, four and five, in sequence. Those buildings erupted too, sending building pieces flying in all directions. Another pop went off in the trees, and another assassin succumbed to a cloud of incapacitating gas. Reaper didn't know if the gas was deadly or just had a sleep agent. He didn't dare go over and look, as his sidekick with the Gatling gun was throwing lead all over the place.

Barnes had been in the rear of the group, not wanting to take fire. He had a safer strategy of leading from behind. The assassins took up positions in the other cottages. Some hid behind trees while others ran into the administrative buildings.

Several of the assassins were shot and lay dead in the middle of the compound. Several were climbing into the chopper trying to get the pilot to take off. He refused, so they put a gun to his head. He changed his mind.

Reaper, seeing the helicopter trying to escape with some of the assassins, and possibly with armaments that could take out the APC plus Wolfe and his crew in Phoenix Cottage, picked up his rocket launcher and fired a rocket-propelled grenade into the open door of the helicopter. The grenade struck the opposite door of the chopper, resulting in an explosion that destroyed the helicopter.

Barnes looked up just in time to see the chopper burst into a ball of flames and head to the earth practically on top of him. He jumped up and ran as fast as he could, tripping and falling as he scrambled to try to get away from the burning chopper. He jumped behind a big pine tree just as the chopper crashed and another explosion shredded the remainder of the helicopter into a million pieces.

# chapter 82

Barnes quickly assessed the situation. He still had not found the professor and his inventions. If he could find him, all was not lost. He checked for his weapon but it was gone, lost in his struggle to find cover and abandon his troops. He didn't know how many of his assassins were left, but by the count of bodies lying in the open compound, he guessed not many, if any.

He ran to one of the dead assassins and grabbed his automatic weapon. He grabbed one of the full magazines from the dead man's body armor, ejected the expended magazine, and slammed the full one in place. Then he racked one round into the chamber and was good to go. He had to find the professor.

Just then, General Birchmont called him on his sat phone. "*Barnes*," he shouted into the phone. The noise of gunfire was nearly deafening.

"This is General Birchmont. Status report!"

"We've met some resistance we hadn't planned on. Some kind of military response. I have no idea who they are, but we're pinned down."

"And the professor?" said Birchmont, clearly angry.

"He's still here, and I'm going to get him. Don't worry. I'm very close," shouted Barnes.

"Report back when you have the professor *and* the inventions. Not before!" Birchmont terminated the call.

General Birchmont decided he had to cut his losses. This situation was all out of control. Barnes had lost it, and who knows what was going on at the compound. He picked up his phone and talked to the commander who had an attack force ready to go on a moment's notice. Birchmont had prepared a cover story for exactly this situation. Professor Dejanovic was now a rogue scientist who had created a biological weapon that was a danger to the planet. The only way to destroy the weapon was to burn the entire compound.

"Do it!" he said. "Level the damned place. No one leaves alive and no buildings are to be left standing. And," he continued, "burn the area so that even the rocks are melted. And do it now!"

The commander complied and gave the order to his team. "Damn!" said Barnes. He looked around and saw one of the few remaining buildings, which was the rec building. He ran toward the building with singular intent. If he didn't get the professor right now, it was over for him.

Coming to the front door, he kicked it in and ran inside, looking all around as quickly as he could to see if he could find the professor. "Professor!" he shouted. "Where are you? I'm here to help you!"

He kept looking around and finally saw the top of the professor's head slowly peeking up over the top of the table. "Professor! Come here!" he shouted.

The professor stayed crouched under the table. "I'm staying right here," he said.

"The hell you are!" said Barnes and ran over and put the machine gun in his face. "Come with me now or I swear I will blow your head off!"

Professor Dejanovic curled up into a fetal position and refused to budge.

"Have it your way!" said Barnes as he shot the professor at point blank range. "Well," said Barnes, "the General said, dead or alive. I guess it's dead!"

Back at Phoenix cottage, Wolfe got a call on his sat phone from Reaper that there had been an airstrike called in on the compound.

Wolfe shouted into his phone. "*Reaper!* Get Viper and your crew out of here, fast! That's an order! We've got a bomb shelter here! We'll be OK! *Go!*"

Reaper responded. "Copy, Commander. Looks like all assassins are dead or disabled. But there may be a couple still on the loose, so be careful."

Viper said, "Copy! We're outta here!"

Wolfe turned to Terri and the others. "The professor!" he shouted. "He's still in the Rec Hall! I've got to go get him," and he turned and ran back out the door. But as soon as he did, he saw Barnes staggering out of the Rec Hall, coming towards him.

# chapter 83

Both Viper and Reaper ran back to the marina, dropping all their gear so they could move as fast as possible, not sure if they were going to get away, but they'd get back into the APC and try their best.

Just then a loud roar came from the lake just off shore. It was a U.S. Navy fast boat and it was roaring towards the marina, and way faster than wake speed. The APC gunner and driver jumped out and dove into the water along with Reaper and Viper, and swam for all they were worth over to the boat that was now only a few yards away. Crew on the boat pulled them all in, and the boat took off at full power, heading away from the compound.

"Where are we going, Captain?" asked one of the APC crewmen.

"As far and as fast as we can before hell shows up," said the captain.

"I hope it's far enough," said the crewman.

"You and me both," said the captain.

Barnes stepped out of the Rec Hall and immediately saw Wolfe coming out of Phoenix cottage. He stopped and shouted at Wolfe.

"Too late, *Clayton*," he said in a mocking manner. "The professor is dead! He wouldn't play ball, so I killed him. Game over for him. And now for you. Your days of being the biggest pain in my ass are coming to a swift close. Get ready to die!"

Barnes raised his machine gun, but when he pulled the trigger, his weapon jammed and wouldn't fire. "Piece of crap!" shouted

Barnes as he kept trying to rack another round into the firing chamber.

Wolfe saw his dilemma and started toward him. "Having a little trouble, *Barnes*?" he taunted. "Haven't learned how to fire a weapon yet? Need a refresher course? Maybe the Boy Scouts have a Marksmanship merit badge you can work on." Wolfe continued to walk towards Barnes as he taunted.

"You're the piece of crap, Barnes," he continued. "Not the gun. You're a novice. You can't tie your shoes under combat conditions without your Mama's help." Wolfe was now moving swiftly, taking long strides, but not running—focused on Barnes, watching in case he cleared the stuck round before Wolfe got there—ready with his plan B.

Barnes was furious, yanking on the weapon, beating it to try to dislodge the errant round. He kept glancing at the advancing specter of Wolfe looming larger and more dangerous than ever as he got closer.

"You're gonna die, Wolfe!" he shouted. "Here and now. And I'm gonna be the one to take you out—man to man!"

Wolfe said, "Man to man? Where's the other man? I'm here, but what other man are you talking about? It couldn't possibly be *you*." Wolfe kept talking, working on Barnes' emotions, getting him rattled, angry—not thinking clearly. And while he was doing this he was moving forward.

Ever forward.

Eyes locked on Barnes' eyes.

Now he was only steps away, and Barnes, blind with rage, threw his weapon at Wolfe and charged at him like a bull, head down.

Wolfe was ready for him. He watched Barnes carefully, as he was known to feint like he had no weapon, and then at the last moment, pull a nasty knife from some secret spot and stab his victims to death.

True to form, Barnes appeared to be out of control, but as he was in striking range of Wolfe, he reached around his back and produced his legendary knife and thrust it straight at Wolfe.

But Wolfe was ready. He grabbed the wrist of Barnes' knife hand and twisted his arm up and around in an unnatural position in a way that was not anatomically possible. His shoulder dislocated and ligaments torn, Barnes let loose a piercing scream.

As the momentum of his charge at Wolfe drove him further and further away, Wolfe still hung onto his wrist, twisting and pulling, causing Barnes even more intense pain, if that was possible.

Barnes had dropped the knife, and was now in shock. He was running on pure adrenalin. His right arm was now useless, but somehow he managed to find the knife on the ground with his left hand. He gripped it tight, stood up, and insanely charged Wolfe again with a blood-curdling howl.

Wolfe was ready for that one as well. He repeated the same maneuver, except that he added a head-butt to Barnes' face that broke his nose and several teeth, and finished with a blow to the ribs. That had to crack at least two of them, thought Wolfe.

Both arms were now out of commission as Barnes lay on the ground, unable to get up. "Go ahead! Shoot me, you miserable bastard!" shouted Barnes. Wolfe looked at him, and then heard the attack planes getting louder. He only had minutes.

"No, Barnes. I'm not going to shoot you. That would be too easy on you. You can lay there and contemplate your relatively short future as the planes and helicopters you caused to be brought down on this place will exact more revenge than I could ever inflict."

"Shoot me! Shoot me, you coward!" shouted Barnes. But Wolfe had already turned and was running toward the front door of Phoenix cottage. Eino was holding the door open and yelling at Wolfe.

"Hurry!" said Eino. "Quinn has an escape hatch but we gotta get down there now!"

While Wolfe had been battling Barnes, Quinn had been leading the others into the basement of the cottage. There, in the middle of the floor, was a metal trap door. Quinn and Josephs had lifted up the heavy door. It was ten inches thick, and used a hydraulic lift arm to help move it to an open position. But even so, it was still a handful. Eino quickly climbed down the stairs with Wolfe right behind him. As he was climbing down the steps, Quinn yelled, "Hey Wolfe! Press the yellow button on your left after you clear the opening!"

Wolfe looked to his left and saw a large, yellow button that said, "Close" on it. He made sure his head was below the opening, then he hit the button. A mechanical hum sounded, and then the thick door slowly swung down into place with a resounding thump. Then there was a sound of a metal lock sealing the door. Wolfe stopped and looked back, then shook his head and kept on going.

The raid had started and bombs were beginning to drop. They could hear the sounds of explosions and forest fires raging and the staccato of gunfire, everywhere, as if the hinges of hell had just blown open. Wolfe even thought for a moment that he could hear Barnes screaming his name with a string of obscene epithets. But only for a moment. Then his attention was directed to Quinn's voice.

"Quickly," said Quinn. "This way!"

They all ran down a tunnel behind Quinn until they came to an opening that caused them to stop and stare.

# chapter 84

W hat they were all staring at was a large tunnel, twelve feet in diameter, with some metal tracks on the ground, heading into a dark abyss. Sitting on the tracks were five metal cars for hauling ore, open at the top and large enough to hold a person sitting in them, facing front.

Quinn was standing in front of them. "See? We have transportation out of here. Just enough for the six of us."

They all looked at each other. Sparrow said, "I'm not getting in *that*. No way. A rust bucket? You've gotta be out of your mind. No offense, Quinn."

Quinn just smiled. "We can't stay here," he said. "From the sounds of it, there are big bombs going off up there. And I don't know whether that trap door can withstand a direct hit. Do you?" Heads shook. "I thought so," he said. "Let's load up and get out of here." He looked at Wolfe, raised his eyebrows, and shrugged his shoulders.

Wolfe took command. "Let's start loading into the cars. I suggest that Eino, being the tallest, and with the miner's light stapled to his head . . ."

"Not *stapled*, Wolfe," said Eino, taking exception to Wolfe's statement. "Just because I'm the only one prepared for this trip, you don't have to . . ."

"Fine," interrupted Wolfe. "Eino will be in the back car. Because of his height, his light will shine above everyone's collective heads and should illuminate our way forward, even though we will have no choice in the matter of direction. We go where the rails take us. Right, Quinn?"

Quinn nodded. "Right. But don't worry. I've been down there quite a bit before. You all will be safe once we get there."

"Once we *get* there?" said Terri. "What does that mean? That we're not safe between here and wherever we're going?"

"Let's just say, we'll be safer there," said Quinn.

Eino was looking curiously at Quinn. "How do you know all these things? Aren't you like, *ten*?"

"Time and place, Eino," said Wolfe. "If we don't get going, this could all be a moot point, and soon."

"With you Wolfe," said Eino.

"I'm in. Last car." Eino climbed in.

"Great," said Wolfe. "Sheriff, let's put you in the next to last car."

"Fine," said Josephs, who climbed in as well.

Wolfe nodded. "Terri, since you have kind of adopted the role of caretaker for Quinn, and he seems to like you, take the third car and Quinn can sit on your lap. You can be his protector."

"OK by me," said Terri, smiling at Quinn, who nodded and smiled back.

Wolfe pressed quickly along. "I'll be in the front car and Sparrow will be right behind me in the second car. Any questions?"

No one spoke, thinking of the seconds ticking away.

"OK. Everyone else load up."

Quinn remained outside the cars, giving last minute instructions. "OK, listen up," he said, sounding more like a drill sergeant than a ten-year old kid. "There are no brakes on these things, to speak of. Each car has a vertical metal bar on the left side, which, if you pull back on it, will provide some braking effect on that individual car. It is just a metal bar on metal wheels, but if you pull it hard enough, it will slow the cars. But it is imperative that the cars stay together. Because if any distance begins to separate the cars, if one front car needs to brake, the rear car could crash into the front ones and cause a derailment. That would be catastrophic."

"So we stay together," said Eino.

"As close as possible," said Quinn.

"Finally, there is nothing keeping the cars from rolling down the track right now, except a chunk of wood in front of the front wheel of the first car. There's a rope attached to the wood, which I am handing to Wolfe." He did so. "Once we're all ready to go, Wolfe will give the signal and will pull the rope, freeing the piece of wood. After that, it's all downhill, so to speak."

"Just wondering," asked Josephs, "how fast will we be going, and how long is the ride, and what will stop us at the end of the trip?"

"All good questions," said Quinn. "Hard to say what the speed will be, since it is largely dependent on the weight of the load. The heavier the load, the faster the speed."

"And how about *this* load?" said Josephs.

"Compared to a normal load going downhill, much heavier, considering they normally go down empty."

"So, you don't know," said Josephs.

Quinn looked at the Sheriff. "Let's just say, we'll be going down fast. It'll start out slow, but speed will keep increasing for the duration of the trip, until we get near the end. Then the slope will decrease and we will slow to a stop."

Wolfe took command. "Enough questions. Hop in, Quinn. Let's get this train rolling."

Quinn jumped into Terri's car and sat on her lap. She put her arms around him in an instinctive move, and hoped she could keep him safe, since there was nothing to buckle them in.

"Ready?" said Wolfe. "OK then, I'm going to pull the rope." And he did.

The chunk of wood sprang free. Wolfe threw the rope over the side, and grabbed onto the sides of the ore car.

The cars didn't seem to move at first, but slowly the wheels began to turn and the cars began a slow roll down the dark, foreboding tunnel.

The cars began picking up speed, and the light cast by Eino's miner's light was no longer strong enough to penetrate the darkness before they arrived in it. They were rapidly dropping into an unknown world at an ever-increasing rate of speed, and all they had to hold onto was faith in a ten-year old boy, who seemed to be much, much older than he was.

# chapter 85

The train of ore cars with their human cargo sped down the tracks, faster than they ever had before. Fear gripped most of them because of the unknown—except Quinn.

Sparrow shouted at Wolfe, who sat in front of her. "This is like the most *demented* amusement park ride I have ever seen!"

He said, "I agree!"

The train of ore cars was going faster and faster and it seemed like the slightest curve in the track would immediately derail the whole group and cause a cataclysmic crash.

Suddenly there was a muffled but distinct, *boom*, and the tunnel shook. Debris dropped from the top of the tunnel onto their heads and onto the tracks—but not enough to impede their progress. The cars lurched left, then right, then back again.

"What was that . . ." began Josephs.

"Big bomb," said Quinn. "But I think we're far enough underground, so don't worry."

"Oh I'm not worried about that, anymore," said Josephs. "It's the terminal velocity of this train wreck that's coming that has me concerned."

Wolfe shouted back to Quinn, "Have you ever gone this fast before?"

"No," said Quinn. "And I'm getting a little nervous. The cars are getting a little unstable at this speed, with all of us in them.

We may have to slow down a little—or a lot. I think now would be a good time," he finished.

Wolfe turned his head and shouted at Sparrow—"I'm going to pull back on my brake lever until it hits the wheel, and as soon as I do, you do the same. Pass it on to Terri to do the same, and then on to Josephs and Eino. That way we will all remain together. First one, then the next one, and so on. Go ahead pass it on. When everyone has been informed, let me know and I'll begin."

She did as instructed. Then the word came back up that everyone was ready.

"OK, here I go." Wolfe pulled back on the lever and the sound of metal screeching on metal made a horrible racket. Sparks were flying all over. Then each person in turn did the same, and each time the sounds added a higher level of screech like Banshees from hell. Combined with the sounds of the wheels on the rails and the wind blowing past them, talking was now almost impossible, and made fearsome conditions as they careened down the pitch black tunnel.

"I don't think we're slowing enough," shouted Quinn.

Wolfe turned his head to shout at Sparrow. "Pull harder! Pass it back!" She did.

None of this seemed to have much effect, except to crunch the cars together so there was absolutely no space between them, and to produce a noxious smell of burning metal and more sparks that now added to the already claustrophobic conditions of their terrifying flight down to—where?

"More braking!" yelled Quinn.

"Pull harder!" shouted Wolfe. "Pull as hard as you can!"

The call made it back to Eino and he and Josephs did the same.

Everyone was straining just as hard as they could to slow the train of cars.

The cars were now rocking violently back and forth, and the small imperfections in the rail fittings were greatly magnified by their speed, causing dangerous bumps as the cars went over them.

"Harder! Harder!" yelled Wolfe as the front car started to be-come unstable. It felt as if it was about to be lifted from the tracks. It seemed impossible that such a heavy car loaded with its occupant could become airborne, but now Wolfe wasn't so sure.

"Harder, harder!" yelled Quinn.

Josephs was straining with all his might. "C'mon, Eino! You can pull harder than that. I feel like you're pushing me!"

Eino shot back. "Stuff it, Sheriff! I'm pulling as hard as I can. I even think I bent the lever!"

The cars were bouncing and rocking and seemed about to leave the tracks entirely, when suddenly it felt like the cars were slowing. It wasn't that perceptible at first, and Wolfe wasn't sure it was really happening.

But then Quinn shouted, "We're slowing down! We're almost coming to the end!"

Sure enough. The train of ore cars with their precious cargo began slowing.

"Let off on the brake levers now," shouted Quinn. "The cars will slow naturally from here on in, so you have nothing to worry about."

"Yeah, that's what he said before we started on this horror show," Eino said to Josephs. Josephs was still trying to slow his breathing down to a manageable level and couldn't talk at the moment.

The train of ore cars began slowing more as the grade decreased. There began to be some light ahead, and the tunnel seemed to be opening into a much larger cavern. Finally they could see the bumper at the end of the tracks, and they all breathed a collective sigh of relief. But that relief was replaced with amazement at the scene that unfolded to them. They all just stared with eyes wide and mouths agape.

They were totally speechless.

# chapter 86

When the cars finally stopped, they all stared until they could regain their powers of speech. Finally, one did.

"What *is* this place?" said Terri.

"Yeah," said Eino.

"Well said, Eino," replied Josephs, a trace of sarcasm already seeping into his voice.

Quinn hopped out of the car and helped Terri out. The others got out of their own accord, including Sparrow. Wolfe was the last to leave.

"C'mon," said Quinn. "I'll explain everything—or *most* everything."

The train of ore cars had come to stop in a great cavern, hundreds of feet high and equally as wide. It was lighted in soft pastels, but the light fixtures could not be seen. However there was enough light throughout the cavern to see everything clearly. There were machines of unknown purpose scattered around, and also groupings of furniture for casual seating, as well as tables that appeared to be like café chairs and tables, with colorful umbrellas, much like a French outdoor café. There was a fountain of water in the center of the area that was obviously artificial and that produced multiple patterns of spray that changed every minute or so. The fountain looked Italian.

There appeared to be a section of the cavern that was devoted to technical work, like a workshop with parts and supplies scattered around, and partially built devices of one kind or another.

As they were staring at it all, a man walked into the room from a doorway behind a wall, and up to the group. He was tall, well built, of Nordic background with blondish hair. He had on casual, comfortable clothes. Quinn walked up to him and gave him a big hug. Then he turned to the group and said, "Everyone, this is Raimond Anker—my father."

Back in Washington, General Birchmont was watching in real time what was going on at the compound, via a live spy satellite that he had requested be tasked for this operation. He watched as the bombs dropped, and the place caught on fire in an inferno the likes of which he had never seen before. Everything was incinerated.

"Nobody could have lived through that," he said to an officer standing next to him.

"No, sir," said the man.

"Not even the rocks could survive," General Birchmont continued.

"Not even," said the officer.

"General," said the Secretary of Defense, "the President considers this incident closed."

"I agree with the President," said General Birchmont. "Get all the tapes and recordings of this incident and destroy them. That's an order. There is to be no record of any type of what happened there today."

"I agree," said the Sec Def. "This never happened. Just an unfortunate forest fire."

Birchmont nodded. "Smokey the Bear was asleep at the switch."

"Indeed," said the Sec Def, as he turned and left the room.

Birchmont sighed with relief, and thought to himself, Good thing my cover story about a rogue scientist and a biological weapon held up. If the President ever finds out what really happened, there will be hell to pay.

Back in his own office, General Birchmont picked up his private line, and called his personal stock broker. "Jim? This is Chet Birchmont. Let's buy those energy stocks we had talked about. I think they're gonna be a good bet for quite some time. Yup. The amount we mentioned. As soon as possible. Good. Thanks a bunch, Jim. Talk soon."

# chapter 87

"This man is your father?" said Terri.

"Yes," said Raimond. "I'm Quinn's father. His mother died years ago, so I've been his only family."

"But," said Terri, "he's been wandering around alone—homeless—outdoors without a jacket, dirty, hungry. I mean, I can't see how you've been taking care of him. Especially since you're down *here*."

"It's a long story," said Raimond, "but it's not as bad as it looks. There are other ways to get topside. It's very easy. So don't worry about that. These things you've just described have been staged and set up to gain entrance to Professor Dejanovic and his research. You see, he was never on the right track with his inventions.

"Quinn and I have been secretly providing tips to the professor to get him on the right track so he could 'discover' the access to dark energy and make it available to the world. We knew his philos-ophy and desires to make it available, and we wanted to help him, to see if he could make it happen. To see if the world was ready for it."

Glancing up symbolically to the scene of the airstrike, Josephs said, "Apparently it's not."

"Clearly," said Raimond. "It appears that the powers of this planet would rather die than share a gift that would free mankind from the privations of restricted energy. When you think of what would happen if you provided a free energy device that could operate in the middle of the desert, or in the rain forest, on in the mountains, or under the ocean . . ."

"No way that's going to happen now," said Eino. "The circuits are blown to atoms, the professor's dead, and any inventions he had are long gone."

"Not necessarily," said Raimond.

"What do you mean?" said Josephs.

"What do you think is providing the electricity for us down here? Powering the lights and everything else?"

They all looked around. "You mean you . . .," began Sparrow.

"Yes. As difficult as it may be to believe, dark energy is providing our lights and all our electricity in this area—and elsewhere." He looked at the puzzled faces. "Come over here," he said, leading them to the area that looked like a workshop. He showed them a metal box sitting on the floor, approximately one foot high, one foot deep, and two feet long. "That's it," he said. "The power source for the whole area."

"But there are no wires connecting it to anything," said Eino.

"Don't need any," said Quinn. "As Nikola Tesla had proven decades ago, electricity can be sent through the air, through space from one point to another, or from one point to all points. And even through the ground," he continued.

They all continued looking at the box. "But it doesn't make any noise," said Sparrow.

"No moving parts," said Raimond. "Nothing to turn on or off once it's started. A perpetual motion generator," he said. "Something the United States Patent Office would not patent because it says perpetual motion doesn't exist. It's impossible." He smiled. "You think maybe they were wrong?"

"Wouldn't be the first time," said Wolfe. Then he made a startling revelation. "I've known about this place and this operation for a while, and offered to help Quinn and Raimond try to introduce these generators to the world through this deception. But apparently human greed knows no bounds."

"But we're not done yet," said Raimond. "There are other ways to cut the energy stranglehold precipitated years ago by those in power. The world needs free energy."

Terri was looking at Wolfe strangely. "You mean, you've known about this all along and you didn't tell us about it?"

"He couldn't," said Raimond. "I made him promise that he wouldn't reveal any of this to anyone for any reason. Especially my identity."

Eino said, "Wait a minute. What do you mean about him not revealing your identity? We don't know you from Adam. So why would that matter?"

"It mattered to you," said Raimond. "Several of you kept asking him to reveal my name to you."

"We never. . ." began Josephs. Then he stopped and looked at Wolfe, and then at Raimond. "Wait. You mean . . ."

Wolfe looked at Raimond and Raimond nodded. "Raimond is my benefactor. The supplier of condos and cars and weapons and airplanes and . . ."

"Holy crap!" said Eino. "*You're* the guy."

"Guilty," said Raimond.

"You must be rich," said Sparrow. "Where'd you get all that money?"

Raimond smiled. "I own several mines that contain precious metals."

"You mean, like gold?" asked Sparrow.

"Yes," said Raimond. "Gold, silver, platinum, palladium, copper, and other elements, even more rare. So you see, I have plenty of money to fund this endeavor indefinitely. And I plan to. Free energy is the future. It will save mankind."

"Yeah," said Eino, "if we can keep mankind from destroying itself. As we can see, no easy feat."

"True," said Raimond. "But doable."

"What about this place?" asked Josephs. "Where did it come from? Who built the tunnel, the cavern?"

Raimond walked over to the comfortable furniture area and sat down, indicating everyone to do the same. "There are mines all over Northern Michigan, and particularly the Upper Peninsula," he began. "An ancient civilization long since gone had mined for copper, particularly in the Keweenaw Peninsula, but other places as well. They left relics behind, but no trace of themselves or their civilization."

# chapter 88

"Strange," said Terri. "Is it true?"

"It's true," said Raimond. "At least as far as we know. But it appears this mine was started well before the house was built. When the builders saw the tunnel, they simply built the house over it, leaving the trap door so they could explore it at a later date. The door was later updated to be a blast door when everyone was building bomb shelters."

"Yes, but those ore cars and rails, and the long tunnel to—well, here. Who built those? Certainly not this ancient civilization," said Terri.

"Right," said Raimond. "The ancients, as far as we can tell, started digging and found some ore, but after some initial exploration, they suddenly disappeared with the rest of their civilization."

"So I ask again," said Terri, "where did the rails and the rest of the tunnel come from?"

Raimond paused, unsure whether he wanted to say any more.

"We don't know," said Quinn abruptly.

"What?" said Eino.

"All we really know," said Raimond, "is that they were here when we first got here, and we have no idea who made them or why. Although, seeing as the metal cars on them are evidently for hauling ore to the surface, we speculate that that is their likely use and purpose."

Sparrow, the resident sceptic, continued the questioning. "OK, I guess that makes sense. Kind of. So, if I might ask, what brought you down here? And how did you find it?"

Raimond smiled patiently and answered. "One of my, ah, associates is—was—a member of the association that owned this property when it was still an exclusive club. One day he invited me here and asked me if I wanted to see something interesting. I told him, yes, of course.

"So he brought me to the Phoenix cottage and showed me this hidden passage to an underground cavern. I was intrigued. I had needed a place to continue my research and experiments in privacy, and this seemed as likely a place as any. My friend, who had explored this area secretly and extensively, showed me another way to get down to the cavern and back up much more easily, so he took me down and showed me around. It was at that point that I felt that this would be the perfect place for Quinn and me to live and work on our inventions in peace and safety. As you can see, such precautions were not unwarranted," he said, smiling.

"So how did you get all your supplies down here? You didn't bring them all through the Phoenix cottage, I imagine."

"Correct," said Raimond. "The other entrance to the cavern is not too far from here, but it is on land that is uninhabited but not too difficult to access with the right equipment."

"Which you had, of course," said Sparrow.

"Of course," smiled Raimond.

Wolfe, knowing the history already, remained silent while others satisfied their curiosity.

Josephs then spoke up. "So, you made all these improvements to the cavern, then? All the electricity, furniture, food, even the fountain?"

"We did," said Raimond. "Quinn and I did. Nobody else."

"Quite a feat," said Josephs, looking around admiringly.

"Not as difficult as you might think. Less than a year and we were pretty much set up as you see us now. Actually, it's self-contained and quite livable, if you think about it. We create artificial sunlight or grow lamps that enable us to grow our own food, generate oxygen and light. Clean water, filtered by the earth, is in ample supply as well. There are plenty of metals and we can manufacture pretty much all we need to do our work from the elements that surround us. We can stay here indefinitely, if we need to."

"But don't you miss the sky and fresh air?" said Terri.

"No," said Raimond. "Because we can go topside anytime we want. We use the alternate entrance I told you about. It's much easier to traverse."

"If you say so," said Sparrow doubtfully.

"One more question," asked Terri," for now at least."

"OK," said Raimond. "Go ahead."

"How is it that Quinn is so smart for such a young boy?" Terri looked over at Quinn who was looking at her with a playful smile on his face, that said, *what*?

"It's not much of a mystery, I'm afraid," Raimond responded. "His mother and I were both blessed with extremely high IQs. We were given excellent schooling for gifted children, and then provided the same for Quinn when he was born. Although, I must say that Quinn has talents as a child that neither his mother nor I had. He's really quite an exceptional young boy."

"That's saying a lot, coming from you," said Terri."

"I suppose you're right," said Raimond.

Eino chimed in. "What are you planning to do now?" he asked.

Raimond gave a thoughtful look for a moment, then said, "Our work is not done regarding free energy," he said. "We have many more experiments to conduct, many iterations of dark energy that need to be explored, and we must continue to find ways to make it available to civilizations around the world.

"We have some ideas on how to do that, and so we will continue with our work."

"Raimond," said Terri, "you keep saying *we*, when referring to your work. Do you mean just you and Quinn?"

"I do. Quinn has been the discoverer of many of the aspects of dark energy. He is quite adept at working in a variety of areas, including architecture, metallurgy, communications, and vehicles of all kinds, plus technology such as computers which are now only in their infancy.

"I think that's enough for now," said Raimond. "We can deal with other questions you may have at a later time. For now, we should get busy. We've things to do, and I expect you do too."

Wolfe nodded. "We do, and we'd best get to them. And the first thing I will do, once we are topside, is to call the President and tell him what really happened. I think General Birchmont will have a surprise in store for him."

# chapter 89

Wolfe took Terri over to the workshop area where they sat down on a padded bench behind a wall, out of sight of everyone. Terri hugged Wolfe tight.

"I don't care about Jenny," she said softly. "Or Sparrow or Vikki, or anybody. I don't care about your secretiveness. I don't care that you didn't call me. Well, I care a *little* about that." She smiled. "But Clay, through all this, I realize that I still love you. Brent was a placeholder only. I love *you*. And I hope you love me too, because I want to be with you—from now on. *Always.* Understand?"

"I do," he said. "And I feel the same way about you. I missed you so much when we were apart. All I could think about was you. But I had assignments that I had to take care of and I couldn't endanger you by involving you in them.

"But I see now, that life itself is dangerous, no matter which path you choose. And I'd rather be with you through those dangers, than without you. I love you too, Terri. And I always will."

"I believe you," she said. "And *always*, sounds good."

"And Brent?" he asked.

Terri smiled. "I'll call him right away and break it off." Then she looked around. "That is, as soon as I can find a *phone*."

They laughed, knowing that they were still in a precarious position, but also knowing they would find a way out—together.

# Acknowledgments

To Jennifer Tacbas for her excellent work on my author photo, her outstanding and invaluable work as my publicist, and her willingness to assist in the many details that go into marketing and success of this book;

To Phil Oppenheim and Fred Firks for their help and suggestions regarding aviation, firearms, and other aspects of the novel;

To my sons, Jeremy, Ryan, and Nathan, who have given me wonderful support and assistance throughout the process of writing and publishing this novel;

To my sisters, Linda and Mary, who have been so supportive of my work for many years;

But most of all to my wife, Cindy, whose expertise in editing, thoughtful suggestions, and continued support through the many years have greatly contributed to my success and the success of my novels. Without her, this novel simply could not have been written.

www.ingramcontent.com/pod-product-compliance
Lightning Source LLC
Chambersburg PA
CBHW050911250626
47155CB00001B/185